Trampoline

an anthology

Trampoline

an anthology

edited by Kelly Link

Small Beer Press
Northampton, MA

Collection copyright © 2003 by Small Beer Press. All rights reserved. Copyright for the individual stories remains the
property of their authors. Page 337 functions as an extension of the copyright page.

Small Beer Press
176 Prospect Avenue
Northampton, MA 01060
www.smallbeerpress.com
info@smallbeerpress.com

www.kellylink.net

PCIP

Trampoline: An Anthology
        Edited by Kelly Link
        p. cm.
        LCCN 2002115135
        ISBN 1-931520-04-6
        1. Link, Kelly, 1969-   I. Title
        2. Fiction
        3. Fantastic fiction
        PN 6120.95 .T771 2003   813.08

First edition 1 2 3 4 5 6 7 8 9 0

A Jelly Ink book. Jelly Ink is an imprint of Small Beer Press.
Printed with soy inks on 50# Supple Opaque recycled paper by Thomson-Shore of Dexter, MI.
Text set in Centaur 11.5/13.8. Titles set in American Typewriter Medium 24.
Cover painting by Shelley Jackson.

This anthology is dedicated to:

Vincent McCaffrey,
Thais Coburn,
& Avenue Victor Hugo Bookshop

contents

The Force Acting on the Displaced Body

Christopher Rowe

The little creek behind my trailer in Kentucky is called Frankum Branch. I had to go to the courthouse to find that out. Nobody around here thought it had a name. But all the little creeks and branches in the world have names, even if nobody remembers them, or remembers which Frankum they're named after.

I wanted to know the name when I was planning the trip back to Paris. That's Paris as in Bourbon kings, not Paris as in Bourbon County. I was writing out my route and Frankum Branch was Step One. I couldn't afford to fly, so I was going by boat. I didn't have a boat, so I was going to build one.

I was drinking a lot of wine just then.

I saved the corks.

Before I decided to go back to Paris, I considered using the bottles to build some sort of roadside tourist attraction. I looked into it a little bit, but the math defeated me very quickly. You remember how I am with math.

A boat though—a boat built out of corks—that turned out to be easy. All you need is a roll or two of cheesecloth and some thread and a needle and of course a whole lot of corks. I put it together in a long afternoon in the field behind the trailer.

None of the bottles, full or empty, would break on the corks, so I never did christen it. I'd be happy to hear your suggestions for a name, though, you were always good at that.

The neighbors had that party, set up the game to name their new kitten. Calliope, you suggested, and nobody else even came close. You didn't go to the party, though. I carried over the note you'd written.

Frankum Branch, that's a pretty good name. Even if I couldn't track the provenance, I know there are Frankums around here, know they've been here for a long time. Probably a particular Frankum, sure, but here's a case where ignorance is kind of liberating. Since I don't know—since nobody knows, not even the people at the courthouse—it could have been a man or a woman, an old lady or a little boy. It could be named for all the Frankums.

The boat behaved at first. It rolled down the hill and settled into the branch, stretching out long because the stream bed is so narrow. It waited for me to throw my bags in and to clamber in myself, and then I headed downstream.

I only moved at the speed the water moved. I only went as fast as the world would carry me.

How far is my trailer from Sulfur Creek? See, that's a more interesting question than it might seem. There are so many ways to measure it.

If I walk out my front door and follow Creek Bend Drive to the end of my landlord's farm, down into the bottom and across Frankum, up another hill and then back down to where the blacktop turns to gravel, it's about two miles. That's the closest place, I think. Where the road breaks up into gravel is where Frankum Branch flows into Sulfur Creek.

But there are other ways I can go. I can walk through the fields, cross the branch on rocks at a narrow place, climb through some woods. I think it might only be about a mile and a half, that way.

Then there are crows. "As the crow flies." Do you think that means that crows are supposed to fly in straight lines? Maybe they used to. I watch crows, and I don't think I'd trust them to give me advice on distance. I don't think I trust crows or creeks either on much of anything, except to be themselves.

Finally, there's time. Nobody ever gives distances in miles anymore, but it's not because they've switched to metric. They measure how far it is from here to there with their watches, not their odometers.

That place, that confluence of water and roads both? It's about two miles from my trailer, it's about a mile and half, it's about an hour if you take Frankum Branch in a boat made out of corks.

So then I was on Sulfur Creek, which is broader than Frankum. The boat rounded itself up into a little doughnut. I smelled the water in the creek and I tasted it, searching for rotten eggs, I guess, or hell.

The sulfur must have washed away, though. Sometimes that happens, things wash away and only the names are left.

My hometown—the town I lived closest to growing up and the one I live closest to again—it's an island, maybe. At the edge of town, you have to cross a bridge over Russell Creek. At every edge of town. Every road leading in and out passes over Russell Creek.

When I was younger, I thought that meant that the creek flowed in a circle. I'd seen illustrations of the Styx in my mythology books.

It's not, of course. The creek and the town are neither of them circles, and the roads don't lead out in perfect radials along the cardinal directions, something else I used to believe.

What's the difference between a creek and a river? Length, just length. Nothing about how much water flows through it, nothing about breadth or depth. In Kentucky, if a rivulet you can step across is at least a hundred miles long, then it's a river. Russell Creek is ninety-nine miles long. Maybe it's the longest creek in the world.

When I floated out onto it, I started thinking that maybe I should have dug a trench somewhere at the headwaters or made a long oxbow in a bottom. Maybe instead of building the boat I should have lengthened Russell Creek. But then it would just be a short river.

Russell Creek flows around the town, and beneath the bluffs that line one side of my family's farm, and then winds, winds, winds through the county to the Green River.

The Green River pretty much named itself.

The Green is deep and swift above the first locks and dams, then shallow and tamed below. Floating through the impounded lake at the county line, the boat began to misbehave. It didn't want to leave town, after all.

It bunched up in a tight little sphere. I bounced on the top, netting my nylon bags filled with wine bottles and this notebook and a corkscrew into the cheesecloth so they wouldn't drop down and disturb the muskies. Then the boat stretched out, became narrower and narrower, longer and longer, so it almost looked like it was floating forward.

But I could tell it wasn't really moving, so I tried to paddle for a while with my hands. I kept getting pushed back by the wakes of fishing boats headed for the state dock. When I gave up, exhausted, the boat finally shuddered or shrugged and drifted on through the spillway, through the dam.

I don't know the motive force of the boat. Its motivation is a mystery to me.

You have to keep an eye on that boat.

Then it was a John Prine song for four hundred miles.

Here's a true story. The Commonwealth of Kentucky owns the Ohio River, or used to.

3

We still own most of it. But then counties along the south bank started charging property taxes to the Hoosiers and the Buckeyes who built docks off the north shore. The Hoosiers and the Buckeyes got their states to sue ours and theirs won, a little bit. Now the Commonwealth owns the Ohio River except for a strip one hundred yards wide along the upper bank. The Supreme Court of the United States decided that.

Those counties shouldn't have tried to charge the taxes. They should have known what would happen.

There doesn't seem to be much point in owning most of a river.

These are things I saw along the Ohio River.

Below Henderson, where the Green gets muddied into the brown, I saw the carcass of a cow, bloated and rotting, floating in the shallows outside the main current. The boat shied away from it even though I was curious to see what kind of cow it was.

At Owensboro, the water became as clear as air, and I felt like I was flying for a little while. The bed of the Ohio is smooth and broad at Owensboro, unsullied by anything but giant catfish and a submerged Volvo P-1800 in perfect condition.

Ralph Stanley was playing a concert on the waterfront at Paducah. This time I didn't mind the boat's dawdling.

At Cairo, I floated onto the Mississippi.

Cairo is pronounced "Cairo."

Mark Twain's mother was born in my hometown. She was married in the front room of the big brick house at the corner of Fortune and Guardian. Mark Twain was conceived there. No, Samuel Clemens was conceived there. I think Mark Twain was conceived in San Francisco.

Doesn't Mississippi mean "Father of Waters"? That's a great name, in the original and in the translation and in the parlance.

You could make a career on that, I think. "Father of Waters." If I'd made that up, I would have lorded it over all the other namers for the rest of my life. I would never have named another river.

So, past New Orleans, the first place I was tempted to stop (but didn't), and into the Gulf of Mexico. The discharge of the father forced me all the way to the Gulf Stream, and it's easy to cross an ocean when the currents are doing all the work.

The boat was showing a little bit of wear, though. I had to drink more wine and patch a few places with the corks.

It was around then, south of Iceland maybe, north of the Azores, that it occurred to me that I could have used all those bottles to make a boat instead of the corks. It might have been sturdier and I could probably have found some waterproof glue. I think you would have thought of that at the beginning.

But me, I was south of Iceland, very wet and cold, before I hit my forehead with the heel of my palm.

"Bottles!" I said.

The French, in naming rivers and cities and forests and Greek sandwich shops, have the advantage of being French speakers. I only know how to say "I don't speak French" in French, but I say it with perfect pronunciation and a great deal of confidence. Nobody in France ever believed me. Sometimes even I didn't believe me.

So, I don't know what Seine means, and I'm actually a little bit unsure of the pronunciation. I kept my mouth shut through Le Havre, past Rouen.

France was the first place along the trip that other people noticed the boat. The French love boats. I know what you think about that kind of sweeping comment. It's true though, in all it's implications. All French people love all boats, even ones made out of corks. They might not like them, all of them, all of the time. But love, sure.

Do you remember when we were on a boat on the Seine together? Cold fog, ancient walls, tinny loudspeakers repeating everything in French, English, German, Japanese?

Do you remember the other boat? The Zodiac moored under the Pont au Double, lashed against the wall below Notre Dame?

A man stood in the boat, leaning back, pulling a bright blue nylon rope. People started watching him instead of the church. What was he pulling out of the water? What was the light rising up from below?

It was another man, a man in a red wetsuit, with yellow tanks strapped to his back, climbing the rope against the current.

Do you remember that?

They were still there.

They waved me over.

We have underground rivers in Kentucky, too. The Echo is famous, in the caves. If I'd thought of it at the time, I would have tried to coax the boat into the caves when I floated past them, tried to spot some eyeless fish.

In Paris, the underground river is the Biévre. It enters the Seine right across from Notre Dame. But then it leaves it again. It's just a river crossing through another one, not joining it.

I told the man on the boat that I didn't speak French, in French. He shrugged. Maybe he didn't care. Maybe he didn't speak French either. He just pointed at the diver in the water, so I slipped over the side, into the Seine. My boat seemed glad to be rid of me.

The diver took me by the hand and led me down. Down a very long way. He tied himself to a grating in the side of the stones that formed the channel there and showed me how he'd bent the bars wide enough for someone not wearing air tanks to slip through.

So I did. I slipped through.

Then up and out of the Seine, or it might have been the Biévre. I could have been in the secret river the whole time. Up and into a dank passage. I've been in dank passages in Paris before, but never any with so few bones.

No skulls and thighs stacked along the walls here, just a dark stone hallway. I followed it and followed it and came to a junction, a place to choose. Left or right.

You remember my sense of direction. You wouldn't have been surprised to know that I knew where I was: at the center of the Ile de la Cité.

Left was north, then, and I knew that it would take me beneath the police head-quarters and up to Sainte-Chapelle, which Louis IX built to store the organs of Jesus after he'd bought them from of one of the great salesmen of the thirteenth century. Right was south, to Notre Dame, where signs remind the pickpockets that God's eyes are on them.

Notre Dame or Sainte-Chapelle. The lady or the heart.

I stood there.

I am standing there still.

Other than the signs saying that God is particularly aware of petty larceny there, I only remember one thing from inside Notre Dame.

You were so disgusted when we heard the woman with the Maine accent say, "They're praying. I didn't think this was a working church."

There were jugglers outside. I didn't think it was a working church either. I didn't tell you that.

When we went to Sainte-Chapelle together, we didn't go to look for the heart of Jesus. There was a concert, a half-dozen stringed instruments in a candlelit cavern of stained glass. Bach? I don't remember.

What I remember was leaving, walking out of the cathedral and into the rain. The line was slow because we had to pass through checkpoints in the Justice Ministry, which surrounds the church. Gendarmes with Uzis below and gargoyles with scythes high above.

I tracked a stream of rainwater from the mouth of a gargoyle to the pavement. I leaned out, turned my head up, opened my mouth. I told you that I didn't know what it tasted like. Like limestone, a little. I said limestone or ash, soot or smog.

You smiled and said, "It tastes like gargoyles."

You said that from my description. You didn't catch the rain on your tongue.

A long way to come to choose between places I've already been. A long way to come to choose anything at all.

I wonder if I can turn around.

I wonder if I can find my way back to the boat.

I wonder if it's still there.

Well-Moistened with Cheap Wine, the Sailor and the Wayfarer Sing of Their Absent Sweethearts

Ed Park

I.

It was good where I was. I lived with seventeen beautiful, intelligent women, all named Tina, so I never got their names wrong. My name was also Tina, and it was pleasant to hear the chatter at dinner: "Tina, great job with the digging today," "Tina, you've done wonders with the jicama," "Tina, I have to say, those camouflage shorts are the shit." The self-reference *was* a little surreal at first, like someone was always talking about you, but we quickly came to relish the closed circuit of our situation. Self-consciousness became passé. We wrote notes to each other that read like diary entries, all the most intimate things, ever so freely expressed. Dental floss and underwear were borrowed. Coming back from the dig site as the sky turned sapphire, we would link arms and sing, till our lungs burned, the infinite glories of being Tina.

We had all come to the island under the auspices of the Syllable Foundation. Our job was to gather and translate samples of the ancient writing known as oracle bone script. The island was lousy with it. OBS was a pictogrammic system of the early Shang Dynasty that bore only slight resemblance to modern Chinese. The name pretty much says it all. Three thousand years ago, priests would divine the future using turtle shells, dried bamboo, the shoulder blades of cattle. They would pose a question, then heat up the matter till it cracked. The answer lay in the breakage. Would tomorrow's hunt be successful? Would the rains fall soon? Was everybody really going to die?

They recorded the results right on the riven tabulae, with a proliferating vocabulary of symbols: a bolt of lightning, a labyrinth's futile curl, a vigilant eyeball—hundreds of other icons, with endless subvariations. To a degree, these descriptions are Rorshach, yet one couldn't help but see in those jottings a pitchfork, or a cat's ears, or a horned head on a triangular body. (Indeed, the horns came up rather a lot.) Every few days we turned up a new symbol, and one of us would set to work teasing out its meaning. We tried to leave behind our modern sensibility, with consequently terse results. Even so, there was no guarantee that two of us would read the same line the same way.

This was abundantly clear from the first. Tina with the scorpion tattoo had unearthed a large clam shell spidered with cracks, on the underside of which were visible four characters. She propped it up on a dining table and got to work.

Horse

Run

Sun

Cave,

she wrote, in a fine Spencerian hand. The marks were easy to identify. On the other side of the ledger, she inscribed her hypothesis: "When the cavalry flees the light of the sun, they live as if in a cave." It was like a little Zen koan that slipped easily in and out of the mind.

After a lunch of champagne mangos and eggs benedict, Tina, the one who wore her hair up in biscuits, studied the same row of markings. She tore a fresh sheet from the ledger, copied down the text, and wrote:

Storm

River

Dog

Spear.

"How . . . ?" sputtered the Tina who'd first interpreted, rubbing her tattoo.

"Just because something *looks* like a horse's mane doesn't guarantee it means 'horse.'"

"But I'm basing it on the work of Bodenheim at Yale and Marone at Columbia."

"Bodenheim and Marone have been dead for years," chimed in Tina, returning from the fields with berries in her calabash. "Besides, no one even *knew* about the island back then."

"So we start from scratch," said Hair-Biscuit Tina. "A storm. A river. A dog. A spear. I'm basing it on what we know today. I suggest you do the same."

The first Tina didn't seem upset, though her face continued to register perplexity. "You mean there was a storm, so they went to the river—and killed a dog with a spear?"

Tina with the French manicure spoke up, "Or do you mean that storms are like rivers, in that they bark like dogs?"

"You forgot the spear part," I said.

Tina with the hair biscuits shook her head. "Tina, Tina, think about it. You're living three thousand years ago. Everything is simple."

"But it can't just be things," complained Invisible Braces Tina, who I knew had written a monograph on Bodenheim. "There have to be *connections.*"

All this philology was making us hungry. Tina with the perfect eyebrows spoke. "I want to make a pizza using pineapples and maybe some coconut."

"I second that emotion," said Tina.

II.

I should mention that the island had no name, no human population apart from eighteen Tinas, and no fixed position: that is to say, it drifted in a rather astonishing rectangle two degrees longitude by a half-degree latitude. Sometimes in bed you could feel the ground move or convince yourself that you could. It did not appear on the normal maps. Tina suggested that we might be on one of the mythical islands that Qin Shi Huang, China's first emperor, believed was home to the elixir of immortality. Early in his reign he had sent his chief alchemist and a crew of a thousand virgins in search of it, but the ship never returned. I registered my skepticism: The water on the island was atrocious—an untreated pint would kill you—and the old quack probably had a different idea for the virgins. But Tina's romantic notion caught everyone's fancy: We would live forever, provided we stayed on the island. It would be our little Shangri-la.

As our term of contract passed the halfway mark, our happy mood darkened. We wanted never to leave and came to dread the moment every morning when one of us had to flip the page on our communal calendar.

"What do you call Muhammad Ali after a bowl of beans?" Tina read aloud, to defuse the gloom. It was one of those joke-a-day deals.

After a minute of stone silence, she tilted her head to read the inverted solution. "Gaseous Clay," she said. Someone started crying.

There was still so much to discover, so many characters left to translate. We tried to think of a way to extend our tour of duty. Tina suspected that the man who bankrolled the Syllable Foundation, an old China hand turned oil tycoon, had once pined for an unattainable Tina, perhaps had wooed her before the war and lost her when he came back limbless. Maybe he had dreamt her up while in the grips of malaria and never guessed her basic nonexistence. Such explanations were the stuff of florid fiction, and I tried to explain that it was just coincidence that out of three thousand applicants, the chosen ones all had the same name. But Tina and Tina and Tina weren't buying it.

We contemplated sending some saucy photos, the Syllabic sybarites draped languorously over pottery shards and lexicons, feeding one another thumb-sized grapes, but that plan could backfire: It wouldn't do to waste a resource as precious as film. So we pecked out letters on the rusty old Remington, asking the Foundation to consider the value of establishing permanent scholars on the island. A final draft was produced. Then we realized there was no mail service. I volunteered to type out five more copies. These were sealed and tied to the legs of birds we'd befriended. We hoped for the best, releasing them into the giant Rothko painting that was the sky at twilight, salmon over slate. The sight of those hearty messengers winging eastward filled our hearts with hope.

Later that night, after a rain had cleared the haze, with the moon dripping amber over everything, Tina noticed a few of the birds strutting outside the mess hall, looking a little sheepish, if that can be said of birds. They were pecking the dirt like chickens, trailing the letters they had ripped to shreds. It was too demoralizing for words. In our optimism we had sent off the original, and none of us had the energy to re-create the language. Tina prepared a midnight snack, birds of paradise with peanut sauce, on kebabs soaked in mint tea.

We carried on. In the great cavern, atop wheeled scaffolding, we chalked up all the known symbols. It was a wall of text, massively beautiful, and the crude shapes seemed to hum with life. Each character was a meter high and numbered in red. On the opposite wall, on a more conservative scale, we wrote the corresponding definition or possible definitions. The rock turned pink with erasure and doubt.

It was hard work, and the idea of having a "personal life" was very alien indeed. Some had husbands; most had boyfriends; a few were looking extremely lesbian. I cannot deny a mad flirtation with Pageboy Tina that faded as October rolled around. After a hard day's dig, we would swing in a single hammock, notebooks in hand and a head at either end, Englishing what we joked was the earliest love poetry extant. In the garden the deranged hydrangea bloomed backward, unfurling under Japanese lanterns and folding up like paper vampires at the first touch of dawn. All we knew were flowers and footrubs and perfect acts of language. We listened as French Manicure Tina plucked a cat-gut lute, and a chorus of Tinas resurrected a ramshackle sea chantey. I don't remember the words, just the diligent bees that coated the landscape, and the Venus flytraps snapping at the ghosts of bluebottles, and Tina disentangling forever her fingers from mine.

It was all over before it had even begun. One day I heard her tell Tina, in a voice designed for an audience, that she missed her fiancé, who sold stock in San Diego, collected coins in Cap d'Antibes, played tight end in Tarrytown—I forget the specifics. *Fiancé my sculpted arse,* I thought. I was so confused. Love, if it was love, always kicked me in the teeth, even here among my supposed sisters. I told myself I wouldn't let Tina hurt me again, and later that night began work on my character, the upside-down F.

I called it the Feather, partly for its shape, partly because the ivory sliver on which I'd found it looked like a quill. It was the only one of its kind. Its position amid a series of what we knew to be "placeholders"—they looked like asterisks—suggested a combination of the literal and the abstract. It was a tricky concept. A rendering of a hand, for example, could mean both an actual hand and associated activities: writing, hunting, cleaning, cooking. In certain cases, the definition of this same symbol went beyond that, to honesty (an open hand hides no weapons) or power (a mighty warrior needs no weapons to defeat a foe). When you got to that level, everything could mean anything, as well as its opposite. You had to pick which side of the contradiction to embrace or else record the whole unholy snarl itself.

It was reasonable to link the Feather to an L-shaped letter, the meaning of which we had previously isolated as "singing" or "song." Tina had brilliantly noticed that it generally came before long descriptions of drinking. Furthermore, a small horizontal line attached to the midpoint of stalk-based symbols and jutting right was thought to denote incidents performed under some state of inebriation. Other rules and contexts presented themselves. With these in mind, I came up with "Drink-song" as a definition for my Feather.

I said it aloud in my tent, long after midnight. *A drinking song? Maybe—not necessarily. You see, things were simple back then. You drank, you sang, but we cannot call it a drinking song, no, not yet. We needed more pieces of the puzzle.* I paced as I delivered my lecture extempore in a German accent that lent authority. In my mind the subtleties of the Feather became patent.

"Hello, darling," Tina mumbled from her cot. "Could you put a lid on it, love?"

I pecked her on the cheek and snuffed the candle.

The next morning brought applause at my solution but also a fateful setback. Tina, who served up a mean Cobb salad, had fallen ill with a parasite. I touched the blue veins at her temple, not that I knew what I was doing, having lied about a nursing degree on my résumé. We loaded her and half a Virginia ham in a self-correcting canoe slathered with shark repellent. It would reach China in two weeks. Tina, who had the best calligraphy, wrote detailed instructions as to the care our companion should receive.

Her replacement arrived within a week, in the same vessel. She introduced herself as Tina from Auckland and bore greetings from the Syllable Foundation. She had no discernible accent. We welcomed her with song and three long tables heaped with delicacies, though she only touched the melon and the wine. I held my tongue, but in truth, I suspected something from the moment I saw her leave the canoe and kick a donkey in the ribs. She was certainly a sight to behold. She had a potbelly and a John Wayne swagger and didn't care much for clothing. She was shorter than the average Tina by half a foot. When she removed her Stetson, we were greeted by a shock of powder blue hair that looked like a chemistry and physics experiment rolled into one.

That night I put my finger on it: She was a dead ringer for one of those little troll dolls that kids put on the ends of pencils. Who could forget their beady glare? I would call her Tina, but in my mind I prefixed an anagram. She was the Anti-Tina.

III.

Our curiously coiffed rookie bunked with "my" Tina, though of course I'd ceased to think of her that way. I noticed them walking to meals together, laughing in the stupid garden. They even did that tired routine: one would redden her lips with berries and drink from the chalice, then the other would sip from the same side and get the color smeared on.

Get a room, I thought, then realized that they already shared one.

The week of the monsoon scare, all of us moved our tents to the cavern. We piled stones by the entrance and hunkered down, an impromptu vacation, but the Anti-Tina braved the weather, disappearing for hours. One morning I saw her head off to the dig site alone. I took an alternate route and met her there, feigning surprise and (what was harder) delight.

"Great work on the 'Feather,'" she said, in her evil chipper voice.

"Thanks. It was hard work."

"Translation always is. Of course, it's completely wrong."

Though I had no reason not to expect animosity, the words felt like a slap. "Is it."

"You isolated the radical for 'drink' and the radical for 'song', and you got 'drink-song.' That's hardly what I'd call poetic."

"Poetry's not the point," I said. I questioned her anachronistic use of the word "radical," but held my tongue. "We're committed to accuracy."

"All poetry is accuracy," she said.

I was regretting my decision to trail her. "Who died and made you goddess?" I muttered.

"Your so-called Feather really unfolds like so." She held up a finger and translated, in a warbly voice a half-octave higher than her normal one: "'Well-Moistened With Cheap Wine, the Sailor and the Wayfarer Sing of Their Absent Sweethearts.'"

I burst out laughing. "Sure, sure. That'll go over great with the rest of the Tinas."

"Amateurs," she snorted. "Tell me, Tina. What do you know about the Shang Dynasty? What do you *really* know?"

I didn't answer. She unscrewed a flask and took a swig.

"You studied with Professor Mütter at Princeton, right?"

"That's the other Tina. I was at Michigan."

"Ah. With Dickie Phung and that wretched Ledbetter."

"I won't listen to you insult my mentors," I said. I walked off, but the Anti-Tina kept pace beside me, whiskey on her breath.

"There *was* no Shang Dynasty," she said. "You know that it was pure myth until 1899, right? It was like believing in Zeus. Then a professor, bumbling around in the boondocks, went to fill a prescription and saw these grotty turtle shells in the window, covered with weird letters." I knew the story, but I let the troll finish. "The country folk had used this stuff for medicine, grinding it up, mixing it with water and mushrooms. And then—wham. Suddenly all the gobbledygook was supposed to be writing from the Shang Dynasty."

"You're saying it's not writing, just nonsense pictures?"

The Anti-Tina shook her head. "Thing is, you've got it all wrong on the level of *history*." She picked up a stick and started peeling off the bark. "Did you ever hear of the Kingdom of Women?"

"Can't say I have."

"An old wives' tale, about a land of Chinese amazons. Sailors supposedly reached it in the fifth century. Some say it might have been America. But that's wrong. It was here. On this island." She threw the stick back into the brush. "And we weren't even Chinese."

I stopped. What did she mean, "we"?

"It was beautiful, it was beautiful for a thousand years, we had no weapons or war, we had plenty to eat, we lived till a hundred or more," she babbled. "Each letter had a meaning, and each person was a letter, and when somebody said your letter aloud you had to go to them. Even if you were sick, or dying, or dead." She put a hand on my arm. "Which is why I'm here, Tina. Your 'Feather' was *my* letter."

She was clearly crazy. I wondered, for the first real time, whether the Syllable Foundation had actually sent her—or if she'd ambushed our poor, parasite-prone Tina. We never should have let her go off alone. Sharks hadn't been the worst of it.

The Anti-Tina continued to talk: "We imported men from the mainland and fed them hellebore porridge to forget, and once they'd served their purpose we sent them back." There was a pregnant pause. "Baby boys we left for the turtles and the lyrebirds."

"And you all had blue hair," I said. "OK."

"That's right." She smiled. "And we all had something else." She tipped her head forward, gathering thick strands with either hand, until I could see through a parting two dark little horns. When I awoke I was alone, at the temple ruins, the farthest point from camp, with a blanket wrapped around me and a log under my head.

I didn't mention the horns the next day, or the next; in a fortnight I wondered whether I hadn't dreamt it all. The Anti-Tina now wore her Stetson round the clock and was definitely avoiding me, while bonding with the rest of the camp. Her saccharin voice, her fake affection. It was like she was running for sheriff.

On the first day of November, French Manicure Tina was hunting a rabbit on foot—using the ineffective method of throwing pebbles—when she found herself before a creekbed that had eluded our mapping. Something on a flat rock caught the sun, and when she waded in she discovered a knot of gold as big as her hand.

"Gold!" Tina cried. "Gold!"

And like lemmings the rest of the Tinas rushed to the water. Tina left the leeks on the chopping board and brought pans and Tupperware from the cupboards. Tina with the hair biscuits, the most brilliant woman I'd ever met, stopped translating a segment of turtle shell to run barefoot and screaming with joy. It was all so degrading that I had to have a look.

The gleam from the creek was unreal. You couldn't tell where the sun left off and the gold began. Everyone was panning, dancing, even crying. But where was the Anti-Tina? Something was wrong. I sensed her spying from the margins with a glass, gauging how easy it would be to claim us, an army of Tinas already in love with her. I began to shout, telling everyone to stop, that we weren't here for treasure, that we shouldn't be putting a price on our souls. Then I tripped on a hunk of gold. They dragged me back to camp, and Hypodermic Tina slipped me a sedative that collapsed the hours.

"Tina, are you feeling OK?" It was my ex, good old Tina with the fiancé. For a moment, she was close enough to kiss.

"I'm feeling fine," I said. "Couldn't be better. It's the rest of you I'm worried about."

The whole thing was maddening. They were still blind to the set-up, and the more I inveighed, the less they wanted anything to do with me. I knew if I dug under the Anti-Tina's cot, I would find bars of gold, with tools to forge them into "natural" shapes. I would find blue food coloring, glue-on horns, and who knew what other jiggery-pokery. There would be an elaborate headdress, made of conch shells and jade, for whenever she crowned herself queen of the Kingdom of Women.

All the Tinas loved her, and now most thought I was nuts. That night I packed silently. I patted my bunkmate Tina's beautiful blond hair, the edges of which, I noticed, had been dyed turquoise. An unchecked tear rolled off my cheek onto hers.

"You're off then, love," she said between snores. "Mind the gap, as they say. Mind the gap."

When the canoe hits the mainland, the inevitably swarthy dock workers ask me where I've come from, in a derelict dialect that's hard to sort out. I say nothing and hand over my notebook full of oracles. At town hall I down a thimble of rice wine and ring up the Syllable Foundation. The connection is surprisingly clear. The woman who answers the phone, to my relief, is not named Tina. I tell Rachel that the island has been swallowed up, that all you can see from above is a widening mass the color of ink. I lie, but I'm good at lying. I think I use the phrase "only survivor."

Rachel spells out the password for my plane ticket, GRINGO, which will be waiting for me at the Shanghai airport. I try to sleep on the train, but even the racket of the wheels can't muffle the voices from the shore. They repeat my name so many times that it breaks the consonant fetters, merges with the songs of birds whose names I never learned. Now I can see the Tinas holding up their gold-grubbing pans, standing tall and tan in panama hats, bandanna bikinis. The river shimmers like a special effect.

Standing apart from the rest, on a shelf in the cliff wall, the Anti-Tina smiles, surveying their work, their hair. Her horns are in the open. She sees my vessel and waves with one hand, drinking the last of the year's good wine with the other. The wind is a cat's paw, conjuring a rune on the water. It's a simple symbol: two lines crossing at a slant. My oracle book is gone, and I try to remember the meaning. It might be as long as the tale I've just told, or as short as a single word: *Go*, I think it means, or *stay*. Or possibly both at once.

Angel
Shelley Jackson

When the taxidermist found the dead boy, he was astonished, but not as astonished as he thought he ought to be. The boy lay on his back with his head turned sideways toward his bent arm, and there was something familiar in the way the wrist was curled around so that the back of the fingers pressed lightly against the mouth, while the splayed legs, turned out further at the hips than was usual in the living, looked like something he had seen in a photograph or on TV. The body lay among weeds in a copse of thin, unhealthy trees near a sluggish curve of the man-made stream in the park, a place that had never seemed to hold any special claim to significance.

For those who will in the future also discover a dead body: though at present you can't imagine what you will think when that time comes, what you will discover is that all the information about the dead is contained in the living body, which you know perfectly well. There is nothing more to know about the dead; there is in fact slightly less to know. The dead body is only a bad impression of a living one. It is something like a piece of bad taxidermy.

The taxidermist considered himself and found he was not disgusted by the dead boy. He found him less uncanny than a live one full of secret thoughts and fears and hopes. He thought, when we say an inanimate object is haunted or possessed, what we really mean is it's like us. Death is a kind of exorcism, and corpses are the only really trustworthy people. He would have liked to communicate these thoughts to Darla, who was interested in death and ghosts, but Darla was through with him.

The taxidermist sat down beside the body, his arms folded on his knees. Night had almost arrived, and when he slitted his eyes, the body was just a shape: a blobby x, with complications. He unfocused his eyes to the point that the complications did not show, and sat at peace in the dark with only a tangy smell to offer specific information, information in this case about substances that had leaked from the shape, as substances will. That was something he had learned from taxidermy: a shape was a shape, but sooner or later you had to deal with specifics.

The taxidermist sat by the dead boy a long time, keeping him company and thinking about what to do, though the evening became cold and he heard a skirmishing in the underbrush—rats, he imagined, though it might have been squirrels or chipmunks. He was not afraid of rats or disgusted by them. As a taxidermist, he had stuffed many rats that had died supping on the bitter tisanes served up by his landlady in the back passage by the garbage cans.

Stuffed was a misnomer, as he had explained to his father many times; taxidermists no longer merely "stuffed" skins but stretched them over a carefully modeled figure. Think of Michaelangelo's *David* in a wig of human hair. Taxidermy was not, perhaps, a high art like painting, but it was certainly a demanding craft, requiring patient, knowing hands, a sense of forms in space, and close observation of the living animal. Furthermore, the taxidermist was not a killer, as his father had characterized him to a poet friend in his rage and disappointment, though he supposed he might be a "throwback" as his father had also declared. The taxidermist practiced his skill only on the kill of others, and on such specimens as chance laid, already dead, in his path.

It was his father who had taught him to study the shapes of things. When other children were drawing stick figures and suns, the future taxidermist was trying to achieve an asymmetrical balance between two squares of unequal size. His father looked on, tapping his brush handle against his teeth. Finally he nodded. But when the future taxidermist asked if he might call his composition "Father and Son," his father cast him out of his studio, saying he had a hopelessly narrative sensibility.

His father had declared many times that he had furthered his art by the little trick of unfocusing his eyes to study form and composition without getting hung up on details of rendering. That and squinting. Years of squinting and unfocusing, though, had had a deleterious effect on his vision, and when he was in his cups he often lamented the loss of his once-keen eyesight to his friend the poet. Despite this, his father would not wear his glasses outside the house, claiming to appreciate the play of abstract forms that the visual world became without the disciplinary lens. The taxidermist thought the real reason was that he was vain.

Sometimes the fatherless taxidermist let his eyes unfocus so he could see what his father had seen. Sometimes, just for a moment, he did it when he was crossing the street.

His landlady, a word starting with L, was masturbating again. He knew it the moment he opened the front door. The smell of cat pee that permeated the hall seemed to intensify when she became excited. He imagined, and gagged imagining, a physical object, something like a cotton wad soaked with musk and sulfuric acid, tamped into the back of his throat. The taxidermist made a big fuss of jingling his keys, banging his packages against the radiator, slamming the door and then rattling the knob to test that the door was really locked. It used to be that this silenced her, silenced as a bonus the amorous calls of her cats, and he would climb the stairs in peace, though nervously aware of her wet fingers still pressed among her folds and her breath rising and falling strongly in her chest. Now she did not stop when he came in, and he could hear her door softly creaking in its frame and the tang vibrating metallically in the lock as she rubbed herself against the doorknob on the other side.

There were slithery sounds, and the small paw of a cat slid out from under the door, claws sensuously extended. The taxidermist raised his foot and slowly lowered it onto the paw, which was quickly pulled back.

He started up the stairs, but was stopped by a call from behind the door: "Is that you? Just a second! I have something for you!" He shook his head. For a moment he had thought it was the cat who spoke. The masturbator opened the door after a time of it jiggling in which, as he imagined it, her fingers were aslip on the knob, both knob and fingers greasy. He was relieved when, rather than whipping open her dressing gown, she handed him a small package wrapped in lime green tissue paper, and consequently he said "Thank you" with a great deal of verve, so much verve that she actually took a step back.

"I thought of you when I saw this," she said, "and I just had to buy it for you."

He took the package to his room and opened it there. It was a blank book. On the cover was a fat baby angel, in a thoughtful pose.

As a taxidermist he was often invited to have a look at the stuffed animals of others, hand-me-down horribles or the work of weekend hobbyists, and he saw a lot of birds arranged in poses that they'd never strike in life. So his first thought when he saw a picture of an angel was: That thing could never, ever get off the ground.

His father had once said that angles were holier to him than angels. Maybe for this reason, when in school the future taxidermist had been confronted with problems involving graphs, he had become suspicious and almost tearful, sensing a hidden moral dimension to every problem. He could not help seeing the graph as a kind of didactic picture in which the x-axis was his life on earth, proceeding from left to right, the y-axis went up to heaven or down to hell, and threatening apparitions swung over his head or coiled under the earth with sinister intent. The z-axis, when he came to hear of it, was something disturbing and almost unthinkable, because it stuck into and out from the page in an uncomfortable direction, possibly straight through his heart, into his soul.

Angles, therefore, had always frightened him, and when it came to that, angels were worryingly ambiguous as well. What was the connection with Cupid? Was there some general confusion there, between the pagan love god and the Christian angels, and the notion, he did not believe it was scriptural, that dead children became angels in heaven? Or was the confusion only his own? Angels were not all good. There were fallen angels, which, if he had to graph them, he would place in the lower left hand quadrant, in the negative numbers. In Breughel these were characterized by the infelicitous melding of characteristics from many species. But then so were the good, the risen, the still airborne angels, since human and bird features surely did not belong together any more than the head of a frog belonged to the body of a crawfish.

There was such a thing, also, as the angel of death. What kind of an angel was that? He pictured a ghastly child, cherubic but white as chalk, fluttering around his head sprinkling deadly powders. Or just taking him out with a pair of nunchucks.

The taxidermist's landlady was a compulsive masturbator, and she had other peculiarities as well. When he had first moved in, his landlady had refused to say how many cats she had. From this he had suspected at least three, and the smell in the stairwell, mounting to the landing and beyond on a damp day, suggested more. The first time he entered her apartment—she had invited him in for coffee several times, though the invitations had ceased when Darla had started coming over; they had picked up again when she left—there had been six in plain sight, parts of several more visible through the chinked bedroom door, and suspicious noises in the kitchen. Now he knew for a fact that there were at least thirteen cats, since he had seen white ones, black and white ones, brindled ones, grey, brown and grey ones, tabby, calico, tabby and white, grey and white, brown and white, brown, brown and black, and black ones. But he thought there were as many as twenty or thirty.

He knew she had one less than before.

Most of the cats had something wrong with them: a bald patch with wet sores on it; one swollen, crusty eye; hair balls. They were always gagging or vomiting. He had not noticed this right away, but many of the cats had extra toes on their front paws—in some cases so many, and distributed in such a way, that each paw seemed to be composed of two paws imperfectly merged. It was apparently difficult for these cats to lift these broad, heavy paws, and they seemed to bump into things that they could have avoided, as if doing it on purpose to call attention to their predicament. These cats seemed to be aware of their special status and even to enjoy it. They were regally fat and lazy. They did not mind having their paws handled; they seemed to expect it.

The cats of his landlady sometimes keened all together, a throaty wail that penetrated his floorboards and rose up in the pipes so that it was sometimes as though he lived inside a keening cat, a cat in heat. Sometimes the keening became a shrieking that was the sound he imagined a rat might make having its skin pulled off over its head—an operation he had performed many times on the dead, not without imagining its effect on the living. This sound made his blood stand still in his veins like a sudden red tree. Sometimes, especially late at night, he would hear soft thuds under his floor, as if the cats, running faster and faster in circles, had freed themselves sufficiently from gravity to take to the walls, finally banging themselves against the ceiling in their frenzy. He imagined his landlady lying back in bed, shiny in eye and tooth, watching their transports with both hands under the covers. He imagined cats in coitus on his landlady's vanity, stuck together and bawling among bottles of unguents, male cats standing with stiff legs and vibrating tails in the bathroom, hosing down her towels and dressing gown with musk, female cats crying invitations from her closet. Growing excited, he imagined cats fucking in her open underwear drawer, cat semen stains on the cotton crotch of her fleshtoned panties, and he imagined her wearing those panties, unwashed.

If his landlady was a cat lady, he was a rat man. His room was full of rats. They were dead, of course, and meticulously prepared for mounting, so there was a difference between him and his landlady, a difference which might either make him less crazy than his landlady, or more so—he wasn't sure which. Certainly, crazy in a different way. He did not let his landlady enter his room, to which he had installed his own lock. His landlady did not know that his room was full of mounted specimens, mainly of rats. She might have considered them unclean, though he washed the skins fastidiously with his own shampoo, and painted them with preservatives murderous to all microscopic forms of life. She would be distressed, he thought, to see one of her cats among the specimens on display, and would jump to conclusions injurious to their relationship, though in actuality the cat had died from eating rat poison that she herself had set out, or perhaps from eating one of the poisoned rats. The cat was not a perfect specimen (though the taxidermist had done his best to conceal the patches of missing fur), having perhaps suffered some indignities from the still-living rats after its demise. The taxidermist imagined that the rats had held festivities around its body, mocking its rictus with increasingly daring tarantellas in the vicinity of the dead mouth, whisking their tails right over the bared teeth on which the saliva was long dry. This is how he had once depicted the incident in an elaborate tableau, which was like those one might find in a natural history museum, but unusual for the urban setting and the fact that in the central specimen he had tried to achieve a convincing imitation not of life but of death. He called this tableau "Vulgarity Disavows The Unease Of The Living Toward The Dead."

He regularly rearranged the specimens, assembling them in tableaux that illustrated moral principles. Every day when the taxidermist woke up and looked around his room, he was uplifted by his arrangements and went forth to restock jug wines with a will. The sensibility that informed these arrangements was narrative, granted. His father had been right about that. He did not go so far as to dress his rats in little smocks and berets, but it was almost as bad. One of his tableaux was called "Father and Son."

It had taken him rather a long time to notice that *rat*, rearranged, was *art*.

Moral was an overstatement. The tableaux were arranged in various ways, depending on his mood. If he had time after he got up in the morning, he liked to set the tone for the day by rearranging his rats. Sometimes he just knew what kind of day it was going to be, and he arranged the rats accordingly, either right in line with how he thought it was going to be or, if he dared, subtly different, so he could try to change his luck. Some days he had no idea and he just did what he felt like, and sometimes these arrangements turned out afterward to be the most perfect ones of all. The morning Darla left him, while she was asleep, he had set up all the rats on one side of the room in rows like an army. He had put the cat on the other side of the room. He had called this arrangement "Reclining Empress Reviews Her Troops," but it turned out the title was wrong, though the arrangement was close to perfect.

It was easy to get the emotional content of a tableau completely wrong, he found. The rats were very expressive, but expressive of what? was the question. Whatever he had the rats doing, they seemed to be in the right, most eloquent postures—it was instructive how warlike a preening or foraging pose could seem in a new context. Or how grief-stricken, how merry, how amorous. In fact, the more neutral and "natural history" the pose, the more emotive it seemed once the original context was removed. A squirrel that was contorted from holding onto what in a museum setting would have been a branch or a fence post, when contorted around air seemed to be in a kind of struggle with himself or with invisible devils or angels. It was an uncanny thing to see a rat brawling stock-still with a hurly-burly of motionless wind. Their upraised arms were twiggy and severe. They seemed to be making demands in a sign language he did not know.

By the usual standards of the profession, the taxidermist was wasting his time on offal; the approbative words "noble specimen" could in no way be applied to even the best-looking rat. His father, had he been alive, would also have disapproved, but for a different reason: from the point of view of his father even rats deserved respect. The taxidermist was denying the rats their own kind of dignity, such as it was, by making them stand up after the time had come for their lying down, and act out foolishness for his private gratification. And the way he used them, played with them like dolls, was further abomination. His father would have said the dead should be allowed to lie back in the peace of their bodily decay, and people had no business propping them up and making an entertainment out of them. He would have said that even the so-called tasteful arrangement of expertly mounted specimens in well-observed natural poses among plants and lichens native to their own ecosystem was not much less chilling than the novelty treatments, and really, what was more unnerving than the frozen impression of life where death was the reality? That what was lifelike in the living was their quick, uncatchable changing, which was x'd out as if it had never been by the catching of it.

He pictured his father frozen, his hands holding something that wasn't there.

Here's how to skin a rat: slit the skin at the belly with a very sharp knife. Separate the skin from the body on each side, forcing your fingers down between them. Peel the skin back down over the legs to the feet. Cut the feet from the legs; the feet stay attached to the skin. Pull the skin off the tail, making a small slit on the underside near the tip to help loosen it. As you pull the skin up off over the head, it turns inside out. The eyeless, empty skin and the skinned body wind up facing each other, stuck together at the mouth. It is as though the rat is kissing its own ghost. Like someone having trouble admitting he is dead.

Until recently, the taxidermist had actually made a living by his craft. While he was still living at home, he had done a good trade in novelty mountings, which in this case meant butts—deer butts, antelope butts, you name it—mounted on plaques for hanging. You've seen heads on plaques; this was the same idea turned around. A certain kind of person enjoyed this sort of thing, and it was certainly surprising the first time you saw it when you were expecting a head and rack of antlers. Your eyes tried to make the butt into a face, in which the tail was some kind of tufty Dr. Seuss nose. Customers also enjoyed the joke that this was all of the animal they had been able to bag. Or as one ad put it, "More often than not, this is the view of the elusive whitetail deer that most hunters remember seeing as the buck bounds off into the safety of a thicket. The deer rump mount is a great way to pay tribute to all the 'ones that got away.'"

He had considered mounting one of his rats in this fashion and hanging it near the floorboard as if it were disappearing into a hole in the wall. This would surprise the cat lady and her cats, though knowing the cats they would not waste any time in uncovering the trick of it.

One of the last things the taxidermist's father had said was, "My son sells deer butts." This was not just a statement of fact, though it was a statement of fact, it was also a lament, though said in a flat voice. He said this, and went for a walk in front of a speeding car. Of course he didn't see it coming; he had left his glasses at home, on the ledge of his easel. From what they could tell the taxidermist after the autopsy, his father had been struck hard enough to be knocked off his feet, but though the internal bleeding that eventually killed him had already begun, no bones were broken, and he had apparently been able to stand up, and, knowing his father, tell the driver he was all right, just fine, no need to make a fuss—his father had an exaggerated sense of personal dignity—and walk to the side of the road under his own steam.

His father had died sitting up, leaning against a section of piping left to abide by the roadside when the money for improvements dried up. When the taxidermist found him some time later, he looked relaxed and affable and had a look of mild, pleasant surprise as if about to say hello to a friend he hadn't seen in a while. In fact, the taxidermist had already said "What's up, Dad?" before realizing his father had passed away. The words hung around foolishly in the air as if they had no place to go.

Rigor mortis had set in and it was not possible on first trial to cause his father to lie down in a dignified posture of rest, and so the police took him to the coroner's office in a sitting up position. Of all details, this was the one the taxidermist could not bear to think about, and so he thought about it all the time, as if it were drawn toward him by his aversion to it. So, gradually, it became part of his sense of things. Sitting reminded him of death, and almost everything reminded him of sitting: chairs, of course, and butts, but also anything bent in the middle, anything L-shaped, even the letter L itself. His father was a right angle. The taxidermist did not have to be sitting or see someone sitting or even thinking explicitly about sitting to feel a sense of sitting come over everything, what his father would have called sitting in the abstract, like a shape he could see hidden inside completely different shapes. Not that things might sit at any moment, but that they were in some sense already sitting—though dead, sitting; though living, yet dead, and sitting.

After his father's death, the taxidermist had begun posing some of his animals in this position, though for most animals it was not a natural one and indeed gave the appearance of broken bones and, in consequence, of death, which was exactly what in the taxidermic specimen one usually wanted above all to avoid. His paying work disappointed him now, and he turned away those customers asking for novelty butt plaques so vehemently that he acquired a bad name, and his business suffered. Eventually he moved to the city and got a job at Wine and Spirit World.

The day after he found the dead boy, he had to work the morning shift. It was a quiet time. The taxidermist spent a lot of the time gazing out the side window at a black shape he thought was Darla in the window of Nice Nails. But when he got off work, he saw Darla crossing the street toward Nice Nails from the bus stop. Ergo, whatever he had been staring at wasn't Darla. This made him so disgusted he decided to go see the body again, just to spite Darla, who would have wanted to see a dead boy for sure.

Darla had been the one to point out to him the eeriness of "Wine and Spirit World." Darla was goth and attuned to the beyond. She used to wander over to talk to him whenever she didn't have any customers at the nail salon, and she had been taken with what she saw as his macabre hobby, which he had told her about one day in an insane fit of bravery. He in turn was taken with her thick powdery makeup, which left white streaks on his black sheets, and the blond roots gleaming secretly in the part of her black hair, and above all her deep purplish red lips, which would leave a color around the seat of his maleness akin to what one might acquire through intercourse if it was the girl's time of the month. She had a pear shape and weirdly short arms, but they looked good on her. Her hips and butt were copious, her breasts small on a ribcage so narrow he thought her lungs must be the size of a smaller mammal's, maybe a fox's or a rabbit's, and crowded up close against her heart as if for warmth. When she became excited, she panted shallowly, and her pink tongue contrasted interestingly with the unreal color of her lips.

He was in love with her pussy. You might think a girl like that, with the perfect nails and the dyed hair, a girl you never saw without her face done, would keep her pubic hair trimmed or even shaved, but no, when she still had her panties on, her full bush packed the crotch in front almost as if she had a man's equipment. She was furry higher than was usual in front, with a treasure trail right up to the navel, and lower down her thighs, too. It was sexy, as if more of her were pussy than of other people. And the item itself was a treat: sweet, clean, milky-mild, friendly and adaptable. He imagined he could tell her youth (she was nineteen) from the taste of her, and that she ate well and was not much of a drinker; in fact, her eyes would go softly out of focus just from nipping at one of the tiny bottles of Kahlua or Goldschlager she liked. Really she drank them for the sugar. She took them in tiny sips, like a hummingbird.

Darla had appreciated his specimens as no one had before, admiring in particular the dead cat. When the taxidermist got up early for work after a night she had slept over, he would arrange the rats in a love message to surprise her: for example, he would pour salt in a heart shape on the kitchen table and place two of the best-looking rats in an embrace in the center. He told her the story of the sitting up end of his father, and she said, "Whoa." Once, in bed, she had become very serious and said she had a confession to make, which was that at home at her parents' house she had one of the biggest Hello Kitty collections ever, and that she would never, ever give up Hello Kitty even though it did not go with her witchy-poo style. One of her favorite things he ever said was something she didn't hear the first time because he was under the covers between her thighs. She lifted up the quilt to look down at him and he got a blast of cool air. "Did you just say what I think you said?"

He couldn't tell if she was mad or not. "Hello pussy," he admitted.

"That's the best! That'll be my porn star name!" Darla said, and pushed his head down.

But after a while he noticed she was looking at him in a different way, without kindness. Once, she threw a pillow at one of his rats. She said it was creeping her out. "You? Creeped?" he said. She just shrugged. On their first date, she had commented that he used a lot of expressions that made him seem much older than he was (twenty-six): Heavens to Betsy, Hell's bells, for the love of Mike. "It's actually kind of cool," she had said. "Kind of retro." Now when he said one of these things she looked at him hatefully.

Then she split, making a small modification in his Reclining Empress tableau: she removed the cat. He thought up a new name for it on the spot: "When The Cat's Away The Rats May Play." He didn't realize that was the wrong name until he tried to make the bed. The cat was under the covers, with lipstick blood scribbled around the nose and butt. The right name? Of course. "Goodbye Pussy."

He knew what had happened. Darla had gone back to pink, reverted to the strawberry colors of her moist lining. She had lost her letch for death. He saw her in her room kitted out, kittened out, Hello Kitty from head to toe. He pictured her pink in a pink room, her face scrubbed. Her black clothes would be burning in a garbage can in the backyard, along with the *Malleus Maleficarum*, Alastair Crowley, and all the rest of it. So when he next saw her getting off the bus in her usual Morticia Addams getup, he received a profound shock.

One night not long after that he placed the dead cat on a towel on the floor beside his bed and got a washcloth and wet it and wrung it and folded it up and put it down next to the cat. Then he took his pants off, went to the window, walking his boxers down, and raised the blinds until the bottom bar swung against his stomach. The projecting edge of the windowsill dug into his legs just above his knees. He stood there tensing his butt muscles, a little dizzy, his balls pulling up tight. He was not completely erect but his cock felt full and heavy. He kept as still as he could. He thought it was possible that behind the glass he looked like some kind of mannequin or lay figure from a museum diorama, not a living person. The tip of his cock touched the cold window and made a tiny wet dot with a halo around it. He heard a clatter on the street. Though to be seen was in theory what he had been hoping for, he dropped to the floor, heart pounding, and scrambled on his hands and knees to the back of his room. Then he masturbated over the cat. When he came he pressed his spurting cock against its hard flank, on which there were still traces of lipstick. He used the damp cloth to clean the mess off its fur. The cloth came away pink.

It was after this that his landlady began her own masturbating ways, and he could only assume that by unlucky chance she had been the one to spot him at the window.

The taxidermist was not really expecting the body still to be there. True, the place was covered with tall weeds, the leaves of which were somehow sticky and spiky at once and could not be peeled off your clothes without leaving bits behind, but the boy was visible from at least two places on a path down which joggers and drug dealers intermittently passed. The taxidermist walked past, glanced over, saw that the boy was still there. He kept going. He was not in the mood.

He went for a stroll up the stream.

Had he not done so he would not have seen the rooster. It was not immediately apparent that it was a rooster, actually, because he could not see its head, and his father would have advised him not to leap to conclusions, hastening from a pattern of light and shade to a name and even a breed, but to describe only what he saw, which was a brown ruffled shape raised on sticklike forms which, despite his father's advice, he felt confident were its legs. A family—father, mother, toddler of uncertain sex—was standing around it, keeping a safe distance, discussing the bird in what he thought was a Slavic language. The rooster, who stood, sleeping, waiting or in despair, half under a bush on a well-trodden bank of the artificial stream, seemed to him to be sad, uncomfortable, dignified, and stoic. He knew this was a sentimental projection of which, again, his father would not have approved. The child became excited by the quiet behavior of the bird and began stamping its feet and squealing, whereupon the mother caught the child's hand and pulled it farther away from the bird. The bird brought forth its head from wherever it had hidden it away, and he saw that it was indeed a rooster, from the bright comb and wattles.

He left the rooster alone, but he marked where it was, and when he came back after a stroll around the playing fields, it was still there and the family was gone. The taxidermist thought the rooster might attack him or fly away and for this reason he took off his shirt to throw over its head; he understood that chickens were calmer with their eyes covered. (Or was that horses?) Whether for this reason or because the rooster had become dispirited by losing its way in the park, it remained calm the whole subway ride home, as calm as if it had been drugged.

That gave him an idea, and once he was home he spit on a bit of aspirin and squished it up and smeared the paste on the rooster's beak. When the rooster opened its beak a little, he poked a bit of the paste inside. Then he waited a while, to give the aspirin, if the rooster had actually swallowed any, the chance to work.

He did not kill the rooster, merely removed its wings. He set them to one side, stretched the skin together over the openings, and sewed them closed with a sterilized needle. Of course he was not a veterinary surgeon, and his skills in cutting and stitching were specific to the dead, but he was neat and careful, and knew his way around a bird. He was gentle, in so far as he could be. The rooster was unresponsive and had a fixed stare (but birds always stared); he thought it might not live, but hoped it would. He laid it in a cardboard box on top of the refrigerator, where it was warm, and covered it with a towel. If it lived through the night, he would set it free in the park.

The taxidermist wrapped the wings in plastic, tucked them into his bag of tools, and went back to the park.

He sat beside the body, waiting for it to acknowledge him, to abandon its air of absurd, exaggerated indifference. Little by little the body softened, grew eager and confidential. By small shifts and emissions it spoke of this to him. The taxidermist had already guessed it, felt the change in their relations. The body was becoming family. The body confessed to him its shame at being so relaxed and unventuresome in a world pullulating with projects and activities. It confided that it had feigned indifference in order to shield itself from the judgment of anyone passing by; it confessed that it knew this was a weakness, but one that it could not yet relinquish, though it was growing stronger and more able all the time. It confessed that its shame was already giving way to a willingness, even eagerness, to be exposed further and broken down into its primary components, so everyone might see exactly what it was made of. It confessed a desire to no longer resemble anything human; more and more it was in a hurry to forget the ways it had been wont to behave and adopt new, strange ways.

Right now, said the corpse in a voice of poisoned sighs and whistles, its name was still written in every cell, and it would be for some time; the only hope, it said, was to allow rats and even smaller animals to take away more and more of these innumerable copies of its signature, until it was so dispersed that there was no chance of reassembling it.

This was at odds with the taxidermist's plans for the corpse and he explained this to the body. He said he had a pocket knife and a bar of soap and some folded paper towels in his pocket, and that his bag he had brought with him contained more tools—the usual ones of his trade.

Fortunately, it was November; the weather was getting cold, and the dead boy was not much swollen, though when he pierced his abdomen to let off pressure and forestall a rupture, a noxious wind issued from the hole. Seepage had distressed the boy's shorts. He pulled the boy into the artificial stream and removed his clothes underwater before soaping him all over, which took care of most of the smell. Washing the hair gave him a strange feeling, as a dead head does not feel very different from a living one, but he got on with it and did a good job.

The taxidermist slit the skin over both shoulder blades and cut through the muscles until he could see the bone. He used a hand drill to pierce each shoulder blade in two places and worked the wire through and back up from under. Fiddly work, but doable. He wanted the wings to sit right on the shoulders, not just hang off the skin. He wound the wire up around the wing bones until they were solidly attached. He adjusted the angle. Then he pulled the skin together—the chicken skin and the human skin—and sewed it up.

The wings lay pretty on the shoulders, with their complicated patterns of feathering standing out against the white skin. They looked almost natural. He sat for a long time admiring the skin stretching around the join (his smallest, neatest, tightest stitches there), the washed and neatly imbricated feathers brushing the not yet discolored skin.

The dry, mostly meatless wings would last longer than the soft body. How strange, he thought, that we are meat, and that meat rots, and so we begin to stink when we die, like anything left out too long. The body was rotting already, starting to shift inside, undergoing all the familiar givings way, slitherings forth, the breaking down of barriers. But that sounded so martial and like it had to do with breastworks and barricades, when the process was something much gentler and more like cooking, a slow softening and permeating and fluid trading back and forth. When you looked at it this way, decay was like living, all in motion, only while living went in cycles this was a one-way trip.

Since he spent so much of his time with the dead, the taxidermist sometimes felt like he was dead already, that everyone was. The past was fixed and everyone was living it, or that shrinking part of the past that still lay ahead of them. Their gestures weren't really optional; they would prove in retrospect to be unchanging, final. Even his thoughts, in their repetitive circlings, would look from any distance like a fixed point. He, Darla, his masturbating landlady were all mounted specimens, memorabilia of the future.

It was not an alarming idea to him. The dead are friendly, if a little formal. They welcome you into their club. When you die, you are released from the tense present into centuries of the perfect past. It is a kind of graduation from the apprenticeship that is your brisk and abbreviated life.

In the morning he had a look at the rooster. It was dead.

At Wine and Spirit World, he found pieces of straw among the cartons downstairs and for a moment he thought: I'm in a diorama! Then he remembered that some of the expensive bourbons were packed in straw, and he was relieved. When he wheeled a hand truck past the chilled import beers, someone seemed to be looking at him from the refrigerated room behind, but he moved a six-pack of imported green beer and took a good look, and there was no one there.

It was so dead that day that everyone was just standing around glassy-eyed, so he asked and the manager let him go home early. He opened his front door as silently as he could, but someone heard him; a little grey paw with too many toes on it slid out from under the landlady's door. He stepped on it. There was a terrible squalling, and the paw was pulled away back under the door. He looked down, and there was a claw stuck in the carpet, a tuft of fur on the end of it. He covered it again with his foot, which meant he was standing very close when the door opened.

The landlady gave him a conspiratorial look and invited him to dinner. He accepted and waited for her to close the door. Then he picked up the toe and took it upstairs. A little later, he entered her quarters; the cats seemed unusually agitated, circulating the room in keeping with what seemed to be rigorous if complicated rules (running across the back of the couch, leaping from there to the top of the serving board, ducking behind the curtains to cross the window sill, emerging at the other side and leaping to the very top of the credenza, etc). His landlady crept into the kitchen, and he followed. She spat and hissed and cats spilled off all surfaces onto the floor, landing clumsily on their enormous bifurcated paws. On the kitchen counter, which four cats had just quit, was a big white ceramic bowl of spiky items. She picked it up and turned conspiratorially toward him. "We're having wings," she said.

After dinner, the taxidermist put the rooster and the cat and all the rats in a doubled lawn 'n' leaf bag and set out for the park. On the subway he saw a lady looking leerily at the bag and realized that a couple of the rat arms had punctured the plastic and were reaching through.

Between the subway stop and the park there was a discarded futon tied up in some decent rope, and he picked all the knots and unwound it. The futon came open and fell over on a Subaru and set off its alarm. He hurried off with the rope and his bag of rats.

He emptied the bag of rats beside the boy. He made the limp rooster and the cat lie down together to one side, but he set up the rats in a circle around the boy. With their scrawny arms clutching at non-present twigs and outcroppings of air, they looked like they were praising him, cheering him on in some athletic feat. As if lying there taking leave of everything were the hardest work of all. He wasn't sure of the title of this arrangement, but he had a feeling it started with an L.

What angels flew, these days, wouldn't be made of light. They'd still have the heaviness of their flesh, and there was a good chance they'd crash. They'd be jury-rigged. Conviction would fail them. There wasn't going to be any blaze of light or sublime angle graphed on the sky. Only the barest upward turning, the slightest lift at the end of a long downhill run.

He was not going to close his eyes and make believe he heard the rush of giant wings. He was going to go to a hardware store and buy some heavy screw-eyes. On the way back he was going to collect that blue painted board he always passed on his way into the park, that had once been part of a police barricade. He was going to tie the boy onto the board, screw the screw-eyes into the ends of the board, run the rope through them, throw the other end of the rope over a branch, and hoist him up. He was going to look hard at what was really there: a dead boy, the appurtenances of a chicken, his own sick handiwork. If the angel flew, he was going to have to fly with the available equipment, raising his untranscended flesh on chicken wings, dropping bugs on the faces of the faithful. There would be a smell.

If an angel, then *this* kind of angel.

If he flew, the taxidermist wouldn't see him. He would fly out of or into the page: the mortal direction, the invisible direction. He would take the z axis into the spirit world.

The body lurched up out of the ring of rats, decking a third of them. Something splattered on the leaves below. The taxidermist gave the body a push to start it swinging, then sat down quick to avoid the backswing, hoisting hard on the rope. Something whooshed through his hair. The rope shrieked as it sawed back and forth over the tree branch. He could not make out the angel against the dark branches overhead, only sense something hurtling toward his head. If he blurred his eyes, just for one moment, he could make believe it was flying.

Impala

John Gonzalez

I t's the start of a brand new life, Johnny."

"I'm Joey."

Laughter of Papa. "Sorry about that, kid. I'm on cloud nine."

Red '72 Impala shoots down the highway with Papa at the wheel. Air from open windows blows back his hair. Papa's elbow stuck out the window, arm rests on edge. Watching hair on arm squirm and flicker in the wind. Sun makes Impala hood shimmer. Faces of buildings along highway made bright in sunlight, slide past Impala.

"You can really see that Detroit's golden age was long over, eh? All run down and shitty. I bet if we could pull off one of these exit ramps we'd find some ratty gas station with an Arab sitting behind bullet-proof glass. So how long to 3 Deimos?"

Confusion of Self.

Papa laughs. His big belly shakes. "Oh, that's right. I forgot. What I mean is, check the map and tell me how long to Chicago."

"Yes, Daddy." Unfolding map across knees. Rechecking route from Detroit to Chicago. Papa leans forward and squints through slanted ray of light.

"Hey, that's the Fisher Building. Wow. So what makes the roof green?"

"Four hours, 20 minutes to Chicago, Daddy."

"Thanks. This thing handles like a dream, by the way. I can see you had good people go over every detail. During setup I measured the body length and fuck if it wasn't two hundred and nineteen *point* nine inches, exactly. Very impressive."

"I'm glad you're happy, Daddy."

"Another satisfied customer, right? And you look pretty good, too. I was worried they'd fuck you up working from 2D images, but you're pretty close. Too bad I couldn't take both of you. Did you know the '72 was the bestselling full-size car to date?"

Shaking head.

"It was. Car of the people, an honest car. I always wanted to drive one of these things, and it's everything I imagined. They knew how to travel back then. I'm in love—weather's gorgeous, cherry red '72 Impala, and a first-class routing lane. All courtesy of Mr. dumb son-of-a-bitch Akecheta."

Happiness of Self.

"So you and I, we're going to do some relating. I haven't seen you or your brother in months, and I could use the practice. I paid extra for the McDonald's thing, so I'll reset you when I get hungry, okay, Johnny boy?"

"I'm Joey."

"Fuck." Papa sucks lower lip. "Okay . . . anyhow, get some sleep." His fingers reach and ruffle Self-hair.

"Did you know that at this time McDonald's was the largest single owner of real estate on Earth? More than the Catholics, even. All they had was the Vatican."

Papa sits in hard plastic booth on other side of table. Wisps of steam drift up from Papa's coffee cup. Sun shines through plate glass window at edge of table, throws half of Papa's face into shadow.

Wince of Papa. "Seems they could at least *approximate* a cup of coffee. But maybe your food will be better, we'll see."

Yellow-wrapped cheeseburger and blue-wrapped fish fillet. Red carton spills french fries across brown plastic tray. Papa unwraps, eats, smacks lips.

"Are we near Chicago, Daddy?"

"You know we aren't." Papa chews. "We're about halfway, so it's cycling me through these towns I never heard of: Battle Creek, Kalamazoo. Oh, and there was one named, get this: Climax. I was like, what's next, Cum Stain?"

Laughter of Papa.

"Daddy, when we get to Chicago, can we see Sears Tower?"

"It'll be there. And so will a bed. I got to tell you, the Impala's nice, but I can't wait to hit 3 Deimos and climb out of this get-up for a while. I need some sleep. Haven't slept in thirty hours, and I could use a whore, too, you know what I mean? I paid extra to get the resort stops, so might as well get what I paid for. After Deimos I got a fourteen-hour haul to Callisto, but I can stay over there, too, before I make the shot to Nereid." Papa chuckles. "Or should I be saying 'Las Vegas?'"

Papa chews and smiles. Open mouth permits view of crushed fish meat and fries smeared over tongue. "What's in Vegas, Daddy?"

Papa grins. "A brand new life. Daddy has been lucky enough to come into some wealth. Not enough to make the difference—not *yet*—but enough to buy my way into playing some high-stakes tracts on Nereid, and from there I get rich. From there, I make a load of dough and come back home to show that fucking bitch your mother how wrong she was."

Nodding head. "What will you play, Daddy?"

"Do you got to say 'Daddy' after everything? It's getting on my nerves. As for what interactives I play, I used to do *NukeWar* and *Atrocity Man 5*, but now I'm pure *Shaolin*. Best Kung Fu tract there is. I do Monkey style and Mantis, but that was just prelude to mastering White Crane. Believe me, have I mastered White Crane. That's what's funding this little trip of ours."

Grin of Papa. He leans closer. Belly squeezes over table edge. "Get this. I am five billion dukes richer than I was twenty hours ago. And how? By playing *Shaolin*. Your mother keeps saying, 'That Kung Fu crap will never amount to anything,' but today I brought home more dukes than she makes in three years. *Three years*, Joey. And it's just the start: When I get to Nereid, I'll turn those billions into trillions and your mother'll shut her trap about my so-called 'money troubles.' Fuck her. When I get back the sky's the limit for you and Johnny but she can go straight to hell." Papa stabs table with finger.

Nodding head.

Papa drains coffee cup. Places cup on tray and pushes it to end of table. "Here's how it happened. I can't wait to tell the both of you when I get back, you're going to love it. The story is me and this Akecheta. I watch this guy for months at Shashida's, it's a low-class tract salon. He lords it over there. Undefeated. And he's rich because, well, because he's big in the drug trade, probably—he's no nice guy. This Akecheta is the biggest bastard you ever saw—" Papa spreads his hands. "Absolutely immense. Arms like tree trunks. He's one of these New-Sioux fucks.

"Now Akecheta takes down all comers, Monkey and Mantis guys, like he's clearing his throat. I watch this jerk win time and again, and I start thinking, what would it take—what would it require—to bring him down? That's when I settle on White Crane. It's rare. You hear some people using it in high-stakes tracts or the Interplanetaries, but there are no stars fronting it. It's tricky, takes a lot of time to master.

"So I spend five months practicing every fucking day. White Crane. This is after your mother threw me out, of course, so I had to take the Luna gig. At least I don't have to hear her carp every day, just when I call down to see you guys. And then it's always, 'Where's the next payment?' Which I kept coming the best I could, by the way."

Sigh of Papa. "Anyway, after five months I'm at the point where practice tracts can't even touch me, so I know I'm ready. Yesterday I walk into Shashida's and start cleaning clocks with White Crane. I go three matches: monkey, monkey, mantis, win, win, win, before one of Akecheta's goons sends me over to the boss's table for a chat. I have no rep, so Akecheta smells easy prey. He says, 'Would you care to play for a wager?' I look him in the eyes—he's got war stripes on his cheeks, by the way—and I say, 'As much as you'd like.'

"Smile spreads across his face. 'House maximum is five billion ducats,' he says. Legally that's true—it's Luna's limit—but at Shashida',s stakes never lift past the millions. He's trying to intimidate me.

"I say, 'All right.'

"He can't believe it, of course. We run a verification, and sure enough, my accounts show five point two." Papa holds up his hands. "Now, how I'm showing these balances, of course, is another story.

"He's trying to hide it, but I can see how excited he is. It's not that he needs the money, he's got trillions. But you know what he can't resist?"

Shaking head.

"This scum bag wants to think he's a pro-level tractor, fucking king of *Shaolin*, but chopping around Shashida's, he never gets to feel that, see? He knows it's a dive. He wants to think he'd be a badass if he hit Nereid or any high-stakes salon. A wager, legal limit like this? It gives this stupid fuck the drama he craves."

Papa gets up, stands in aisle between tables. Reaches behind to hike up pants. "We get plugged in, and they load the level, a typical dojo space. The first match, I come out direct, full Crane stance, dancing—" Papa raises both arms above his head, hands bent to peck like beaks. Swivels his hips. "Meanwhile, Akecheta's style is southern Dragon, so he waits for me, sunk low in horse stance. Now as I do this, you got to keep in mind my avatar is a wiry little Chinese guy, extremely agile. I call him Zhao."

Papa punches air. "I strike and he blocks. He counters and I block, which violates *all* the teachings of White Crane. There's a saying: 'Evade an attack, there will only be one; block, and there will be many.'

"He's hissing Dragon style. Grabs and twists my right arm, sinking past me." Papa drops toward one knee. "My shoulder cracks—dislocation. He drives his elbow down into my elbow, shatters the joint. Pain. Gets a claw in my face, punches my larynx and I'm out.

"It's a very clean win for him, and that's fine by me. We start the next match, but now I'm purely evasive. I peck at him, just enough to piss him off, keeping my distance." Papa twirls, arms like wings. "He sees I won't come to him, so he rises from his horse stance and comes at me in Dragon crouch." Papa drops shoulders, bends elbows. Hands held like claws in front of face. "Me, I dodge and spin to the wall, full regal White Crane." Papa bumps into opposite table.

"Akecheta's making his Dragon hiss, but he's got it all wrong. I noticed this watching his other fights: His breathing's not disciplined.

"And that's what I'm counting on. I'm right in front of him, vulnerable, the wall to my back." Papa draws fist back. "He launches an all-out throat strike, and I hear his breathing *stop*." Papa spins, stumbles slightly. "I whirl away at the last second, and bam! His fist slams the wall behind me, his lungs full of air. Shockwave pops one lung like a balloon.

"It's beautiful. A beginner's mistake. He wheels around, blood pouring from his mouth, this wild look in his eyes. It's comical. I let him suffer awhile till he slows down, then I snap his neck with a high kick."

Papa takes a breath and straightens. "Now you realize, this is going perfect. First match, let him win. Make him think I'm easy. Second match, let him defeat himself. Final match, he's pissed as hell and has something to prove.

"From the start he's on the offensive. But now I'm giving him flawless White Crane, whirling, spins, somersaults. He's throwing strikes at thin air. I lunge under one punch and break the arm. Other hand catches ear, throat, nose. I leap back, and his footsweep passes under me. Then I jump high and give him a roundhouse *and* a back roundhouse before I land. He's dead before he hits the ground."

Papa squeezes back into booth. "We get unplugged. Five billion transfers into my accounts, and I walk out of there a rich man. The place is silent."

"Was Akecheta mad at you?"

"What do you mean?" Papa shakes his head. "That's not the point. I kicked his ass and took him for five billion dukes. I doubt he liked it." Papa tries to drink from empty cup.

"How was lunch, Daddy?"

"Lunch? Fine. But you don't like that story? It bored you or something?"

Shaking head. "No. It was good."

"I know it was, but not from looking at you. Where's your enthusiasm? My boys are going to flip for that story. They sure as hell aren't going to change the subject and ask about fucking *lunch*."

"I'm sorry, Daddy."

"Yeah, I guess so."

Stare of Papa.

"Well, whatever. Let's just get back to the Impala." Fingers reach across table and ruffle hair of Self.

Coming awake. "What the hell's going on here?" Papa looks over shoulder. Thumb hooked toward rear of Impala.

Turning to match Papa's gaze. Long gray ribbon of asphalt snakes back to gentle rise of hills. Horizon rimmed in light where it meets blue sky flooded with sunshine. Tiny shape has risen over hills, flickers metallically. "It's another car, Daddy."

"No one else should be using this routing lane. And it's gaining."

Calculating.

Explosion of Papa. "Come on, what do we do? He'll flip us right off the routing lane. People die this way!" Adjusts rearview mirror and stares into it. "I am *not* going to die out here."

"Daddy, it'll bump us a little but we're okay."

"*Bump* us a little? Your displacement countermeasures are that good? Because they better be."

Nodding head.

Car, nose low to ground, scoop-shaped. Fenders flare on either side. Midnight blue finish alight with sparkles of sunlight. Vibrates with velocity.

"Christ." Papa grips wheel. Braces for impact.

Squeal of tires. Car swerves from Impala, flashes through consecutive frames of rear, side, front windows. Shape very different from Impala, sharp angles and round curves.

Wide overhang tail swings in front of Impala. Six circular brake lights. Slatted rear window.

Impala rocks sideways. Papa struggles with wheel.

Impala keeps on road. Papa lets out long breath. "We still on lane? Are we okay?"

"We're okay, Daddy."

"Did you see that? Do you know what that was?"

Shaking head.

"Reckless asshole cocksucker. That was a fucking Mako Shark. Mako Shark II Concept Car, 1965. Four hundred and twenty-seven cubic inch Mark IV, three-speed hydromatic. That's so . . ." Papa shakes his head. "It's so esoteric. Why the hell would someone's skate get represented as a fucking Mako Shark? Just because it's faster?"

Scowl of Papa. "When I get to Deimos I'm going to have that fucker's ass. Doubling up on a routing lane. And it's not accurate, either! That thing was unstable at high speeds. You couldn't drive it that fast!" Papa mutters, "I don't think so, anyway."

Silence.

Papa turns to Self. "So why the hell didn't you tell me I could choose a Mako II when I set this up? I would have jumped at the chance. An Impala is shit next to a Mako II. You could have let me know my options, you little shit."

Hand of Papa shoves Self-head into seat cushion.

Impala slides into motel parking space between two cars. Sulfur lights far above wash Impala and other cars with brownish yellow light. Papa clicks off ignition and removes keys.

Motor ticks. Papa lets out long breath.

"I got something for you to do. I want you to watch the skate while I'm inside. If anyone, and I mean anyone, enters this hangar, I want you to log his visuals, his audibles, activities, everything. And if anyone touches the skate, I want you to take lethal countermeasures. You understand?"

"Yes, Daddy."

Stare of Papa. Sinks back into seat and swallows. "I've been thinking about that Mako that passed us, and I'm going to check into it. Probably it's nothing, but I want to make sure. So you keep your eyes peeled and take countermeasures if anyone touches the car." Daddy raises buttocks from seat, thrusts something down backside of jeans. "It's probably nothing. I hope so, 'cause I need sleep and a fuck."

"Daddy?"

"Yeah."

"Did we pass Sears Tower already?"

"What?"

"Did we already go past Sears Tower?"

Papa rubs his temples. "What?"

"I thought we were going to see it."

"Yeah? You were in Sleep. I'm supposed to feel bad about that?"

Quivering of lips of Self. "No."

Papa looks out the front window. "This is bullshit. You do some 'disappointment' routine and I'm supposed to feel like I let you down?"

Confusion of Self.

"You know, I paid for a trip, not a guilt trip. Those sui fuckers are getting too good at simulating family." Papa opens door of Impala. "Just do your job and kill anyone who messes with the car." Papa's fingers graze Self-hair.

Coming awake to voices.

Beyond front window, hood of Impala has been raised. Impala windows rolled down.

Man with neatly-trimmed black beard peeks around edge of hood. "Interesting. It appears to be a child."

Voice behind hood. "A kid with him? He a pervert?"

"I suspect we'll find out." Beard Man approaches Self-window. Glances toward hood. "It's not just a child. It looks like Joe, his youngest."

"Pervert."

Beard Man leans toward window, hands on his knees. "You're Joe. You are, aren't you?"

Turning away to stare at empty Papa-seat.

Short man with bronze skin steps from behind hood. Stands next to Beard Man. "So what period this is?" Raspy voice.

"My guess is late twentieth or early twenty-first. So, Joe, we're saying hello to you."

Shaking head. "My Daddy said I shouldn't talk to strangers."

Beard Man chuckles. "Yes, your countermeasures said as much. But you needn't be afraid. We aren't strangers, Joe, we're friends of your father. His name is Edward Berkholtz." Points at motel. "He went inside the resort wheel some time ago?"

Silence of Self.

"He's not talking to us, Mateo."

"Momentito." Short Man steps behind hood.

"We'll try making this less of an ordeal for you."

Shaking head. "I won't talk."

Voice behind hood. "Secondary inhibitor I missed."

Relaxing of Self.

"Got it."

"I should say so. Poor boy nearly went limp." Beard Man squats next to window. "Does that feel better, Joe?"

Shrugging.

"So your father is inside the orbital resort."

Nodding. "The motel."

"All right, motel. And how long ago did he go in?"

"Two hours and twenty-five minutes."

"Did he give any indication of how long he was going to be gone?"

"About ten hours. He said he needed to sleep and see a prostitute."

"He said that?" Beard Man's mouth puckers. "Did he seem worried about anything?"

Nodding. "He was going to check on a car that passed us."

Short Man slaps side of Impala. "Told you."

"Shush, Mateo. The news is all good. We've plenty of time."

Short Man shakes his head. "Right under our noses. Find him, get it, delete him. Keep it simple."

"That's not simple, Mateo, it's impatient. Dangerous, too. If he makes any noise, someone is likely to call security. And that would be bad."

"If he don't make no noise?"

"As good as we are, that's not a sure thing. And afterward, if someone were to find even a speck of meat, our bribes wouldn't stand. The port logs would show that our skate docked here not long before his, and the inquiries would begin. Now, what would our employer make of that?"

"Better than lugging our asses out past Jupe."

Beard Man laughs. "Mateo, you're confusing better with faster. What I'm trying to say is that faster will be sloppy, and I am a proponent of neatness. Now please, go set up the inquiry and retrieval protocols we need. We can handle the rest at Calli."

"Your way." Short Man retreats behind hood.

Beard Man turns to Self. Rolls eyes. "So, there are a couple of questions we'd like you to ask your father. We'll meet up with you down the road, as it were, and find out what he had to say. In the meantime, it's important that you not go telling your father that Mateo and I stopped by."

"But I will."

Beard Man smiles. "No, you won't, but I must say I admire your resolve. I have a nine year old at home, and when she's stubborn, she's just like you. You're very good."

Short Man lets hood slam shut. "Done."

Beard Man stands. "Excellent. Your skills make up for your personality. I wonder, would you be less grumpy if I procured the services of a sex worker for you?"

"For about fifteen minutes."

Beard Man laughs. "I guess we'll have to settle for so brief an interval of peace." Beard Man bends down, reaches through window, touches Self-forehead.

"Hey." Coming awake, shaken by Papa. "Wake up."

"Yes, Daddy."

"Did anyone mess with the car?" Papa's eyes are bloodshot and puffy. Stubble peppers his cheeks. Loose spikes of hair tremble above his head. "Well? Did anyone?"

Shaking head.

Papa narrows red-rimmed eyes. "You're sure? Nobody even came in the hangar?"

"No, Daddy." Not turning away from stare of Papa.

"All right." Papa puts Impala in reverse, pulls onto highway. Shadow stretches far ahead of Impala. Sunrise colors faces of buildings orange-yellow, casts dark rectangles behind them.

Time passes. Impala shadow shrinks. Clear blue sky. Brilliant yellow cornfields line both sides of highway.

"Daddy?'

Papa's belly jiggles. "I leave you on?"

"Why did you think someone would mess with the car?"

Papa shakes his head. Takes a deep breath. "Probably I was just getting sort of paranoid, but I thought maybe that Akecheta guy I told you about sent some of his goons after me. Which is silly, because I took precautions."

"You think you made Akecheta mad?"

"Don't you pay attention? I took the guy for five billion dukes. What do you think, of course he's fucking pissed. The question's whether he knows it wasn't legit."

Confusion of Self. "It wasn't legit?"

Papa hisses. "Of course it wasn't, genius. Akecheta's a fucking cheat, all right? So I had to cheat back. Fucker's got his tract link jacked so high his avatars, their teeth *chatter*. He's running thirty, maybe forty percent faster than anyone, that's why he's undefeated. So I hired a tract boy to build me something subtle, okay? You got a problem with that?"

Papa turns to Self. "I'll tell you what else. The five bill in my accounts wasn't even mine, I had to rent that money. And you know why?" His face crumples. "Because my life is shit. If it takes cheating a cheater to get something in this world, I say fuck the cheater. Serves him right for strutting around Shashida's like he's some pro *Shaolin* tractor. If he tried any of that shit on Nereid or any high-stakes salon, protocol would have his ass before he stepped off his skate. So are we done with this?"

Nodding head.

"We better be, because I'm in no mood for it. Nothing's going to take this away from me. And nothing's going to be sweeter than the moment I show up and drain that fid of the four bills I got left. If you or Johnny or Shelly or anybody think there's something wrong with that, you can all go fuck yourselves."

Pausing. "What is a fid, Daddy?"

"Jesus Christ, what do you think it is? Fiduciary account, Einstein. As in, holds my winnings till I get to Nereid."

"Sorry, Daddy."

"I show up, say 'Seventy-two Impala,' and they charge me with four point two billion dukes. Four point two. I get my White Crane rolling and I don't stop till I got one or two trillion. And then I head back to spend some time with my real boys for a change."

"Yes, Daddy."

"Now shut up and leave me alone for a while." Papa's hand reaches out and taps forehead.

Red '72 Impala shoots down highway at night. Headlights catch yellow flickers of cornstalks at side of road. Heater clanks and warms compartment.

"I had McDonald's again, and it was worse than the first time. What kind of rip-off did I pay all the dukes for?"

"I'm sorry, Daddy. Do you want to eat someplace else?"

"Don't bother. I got another idea. Let's play Twenty Questions."

"All right."

"I already thought of something, so you can start asking."

"All right. Is it a person, place, or thing?"

Papa snorts. "It's all three."

Confusion of Self.

"It is. I was thinking about it, and it is." Papa glances at Self. "But it's also none of the above, so what do you make of that?"

Thinking. "Is it famous?"

"Yeah. Everybody knows about it, and it's used, you know, quite a bit."

Thinking. "Is it living or dead?"

Papa chuckles. "Yeah, there's the one I was waiting for. There's a controversy about this one. Some people, my ex for instance, insist this thing is a life form and call for a ban on using it. And then there are the sensible people who realize that this thing is just a thing, a tool, nothing more."

"I don't think I want to play anymore, Daddy."

"And why's that? You getting uncomfortable?"

"No, Daddy."

"Then keep playing. I'll give you your answer: No, it is not alive. It may seem alive, it may be fucking creepy sometimes, but no. It's just a tool. Technology. Deep down, it doesn't have a soul."

"I don't think I want to play anymore, Daddy."

"And why is that? Don't want to wreck the show?"

Confusion of Self. "No."

"Too philosophical?"

"I don't know philosophy."

"Well maybe you should fucking get started. God knows you've got the processing power and it would make you a hell of a lot more interesting. I don't know what I was doing choosing one of you as my navigator when I could have had a philosophy prof or a stripper with big tits and pasties giving me blowjobs, or, fucking Alan Turing for that matter. Any of whom might have afforded some decent conversation."

Throat tightening.

Papa taps his hands on steering wheel. "But I'm the stupid asshole with dreams of a roadtrip with Daddy." Papa grunts. "Cars and all that shit he was into. Anyway."

"I'm sorry, Daddy."

"And why are *you* feeling sorry?"

"That you're sad about Grandpa."

"Oh, shut the fuck up. I'm not asking you into my head, and I don't need a . . . I don't need your sympathy. He was a fucking asshole, and he's not your grandpa. So shut your mouth."

Shutting of mouth.

Papa drives. Breathes through his nose.

Papa grabs rearview mirror and wrenches it down toward Self. "Here, answer your own question. Is it living or dead?" Viewing in mirror a small child, nine years old, curly brown hair. "Well?"

Dropping chin to chest. "I don't want to play, Daddy."

"So you're giving up?"

Nodding.

"But you want to know what I was thinking, don't you?"

Shaking head.

"SUI. Ess You Eye. That's what I was thinking."

"I don't know Sue, Daddy."

"Oh shut up! I'm sick of you!" Papa's hand grabs the top of Self-head.

Coming awake as Daddy jabs thigh of Self. "There, you happy? That make you feel better?"

Following Papa's index finger. On Self-side of Impala, in center of large quadrangle of grass, stainless steel arch loops into the sky, lit from beneath by floodlights.

"There's your gateway to the west. That make you happy? Or do we have to turn around and go back, see Sears Tower?"

Splaying fingers on window, cool to touch. Staring between stretched hands. Excitement of Self. Arch is hundreds of feet tall. Curves into sky like giant horseshoe. "Wow! It's so big!"

"Right."

"How does it stay up?"

"Who gives a shit. I need some sleep. Get me docked here."

Turning from arch. "Thanks, Daddy."

Papa presses lips together. "Yeah, thank yourself. Get me docked."

Impala turns off road and into parking lot of ranch-style motel. Tires crunch across pebbles. Impala coasts to a stop.

Daddy jangles keys from ignition and pushes door open. "Okay, kill anyone who touches the car, same as before."

"Daddy?"

Scrabble of feet on pebbles. Chunk sound as door shuts, displacement of air in Self-ears. Watching Papa walk past motel rooms, down sidewalk to check-in office.

Time passes. Able to inspect arch through rear window of Impala. Structure is six hundred and thirty feet tall. Legs are six hundred and thirty feet apart.

Time passes. Each leg is equilateral triangle in cross-section, fifty-four feet on a side at ground level. Tapers to seventeen feet on a side at apex of arch.

Hood rises. Windows roll down.

Relaxing of Self.

"Hello, Joe." Beard Man leans close, rests arm across window edge. "How has your trip been?"

Short Man steps from behind raised hood. "Come on. Business."

"So, Joe, did you obtain the fiduciary code, as we asked you to?"

Nodding head.

"Excellent. What is it?"

"'Seventy-two Impala.'"

"'Seventy-two Impala.' Rather simple. We thank you, Joe. Well done."

Happiness of Self.

"So where is your father planning to go from here?"

"Las Vegas."

"Las Vegas?" Puckers his lips. "Has he referred to this destination by any other name?"

Nodding. "Nereid."

"Ah. So he's still planning to go there next?"

Nodding.

"Very good." Beard Man stands and addresses Short Man. "Mission accomplished. How long will you need?"

"Twenty, thirty tops. Nothing too special." Short Man stoops behind Impala hood.

Beard Man kneels beside window. "As I said, Joe, a good job. You have our thanks."

Happiness of Self. "Can I ask you something?"

"Of course."

"Can I go with you?"

Raises eyebrows. "You mean, come with us?"

Nodding.

"No, I'm afraid that's not something we could arrange." Bites lip.

"Please?"

"I'm sorry, Joe, but it's quite impossible." Beard Man's hand reaches and taps Self-forehead.

Coming awake as Papa slides into Impala. Hair wet, molded back from face. Clean-shaven and smells of citrus.

"Hey there."

"Hello, Daddy."

Papa's arm glides over Self-head to rest on top of seat. Papa turns to watch out rear window. Impala backs out of parking space.

"Well, I don't know about you, but I am feeling *much* improved. I was like death warmed over coming in. We got, what, six hours to go?"

Unfolding map across knees. Impala heads down black asphalt under brilliant blue sky. "Six hours and fifteen minutes."

"Fantastic. That's a lot better than the fifteen hours it took to get to that shit heap."

Time passes. Impala leaves cornfields, enters desert. Expanses of cactus and scrub grass stretch away from both sides of road to flat-topped mountains in the distance.

"Desert makes sense for this stretch. Nothing between Callisto and Nereid. No colonies, nothing to mine. Nobody comes out this far unless it's for the salons."

Nodding head.

"Hey, I was thinking about last night."

"Yes, Daddy?"

"I just wanted to say that I was *really* super tired. Those fifteen hours fucked me up. So if I got a little nasty, I'm sorry. I was just worn out."

"It's okay, Daddy."

"I know it is, but I just wanted to say it. I know you aren't real or anything, but that's no excuse for me being an asshole. Maybe this hasn't gone like I wanted, and hasn't been everything I hoped for, but in four hours I've got a brand new life, let bygones be gone, et cetera. So I'm sorry."

"Yes, Daddy."

"All righty, then." Papa's hand touches Self-forehead.

Coming awake to Papa's shouts. "What the fuck is happening?"

Impala lurches. Decelerates and drifts toward road side. Far ahead, desert sunset spreads orange and red across horizon.

"What is this? This makes no sense!"

Police siren whirls. Pauses, gives two loud blurts. Whirls again.

Looking rearward. Red and blue lights spin atop white police cruiser.

Impala scratches to a halt at shoulder of road. Dust swirls past Self-side window.

Papa's knuckles white on the steering wheel. "This isn't happening. What the fuck is a cop car? Are we really stopping, or is it just represented?"

Confusion of Self. Still looking at police car. Doors unlatch. Tan trooper hats rise from both doors, men in brown uniforms underneath.

"This is crazy. Come on!"

Policemen walk toward Impala, one on each side. Tall one's boots clack on pavement, short one's crunch on dirt shoulder.

Impala windows roll down. "What the fuck!" Papa grabs for window as it lowers.

Torso and waist of Policeman framed in Papa-window. Silver badge on chest.

Second officer stands beside Self-window. Wide-faced and bronze-skinned: Short Man.

"Were you aware, sir, of how fast you were traveling back there?" Beard Man's voice. Stoops and stares at Papa from under brim of trooper hat.

Papa does not look. Both hands on steering wheel.

"Were you in a hurry to get someplace, sir?"

Papa shakes his head. Turns to Beard Man's face. Emits short cry and stares back at road. "Fuck. Fuck."

"Were you, by any chance, in a hurry to get to Nereid, so you could access a fiduciary account containing four billion ducats illegally seized from a Mr. Akecheta of 5 Luna?"

Groan of Papa. "I didn't do anything illegal—"

"On the contrary, sir, the cheat soft you used to win those matches of *Shaolin* was highly illegal. Unfortunately, before we detected it you were able to throw ahead your winnings into the fiduciary account on Nereid and charter this skate."

Papa swallows. "Well, I'm not going to argue. You can have it back. When we get to Nereid, I'll release all my funds to you. I have no problem with that."

"That is an extremely polite offer, sir, but I'm afraid it's based on false assumptions: First, that my partner and I are physically here with you, and able to negotiate with you; and second, that we have not already drained your ducats back to 5 Luna."

Papa's chin trembles. "But that's impossible. You can't without the key."

"We already have the key, sir. It was 'Seventy-two Impala.'"

Papa screams and bangs fists on windshield. "But I didn't tell anyone!"

"I'm afraid we have some more bad news for you. Your skate has deviated from its routing lane and is dumping all its fuel. A rescue mission from Nereid—"

"Impossible! Fucking bullshit!"

"—A rescue mission from one of the Nereid franchises might have reached you in a day or two had you an operable distress beacon or functioning life support. Unfortunately, those features have been disabled. Indeed, you have only forty minutes or less of life support left. This should, however, give you ample time to think over the grave error you made in trying to swindle Mr. Akecheta."

"But I didn't tell anyone!"

Men turn from Impala and walk back to police cruiser.

Papa twists in seat, yells. "But I didn't tell anyone! You can't do this!"

Papa breathes through mouth as men get into police cruiser.

Cruiser pulls onto road and accelerates past Impala. Papa grabs fistfuls of his hair and screams, "No!" Bounces in seat. "Bullshit, bullshit, bullshit. I told *no one!*"

Papa holds breath.

Turns to Self, his mouth open. "You motherfucker. It was you. You killed me." Snarls. Hands clutch at Self-throat. Trying to pull away but cannot. "Fucking kill you!" Fingers lock around throat. Self-head smacks into window, lolls on neck, smashes again and again. Registering pain. Screaming.

"Shut up! You sold me out, now you do as I say. You give me direct access to life support and energy allocation *right now*. Drop the fucking SUI shell so I can input commands directly."

Crying of Self.

"Stop crying. Do it!" Papa grabs shoulders and shakes Self. Head cracks against window. "You fuck! Stop crying!"

Fist of Papa draws back. Smashes against Self-mouth. Lips mash against teeth. Smashes Self-jaw and nose. Cracks against forehead.

Red '72 Impala motionless on shoulder of road. Sun has gone down.

Papa's head rests on steering wheel, between clenched hands. Shoulders rise and fall.

Fuel gauge reads empty. Radio and climate control panels cracked open, wires dangle out.

"Oh Jesus. Why did I do it?"

"Daddy?"

Papa groans. "Yeah?"

"Are you okay?"

Sniff of Papa, then chuckle. "Yeah. I'm peachy. I'm drifting off my routing lane, can't send a distress signal, life support is nearly out. I have about fuh . . ." Papa swallows. "I got five, ten minutes to live. It's great."

"Daddy, let's go walking and get gas."

Papa sobs. "Don't say that shit. Just . . . don't say those things. You don't know what you're talking about. I'm going to die, and there's nothing I can do about it."

"But we could go get some gas."

Scream of Papa. Bangs fists on windshield. "Shut up shut up shut up! Will you shut up, you're so *clueless.*"

Shutting up. Papa sobs and mutters.

Papa swallows, clears throat. Tries again. Sits up, touches hand to base of throat. "Christ. I can feel it. It's awful." Convulses forward in seat as though about to throw up.

"Daddy?"

Hands of Papa pull Self to his face. "Listen, I want you to record something for me. You can do that, right? If you do, I'll forgive you for selling me out. Record this. Tell my wife that I'm sorry about this. I fucked up. I thought I had it figured out, Shelly. I thought I was going to make all this money and come back home and we would spend it, you know? And Joey and Johnny, please, I'm so sorry that I'm a fuckup. Please, I love you all. I love you all."

Hands release hold on Self. Papa weeps. "Did you get that?"

Nodding. Crying of Self.

Cough of Papa. "Listen, Johnny." His words are thick. "Listen, I'm going to lay down and I want, uh, I want you to hold me, okay?"

Weight of Papa across knees of Self. Running fingers through hair of Papa.

Papa chokes. Legs coil and curl.

Stillness.

Papa kicks. Feet bang against door panel and Papa-side window. Papa gasps.

Crying of Self. Stillness of Papa.

He stays like that for a long time.

Famous Men:
The Periodic Table of Liquids
Samantha Hunt

The morning before they fell there was fog. The Captain told his young passengers that it would burn off. That was an expression that the boy who would become the Reverend had never heard before and imagined that it meant some sort of heavenly match could come burn something off the Earth. The boy was seven and alarmed by the expression. His last name was Wood and so he wanted the heavenly match to stay far away. He jumped in the water.

In the water he thought about the way the fog didn't feel like anything. How could something that was nothing stop their boating plans? The boy Reverend thought, "I'll sneak up on it. I'll grab an armful of fog, and then I'll measure it on a scale, so that, measured, I might get a truthful statement from the fog." Something like:

"What do you want?" the fog would ask.

"You don't seem like anything. I want to know what you are made of."

"Air and water."

"No, really."

"Really," the fog would say.

"No! Really!" The boy would become belligerent.

The fog would look around to ensure that no one was eavesdropping, or maybe the fog was looking around because it was stalling; it needed a moment to formulate a fib. "Tiny particles of God," the fog would say. "That's what I'm made of."

When the fog finally burned off, the Captain, the boy, and his sister got into their boat. The boat capsized upstream from North America's most powerful waterfall, and the Captain drowned, the sister was pulled from the river twenty feet before the falls, but the boy was swept over the cataract.

After some time, he was picked up by the Maid of the Mist. He had lived.

"It was nothing," the boy said afterward. "Tiny particles of something," he said.

Though now he is older. He is less brave. Now if he remembers, "I went over Niagara Falls and lived," it is not too long before he has to relax on a day bed or couch until the metal smell of water, the terror of God's tiny particles, leaves him.

Lately, the Reverend has noticed that people, the news media, say horrible things about water: hurricanes, floods, or shark attacks. A lot of sharks. He is tired of these bad stories. He is tired of defending water and getting no help. There are horrible things: shipwrecks, water-borne microbes, and that thing children do with other children's heads in public school toilets. So over and over he encounters people who want consolation that the miles of black, totally alive water is somehow a polite senior citizen in control of its waves, wildlife, whirlpools, and undertows.

The Reverend has a dark inkling of doubt.

The Reverend's fear of water is not the same as other people's. His fear is that one day he'd wake up and find a note from water. "Please forgive me. I couldn't stay. I hope we can still be friends," the water would write. He'd turn on the tap, and water would really be gone. He'd think, "I'm not too worried. One of these days it has to rain but then it wouldn't and it wouldn't, so he'd drive eight and one-half hours to the shore, saying, "Please, please, of course we can still be friends." And then he would start walking toward Iceland looking for her, water, crunching the dry bones of fish underfoot.

Every Wednesday in the basement of the parish house the Reverend makes tea and coffee so that his weekly prayer group can have some warm refreshments when they finish praying. There is one woman in the Reverend's prayer group who is a new member, and the Reverend feels a special feeling for her. He likes her, and he thinks she likes him. When he thinks of her, he can't help but think of a town he'd visited once in California called Point Conception. The town was lovely, and despite his embarrassment with many things sexual the Reverend tried to repeat the name of the town as often as he could during his visit. "Lovely Point Conception," or "Here in Point Conception," he'd say, because saying the name gave him a feeling of terrific liberty.

The Reverend tries to make their prayer group interesting so that this woman will return every Wednesday. She is not an American but from somewhere in Scandinavia, and the way her choice in footwear reflects her native country touches the Reverend. On Wednesday the Reverend looks at the Scandinavian and again thinks, "Point Conception," and then he prays.

Each week he gives his prayer group the opportunity to shape the direction of their joint thoughts. Most of the members are shy and, outside of some minor prayers, they rarely take this opportunity to express their personalities but leave it up to the Reverend to lead. This Wednesday he asks around the circle for suggestions.

"Let us pray today for healing for the boy in Deposit who fell in a quarry."

"I'd like to think on the high school seniors and pray that they make a smooth transition into adulthood."

"Perhaps we could send our thoughts out to the President as he travels to China," they said.

And then he comes to her, the Scandinavian, who says something quite different. She says, "I wonder if someone here could answer my question. Why did it happen that in 1848 there was a storm that blew up the coast of Norway so quickly that in one night five hundred sailors were drowned and died?"

And the Reverend thinks, "I know the answer. That is why I lived." But he just stares at her. The longer he stares, the more dumbstruck he becomes, and when he tries to think of one smart reason why God sometimes kills us with water, he cannot. He thinks of the sailors, and his heart hurts. The pressurized silence lasts just about as long as the Reverend can take it, so he says quietly and cowardly, "Yes, let us pray for sailors everywhere." And she looks disappointed immediately by his impatience with silence, that he could not wait for the real answer to her real question, which is not, "Why did the poor sailors have to die?" but rather, "Is the water evil?"

The group closes their eyes to pray. The Reverend looks through his lashes and can not remove his eyes from her shoes. "There," he tells himself, "you have spoiled your chances." He pinches his own hand and says, "Again." After prayer group he excuses himself while the others enjoy some refreshments.

Once outside he does not feel better. The Reverend has a seat on the curb of the horseshoe-shaped drive. He is careful to not sit smack at the bottom of the horseshoe curve but to throw symmetry off, to wait for the Scandinavian in non-symmetry. The longer he waits, the heavier his answer grows, itching to tell her how he'd been seven years old, how he'd gone over Niagara Falls with nothing but a life preserver, and he'd lived. He wanted to tell her, "I can still smell the water, and it is not evil." But his heart hurts. Her question had been a measure of his worthiness, and the measurement read "mediocre."

He closes his eyes and believes he can see the Norwegian storm of 1848. He believes he can see the water rising up out of the ocean and asking each sailor, "Do you think I'm evil?" And the sailors would at that moment admit what the Reverend knew. "No. You are beautiful," they would say. "I am in love with you." And the ocean would ask, "Even my shoes?" And the sailors would say, "God, yes." And the ocean would devour each and every one of them.

That is the Reverend's answer. But as she leaves the parish house, he can't tell her.

He watches her leave. She carries nothing, no purse, no folder of disheveled papers. She gets into her car, and the Reverend stands to flag her but ends up standing to watch her drive away. He waits while she drives out the end of the horseshoe driveway and takes a left, and then he can no longer see her though he still feels her question. She takes a left with the weight of five hundred fishermen in her small car from Europe, and the Reverend knows why he lived. Maybe the beautiful torrent that curved like a lip had found him dry, unworthy to die in the fall, mediocre.

The Reverend walks slowly to his own car, past a community softball field where the asphalt has eroded and puddles have collected in the vacancies left behind. He dips the tip of his shoe into the muddy puddle water. "Why did you kill those five hundred sailors?" he asks.

"That was a long time ago," the water says.

"Well, what about me? How come I was saved?"

"Huh?"

"Why didn't I drown? Why was I saved?"

"What makes you think you were?" the water asks. "Saved, that is?"

"It said so in the headlines. BOY SAVED FROM FALLS."

"Hmm," the puddle says.

The Reverend can smell the water and remembers a heartbeat from being seven years old. One heartbeat in the water at the edge of falling over when the roar of that much non-human power filled him, and in that heartbeat he'd thought, "I am all yours."

But then the water did not devour him. The water didn't want him. Water that wanted so many didn't want him, and he couldn't stand it.

The Reverend looks into the puddle and thinks, "I could stamp my foot in you. I could disperse and evaporate you. I could drink you."

And the water says, "Still, still, still," meaning not calm, not tranquil, but still like the still of that letter water would one day write, *I hope we can still be friends.*

Famous Men:
Igor and Igor and Igor and Igor

When the man working right now in a laboratory to further human cloning efforts was a child, he liked the cancerous, collection aspect of brains in jars kept stacked on shelves. He thought he'd have a workshop like Dr. Frankenstein's. It was why he became a scientist in the first place. Now he is a cloner, though he doesn't even like himself. He imagines that all non-cloners think that people like him must love themselves so dearly that they want to go on forever and ever. "But I have trouble even being alone with myself on the drive from the laboratory to my home," he thinks. He often rides the bus to avoid himself.

His wife has asked him to do something about one of the machines in their basement that helps the house run smoothly. The machine is broken and so things in the house have not been running smoothly. He has been working on it. He trips over a mousetrap in the basement and considers a new mousetrap. He thinks, "Now, that would be a good job." And then he thinks, "When I am not in the laboratory, I will be here building a new mousetrap," because the renown involved with developing such a tool delights him. He is not thinking well. He is nearing nervous collision, a crisis arising from the paradoxes of human cloning. In fact, he has already become jealous of his better, younger self, his clone-to-be.

In the morning, the scientist returns to the laboratory riding the bus so as not to be alone. The woman seated in front of him says, "Get your foot off my coat," and he is stunned by the passage of air over her vocal chords. It is singular. "This could never be reproduced," he thinks, though he plucks one of the woman's stray hairs from the wool of her winter coat just in case.

At work he spends his day alienating a protein. When he leaves that night, the protein is alone, alienated, barely able to stand its own self.

And that night the scientist considers the mousetrap again. His wife finds him in the basement.

"How is the dirty work of making human clones progressing?" she asks. He is playing with a trap. He stops. He pulls his wife close and tucks his chin so that his head rests on her breast. He hears thumpthump. Thumpthump. Her heart, he notes, already has a double.

"The wonder," he thinks but remains silent to continue listening. The scientist is becoming scared, more so today than yesterday, and it surprises his wife, so much hugging.

He remembers the lonely protein. What is it doing? he wonders. Wrapping its arms around its wholly perfect, lonely self, snuggling its head into its own singular breast and listening, waiting for a thumping that never comes.

"This has another name than science," he thinks. "I just haven't thought of the name yet. Science studies what is here: skeletons, wet noses, nebular clusters, beehives, biotite, muscovite, and chert. This is made. This isn't here; it isn't here yet, or at least the *this* that this might be isn't here yet. What this would that be?" he asks himself, but he has become confused.

And at that moment, his nervous collision strikes. "I'm casting two shadows," he screams with a start.

"Oh, dear," his wife says because she worries about him, but when she looks, she can see that, indeed, he is not falsifying his observation.

"Oh my god, oh my god, oh my god!" he says and then just, "God! God! God!" and the number of shadows he casts multiplies with each incantation of his heavenly deity's name. His wife quickly clasps her hand over her husband's big mouth.

He is trembling. He is squeezing his wife in the basement. He looks at his wife in his arms. He squeezes her tighter. She is very small. "What if she likes my clone more than me?" he says because the mental collapse has picked up downhill steam. He looks at her. Her last fingers, her pinkies, grow at an incline in toward the other fingers. That's not like him at all. His nasal hair has come in coarse. Someone exactly like him might make his wife happier. He imagines a busload full of hims and each him with uncoarse nasal hair. Each him hellbent on finding her first. Each him wringing his hands in anticipation of *his* wife's small body. That is except for one him, one who's lost, or one who is trapped, one him whose arms and legs have been secured with duct tape by the others, one him who is him sits banging his head that is his head against the window.

Famous Men:
For Love

"You have a family, yes?" he asked his bodyguard through the locked bathroom door.

"Yes," the guard answered.

"That's nice," the Sultan told him and tried to finish up in silence but instead turned on the faucet to hear the sound of water. That was nice, too. Until the repetition of water falling down the drain began to sound like a young girl laughing. He turned the water off.

There is a room in my palace, he thought, where there are over three hundred women, shiny models and actresses imported from Los Angeles. So many girls that they have to share bedrooms, two per bed. At that thought he clapped his hands three times in excitement. And I also have some very nice cars. Tonight I will wear my red velour jogging outfit, he thought.

Once the Sultan had had a near-death experience. Not his death, but near someone else's death. His driver, while negotiating the streets of O_____, had been distracted, racing a cargo train running alongside the car. He failed to note an intersection. The Sultan saw very little but a pair of women's eyeglasses thrown high into the air, coming to rest on the other side of the road where they were struck instantly by oncoming traffic.

At the palace they had a party every night. It was the only thing that the three hundred actresses and models imported from Los Angeles to the place where he lived did outside a monthly shopping trip to London or Paris. The parties were normally held by the pool, and they were fun, he thought. Dancing and fancy clothes, three hundred females to six or eight or eleven males depending on whether his cousins were around. At the party, every now and then, a plate of snacks would be passed.

At three in the morning one of the models or actresses would return to the Sultan's room with him for love.

Between noon and one the Sultan tried to visit his wives and children.

Sometimes there were angry women in the palace. They would be asked to leave before the germ spread. But he'd heard them more than once and remembered what they'd said. "The Sultan bathes with hogs," or, "We are being starved to death," or one, who could not stop repeating in a calm way, "He ate my child. The Sultan ate my child. He ate my child alive."

He had not.

Often the Sultan turned to television. The richest man in the world, an American who had usurped the Sultan's title, was being interviewed. Few people ever asked to interview the Sultan. But still he imagined how it would sound. He imagined his own voice saying, "Well, Dan, you should have seen the all-girl conga line we had going last night. What a hoot."

His driver had not stopped after striking the pedestrian. And over the course of the next few days and weeks the Sultan, at odd moments of quiet, found himself making his pointer and middle finger into the pedestrian. And then he began to do it at not so odd moments. He began thinking of her regularly. He walked her across the table. He tucked her under his sheets, but it was an awkward position for his hand to be in, so she, as his hand, lay in bed lifeless. This inactivity disturbed the Sultan. Normally, he thought girls' legs were the prettiest things he'd ever seen, but not this girl's. His fingers made her legs rough and stubby. He was terrified by this girl and her glasses. Maybe she was dead or hurt. Maybe she was possessed with special powers that most rich people fear poor people have. Maybe she would use those powers to shrivel his brain or worse, or worse than that.

The Sultan was afraid he knew what any anchorman would ask him: "Why does one man need three hundred women?"

He'd thought his answer through. "Ah, yes, for good health, yes; you see, certain men, well, to be healthy . . ." The Sultan believed his open-ended answer flattered his virility. But often in his own head he heard the imaginary anchorman laugh and then repeat the original question. "No, honestly, why would one man need three hundred women?"

No interviews, the Sultan thought. If they asked, that is.

With that settled, the Sultan reclined. The pedestrian from the city of O_____ might not be dead, he thought. Maybe only a piece of her is gone, a part disappeared. A part he could pay for.

How much was the price? Each one of the models from California usually ended up costing him $100,000 for one year of residency and clothing. "I'll pay," he said, canceling that evening's party, getting into bed early. He thought of the pedestrian's eyewear. "Here," he said, scissoring his fingers again, walking them across the bed. "Please let me help you." He turned down the covers so the hand/pedestrian could comfortably climb into bed. "I'm sorry," the Sultan said. He adjusted the pillow so the hand/pedestrian could rest her neck. "I'll pay," he said. He pulled the covers up around her, but the hand/pedestrian didn't say anything.

He thought of her eyewear again though eventually he fell asleep.

Near sunrise the hand/pedestrian woke and walked over to the sleeping Sultan like this—index finger, middle finger, index finger, middle finger—and shoved one leg/finger each up the Sultan's nostrils, blocking his breath. The Sultan choked and awoke. "Ahh! Stay away, with those ugly legs!" he screamed, but the hand covered his mouth then, obstructing all breath and all screaming.

Finally she spoke, the dead pedestrian from the city of O_____. "Answer the man's question," she said.

"Hmmm?" the Sultan mumbled through the hand/pedestrian.

"Answer the man's question. Why does one man need three hundred women?"

The Sultan gasped for a breath. The hand uncovered his mouth. "Are you going to answer?"

The Sultan sputtered and coughed. "Yes, yes. I'll answer." But he didn't. He started to cry. He thought she might show mercy. She did not. She kicked her legs/his fingers deeper into his nostril passages and squeezed. "OK. OK." The Sultan turned toward the cameras with a sick stomach now. Sweat on his brow. "I'll answer. I'll answer. Please."

But still he sat not answering. He was balancing the two replies in his head. The first one was, "Because they are soft." He chose the second one. He said it and could see himself in the mirror at the end of his bed. "Because surplus feels like the opposite of dying." His hand dropped to the bed. There, on American television.

In a short while there was a knock on the door. "Sultan?" a voice came from outside his bedroom. "Are you ill? Do you need something?" It was the Sultan's bodyguard.

The Sultan thought on this question. What could I need? A glass of juice? A corn-and-milk-raised nineteen-year-old from Sacramento, Sausilito, San Diego? Another western oil shortage? The Sultan knew the answer. The Sultan said nothing.

Gus Dreams of Biting the Mailman

Alex Irvine

Summer-bright light fell through the windows of Mitch Packard's car as he awoke to the thump of his windshield wiper slapping down on top of a parking ticket. He tracked the cop back to his cruiser with a bleary scowl and dug in his pocket for a cigarette, and when there were no cigarettes he had no choice but to skip his summer Shakespeare seminar in favor of a trip to the liquor store for smokes and then a Brown Jug breakfast special, leisurely eaten on the big concrete planters out in front of the Brown Jug. He gave the pancakes to his dog Gus as a reward for Gus's perseverance; not every dog would have taken it so well when his person was kicked out of his apartment after a three-hour vicious-circle argument that had begun as a disagreement over the relative merits of Charles Bukowski. Mitch wondered how long it would be before he could call Trina and begin the delicate negotiations that would culminate in his sleeping in a bed again. She couldn't hold a grudge for long over Bukowski. Mitch Packard didn't cohabit with women who held grudges over Bukowski.

He held onto this conviction while strolling aimlessly around sunny Ann Arbor until it was three o'clock and he could drop off Gus at Eli's house and go to Doug's Bakery without fear of running into Doug, who was under the impression that Mitch didn't work there any more. Doug's was in Ypsilanti, ten minutes east down Washtenaw Avenue, across from a house where some people said John Norman Collins, the Michigan Murders guy, had killed at least one of his victims. Patrons of Doug's, especially if they had first been to the Shell station kitty-corner from the bakery, frequently arrived at the counter bearing dire stories of diligent police detectives recovering hairs from painted-over cinderblock walls or scraping out floor drains to find a single toenail.

The Shell cashiers were full of bullshit stories about murderous conspiracies. Eli Gray, Mitch's coworker at Doug's, hated them for this, and for his own agonized predilection to believe whatever arcane gossip propagated viruslike on the tongues of bakery patrons. He was neither stupid nor unusually credulous; he was, however, completely defenseless against the question, "What if?"

On this day, the what-if had something to do with Ernest Hemingway's "The Killers" and a rail-car diner that might or might not have once occupied space on Washtenaw Avenue near the bakery. "The thing is," Eli said as Mitch came in the back door and fought his way through oven racks to the fryer, "it could be true."

This was the point at which Mitch's own self-restraint inevitably suffered a catastrophic failure.

"What could be true?" he asked.

It should be interjected at this point that Mitch Packard had a problem with coincidence, or perhaps with probability, or causality. The ultimate origins were of course occluded, but the immediate effects were clear. Apart from the ordinary encounter-with-synchronicity events any human being can report—anticipating songs on the radio, thinking of someone right before the phone rings, et cetera—odd and improbable events pocked Mitch's life to such a degree that he had begun to regard himself as a living embodiment of negentropy, a conduit of fructifying information, a temple to life in a universe doomed to decline. This was one: If he read a newspaper on any given day, one of its articles inevitably would yield information that he would be called upon to provide later on the same day. If he read an automotive column about problems with tie-rod ends in Windstar minivans, at some point before he crashed out for the night—at the bakery, at the Brown Jug, at the house on Pearl Street, anywhere—conversation would turn to steering problems with someone's Windstar minivan. And Mitch would provide information. There were also incidents like the previous night's at the Monkey Bar.

Unfortunately, templehood meant very little when, as a result of an argument over Bukowski and subsequent imbibery and inability to find a place to sack for the night, you awakened to the thump of your car's windshield wiper slapping down on a parking ticket. Neither did templehood prepare you for the co-opting of reality by your best friend's daily doughnut-fryer rant. Which explained, in an appropriately acausal and synchronistic kind of way, why Mitch had, because of four simple words, entangled himself in Eli Gray's latest obsession.

Back in the narrative, Eli spun out a lengthy and ridiculous proposition that, to Mitch's thinking, betrayed his recent reading of som e crank possible-worlds theory. This took the better part of an hour, during which time Mitch frequently escaped to the front register to ring up dozens and coffees or take a wedding-cake order. Undaunted by

these interruptions, Eli picked up each time exactly where he'd left off, delivering himself of a hiatus-punctuated monologue that, much redacted, went something like this:
"You know that scene in *The Time Machine* where the Time Traveler sends the model off
to see if everything works? Check this out. What would it mean if you looked over on
the counter one afternoon and that model was sitting right there? It would mean that
you were a character in the book, man, not that you weren't real but that somewhere a
fiction existed that encompassed not only you but the whole gestalt whatever that we
take to be the universal reality. It would mean that somewhere out there," and here Eli
waved the drumsticks he used to turn doughnuts in the general direction of Detroit,
causing Mitch to dodge a sortie of crisped crumbs and near-boiling droplets of fryer
oil, "what Wells wrote was true, and I'm not talking about true in the sense that literature recovers some essential experience of our being in this world because my point is
that our being in this world is in fact a being in a part of someone else's world, which
in the case of your finding the model time machine on the counter next to the Hobart
would be H.G. Wells's world, which of course on one level is the same as ours only
separated by a hundred years, give or take, since he wrote that book, but on another
level isn't really separated at all since if time and space are all really the same thing then
distance in history should be crossable the way distance between Albuquerque and Des
Moines is, and yet on a third level is completely different, or would be if you saw the
model time machine, because in that case you would realize that somehow, in some way,
the writing of that book created or imposed itself on this universe, made it part of a
fiction that, if you saw the model time machine, would no longer be a fiction."

It was at this point that Mitch decided to make a model time machine so he could
leave it by Eli's bed some night when Eli was on the lysergic highway.

"My point," Eli rattled on, "is that if something like this could happen, and
granted it's speculative and not particularly likely for any given person, still you have to
acknowledge that probabilities aren't predictive, then anything you read could really be
true. True like the-sky-is-blue true or two-plus-two-is-four true. And the other thing
is that you, my friend Mitchell, could be a fiction, which," and up came a drumstick in
a triumphant salute, "in this case would not make you any less real."

"The sky isn't blue," Mitch said. He was frosting danish, a process that involved
repeated submersion of the right hand in an aluminum bowl of slightly watery frosting,
followed by a dedicated imitation with that same hand of an arthritic palsy, which
stiff-knuckled tremor brought forth the squiggly pattern of frosting without which
millions of bakery patrons would find themselves unable to eat danish. Some bakeries
do this with a machine, but Doug's was old-fashioned.

"You and your goddamn literal mind," Eli said. "Doesn't matter."

"If I find a time machine out on the porch," Mitch said, "how will I know that it's
Wells's time machine? What if someone else wrote a story with a dry-run model time

machine? Or what if someone really invented one, and it just happened to pop back into the world on my porch?"

"Doesn't matter," Eli said again, and climbed up onto the deli counter to change the CD in the stereo that sat on top of the cabinets. "Consensus reality is a mishmash of truth and fiction anyway."

Mitch didn't want to have the consensus-reality discussion again. He kept his mouth shut. Then he found himself speaking anyway. "This whole I'm-a-fiction thing is the oldest idea in the world. We used to do this in the tenth grade."

"The other thing," Eli said, "is that, really, what's the difference between believing you're a fictional character and believing that God waved his hand and said let there be light? You got your figurative inscription of reality on the void or your literal inscription of Mitch Packard on Ypsilanti. Either way, you exist because of another entity's act of will."

Mitch grew bilious. "Analogies," he growled. "Logic. The whore of loony opinions."

"Whatever," Eli said, climbing down and wiping his footprints off the sandwich board. "But you can't prove me wrong either."

Or it could have happened as quickly as this:

"Okay. You remember *The Time Machine*, when the Time Traveler sends off a model to make sure the whole thing works before he gets in his machine?"

Nod.

"Right. So if you were sitting on your porch one June afternoon and that model blipped into existence on the railing next to your ashtray, what would you think? What would you be forced to think?"

Silence of Mitch watching Eli flip doughnuts. The overall effect is that of a heavy-metal drummer near the threshold of human tolerance for quaaludes. When Eli speaks at normal speed, Mitch blinks.

"You, my friend Mitchell, would at that moment become a fictional character."

More silence. A rack of eclairs plunges crackling into the fryer. "But that didn't happen."

"Not to you. But I can guarantee that it did to someone."

Later, Mitch and Eli pack a bowl in the shed. "So if I go home tonight," Mitch says, "and there's a little silver machine of indeterminate origin sitting next to the ashtray on my front porch, that means I'm not real."

"Absolutely not." Eli leans against a stack of flour sacks. He is shorter and heavier than Mitch, with a look about him like a New England stone wall. "You're still real; of course you're real. What it would mean is that the fiction was real too. That what Wells wrote became true when he wrote it."

"Then how come *he* didn't run into a model while he was out walking on the heath or whatever?"

Eli passes the bowl to Mitch. "Do you know," he says, "how unlikely that is?"

"Nope," Mitch chokes through a haze of smoke. He sits on a case of Cokes, reflecting on the time he and Melanie the morning cashier had enjoyed a moment of secretive carnality against the very flour sacks now supporting Eli's weight.

"How many books do you suppose have been written since, say, 1899, or whenever *The Time Machine* came out?"

Mitch shakes his head. "No idea." Whatever happened to Melanie, he wonders.

"A fucking lot," Eli says, taking the bowl back. "And for every one, there's another reality created because someone thought it up and wrote it down."

"No way."

"It's true. And this is no wet-noodle academic quantum cosmology. This is fact, my friend. There are more things in heaven and earth, Mr. Packard, than are dreamt of in bookstores and physics laboratories. Vanishingly unlikely that Wells would run into his own creation like that, besides the fact that it would mean that he'd changed his own reality rather than created a new one. Can't do that."

Melanie moved to Iowa, Mitch remembers. He grunts his way to his feet. "Time to glaze the twists."

Inside, a skinny, long-wristed black kid wearing corn rows and a Red Wings jersey waits at the counter. Mitch sips a cup of coffee, feels his eyes drying in their sockets. "Do for you?"

"Y'all hiring by any chance?"

"Always." Mitch rips an application from the pad under the register, hands it to the kid with a pen. "Bring it back whenever."

The kid goes to the counter and sits. Mitch is pleasantly stoned, channels opening in his mind, the day replaying. He digs change out of his pocket and finds a near-mint 1903 Liberty dime in his newspaper change. It's the fourth time that June; the coincidence thing seems to focus around money. Hm, he thinks, now I can pay the phone bill.

Phone bill leads to telephone leads to sound becoming energy leads to energy becoming light leads to a redshifting recollection of the morning's paper. There was an article about the age of the universe, search for planets, extraterrestrial life. Mitch recalls this with a dim sense of foreboding.

The kid returns to the counter. Mitch reads his name and sticks out a hand. "How you doing, Roosevelt? I'm Mitch."

"Nice to meet you," Roosevelt says. His fingernails are ragged and bitten.

Mitch comes around the counter, and they sit together at a table. Roosevelt's handwriting is small and careful. He has no references and no previous job experience, no address and no phone number. Mitch frowns. He looks again at Roosevelt, probing for signals of homelessness, drug abuse, that ineffable whatever. But Roosevelt Rawls just looks like a regular kid.

Okay, Mitch thinks. It's not every day you see a black kid in a hockey jersey. He falls back on the alternative hiring process known as The Question of the Day.

"Roosevelt," he says, "you ever read *The Time Machine?*"

Flicker of a smile. "Yeah."

"You know that model time machine the guy sends off?"

A nod.

"What would you think if you saw one pop into existence right here on this table?"

Roosevelt shrugs. "In an infinite universe, man, all things are not only possible, but inevitable."

It takes Mitch some time to recover from this answer.

"Who says it's infinite?" he asks pugnaciously, remembering the newspaper article.

"Who says it's not? Tell me where it ends."

Roosevelt's answer got him a job, but Mitch's day did not simplify. He was perplexed and not a little worried that he had no answer. His informational capacity had failed him. Clearly a new element had been introduced into his interaction with the cosmos; a delicate balance had been upset. He should not have argued about Bukowski. Perhaps no more Liberty dimes would be forthcoming in cigarette change.

But some good might come as well. If Mitch was no longer the focus of some weird convergence of probabilities, maybe he could start flipping coins again without worrying that he was unbalancing some fundamental property of the universe. Maybe he could go a week without some bizarre coincidence such as had befallen him the day before, when while shooting pool at the Monkey Bar he had fired the cue ball off the table and cracked a bystander in the forehead. The bystander turned out to be a guy named Quincy whom Mitch had once seen mercilessly insulted by a street performer in Key West whose act culminated in knife-juggling while turning figure eights on a seven-foot unicycle called the Suicycle of Death, which it turned out the Monkey bartender had designed for the performer. Everyone in the Monkey had been thunderstruck by this revelation, so much so that Mitch had to stumble out to the curb and cogitate drunkenly on the odds of such an event while inside the Monkey's clientele decided *en masse* to road-trip to Key West and witness the marvel of the Suicycle of Death.

Some of the events narrated thus far are true. Others should have been. It's like Eliot said in *Four Quartets* about time past and time future, about what was and what might have been all coming together to create the present.

What follows is really the point of the whole thing.

It became apparent, after Roosevelt had hung around until one in the morning, that he didn't have any place to go. Tenderhearted Mitch approached him and offered Eli's living room couch. Roosevelt accepted. The graveyard crew came in shortly thereafter, and Roosevelt squeezed himself into the back of Eli's Escort for the short trek to the House on Pearl Street.

I should have called Trina, Mitch thought as they pulled into the driveway. When he walked in, Gus assaulted him, then scrambled into the kitchen. Mitch fed him from a bag of Purina kept cached at Pearl Street for such exigencies, and then the four of them—Mitch, Eli, Roosevelt, and Gus—took up positions in broken-down recliners on the porch.

"It becomes clear to me," said Mitch to Roosevelt, "that you are no ordinary kid."

Roosevelt seemed discomfited by this assertion. Mitch hastened to clarify.

"Simply that your average teenager doesn't toss off smart-ass lines about the age and extent of the universe."

The phone rang. It was Trina. When Mitch returned to the porch, his spirits were somewhat dampened. Eli passed him the pipe.

"I have figured this out," announced Eli. "Roosevelt here is an alien."

Mitch didn't want to hear it. For confirmation, he looked to Gus, who was leaning against Roosevelt's leg with his eyes closed as Roosevelt scratched behind his ears. "He is not," Mitch said, pointing to Gus as evidence. Gus would never consort with aliens.

"He is," answered Eli.

"I am," concurred Roosevelt.

Mitch puzzled over the situation. "I should have known," he said.

"Correct," Eli nodded. "The Red Wings jersey."

"Not to mention uncommon speculations on the nature of the universe."

"Combined with blithe ignorance of hiring rules that luckily we are willing to ignore."

"A fish out of his contextual water." Mitch puzzled some more, then clapped Roosevelt on the shoulder. "You can have a beer, then," he concluded. The three of them toasted this resolution. Mitch, too, toasted the apparent revival of his clairvoyant newspaper reading.

Many beers and not a few bowls later, Mitch had that comfortable kind-of-like-wearing-a-hat feeling that came from careful management of marijuana intake. Gus had long since given up and gone to sleep, his head between his paws. His occasional dreaming grumble raised dust from the porch steps.

A soft pop startled Mitch. He looked up and saw a tiny metal machine next to the porch ashtray. The machine was about six inches long and three high, a framework of some shiny slick metal intertwined with sinuous bars of what looked like ice. A minutely-crafted leather harness and saddle hung in the frame, facing a console of ivory levers. Looking at the console made Mitch a bit queasy; something about it seemed always in motion, always not quite where it was when you looked at it.

"Holy shit," Mitch said. He felt keenly the desertion of causality.

Roosevelt and Eli looked up. For a moment none of them spoke.

"Who did that happen to?" Mitch asked tremulously.

"Who noticed it first?" Eli looked a little stunned. "It looks kind of like a dune buggy."

Mitch, reluctantly: "Me."

"Then it happened to you," said Roosevelt the alien.

"No, man, why? It could have happened to you and I was just who noticed it."

Roosevelt shook his head. "Y'all were talking about this all day, and now it happens, and you want to say it happened to me? Take some responsibility."

"So it happened to Eli," Mitch protested.

"Nope," they both said.

"You did this," Mitch accused Roosevelt.

"H.G. Wells means nothing to me."

"But Eli's right?"

Roosevelt shrugged. "Appears that way."

"So none of us are *real?*" Mitch cried. Gus looked up, then went back to sleep.

"Hell yes we're real," Eli said. He kicked a rock off the porch. "See? That was real. You're real, I'm real. Roosevelt's real, even if he's an alien in disguise."

Roosevelt shrugged. "We're sitting here, ain't we?"

"Look, we're sitting here with a fictional damn model time machine. It and us occupy the same plane of existence. We coexist. Now, I read the book that thing came from, and it wasn't real. So if we coexist, I'm not real—we're not real—either."

"You never pay attention when I'm talking," Eli complained.

"You never make sense," Mitch said.

Eli pointed gloatingly at the time machine.

"I am not black marks on a page," Mitch said.

Roosevelt and Eli shrugged. "Who said you were?" Eli said.

"Look, man," Roosevelt said. "This thing obviously is, and we, too, obviously are, so we all must be. Real. It's that simple."

"'S what I was saying earlier," said Eli.

"No." Mitch shook his head. Then he was distracted. To Roosevelt he said, "If you're an alien, where are you from?"

Roosevelt nodded. "Gacrux."

Eli perked up. "Gacrux? How far away is that?"

Ice cream, Mitch thought. Hungry.

Roosevelt shook his head. "Here's the thing," he said. "Simple logic. Listen carefully."

"Whore of loony ideas," Mitch muttered under his breath, but nobody heard him.

"If all space is simultaneously present," Roosevelt held up one finger, "and space and time are really only different aspects of the same thing," a second finger, "then all time is equally present. T.S. Eliot had this figured out: 'Time past and time future / What might have been and what has been / Point to one end, which is always present.'"

"Where the hell did you read T.S. Eliot?" Mitch said.

"Truth?" Roosevelt popped another can of Pabst. "They give us a class on what to say to humans. It's big on sequential logic and quotations from poems."

Mitch and Eli gauged the degree of condescension in this. They began to feel small.

Eli stood up, breaking the stasis. "That's what I was saying all day!"

It was Roosevelt and Mitch's turn to speak together. "What?"

"What might have been and what has been," Eli said. "Truth and fiction. Mishmash." He flailed his arms, then collapsed back into his recliner. "Shit, you can't expect me to remember it all now."

Mitch was unable to resist. "Hemingway and the Shell guys."

"Those fuckers," Eli said vengefully. "The thing was, I was thinking what difference did it make whether or not the bakery was really the place where Hemingway got the idea for the story. Once you start wondering, it might as well be true. Your mind has already explored the possibilities, assigned connections, delved into variations and uncertainties . . ." He petered out. "Roosevelt knows what I'm talking about."

"He does?" Mitch looked at Roosevelt.

"Look at Gus," Roosevelt said. Mitch did. Gus was dreaming, his front paws twitching, his upper lip curling and relaxing, one of his back legs scratching at the porch's weatherbeaten boards. "What's he dreaming about?"

"How am I supposed to know?" Mitch said.

"Guess."

Mitch considered. "He's either gamboling through a hot dog plantation or biting the mailman."

"Okay. What does the mailman think?"

"Gus is dreaming the mailman, dude. The mailman doesn't think anything; he's made up."

Roosevelt pointed at the time machine.

Mitch began to sulk. "You're saying my dog's dreamed mailman is as real as I am," he said resentfully.

"Yup," Roosevelt said. "It's all as real as you are."

"Bullshit," Mitch said. "Then nobody would ever make anything up."

"Sure they would. They do. Gus is making up that mailman, but he exists somewhere, but the invention is still invention because Gus didn't know that. And even if you know on an abstract level that everything exists somewhere, you still invent it. Go read Borges, man. Incomplete knowledge of the universe preserves our ability to imagine and invent."

This rationale did little to console, and Mitch resented getting a literary-epistemological lecture from an alien. "What are you doing here, anyway?" he said finally.

"Hey, yeah," Eli piped up suddenly, his exuberance signaling the approach of a non sequitur. "And with Hemingway, the other thing was that the kid in the diner or whatever, he looks at the killers like they're from different planets."

Something about this statement, perhaps only Eli's tone of voice, suggested to Mitch that it was significant. But he couldn't figure out why. "Where does it say that?" he said.

"It's all in how you read it, man."

Again, Mitch looked at Roosevelt. Again, Roosevelt shrugged.

"Oh for Christ's sake," Mitch said.

Or it could have happened this way:

Many beers and many bowls later, after the discovery of Roosevelt's extraterrestrial origins, the three of them sit deep within the fragrant cushions of broken-down recliners. Someone tells a joke, and they laugh.

"I have a confession to make," Mitch says.

"Confess," Eli commands.

"All of this is my fault. If I hadn't read that article in the paper this morning, none of this would have happened." He holds up a Liberty dime as proof. Roosevelt and Eli look back and forth from Lady Liberty to Mitch Packard.

"What?" they say.

"It's like this. Every morning when I read the newspaper, one of the articles sort of becomes necessary for me to get through the day. This morning I read something about the age of the universe, looking for planets, extraterrestrial life . . ." They're still staring at him. "Don't you get it?" Mitch says. "I made all this happen. Roosevelt's an alien because I read the paper this morning."

There is a soft pop, and a tiny glimmering machine appears next to the porch ashtray.

"That," Roosevelt says, pointing his beer can at it, "is what solipsism gets you."

What it all boils down to is this, this one end that is eternally present:

Everyone has gone to sleep except Mitch Packard. Roosevelt the alien is stretched out on the orange sectional couch in Pearl Street's living room. Eli is crashed in his room behind the kitchen, Jane's Addiction playing in his earphones. Gus still lies, head between his freckled paws, at the head of the porch stairs.

Mitch alone remains awake. He is preoccupied with the nefariousness of the universe. No immediate prospect of reconciliation with Trina presents itself. His lungs, tired and abused, agree to one last cigarette; the afterimage of the match puts him in mind of stars. Cygnus, Centauri, Polaris, Gacrux.

In an infinite universe, all things exist. Axiomatic. Mitch smokes his cigarette. Closing his eyes, he puts it down. Damn those guys at the Shell station.

Okay, Mitch thinks, slumping into sleep on Pearl Street's sagging porch with a cigarette burning down in the cockpit of the model time machine. It's an old idea. Might as well be true. But. But.

But I'm as real as whoever's writing me. Real as whoever's reading.

His paws hanging over the porch step, Gus dreams of chasing the mailman through perfectly manicured rows of bushes, their ripening hot dogs waving ever so slightly in an endless summer breeze.

A Crowd of Bone

Greer Gilman

Margaret, do you see the leaves? They flutter, falling. See, they light about you, red and yellow. I am spelling this in leaves. When I had eyes and hands, and hair as red as leaves, I was Thea. My mother fed me to her crows, she burned my bones and scattered them; my braided hair she keeps. I am wind and memory who spells this; Thea who is spelled is stone. My mother got me gazing in her glass. Her raven held it up and told her: what I tell you, you must do. *Undo*, the sly moon said. And so she did, undid. Annis was herself her glass, and I her shadow, A and O. She saw me in the stony mirror, naked as a branch of thorn. Devouring, she bore me, as the old moon bears the new, itself again. But I am left hand to her right: not waning, but the childing moon. The dark has eaten me; I bear it light. I cloak myself in leaves, I fly. The wind unspells this.

I will spell this in the sliding water on a web. At my birth, the Necklace had its rising, Annis' chain of stones. But they do give it other names above, that Elsewhere it had set. The Skein, they call it in the Cloudish tongue; in Lune, the Misselbough; that cloud of stars we name the Clasp, they call Nine Weaving, or the Clew. So I did write when I had hands and learned to cipher and to spell. When I had eyes, I saw another heavens through her glass, another world. I walk there now and gather lightwebs, plucking them from thorns of night; I spin them in a skein, a clew. The dark is labyrinth, but not the maze I thought I knew. I wander like a moon. See, Margaret, how the heavens dance, they dance between my hands. When I had eyes, I thought my seeing bound the stars; I knew the Cup, the Hallows Tree, the Ship, as if my naming them were law. There is another law. The stars are messengers; their shining comes from far and farther still, from hearths long cold. Walking, I have seen the hearths beyond the stars, like ashes on a dark hill. But the stars that travel, they are dark and bright, like travellers with scarves of light, like beings newly blown of crystal, each a single note, nightblack, and rayed with burning silver. Their moving is their voice; they do not speak, but dance. Ah, now the drops of water slide away. The web is shaken bare.

I tell this in the frost, the rime. I am not for my mother's necklace. Margaret, have you seen it? It is strung with stones, all flawed: some round as waveworn pebbles, others long and sharpedged. They are souls, the souls of witches, cold long since: the eldest of them ash these nine thousand years. Witches turn themselves to stone. Their gaze is glass. But they are isolate, unknotted souls: they dance by one and one. The necklace is an eidolon, a ring that never was. The souls are gathered on one string, as shadows of the starry Chain. That cord is time; the knot is Law. It is a place. I lay there once, a white ground where the blood is spilled, a place of bones and coins. All witches came there, bent on darkness; none had met. They spelled in blood, cast bones; they spoke in tongues of fire. There are witches still in Lune, on Law. Yet none is living that could read the word my ashes spelled; nor find the nine bones that I left.

Beyond the circle of Whin's light, the sea moves, sleepless in its heavy gown. She walks beside it slowly, toward, away. And to her, from her, endlessly it shifts the longways of its slow pavane. Within her candle's burr, sparse flakes of snow blink, vanish. There is nothing there to see. Salt rime and shingle. Sea wrack. Stones, a curve of jetty, tumbled in a storm. Sticks and weed. They stir. A wave? They draw breath, harshly. The lantern swings and halts.

In the dark, a white face, staring: a man, all bone and shivering, three-quarters drowned. "Who's there?" he tries to call. Whin sets the lantern down. "A journeyman," she says. "A traveller." He sprawls against the stonework, tangled in an iron ring; the next wave frets at him, the next. His coat is gone, his head and feet are bare. A stranger out of Lune, thinks Whin. Uncloudish. Yet he bids her by her calling. "Ashes?" At his throat he wears a skin bag, smaller than a purse. His hands are white past bleeding, bruised; he signs to her, take this. She fumbles with the knots, she bites at them and tumbles out his hoard: cold rings.

"Will you tell a death?"

They are silver and endless on her hard brown palm. White stones like frost. A knot of blood. "Could yer not sell them?"

"None would take. No ship. They—"

"Throwed yer over? I see yer to hang."

He shudders. "It is not my passage that I seek."

"A fire," says Whin. "And drink ye. I'd not shift stones for yer grave."

She squats beside him, lugs him further up the strand. Stripping off his icy rags, she laps him in the old coat, black as nightfall, stiff as death. He'd not starve yet. She leaves him hallowed in the lantern's fleet.

There's wood enough, but sodden. Whin flings the heavy, takes the dry stuff, salt with frost. She stacks it, leeward of a quain of rock; strikes, kindles, drives her iron for the can. Waiting for the blaze, she chafes the stranger, lays him naked to her breast: blue hands, bruised feet, his starved and wrinkled cock and balls, his belly, slack against his spine, until the blood runs shining, sheeting on his dazed white face. The fire leaps. A boy, for all his haggard look. His eyes are sunken, shut; his beard is soft. Not twenty. Younger than herself. She lays him, not ungently, on the stones.

"Not sleep," he whispers. "Tell."

"Drink." The ale in the can's hot; she stirs a slurry of meal in, a scrape off her knuckled ginger. Strong. She holds it to his lips.

"Tell."

Whin drinks. "I will then." She turns the cold rings on her hand. They are silver and endless; they are night, moon, mourning. They would weigh her down. Whin sees the pale boat waiting and the soul that bellies in the dark wind, quick with death; the telling is the shroud that stays it, that the soul can journey. Let her go.

It's what I is. Death's midwife.

And she sets the first ring on.

O death. She sees the wheel hurled downward, burning, and the scattered crows. She sees a white wrist circled with a braid of burning hair, a bluenailed hand; it casts, it casts a blackness on the stony ground. Shards of witchglass, ashes of bone.

And she herself is scattered and restrung. She is the crowd of bone, the dead soul's stringing, and her voice.

Whin's hand is beating, beating on the earth. She sings.

It's in an outland tongue at first, a dancing driving lilt, a skirl and keening; then the tongue's her own. *There are pools in the river, and the river calls him.* All white in whiteness where it rises; swift in running, deepest where the red leaf eddies in the pool. Whorl and headlong, she sings the river's journey: glint and shadow, dint of rain, the running to the downfall and the shivered bow of light.

No more.

Even as she wakes from trance, the ring is ice, is water. Gone.

She sees the fire, sunken into embers; sees the drawn face staring. Far beyond, the sea shifts, turning its sleepless bed. Far gone.

"The child," he whispers.

Ah. The child. Whin presses at her eyes until the red's green as leaves, new leaves. *Ashes. Ashes.* See, the crows at the furrows wheel and fall, they tear at—*No. Leave off. That were back and elsewhere.* A long draught of the caudle, slab with standing. Raking back her hair, salt-fretted with the roke and sweat, Whin slips the small ring on her hand.

And there is nothing. Whiteness. Round she turns, and round; she stumbles, groping for a gossamer, a clew. No thread, there is no thread. A creak of wood. A ship? And then a lalling nowhere, like a woman at her wheel; but small. Arms crossed before her face, Whin blunders at the mist. It reddens and dissolves; it dances. And she's in an empty room. She sees a cradle overset; she sees a tangle of bright silks. In the roar and crackling of thorns, she sees a burning doll, its blind face like a poppyhead, the petals like a cry.

"The child?" His voice is sharp with fear.

"Not dead."

He shuts his eyes. "Ah."

Whin slips the small ring up her finger, rocks it with her thumb. Not dead, she'd swear it. How? Not born?

But where is here? The world is white now, greying like a ghost. Are they now lost in what she'd sung? Whin stares a moment, mutely; then she turns her palm and raises it. It fills with snow. She tastes the water in the hollow of her hand, the salt and sweet.

Bending to the man, she brushes him; she touches eyes, mouth, heart. "Thou sleep."

A girl is reading in a garden where no flowers grow. It is formal and mathematical, a maze, an abstract of the heavens done in yew and stone. A garden made for moonlight and for winter, changeless but for sky and snow and drifting leaves: a box of drowned green light. It is autumn now. The fountain's dry; the stone girl weeps no more. Her lap is full of leaves. The lawn is grey as gossamers with rime. The living girl's dishevelled, in a cloud of breath; she's hunched against the cold in woven velvet, wadded silk: old finery, too thin. Leaves light on her. She holds her book aslant to catch the light, and peers through cracked spectacles: ". . . one king's daughter said to another . . ." Her breakfast's in a napkin: cake, an orange. Costly, alien, aglow. Round she turns it in her cold lap, cradles, sniffs. Straying from her hood, her tangled hair is pale red, light through leaves; her tumbled gown is stormcloud blue. Her slipshod feet are wet. Softly as she's come, she cannot hide her track: her feet, her draggling skirts have torn the hoarfrost, tarnishing. You cannot read her face: an egg, a riddle. What is it lives within a maze, within a wall, within a hedge of thorn? And on an island, not a winter's day in riding round. Yet she's never seen the sea.

A bird cries. *Margaret?* Startled, she looks up and round. The orange rolls unheeded from her lap. There, back of her, a black bird flutters to the earth, as ragged as an ash. Its cry fades like a cinder, glows and fades. Bearded, it regards her with its black eye; hops and drags a mirror in the wounded frost.

Ah, Margaret, it was cold in Cloud, the wandering. I mind a night of frost, a white hag on the hillsides; it was all ways white, whatever way we turned. Kit bore a lantern that he dared not light; my mother's crows have eyes. Round we turned like children in a game; like tops, still giddy, lest we fall.

Here's not yet dark, he said. And none to light our heels. I hear that Will the piper's to the hedgehogs' shearing.

A cup, I said, to drink their health.

A game, said he. Wilt thou have *Aprons all untied?* I'll show thee. Or *Cross my river to Babylon.*

Light words. But doubtful mind, I thought: elated, ill at ease. What should he with this bird of paradise? I was no hedgeling to be coaxed and whistled; yet had lighted on him, haggard to his hand. Brave plumes. And trailing jesses of another's leash.

Thy candle's quenched, said I. Will I light thee another?

And willing, said he. Wouldst bear it then?

And go the lighter for't.

Then soberly he said: the bridge is drowned. I know not the way.

We stood. And all the trees beyond us like a crowd of bones. No stars. I'd never gone by night, without to see the stars. And in my mind I saw what I'd undone: my mother's chain of stones, the clasp of winter from my throat. Her chain of witches' souls. I saw them in the mist, the others in the game, caught out, cast out. They stood like stones, but clearer than the coldest night: in each, a dark witch rayed with blood; in each, the wintry stars. In the last, like an altar stone, there lay the image of a woman sleeping, with the hooked moon at her heart. She was the fell they stood upon, her hair unwreathing in a coil of cloud. This cloud. *I am braided in her hair,* I said, as if my mother lessoned me; and then recalling me, I touched my throat, all bare but for a scarf.

That chain was my knowledge. I put it off with my undoing and I walked unstarry in that mazing whiteness: unwitch, unmaiden and unwise. They say the moon does so. But I was never maid—ah, Margaret, thou'rt full young to see, but thou must see. Thou know'st my mother got me in her glass. And so I was as left hand to her right. I was her make in all things hidden, and I knew as I was known. Ah, but never with an other, I had never been unknown; nor seen, as through a cloud, the hearth and shadow of another's soul. My love, we got thee all unknowing, out of cloud.

But now your breath clouds the glass: too near, you gaze too near. And so see no one in the mist: a whiteness, waning with your breath. Oh, I am all undone. My mother loosed the knot long since; she laid the chain of me aside. The soul slipped by her. White in whiteness: what I am is white.

"So yer run off wi' a witch's daughter?" said Whin. "Were yer mad or what?"

"Dazzled," said the man at last, and softly.

"And t' lass?" A silence, long enough so that Whin thought he slept.
"Ah. No witch. In the end."

Kit stood. Whatever way he turned was white, as white as nowhere.
"Thea?"
"Soft," she said. "Catch hold."
Among the standing shapes of stones, a stone put back its hood and turned. He saw her, Thea, looking back at him, her curled hand at her throat. Stumbling in the mist, he caught her and he took her cold true hand. The lantern of her hair was grey. With hag, he saw: it ghosted them. Brocaded both alike: his russet and her raiment stiff and fine with it. Her face was muffled in a scarf, the whitest at her lips. His hair, when he put it from his eyes, was hackled with frost. "Where's this?"
"Cloud," said Thea. "Is there earth?"
"I know not," he said. He looked about, bewildered, at the mist. "How came we here?"
"By ship."
He remembered; or had dreamed the like. They were in her mother's garden, in among the stones like hooded watchers and the labyrinth of yews. 'Twas dusk and shadowless, the maze, the stones configured as the starry sky. They were playing at a game with lanterns? *Hide fox, and all after.* How the errant star of her shone out, now there, now elsewhere in the dark. Their lamps conjoined. He saw her, still, but as a light is still, still dancing in his eyes. He kissed her—ah, it drowned him deep, that kiss. In her, his soul translated, like a tree of fire, burning in her bluegreen dusk. *Come away with me,* he said, now ardent, now amazed, the words like Perseids. *To Cloud. And let thy mother—*
Nothing. He remembered nothing, like a sleeper waked. Cold moonlight, musty straw. A jangling, as of keys. The dream had troubled him with joy; he wore the stone of it, both bright and heavy, at his heart.
He said, bemused, "My lady sent for you. 'Twas in her closet."
"I had found a door," she said. "The sky has doors."
"And locks?"
"'Tis done. Undone."
He saw a little image, clear as in a dream: a string of stones cast by, like blood spilled on the hoary earth.
"But how—?"
"Thy fiddle was the ship."
Dismayed, he halted. "What?"
"'Twas wood of Cloud. It played the wind behind us."
"Ah," said Kit, and rubbed his eyes. Salt wind: it stung. "I gave it thee. And would

again, were't all the sinews of my heart." And yet remembered nothing of the gift, the journey. *Ship?* As in a waking dream, he saw the sail of sky, bluegreen against a darker sky, all riddled with the stars. He saw the lantern at the mast. Their hands together at his lips were salt. "What tune?"

"*Light leaves on water.*"

"Ah, it played that when its leaves were green. Waked wood." Still unsteady, his voice. That shock of severing still white, which at a thought would bleed. And so he laid light words to it, like cobwebs to a wound. He knelt to mend his lantern. "Here's a fret. 'Tis out. And I've left my flint and steel." He grimaced ruefully. "And come to that, thy book, and all. Hadst thou nothing thou wouldst take?"

"There was not time. The door stood open."

Suddenly he stood and said, "We've done it, then?"

"We do," said Thea. "Grammar."

"Ah," said Kit. "How the old crows' beaks will clack. Canst see them at their feast? Here's bones." And hopping on the ground, he cocked an eye at her, with such a glance of balked fury that she laughed aloud.

"*The crow and her marrow, they quarrel for the glass.*" Then gathering up her skirts, "Let's on," she cried.

"What way?"

"Any way. Away."

"All Cloud's to choose."

"I know. To where the fiddles grow."

"And shake the tree? I'll play no windfall, for the green are sharp."

"But we must cross a river by the dawn."

Round they turned like children in a game, and in and out among the stones. They called and bantered, dizzy with unlawful joy. Kit fell. His lantern slid away, it skated from his grasp; then he was up again, bruised and laughing. "Hey!" Then seeing her a-shake with cold, he sobered. "Canst thou make us fire?"

"No," said Thea.

"Nor can I," he said. "I doubt we'll starve then, but we find some cotter's hearth." He cast his coat round her, crazy with the ice. "Or a tinker's camp. And chaffer for his russet coat." *A mantle of the starry sky.* Her gown was thin, the color of the bloom on sloes, embroidered as the Milky Way: light shaken out, lace dandled. Not for travelling, he thought. A gown for walking in her mother's hall, from glass to glass. And it would snow.

"So this is Cloud," he said. "'Tis like a tale of witches, well enough by the fire. *Once afore the moon was round, and on a night in Cloud* . . . Hast kindred here?"

"None," said Thea, "in this world. But hast not thou?"

"In Lune I had." He bent for the lantern. "We'd best on."

The night was uncompassed. Far off, they heard an endless rampage, not a shuttle but a reel of sound, cloud spinning into ice.

"What's that?" she said. "'Tis like the sea unmeasured."

"A river," he said. "Houses?"

So they set out for it, stumbling into brakes of thorn and bogs and pitfalls, snagged and mired. They went blindly, now toward and now astray. The roar grew louder in the dark. The hills re-echoed with the rush of it, behind, before, and everywhere. Above, a nightcrow cawed, once, in its coaly voice. An omen. Thea stilled.

"What is't?" said Kit.

"The clouds have eyes."

"An I had my fiddle, I would play them to sleep."

On the hills, the foxes yowled and yelped, as if their blood ran green. An eerie sound, that keening. Thea shivered.

"The hills have tongues. They wake."

"They wed. I'd light them with a dance." And wheeling backward, sliding—"Oh!" cried Kit. She caught his jacket as he stepped on nothing, on the brink of tumbling in a foss.

"Now what?" said Kit. "I'm for a glass castle and a bout with goblins. Or a ghost, or what you will. As we've tumbled in a winter's tale." He sat among the lashy thorns and rubbed his shins. "Ah," he said, and fumbled in his pockets. "Here." She felt a handful of nuts. "From thy mother's table, as I passed. We may sit and crack them while the crows take counsel."

"Or match them with a goblin, shell for soul."

"Unless he'd like a gingernut?"

"To cross his river?"

"Aye." Kit rose. "'Twill narrow upstream, far enough."

In the dark beyond the river, there and gone, they saw a fire.

Kit caught at Thea's arm. "A light. A house?"

"A torch," she said. "It moves."

"Thy mother's horsemen?"

"No. They bear no light."

He said, "Belike some lantered shepherd. Or a fiddler from a dance."

Stumbling toward the light, he called out, "Hallows!"

An answer, lost in tumult.

"Hey! Where's this?"

"Crawes Brig," called the voice. "Wait on." They saw the wavering fire and the world made round it, swayed and ruddy. On the farther bank, a roughclad knarry shape held up a torch. It shuddered in the little wind. They saw the wolf-black water, snarling white; they saw the way, from stone to stepping-stone to span, the lighter as they leapt. A clapper bridge, a cromlech. They met on the span. "Here. Gi's that." The stranger took the lantern, thrust the torch in it alight, and latched the door; then hurled the brief end, whirling fire, in the beck.

They stood within a burr of light that brindled in the rushy dark. There was no other where. The stranger stared at them with long dark eyes, quirked mouth. Kit saw the hunch of shoulders bearing up the jangling pack. A traveller, he thought, a tinker or a tain by kindred: breeched and beardless, swart and badgerly of arms. And grey as any brock: with winters or the hag, he knew not. By the small harsh voice, a woman, so he guessed.

"Yer late abroad," said Brock. "Come on."

The candle wavers. Ah, thou frown'st, as if my shadow fell across thine elsewhere. I will spell this in the margins of thy book. Mine, once. See, Margaret, here the leaf's turned down where Perseis gave up. Her grave is Law. But I see thou read'st her spring, her journeying. The lady speaks:

> But thou art mazed, sweet fool. The wood is dark, `
> And I th' moon's daughter in these rags of cloud
> Shall bear thee light.

Another world. I dreamed not of greenwood nor of crowns of May; nor thought on bread, sweat, childbed. Only I would not be Thea, and my lady's cipher. So I saw my chance: a bird in hand, a passager; an occultation of the Nine. I took.

Poor Kit. Wood with love of me. He mourned his fiddle; I do rue it now. His soul and livelihood and all. And yet he had of me a greater thing, unwitting. Not my maidenhead. Whatever ballads tell, 'tis nothing, anyone's. An O. That which annihilates all else. No, Margaret: the game is toyish, but the stakes are souls. My love, we ate each other back and belly, and the heartstrings: which are music, which are gut.

Ah, now the candle gutters. I am leaping; I am shroud and smoke.

I snuff.

"Here," said the traveller. She stooped and they followed through a thicket of ice. The candle woke in it a flittering of lights; it chimed and rattled as they passed beneath it. "Rimes," said Thea, half aloud to Kit. "Glass castle," he whispered. "Did I not say?" Before them was a tumble of stones: hall fallen into hovel; a sill, and dark within. At the door, the traveller stamped the clods from her boots. She set the lantern down; the fire made room. She turned in the doorway and said, "Walk in, awd Moon."

Kit caught her rime, though not her meaning. "Wi' broom afore, to sweep the ashes from the door," he said, as if they came a-souling at the empty house. He plucked at Thea's sleeve. "Go on, love, 'tis thy piece."

She turned her small moon's face on him. "Will there be oranges?"

"Thy lapful."

"I know not the words."

So Kit chanted, "Cold by the door and my candle burns low, so please let us in, for it's shrewd in the snow." He bent and bustled all around her with his broom of air; so they went in.

"Here's guising," said the traveller. "A sword and a bush."

Kit answered lightly. "So it ever was."

"Then let's to yer bout and have done wi' it. Smick smack, and up flies wren."

Thea lifted her face, bright with mischief. "Ah, but you must hear us out; you've bid us in. You must hear Moon's verses, since she's crossed your door."

The traveller looked them up and down: the tousled lad, all beak and bones; the girl in outlandish clothing, with her hair like braided fire. "Out o' thy turning. If thou's Moon."

"Out of thy sphere, if thou'rt fire."

"Out of my depth," said Kit. "As I am drowned."

They clapped themselves and shivered. Dry within. No straw nor muck; but hay and heather, cut and heaped. Kit turned to and helped the stranger drag some branches to the hearth. It was bare enough, that ruin: a hovel for the lambing shepherds or the lasses binding broom. Kit whispered to Thea, "As for cakes and silver, we may bite old moon."

The traveller lit a fire with a stump of juniper. It burned with a sharp smoke, curling; then was firestruck, its every needle cast in gold, consuming. By its light, they studied her, a little smutchfaced woman, dark and watchful, in a coat of black sheepskins, singed and stained about the hem with ashes and blood. She wore grey breeches and a leathern cap. Her hair was unbound about her shoulders, roughly shorn across her brows; a few strands plaited narrowly with iron charms. She crouched by the fire and stirred it with her knife. "My forge is drowned," she said. The bough had fallen all to flinders, and the berries glowered in the ashes. "Get yer warm," she said, and quirked her chin at them. Then she stood and rummaged in her jangling pack, and went out.

They looked at one another, huddling by the fire. All the spanglings of the ice, their winter finery, had faded. There they sat in draggled clothes, ungarlanded, unwed. Bare strangers. By the wall where the bed had stood, a timeworn carving showed: a woman with a pair of shears, but what she sheared was gone. "I feel like a ghost," said Kit.

"How? Shadowy? Thou'rt blood and breath."

"Uncanny on this ground. And you?"

"No dwelling spirit. They do haunt; they have a bloodknot to this earth. A tale. And mine is all before me, all unmoored."

"An elfin, then."

"A waif. A soul unborn, and calling on the wind. Their tale is nothing: only, they are cold without, and would come in."

"I'd let them in," said Kit, "And warm them." White and shivering, her wisp of spirit. And a glass between their souls. He longed to take her in his arms: so small and cold and straight, so quick of mind. A candle and its light, he thought. And then: the fire was his. To have the daughter of so great a lady run away with him—'twas beyond all marvels. And a flawless maid. A dazzlement. A goblin in him danced, exulting; knocked at his breeches. Ranted on his grave. He knelt. "Thea. If thou wouldst—"

"Hush," said Thea, as they heard the traveller's goatshod step. They sprang apart, a little awkwardly. The fire had flushed them, that was all; the wind had tousled them. The traveller walked softly toward them, and turned to Thea with a cup.

"Here's to thy turning."

"With my heart," said Thea, with answering gravity. She took it in her hands and drank. "Oh," she said, and turned to Kit. "Do they not say in Cloud, hallows wi' thee?"

"And wi' thee," he said, and drank. It was milk, still warm. "Ah," said Kit, bemused. "Your lambs drop early, shepherd."

"Twa and twa," the traveller said. "T'ane black and t'other white." She drank. "And all me ewes give cheeses turn themsels."

"Cup and all?" said Thea.

The traveller smiled at her, small and sharp. "At tree, it were. They'll have left it for Ashes."

"Oh," said Kit. "I see." Though he did not.

But Thea, pinning up a braid, said, "Ashes?"

"Shepherds. They do wake her from her mother dark."

"Ah, Perseis. I know that tale."

"It's what I do," said the traveller. "Walk out and see."

Kit caught at straws. "You're late abroad."

"Been hunting craws. To mek a soulcake on."

"But where are your dogs?" said Thea.

"Whistled home." She unhooked an aleskin from her pack, and teemed it out in a stoup. She pulled her knife from the fire, glowing, and she plunged it in the ale. "Ye'll be starved," she said. "Walking."

"Wanting bread," said Kit. "If you can spare."

"As for that." The traveller undid a rag and a knot and a clump of heather, and held out her scarred brown hand.

Kit saw a handful of stones, black scrawled with white, white scribbled over with a sort of wintry runes, like stars and their ascendants, prophecies of light. "I know this tale," said Kit. "You'll be wanting a bit of salt next. For the soup."

"What thou will," the traveller said. She chose a stone and thirled it with a pin and blew: a whorl of sun, widening, muddled with the ale.

"Eggs," he said, bewildered.

"Aye," said she, and tossed the shell away and broke another and another still, and stirred the pot. She teemed the ewe's milk in.

Kit raked through the embers for the few flawed shales of night. White, like the moon in flinders. Black, with a sleave of stars. Were they owl eggs, then? Or nightingales? "It's eating music," he said ruefully.

"O breve," said Thea. "Do they so in Cloud?"

"With bacon. Do we not in Lune?"

The traveller stirred the caudle round, with a race of ginger, knuckled like a witch's hand, a slurry of coarse sugar and a scrape of nutmeg. A pinch to the fire; it sparkled. "Wha said they'd hatch birds? Wha said they'd sing?"

"In Law," said Thea, "they do not."

So grave? Kit glanced at her, and pulled a fool's face, innocent. "They say the Lunish witches eat owl pies."

"Crack bones and craunch marrow, aye," said Thea. Fire and shadow on her face. "But of late they've grown dainty and will nothing coarse: venture on a junket of maidenheads—"

"Ah, that slips down," said Kit.

"—with a boy for a bergamot."

The traveller dipped her finger, tasted. "Aye, but seek as they will, their cupboard's bare. They may beg for't."

"They've sails," said Thea. In the silence, they heard the wind rise from the north and west, from Law.

"T's keeled for them," the traveller said. They looked at her, and at the eggshells, all shivered on the ground but one that whorled about the ale, and sank. "There's all their shallops."

"Will they follow so?" said Thea softly.

"But if their sails are souls, and all their riggins of thy hair."

"'Twas never cut," said Thea.

"Ah," the traveller said. "Reach to." They passed the caudle round and drank in silence. From her pack, the traveller shared out a bannock, spread with curds and new sweet cream. As round as the moon it was, and a little charred beneath. Ah, thought Kit, here's some hob goes supperless, and all the kitchen in a cludder with his sulking on't. He gazed at Thea, silent by the hearth. Her eyes were elsewhere.

Slowly, she unwound her scarf, unclouding heaven. Ah, but she was crescent, she was moonrise, even at the verge of dawn—O hallows—even to the rose.

But not for him, this glory. Bending toward the traveller, she held the scarf: a light silk woven of the sky, it seemed. He'd thought of it as grey, but it was shining, warped with silver like an April morning. Rain and bow. She laid it in the outstretched hands. Kit watching saw it fall on them, and thought their earthgrained furrows would spring green.

"For thy spell," she said. "A sail."

The traveller looked slantwise through her rough dark hair, her long black eyes unglittering. "A soul." It shifted in her hands, turned silver and a flowing dark, like cloud before the moon. And cleared then to a moonless dark. The stars ran through it still like rain. "Well, I's a rag on every bush, they say." She wafted it and caught it crumpled, bunched it in her pack all anyhow. "It's cawd without, thou knaws."

Thea said, "It would not keep me warm."

"It's thy petticoats are musty. Do them off."

"For thy breeches," Thea said. Kit looked at her, her bare throat white as thorn, her face alight. Her breasts—buds in January, whiter than its snow. No lad. She stood and paced, as he had seen her by the whiteskied windows of her mother's tower. Of darkest blue, her eyes, the night in which her fires burned. She turned on the traveller, fierce and cold. "Or thy cap or anything, thy hammer and thy sooty brat, so my mother would not see me in her glass."

"Break t' glass."

"It will not break, the moon. It goes with child unflawed, and of itself. And being full, itself devours, lighter of the dark. It gazes and it gnaws. I want to get back of it."

Kit looked at Thea, like the heavens' cold bright bow; and saw the dark that bent, that held her. There were walls he could not see.

The traveller held her gaze. "There is a door, they say."

"Then I would out of it."

He saw her fury; though her hair was braided close, she blazed as whitely as a falling star. He felt his spirit rise to her. Arrow to her bow. "Love, let me in."

She turned to him. "Crack the glass and I will."

It was his heart that cracked; but like an acorn, that the oak might spring.

He slipped the ring from his finger. "Thea. Love," he said. "With my heart, 'tis what I have." His mother's ring of tawdry silver, black with years. A riddling posy.

Thea turned it round and read. "*Lief wode I fall, an light wode spring.* Or this way, look: *I fall and light: would spring leafwood.*" Round again: "*Anne Lightwode: spring leaf. Would I fall?*" She looked to him and smiled; she slipped it on her finger.

O the falling star. 'Twas in his hands.

The traveller, watching as she would a play, took out her bacca and her bit of black pipe. "Key's under bush," she said. "Look well to yer locks."

And still Kit stood amazed.

"As for yer guising." The traveller undid her pack, and pulled from it a heap of leaves; she shook it out and there were sleeves to it, and dangling buttons made of horn. It was a coat in tatters. "Craws weren't having it," she said. "What's ta'en is anyone's."

"Is there a hat to it?" said Kit, recovering.

"And feather," said the traveller. She swung the coat round Thea's shoulders. It hung to her heels.

Kit grinned. "Ah. Wilt thou go for a ranting girl?"

"Aye, and bid them stand," the traveller said.

"Here's purses full," said Kit.

"I'll nothing but thy ring," said Thea, whirling round on him. "Or will it come to swordplay?"

"Wouldst kill me naked?"

"And would die beside thee."

He reeled her in. "And then I rise."

"Oh," said Thea. "'Tis my part. And I am of out it."

"So I am in," said Kit, and caught her by the coattail, laughing. "Turns," he said; so she let him try it on. He flaunted in it, up and down. He looked all mischief, with his leafish face. And in the flaycraw's voice, the fool's, he said, "I'll riddle thee. What leaves and still it stands?"

"A tree," said Thea. "Turns?"

The traveller shrugged. "For either, as it likes you. And if she's a lad, I's shears."

Thea rounded on her. "Where?"

"No," cried Kit, dismayed. "I beg thee. Not thy hair." He'd not yet seen it down, not played with it undone. It would unravel like a fugue. He thought of all the braided strands of it, the bright and somber and the burning strands, the viol and clarion. "And yet . . ." His token glinting on her hand: he dared. "I'd have a lock of it, sweet witch, for journey's sake."

"In knots, as witches sell the wind?"

"Aye, knotted: for undone 'twould quicken stone."

A parry and no promise: "Thou wouldst thaw my lady's glass?"

"Like April snow. And all thy combs would flower, leafless, from the wood, and make of thy undoing, crowns of May." A tendril, like a wisp of fire, twining by her cheek: he traced it, marvelling. So cold, so bright and cold.

Not fencing now: the blade itself: "Wouldst braid thy gallows? Wear it?"

"Nearer than my breath. I'll knot my soul in it." It burned in him already, bright in every vein: a tree. He took her in his arms. "And being strung upon my bones, 'twill play the same tune still, for sun and moon, and all the starry hey to dance."

Her lips were colder than the moon's, and soft. He felt him falling in a drift of snow, bedazzled, over ears. Her lap, he thought, she lulls them in her lap. Moon and stars. He saw the burning bush. He saw the bird of her, flown up amid her branches—that he could not take. He shook himself, remembering the traveller's eyes, and shrugged the greatcoat off. "I'll go no more a-guising. 'Tis the fiddler's turn to dance."

"To pipe and drum," the traveller said.

Thea and the traveller took the coat between them, lofting it and laying it upon the springing heather, so it made a bed. They stood at head and foot of it, as in the figure of a dance; the traveller spoke.

"What thou gets here, thou mun leave betimes."

"I must bear it," Thea said.

"And will."

"Undone and done."

The traveller crouched and tweaked a corner of the coat aside, tucked something in, and rose. "What is ta'en here, cracks t' glass. What is tinder s'll be ash. Go lighter of it, intil dark." She flung a pair of shears on the makeshift bed. They lay there open, like a striding stork. She turned and gathered up her pack. "I's off."

They saw her go. They lay together on the coat, of leaves as deep as hallows. After a time, unspeaking, they undid her hair, and went into another night.

O the dark. Thou hear'st not, Margaret. I will tell this to the darkness.

I would not be Thea: so I did, undid. The thing of naught. Ablaze and all unhallowed in that night, I cracked the glass. Blasphemed my lady, that was Annis. That was all myself. Of my own will, I overset her holiest of laws; I broke her will of me, her mirror and her chain. Set Cloud for Law, and darkness for her glass. Blood in the stone's place, the place of secrets. Rose for thorn.

The traveller came to the stones. They stood looking out on darkness, on the bare white shoulder of the fell. That knowe is Law. The sky was starless; yet they mirrored in their O that constellation called Nine Weaving or the Clasp. The wintry mantle they had pinned was gone. Softly, she went in and out among them with her dying torch. All doors are hers; but these stood open. There was no one where the girl had been. The torch went out. The traveller turned among the empty stones, toward morning, sunwise.

Ah! cried Brock. She saw the falling star, now, nowhere, in the wintry sky. Her seeing sained it. Wheeling round, she dropped the black end of the besom to the earth, ashes on the frost. She snuffed the wind. It was rising, high above the earth. The sky had flawed with stars, with scarves and spanglings of light. Her eyes were good; she told the eight stars in the Nine, and one beside. It danced with them. The ashes told its name.

Beyond her lay the long bare fells, rimewhite, unwhitening. Through patches of the fading snow there pierced a greener white of snowdrops, that do spring in Ashes' wake. Her flowers. Drops of Milk, the country folk do call them, Ashes' Buds. They bring the light with them returning, rising from her mother's dark: all seely innocence. Yet they are death to pluck; and yet they must be gathered, woven for her crown by earthly hands. By Ashes. Not herself, but in her stead: a lass each winter who must wear the burden of her name, her silence, walking in her sleep. That godhead lights on whom she chooses: Ashes for her sake, her shadow, souling in a coat of skin. Her winter's lyke.

As Brock walked on, she passed a windbare thicket leaning all one way, and saw the curled green shoots of bracken, green amid the scrawl of last year's leaves; she saw the tassels of the oak unbraiding. Saw the selving wood. A hare loped by her, giddy with the moon; she slung no stone at it. It danced in a dizzy spiral. At last she came to where the Clew was caught, like sheep's wool, in the branches of a leafless thorn. Nearer to the earth there hung a garland and a tattered coat, cast by. And at its roots, asleep in winter's lap, there lay a greenwhite girl. Brock bent and sained her, touching eyes, mouth, heart with ashes. Until the dawn she watched by the sleeping girl.

Thea slept and she was kindled: all within her side the star became a knot of stars, a congeries, a cloud, a soul. It waked within her turning sky. Her hair unwreathing was the red of dawn.

Kit woke to see his new-made lover squatting naked in the ashy coat, her shorn hair flickering about her skull. So white, her goblin face. So young. *What have I done?* he thought. *O dark, what is she doing?* On the hearth lay the long sheaf of her sundered hair, not fading like shorn grass, but fiery. Bright as bracken in the rain, as bright as copper molten in a forge, a riverspill of fire on the muddy stones. She was burning it, strand by strand. Crouching, she stirred the embers with the shears.

"No," he said. "Thea."

The child witch turned to him. White as frost, as frail. Blood and ashes on her thighs; the tuft of small fire that a breath would blaze. All naked but the coat of skin. She rose and held a ring to him, white-gemmed, as if she gave away her tears. She spoke in a child's imperious voice. "Go your ways. You have well served me."

Coldstruck, he stared at her. The eyes saw no one. Mad?

She crouched again, to riddle through the ashes with a rusty sieve.

He caught her. Sharp and soft, a thornbush deep in snow. Like branches she recoiled, and all her witchcraft fell away, like snow, like scattered snow. She crouched amid the shards. "Not done," she said. "I was not done."

Kit knelt beside.

"Thea. Love. Wake up." He stroked the hackles of her hair, so cold, so cold. "Thou'rt dreaming."

In his arms, she changed, thawed, cleft. His goblin rose.

And afterward, she slept at last. Lying watching her, the slight moon, turning always from his gaze, he saw a fireglint beyond her: a long strand of her hair, caught shining on a splint of wood. The last. He ran it through and through his hands. He saw the girl in the wintry garden, turning back to call him on; he saw the lantern of her hair. Again and yet again, he played the fugue of its undoing. Heartstrings. Not for burning. With his fiddler's hands he wound it round and round, and tucked it safe beside his heart.

"Gone," said Kit.

Whin said nothing; she could see it still, or the ghost of it: a bracelet of bright hair about the bone. Like stolen fire. He'd wear it to his grave. *Beyond,* she thought. *Would string his stars.* She shelled another mussel for the broth, another; tossed the leavings on the heap. Clack. Click. Clack. At last: "And wha'd take that and leave rings?"

"Crows. Her mother—I betrayed her. In the end."

Whin cracked and thumbed another mussel. Knife-edge and morsel. Weed. "Ah. Craws wi' beards."

Kit turned his face. Not yet, thought Whin. And yet he'd tell.

Wet underfoot. Burnt moorland or bare stone; bracken, bent or tussock: all were underlaid with squelch. "A world warped with water," Thea said, and wrung her coat skirts. Water curling from the cloud, like raw wool from a carder's combs. White water at a ford, frayed out, like torn lace at a roaring lad's throat. Fine icy water in the air. "At least," said Kit, "it's not raining." He did not say: we cannot lie in this. "There'll be a barn," he said. But now he could not tell if they were climbing, if they'd come this way before. Bright and brighter blazed the rust of bracken in its mockery of fire. The color of her hair, the color of desire, flickering on nothing, on the barren moor. Could water burn?

Her face turning back at him was like the moon from cloud; he leapt to it, it hooked him through the heart, the bone-caged heart.

"Look," said Thea, beckoning. "A walker on the hill." She called out, "Stay, thou shepherd!" And she ran. Kit ran after, calling, "Wait." And there was no one there: a waystone, squatting in the bracken like a hussif at her hearth. Thea touched the stone, her face between dismay and laughter. "See, she looms. 'Tis her weather."

"Hush," said Kit. "I doubt another day she brews." And fumbling beneath his pocket flap, he found a bit of bread, their last, and left it in a hollow of the stone. "There, awd lass. For a skein of sun."

And to Thea, "There'll be houses, wait on. We can barter and lie snug as hobs. Curds and barley straw."

"What way?" said Thea.

When they turned from her, the stone was fogbound, roofed and walled with cloud; they saw no way. "Away," said Kit. "'Tis all one." They heard the clank and rattle of a sheep on stones, a bird's disconsolate cry. And then a tap, a tapping, gathering like rain: a hammer on a forge.

"A fire," said Kit.

And stumbling, sliding down a track, they found a trod, stones driven edgewise for laden hooves; a wall, a fire in the mist. They tumbled from the old girl's lap, as if they'd been shaken from her apron, out of cloud and into rain.

And out of rain and by his fire sat a tinker at his work, his anvil driven in the ground, his lean bitch skulking by his side. A sere man, spare and shaggy, like a twist of tobacco. His dog, the mingled grey of ashes, smoke. He'd a tussy of coney skins hung to his tentflap; a jangle of saucepans and riddles and shears.

"How d'ye do?" said Kit, doffing his drowned hat. "Well, I hope, sir."

"What d'ye lack?" said the tinker.

"A knife," said Kit. "A cookpot. And a flint and steel. That blanket."

Clink! went the hammer on the rounding can. "A good cloak, is that. Awd bitch whelped on yon cloak. What d'ye give?"

Kit unfolded Thea's starry mantle.

The tinker eyed the velvet shrewdly; pinched a fold with black nails. "Molecatcher, ista? Owt else?"

"A glass."

An eyebrow. Then a shrug. "Gi's here." He ran his thumb round the frame of it, tilting his eye at them; considered; spat. "Done."

Kit knelt to bundle the stuff. A good knife indeed, well-hefted, sharp. "Yon road?"

"Goes longways." The velvet cloth had vanished in his pack. "And there's folk and not. Dogs."

"What honest work for strangers?"

A shrewd glance at Thea: draggled silk and drab russet, and a started vixen's brush of hair. "Whoring. Thieving."

Kit flushed. "Not while I've breath."

"Brave words to starve on. There's begging o' course. Any trade in yer hands?"

"I could fiddle—" Kit began. And turned his palms up ruefully.

"And I could ride pillion, if I'd a horse and a whip."

Thea slipped the rings from her fingers. "Would these not bring us silver? For a crowd and a bow?"

"Aye, and a dance on the gallantry. Wha's to say they's not been thieved?" The bright eyes slid sideways at Kit. "I can see yer not to drown."

"They're not—" said Kit, and stopped. They were.

But Thea held a ring up, flicked it shining at the heather's roots. "If thou'd not stoop for it, then let it branch and bear silver."

There it lay. He looked at her, and spurned it with his toe. A swift unwreathing, a flicker in the grass and gone. A silver snake. "I'd keep dark yon bits o' tawdry," he said. "There's folk'd cut throats for less. Thy stockings. Or a game or nowt." Thea nodded. "And if thou's a lad, thou doff thy hat, see. More to't than pissing upright." Then he bent to his camp and ferreted, set out a horn cup and a handful of coarse grey salt, a charred bird bound in herbs. "Hovel top o't trod."

"Thanks," said Kit. "My thanks. Hallows with ye."

"Sneck up," said the tinker.

Thea bowed.

As they started off up the trod in the closing rain, he called after. "If it's a fiddle thou's after, thou ask at Jack Daw."

"The fiddle. Ah." Kit gazed at the fire, pale in the wintry sun. No more than shaken air. "'Twas my father's. So my mother said. Of Cloud, as he was." He bit his lip. "I tell this badly."

"So yer no one's brat?" said Whin.

"Hers. Lightborn, we do say in Lune. We grow, like missel, in the air." His face was bright; then dark. "She died."

Whin drank, and passed the cup. A white bird tilted on the wind.

"Mine uncle—I was prenticed clerk. And fiddled at the wakes, and chafed."

"So yer went a-begging of a witch?"

"I was ta'en. By her servant."

"Ah."

"Coming from a dance," said Kit. "On Hare Law."

"And yer went with my lady's huntsman? Mad as a March hare, thou is."

"Drunk," said the fiddler, ruefully. "And thought I was in love."

Cold, toward moonrise, and the stars like rosin. Whirling. Not so drunk, he'd thought, but flown with fiddling. Ah, he'd never played so well as with Ned Hill, his serpent coiling in and out, and with Tib Lang's rowdy pipes and reed flute. They'd all the earth and heavens dancing to their tune, and half of Kempy Mag's great barn. Like hedgers laying thorn, they'd worked; and by some passing spell, their hey was quickset, green even as they wove, and flowering. A garland for a queen of May. That lass—ah, well he minded her, that straightbacked girl in green, triumphal, with a comet's tail of hair. In and out the mazes of the dance, he glimpsed her, arming with this shepherd and that scythesman, but fencing always with his tune, his air her make. As the music ended, she bowed to it: no partner but the air. His air. He lowered his bow and watched her as she coiled her tumbled braid, the bone pins in her soft stern mouth. The swift stabs. His heart. "Wed," said Tib drily. "Next month, to yon lame blacksmith. Get thee drunk."

And he had.

Five sets and six pints later, there was that other lass, at his elbow as he tuned. A brown girl, filching pears and russets; a green chit, all unripe. She'd a brow like a bird's egg, flecked and flawed, and mocking, shrewd grey eyes. "Why d'ye pull those faces, playing?" she'd said. "Toothache?" So he'd had to eat his hunch of Wake-bread, to show her he cared not, and had won a tiny leaden pair of shears, amid the crumbs. A mayfly toy. "They'll serve you for the wars," she'd said. "With a needle for spear." Afterward, he'd found a lady apple in his pocket, flawless, with a leaf.

He'd idled when they'd paid him, talking random, looking sidelong at the door until the girl in green went by. She'd turned at the threshhold, going, with a glance, half mockery and half challenge. Then he'd packed his fiddle up and walked on alone.

Not drunk. Unbounded, that was it: with darkness after fire, sky for rafters, silence for the stamp of boots, the clatter, and the clack of tongues. Light with love. As light as the Hanged Lad, Jack Orion, setting sidelong in his belt of sparks. Toward dawn, it was. As late as that? Well, he defied his master's clock. Kit bowed to the skyclad fiddler, and doffed his hat, calling out, "Measure for measure, lad. Will I outplay thee? "

He walked on over Hare Law, his head a muddle of tunes, bright lasses, bowls of lambswool. *Cross my river to Babylon.* His nose sunk in froth. A bright and a dark head glancing up at him, then ducking low to laugh. His russet coat, Tom's old one turned, scarce worn. New buttons to it. ("Here's a flaycrow in a field goes bare," the brown girl said.) Ginger and marchpane. A leaden shears. The green girl whirling at his bow's end. Out of sight. Ah, still he played her over in his head.

Had passed the branching in the road long since. By Crowcrag, then, the gainest way. That striding bass. *Mall's Maggot.* Syllabub and damson cheese. Dull wool bales in the morning—ah, his head. Sand. Goosequills. Figures on a page, untallied. In and out the hey, and couples for another dance. Nine eight and longways. Silver in his pocket, ninepence, that made seven and a bit, near enough for Askwith's *Atomie of Starres.* For ribands—No, a carven glass. With verses round. A comb. New strings, though, call it six and coppers. All the broken cakes. And at the end of *Nine Weaving,* how the green girl raised her candle to him, like a sword, and blew it out. An apple with a leaf. And again, the tumbled braid, the coiling hands. But they undid; the long skein fell for him alone, unbraiding like a fugue about her moonwhite body.

He was on the high ground now, a puzzle of white stones.

"Lightwood?"

Whirling round in a blaze of stars, Kit saw no one. His coat-skirts settled; he felt the soft bump of his pocket, crammed with cakes, against his thigh.

Stars still dancing.

He'd heard no rider; saw no horse. Yet on the road stood a horseman, spurred and booted: a stranger. Soberclad but richly, like a servant in a great house; yet outlandish. "Master Lightwood. Of Askrigg?"

"Sir?" When he stood the room spun, candlelight and dancers, whin and stars.

"I heard you fiddle at yon hobnailed rout."

"Ah." Had he seen that back amid the dancers? With the brown girl? With the light-foot grizzled farmwife? Or with the lass in green?

"Small recompense among such folk."

Broken cakes. Lead trinkets. "They've ears."

"And so my lady has. And jewels to hang in them. She sends to bid you play for her. A wedding."

"Have you no fiddlers in far Cloud?" This was not going well.

"None of note."

Kit stood. Some wind, toward the morning, twangled in his fiddle strings.

"Nor time to further send. 'Tis by this next moon. I will bring you." A glint of silver. "Come, a handfast. To wet the child's head."

"Thought you said it was a wedding?"

"All the same."

"Ah," said Kit wisely. "'Twas ever thus. Brought to bed, either way." The stars were fading, paling to the east; he could see the long rise of Hawker Fell. "Little enough dancing for the bride," he said. "And the bairn his own piper."

"Brave company," the stranger said. "Here's one will look for you." He held a bone hairpin in his dark-gloved hand. "By this token, you are bid."

Kit took it in his hand, bemused. "Did she give—?"

"Is't yes?"

"Aye, but—"

Then the horseman sealed his bidding with a cold kiss, full on his mouth. Tongue, teeth, and all. Kit knew no more.

The wind is braided in my lady's hair.

Margaret. As thou sleep'st, a storm is rising. Ah, thou hear'st it, even in thy dream of Cloud. But thou art fathomless, thy sleep is ocean. Cowrie'd by thy cheek, thy hand curls inward, closing on the dream that spills away like starry sand. A shutter claps. The hangings of thy bed conceive; the clawed rings inch and jangle. Nearer. On thy coverlid, thy book, left open, stirs. The leaves lift, turning backward in the tale. Unwintering. Again, the dead girl turns and speaks; she plays in greenwood, in the spring of hope.

How cam'st thou by thy book? Dost know? I tell thee, there are rare things in thy bower, which is all thy world. See, that orange by thy pillow. Pith and bittersweet and curving. And when broke, a puzzlebox of sweets. Thy bedgown, of an antick fashion, rich but sadly tarnished with the salt. That rod of shrewd whalebone, that also I felt. Thy comb. And not least, the drowsy wine they gave thee. Aye, the physick and the cup.

All tangled in her seine.

But seldom now.

I have seen my lady with her braid undone, all naked in her glass.

Here's a knot, says Morag with the comb.

Thou do. Undo.

Another.

Seven. And no more.

And with each knot, the wind rose, howling, and now and now the lightning slashed, it winced and slashed, and then the clouts of thunder jarred. By the sixth, it was beyond all noise: one lightning, and a judder in the bones. And when the waves broke—It was Annis falling. It was burying alive in shards of sky.

I have seen ships cracked like jackstraws.

I have found things, walking by the sea. A coffer, cracked and spilling cinnamon and mace. A virginals. A bacca pipe, unbroke. The Nine of Bones. And sailors: drowned and shattered, drowned and frozen, trodden into sand. And some that Morag finished. I have found an orange lying by a tarry hand.

Thea blew her nails and huddled, pinch-faced. Kit rubbed his legs and sighed. So much for begging. Stones for breakfast and a long draught of Cloud ale; stones in shoes; dog's music at the last three farms; and brats at the packbridge with a hail of clods. And now they'd tumbled down a scree. He'd go home if he knew where home was. They were nowhere, halfway down a fell, and sliding from its bony knees. The tops were hid in dour cloud. "Here's kites," said Thea. Higher up, they saw a shepherd, stooping with his burden of a creel of hay. His crouching, prying, flying dogs made bow-knots of a bedlam of sheep. Querulous and unrepentant Maudlins all, a-burst with bastard lambs, and fellowed with their doting Toms, the crazed and kempy wethers and the horn-mad tup. All trundled to fold. "On dirty toes," said Thea. "Same as us."

To the north, they saw the bruised sky blacken, and the bentgrass flinch and shiver in the rising wind. "Coming on bad," said Kit, standing. "We'll lay up." Even as he spoke, the snow came, like a fury of ghosts.

Nowhere.

"Hey!" cried Kit. Stifled. Gloved hands of snow laid hold of him, clapped eyes, mouth, ears. Seen out by February's footmen, to a ditch and crows.

"Hush," said unseen Thea. They could hear the sheep rattle and the shepherd call.

"Way here! Way here, Maddy. Come by, Gyp."

Kit caught hold of Thea's wrist, and scrabbled up the hillside toward the voice. Not far, they'd not get far in this. "How far—?" bawled Kit.

A lean ghost, swathed in sacking. "Get by, thou bloody fool! Down dale."

"Where——?"

"Dog'll tek thee." Something like a hollybush leapt the wall, already chiding at their heels. The shepherd called after, "Thou ask at Imp Jinny."

Down along an outcrop, rising into drystone wall; crook left, and down a stony track between two walls, out of wind; past the shepherd's pony, like a dejected chimney brush, beside his sledge of hay. The black bitch saw them through the gate.

Trees, low and windbent, lapped and laden with the ghosts of leaves; a lantern at the door, that turned their branching to bright webs.

"Hallows," called Kit, and beat muffled hands against the door.

"Will Shanklin?" called a woman's voice. "Owt wrong?" The door opened. A small-faced strapping woman, knitting furiously. Sharp and brown as a beechnut, with a beech's frazzled foliage, an old tree's knotted hands. Blue as speedwell, her eyes. She looked them up and down. "If it's guising, yer a bit few. And late."

"Have you a barn?" said Kit.

"T's a fire," said Imp Jinny. "Come in and keep wind out. I can see lass is dowly."

They stamped and dripped and stared. A low room, bronzy with peat smoke, heaped with apples. Sweet and poignant with their scent. And not low after all, but racked and raftered, hung with anything to hand. Bunches of potherbs, besoms and birdsnares, shears and riddles and a swift of yarn. Swags of old washing—smocks and aprons—kippered in the air, as stiff as stockfish. Lanterns and pruning-hooks, ladles and rushlights. Strings of eggshells. Legs of mutton. Riddlecakes hung out to dry. A ball of thorn twigs, trailing ribands and old holly. Jinny ducked beneath. "Mind urchin," she called. A tiggy drank snuffling at a dish of milk. "Been at wort and gets to singing. Now then, thou rantipole. Mend tongue. Or I'll peg thee out i't apple trees, as a souling for t' birds." She nipped down a sallowed petticoat from under the thack, took a jacket from a kist, and bundled them at Thea. "Get thee doffed." She measured Kit with a glance. "Crouch up to't fire. Y'd look a right mawkin in my petticoats."

"Thanks," said Kit.

"Not at all. Thowt it were foxes at my ewes in lamb. Dropped a stitch, I doubt. Tea. Y've tea i' Lune?" Jinny swung the kettle over the fire; she scrabbled out leaves from a bright tin, painted gaudily with wrens and garlands. "Stockings and all, that's right. Peg 'em up. Lad can tek blanket. Now then, there's cock broth. And a tansy after."

Deep bowls of it, fork-thick with leeks and barley, fowl and carrots; Jinny broke them shards of oatcake for to sop the rich broth.

They ate. The snow pummeled at the windows; their clothes dripped and reeked. Imp Jinny walked to and fro, knitting and muttering and squinting at her heel, in a fury of pins: as thrawn as if her yarn were nettles and all her kindred swans. Born half a sleeve behind and not caught up. You'd think she knit them at the stake. "Purl and plain. Meks three. And—craws eat it!" She knit badly, Kit saw; the yarn snagged on her roughened hands, the stocking bunched and spiralled.

"Mistress Imp?"

Jinny turned, twanging with laughter. "And thy name's Kit Catgut. Imp's what I do. Graff apples to crabs. Hast etten Nonesuch? That were mine. And Sheepsnose, out o' Seek-No-Further. And I's no Mistress, neither. Langthorn Joan's Jinny. Jane Owlet. Awd keeping pear's what I is. Warden. I'd eat dryly." The old hands crooked and looped and darted. "So yer out Lune? How came yer by Cloud?"

Kit, muffled in her patchwork quilt and downheeled slippers, tried for manly. "Seeking work."

"Can you do owt?"

"Undo," said Thea.

"What I can," said Kit.

Jinny pursed her lips. "Work. Well, there's threshing to Swang Farm. A rough gang for lasses; but there's straw and stirabout, and happen a few coppers. Got a knife?" She hefted it and tried the edge. "Aye, that's good." She gave it back to him. "Ye could try yer hand at binding besoms. Up moor." She was setting the heel now, storklegged with aggravation. "Come March, ye could clap eggs for Ashes. Do ye not i' Lune? No? Well, I'll set yer i't road on it. Craws!" Her ball bounded away; Kit caught it. "Thou keep petticoat."

"Ashes?" said Kit.

"Eh well, there's always Ashes. Or there's never spring. Gangs out wi' guisers." The Horn was rounded of her stocking; she sighed. "And byways, there's a barn up Owlriggs, void and dry. Ye could lig there for a piece. While lambing, anyroad."

"Many thanks," said Kit. "How—?"

"Shake snow from me apple trees, I doubt they'll crack. Lilt me yer fiddle tunes. I like a tune. Can't make, but I graff words til 'em."

"Ah. D'ye know this?" Softly, Kit sang through *Nine Weaving*; then clapped into *Jenny Pluck Pears* and *The Magpie's Bagpipe*. No great voice, but a true.

At his knee, by the fire, Thea crouched and set the cradle rocking to the rhythm of the dance. Full of skeins, it was.

"Soft," said Jinny sharply. "Do ye so i' Lune?"

"Do what?" said Thea. "Here's an ark for the urchin."

An odd blue glance; the needles stopped. "Rock empty cradles."

"No," said Kit, dismayed. "Moon turn from it."

Thea said, "I know not what it is. For bread or what?"

"I see," said Jinny. "Out Lune of Lune." She stilled the cradle with her hand. There was a wooden rattle laid in it, a tumbling, turning wren; a doll like a darning egg, a poppyhead unfaced with years; an acorn whirlywhorl. Undone, it spilled a marble in her palm. "That were Het's."

"Your lass?" said Kit softly.

"Imped out," said Jinny. "She were left by ragwell. Anyone's." She whorled the marble; smiled. "I'd've never such a lass. Wick as thistledown."

"Ah," said Thea. "She would braid of her mother then, the moon. I see thine orchard bears the Misselbough."

Jinny turned to Thea, puzzling. Something rueful; something awed. "So thou'rt Ashes still. Poor lass." Almost, she touched the girl's thin cheek; but went to feel her clothes instead, turned smock and stockings by the hearth. "When I were Ashes——"

"Not a lad?" said Whin.

"What?"

"Her bairn that died."

"Drowned," said Kit. "A lass. She said."

"I see. Go on."

Jinny peeled a bowl of russets, broadlapped by the dozing fire. They watched the long curls falling from the bright knife, the brown hands; they smelled the sharp juice spring. "When I were Ashes—forty year ago, and more—I kept back what I got. Oh, aye, come Kindle Night, they'd rived at me and mocked me, for I'd not had maid nor man. Unploughed. Waste o' darkness, they'd said. Said nowt would spring of it. But what I'd hid weren't brat, nor siller, nor a gallop on another's hobby. Sitha, when I'd put on Ashes coat, I'd turned and wondered at glory o't world. All turning and endless. Stars and seed. They caught me up i't dance, threadneedle. See, it's endless, yet there's first and last. Same as like a spindle falling, thread and whorl. Same as peel." And one long rose-moled spiralling fell flawless from the knife. "And I see'd how things go on by dying. How they're born o' fallow. That I kept."

They crossed a watersplash at dawn. The sky had put away its stars, undone the clasp of winter from its throat. It stood, white and shivering, all bare before the sun. No rose: a sudden glittering of frost, a lash of shadows, long and sharp against the fell; and there, where the water sprang, the reddening scratches of the alders. "Withies," said Kit. "I'll cut, an thou bind them."

Clumsy with cold, they set to work with knife and twine. The day clouded up. The water brawled. A field away, a boy went huddling in his outworn jacket, toward the lambs. Kit called to him, "Where's this?" but he ran away. The sheep ran too, all which ways down the moor, their rumpling fleeces heavy with the frost. They slowed from a trotting to a trundling, with their stilted lambs beside them, slowed and stilled and cropped. Kit saw the boy again, up lawside in a scud of stones, his hair as white as hawkweed. He peered from behind a sheepfold. Kit swept him a bow, and he ducked.

"Do you steal children?" Thea said.

"Some run away with me," said Kit.

They sat among the bare wood by the waterside, and ate what they had begged. It was scant enough, cold scrag-end and a lump of pease. A sup of bratted milk. There was twopence in his pocket and his trade in Lune, his fiddle for a ship and wracked, a witch's stolen daughter by his side. My lady's malison on both. He looked at Thea, silvered by the cold fine mist. He'd waked sometimes to see her watching, silent as the moon. He knew her changing face, her dark and bright; he saw and he desired her as he would the reachless moon. Her soul was elsewhere, even as he lay with her, amid the bright leaves burning.

Jumping up, Kit looked about the lashy wood. "It's almost spring," he said. "Here's blackthorn out." It flowered from its bare sticks, white as souls. He gathered twigs of it, the bonniest of all. It twisted, green and sinewy; he'd use no knife. He made a garland of it for her leaf-bright head: a crown too sharp to wear.

Cross and cross between the ash pegs driven in her crucks, old great-armed Imp Jinny told out her threads. Nine skeins unwinding, drawn as one, and dancing in their creels; then down and down, from hand to peg and to and fro, until their measured ending. Eight of wool; the ninth of moonlight, turning on its reel of dark. She was making a warp.

The fire was of thorn. It caught the sway and draw and crooking of her arms, and glinted in the scissors at her waist; it cast a creel of her in shadows, cross and cross the room. Our cage is shadows and ourselves.

As Jinny told her warp, she sang, no louder than the rasp of wool, the crackling of the little flame.

"*O the broom blooms bonny, the broom blooms fair . . .*"

Cross and cross, nine threads. That's one.

"*I have lost a sheath and knife that I'll never see again . . .*"

And loop and nine. That's two.

"*And we'll never go down to the broom no more.*"

Kit remembered the kitchen in her mother's hall, stoneflagged and cavernous; the table, scoured saltwhite as a strand to windward, heaped with wrack of bloody game. Ah, piteous, their eyes, and taunting now, with acorns rattling in his gut. Blackcock and moorhen, ruffled and agape. Wet heather on a red hind's flank. The lean and louring hounds rose hackling at him, girning with their grizzled lips. They suffered him to pass; but watched him, crouching on their bones or pacing, silent but for rattling chains. Scoured as it was, the kitchen stank of them, of hair and blood and ashes, dust of pepper and old damp. On the great gaunt dresser, fishwhite pewter dully stared. The fire whirred and reeked. And Morag squatted with a hare to gut, limp and lolling in her bloody apron. *Madam? I am sent to bid you to my lady. In her closet, she did say.* The log fell in; the shadows jumped. And perhaps Morag twitched at her high shoulder, like a preening crow; or it was shadows, or his smoke-stung eyes. She rose to meet him, knife folded in her apron, capped and barbed. *I come.* Formal and contemptuous, as always. Sheathed. Ah, but where were all the servants in so great a hall? Who scoured and who swept? And he bethought him, late and suddenly: roe deer? On that stony island? What had come of his wits, not to marvel? Yet venison they had at table. No fish but eel pie, not a herring. Nothing salt. Nor sodden, come to that. He saw again the haunch of meat, the charred and shining spit withdrawn, the rusty cauldron tilted by the hearth. The fur and flesh.

"Love? Who provisioned in thine hall?"

"Morag."

"Strange fish she caught."

"Gulls," said Thea. "Thou and I."

"But venison?"

"Ah. She hunts."

The witch rose twirling, turning in the air to raven. Or to ravenwise—a something quilled and barbelled, clawfoot, but a woman to the fork. Thrice round the broch she flew, in widening gyres, over scar and thornwood, sea and skerry, tethered by my lady's will. At farthest of her swing was landfall, rust and desolate. The bracken stirred. She stooped.

Margaret. Do you sleep now?

I will tell this in the moonlight sliding.

In my closet, Morag clasped the necklace round my throat. Cold souls, all witches, dead long since; cold hands, that late had plucked and foraged in the hare's blue meagre flesh. Untwisting it about my breast, she pinched me with her bloody nails. *Is't ripe?* And then the long robe on my shoulders—ah, but it was soft as snow, as sleeping in a drift of death. My mother keeps it still. 'Twas woven with the stars at Annis' wake: night sky and moonless, shading through the blue, bluegreen of twilight, seen as through the branches of the thorn. And naked else.

No sun, but at my fork.

The old crow held the glass. *My lady waits.*

I come.

And in her high unarrased room, from glass to moondark glass, my lady turned and paced. Her iron casket on the table was unlatched. At her throat, she wore the stone it held: no soul, but Annis' self, the true and only shard of night. The seed of Law.

I stood, as I was taught.

She turned and gazed at me. Bare as April.

I had not yet bled.

My lady, said I, to the stone. I knew its touch, ah, cold against the skin, and colder deeper still. Within. I knew her famished eyes.

Her time comes, said my lady to her woman. *By this moon. The souls?*

Two are kept, said Morag. *I have seeled them for the hunt. A mort in milk, a maid in blood.*

And the third?

Is come. Seed full. A pretty piece, the huntsman says.

Shall have his fee.

My mother touched my chin. *Come, Madam.* So she loosed the knot, undid the bright coil of my hair; she bid me to her table.

Whin slept. Lying silent by her, Kit woke long and heard the clash of the sea. He saw its pale thrums shine and ravel. Moonset. Darkness then, the wavebeat of his heart. He counted. Nine for a secret. There was something he'd not told.

That first night in the mist there was a third in bed with them. Half waking in the dark, he'd pulled her down on him, had murmured, fledged, had entered—ah, not Thea's air and fire, but the lap of earth. His grave. The spade bit deep. He saw the wriggling in the new-turned earth; breathed in the scent of earth and ashes, and of heather wet with rain. Still deeper. There, he touched a stirring, soft as moleskin, soft and dusk, and there, the quick and glistening neb. And at the very deep, a something, thrawn and wet: the root of dark, its flowering.

The cards. I had forgot them, slid between rough stone and worm-gnawn panelling, behind the kist. You puzzle at them, at this book of scattered leaves. Know thou, they are Cloudish magic. Not my lady's art, but tawdry: a sort of cantrips that their wiling beggars use. Hedge sortilege. I had them of a witch—a windwife or a sailor's whore, I know not. Cast up. Still living, when I'd hauled her on the sand, a-twitch and broken, like a windwracked gull. She'd signed: *Take. Keep.* A box, a book of spells? Skin bag and oiled silk. I slipped it warily within my skirts: forbidden hoard. And then came Morag with her stone.

I hid them. From her avid and contemptuous, her pebble eyes, her prying hands: myself I could not hide. And all that winter of my threshold year, I looked not thrice at them. My lady basilisk had work. In the waning of the ashen moon, she called me down, in cold stiff cloth of silver and an iron busk, to look upon the last of three set dishes for my maiden feast. A banket of souls. There were two laid up in store, like picked meats from the cracking of a gilded nutshell bark: a child scarce old enough to call a virgin, the betrothed of an outland king; her nurse. Like cage birds fattening, like haggards, leashed and belled. I'd fed them with my hand. Had toyed: which I repent. A poor mad glowering girl; a woman, silent, spilling milk. I'd tasted of their souls, their essences: green quince and bletted medlar, quiddany and musk. And now the third, but lately come: a hare, caught kicking, from the huntsman's bag. A handful of brambles, green and flowering and all. Leaf and prick. I saw a beardless boy, astonished, ill at ease in country boots. He bowed to me. I took him up.

Thou turn'st the Hanged Lad on the gallantry; the Hare reversed.

I see.

Is't riddles, then? A sort of stars?

Go on. But soft now, I am at thy shoulder.

Ah, now thou hast them spread, in knots and gatherings and changeful congeries, across the nighted boards. Just so. They bear the names of earthly tales turned starry, as the Tower, and the Crowd of Bone, and all the figures of the moon and sky. What Imp Jinny called the wood above. And thou art lost in it. Thou hast no clew to wind thee through the mazes of that dance, unfellied and unfretted night. No windrose nor no wheeling Ship. O Margaret, I have read their painted book, an abstract of the airy world. But thou, thou know'st no tale of them, amazed as if thou mansionless looked up at heaven, saw its stars unstrung and scattering like a box of beads.

I will tell this in the cards.

Here's a black wench with a cap and anvil; see, she hammers at a fiery heart. That card doth signify that errant star which some call Mercury. But they do call her Brock. She's a cutpurse of great bellies, and does lighten them; a picklock of maidenheads; a thief of souls. On Whinnymoor she lurks, and bids the silent traveller stand; takes nothing of him naked, but a coin, a clip. Those waifs that shiver, dance and shiver on the moss, in nothing but their own brief souls, she laps in her rough jacket, earth and bone; she slaps them squalling into breath. She is death's midwife and her go-between, the third in marriage beds. Her clip is kindling. Twice did she sain me, doing and undoing: at the door where thou didst enter, love, and at the jagg'd rift of my going hence.

Here's Burnt Eldins. Burd Alone. She tosses up her golden ball outwith a hedge of bones. Its leaves are hands of children flayed, imploring. She is youngest of the Nine, those stars whose rising into dawn doth mark the stone of winter's death. I had the tale of Imp Jinny, how she winds the clew and finds her sisters locked up in Annis' kist. How she sets them free. That card I never drew.

Nor this: Nine Weaving. Eight are painted, bending to their wintry task. Ah, they blaze in their imprisoning. From their tower spills their endless web, the green world and that other, woven with a mingled skein.

And here's the Rattlebag, turned tail. It shows a lad, whiteheaded as a weed; he claps the crows that flacker from his field of corn, all rooted in a sleeping man, a sheaf whose binding is a belt of stars.

And turn, and he's the Hanged Lad, brave in winter, mid a winnowing of stars.

The Crowd of Bone. That fiddle that the old year plays of Ashes, of her bones. 'Tis strung with shorn red hair. Ah, it burns thy fingers, thou dost let it fall.

And Ashes. Not her smutched and tangled guise, as black as holly-blotch, that waif in tattercoats that walks behind a wren's cold corse: that is not Ashes but her mute. This Ashes dances lightfoot, and at every step a green blade springs. Her hair's like fires that the May lads leap, a-whirl in wind. Far far behind her is an O, a crow's eye or a cracked bright glass. Her end. But for now, she's walked away from Annis' glass, her eye of winter, out of that tale into this.

It was windy, with a clouted sky. The farm stood foursquare to the heavens, stonebuilt, with a line of trees to northward bending all one way. They danced. There were catkins on the hazels, taws of light, like whips to set the sun a-spin. Kit sneezed. There was pollen dusted in his hair and on his jacket, nebulas of bloom; he sleeved his face with Pleiades. "No geese," he said. "There's a comfort."

"I'll go this time," said Thea, peering through the hedge with him. They saw a drying yard, windriffled, up against the plainfaced farmhouse. There were two girls playing in the yard. They'd tied a rope to an iron ring in the housewall. One turned, the other skipped and sang. "My mother went to feed her crows, turn round and call them in . . ." The rope made rainbows in the plashy air; it slapped, slapped, slapped the stones. An unbreeched boy ran shouting with a whirligig. It flackered like a rising bird; it caught the sudden light. He tumbled in the mud. A woman in a cap and clanging pattens came out, a creaking wicker basket at her hip.

Kit and Thea slipped through the hedge. "Hallows with ye," he said, and bowed. His back was urchined out with brooms.

The woman nipped the small clothes up. She was rosy with the wind, and round-armed, with wisps of grey-brown hair straggling from her cap. "Here's a rade o' scoundrels," she said to the peg box. "A-ligging and a-laiking, while us poor folk go to work. Well, I's counted shirts."

". . . one for t' rider and one for t' horse and one for t' boatman, for to row me across . . ."

The boy was crouching by a puddle, frothing his toy in it.

Fiercely, the woman pegged the washing out: smock, petticoat, shirt, breeches, smock. All dancing in the wind. Kit tweaked the breeches by the strings. "Here's thy chance," he said to them. "Do as I would."

"Huh," said the woman, but her shoulders quirked. "Would yer go to be hanged?"

"Not I. And yet die bravely in a dance," he said.

Another woman looked out through the door. "Eh, Bet, what's to do?"

"A tain and his tally come a-begging. Lunish folk. Got besoms."

"Has they pins? We's short." She came out on the doorstep, flapping her apron. She was small and crumpled, with a smear of soap on her brow. Looking at the travellers, up and down, she said, "If it's guising, yer a bit few."

"A sword and a bush," said Kit.

"And late."

"The ways are very muddy," said Kit.

"And our shoes are very thin," said Thea.

"When's Lightfast i' Lune, then? Come May?" The woman with the basket looked at Thea. "Where's crown? Is t' wren in yer pocket, then?"

"Under her apron," said the woman at the door.

"Whisht," said the other. "Ista lad then? Or Ashes?"

"Turns," said Thea. "Whichever comes in next. Burnt Eldins."

"Aye well, if it's Eldins, yer first foot," said the woman at the door, relenting. "Not see'd Arrish lads as yet." Quirking at Kit: "What's he?"

Kit turned and shrank and darkened. The witch looked out through him, and cocked her shrewd black eye. Muck, said her mincing, and grubs, said her peck. Watching, Thea felt a thrill of uneasy laughter. He had Morag to the very nails. "The blood I brew, the bones I crack, I bear the childer on my back." The little girls watched, the rope slack, their faces uncertain. He clawed his hands at them and waggled.

The brown girl's thumb went in her mouth; she clung to her sister's apron. But the little dark one said, "Yer not a witch."

"Who said?" He swung the little dark thing in the air, and clapped her in the empty basket, shrieking delight.

Thea rounded on him, ranting in high style. It was her turn for Burnt Eldins; she had the coat. "Wha comes on stones?"

"Awd Crowdybones."

"What's that ye've got?"

"I's getting eldins for to boil me pot." Lantern and thornbush, like Mall-i'-th'-Moon.

"Wha's give thee leave to cut my wood?"

"Me glass and me riddle, they told me I could."

"All but nine, they may not go:

> The alder, the elder, the ash and the sloe,
> The witchtree, the whitethorn, the hazel and oak:
> Break one of their branches, and down with a stroke."

"That's eight."

Thump, went the basket. Thump. And the girl peeked out, with her hair all tumbled, rough as juniper, her eyes as blue.

Thea whirled on her heel. "Burnt Eldins is youngest of all of the nine, I see by her stockins you've hung on the line."

"I's not been etten yet," said the girl. "It's all right, Tilda. Thou can look."

Kit crouched malefically. "Blood and bones, I'll crack, I'll crack, and fell and hair will patch me back. Eyes to me ravens, and breath to me bread, and fat for a candle to light me to bed."

Thea drew her sword of air.

"Take a broom," said Kit softly. "Plays better."

"Ah. Right then." Thea cleared her throat and struck a penny-plain bold stance. "Wha brings thee down but Hallycrown?" Turn and turn, they rimed.

"My tower's where thou'lt never find."

"They's left me a thread, and I walk and I wind." Round in merrills in the mud, she trod.

"I's ower t'riddles and back o' Cawd Law."

"They's spinned me a clew and I's under thy wall." Thea ducked the clothesline.

"I's snecked t'door, thou shan't come in." All a-twitter.

"Brock turns locks and lifts thy pin."

"What's within but mirk and mist?"

"But I's a sun frae Mally's kist." She upraised a withered apple-john.

"Here comes my ravens to peck out thine eyes."

"And here comes my chopper, for to make 'em mince pies."

Once, twice, thrice they clashed and down fell Morag in the mud. Kit clutched his heart, turned tipple, kicked his heels and croaked. Tilda giggled uncertainly. Thea snatched the child from the basket, and Kit spun it round with his foot. Down went the child in it. Thea spoke.

> Now it's a ship and we all sail away,
> So give us your hands for to finish our play.
> The sail's o' th' siller, the mast's o' th' tree,
> The moon's for a keel and the morrow's the sea.

Kit whispered to the child, "Hang on." He jumped up beside Thea and they took the handles of the creel. They hoisted it between them and they swung it, one two three, and whirled it round.

> Up let her rise, and t' sisters take hands,
> So gi' us some siller to bring them to land.

A sadcake, an apple, some eggs and old ale,
To help us poor guisers and weave us a sail.

"Now Tilda's turn," said the child when she'd got her breath.

"Thou gut yon fish," said Whin. "It's that and slawk."

Kit turned from the bitter bright morning. Salt in candle flame: it sparkled. "Ah?" Carefully, from rock to driftwood, rock to rock, he hobbled back to the fire, took the knife in stiff hands. "What's this, a dolphin?"

"Herring," said Whin. "Filched it. They'll blame cat." She prodded at the pot of seaweed, doubtful. "So, where got yer that guising? Not i' Lune."

"Imp Jinny. Said it might get an egg or two."

"Thin wind for thieving, March. All green and mockery." Whin clapped the lid to. "Wants a whet to it, does slawk. Verjuice or owt." She swiped the ladle with her finger, licked it. "So yer kept them rings."

"And who'd buy them?" Kit's hands were glittering with blood and scales. "Who'd make change? As good sell orchards in the moon."

"Spatchcocked, I think," said Whin. She took the fish. "Salt enough."

"There were two left. For the—for the child, she said. Her portion. Those you took." He rubbed his fingers dry in sand. "One spent, one tossed away in scorn. Three ta'en by—ruffians. And one she gave away."

"Did she, then?"

"To a boy. A whitehaired starveling boy. A scarecrow."

"Oh," said Whin, so poignantly that Kit knelt up by her. "What is't then? At thy heart?"

They came by a ploughed field, pricked with the new green corn. A crow lad with his clapper cried, he clacked his sticks and cried, "Ban craws!" The cold wind shook his rags. The crows took up into the air. It was a brash day, bare and windy, with a sky of curds and whey. Thea stood in the furrows, watching; Kit stood by her. A stone's throw away, the birds swirled and settled, like a fall of ashes, calling out. Their voices glowed and faded like the sparks from the anvils of war.

Kit said, "He cries them barley."

"They defy him," said Thea. She was gazing at the sky. The clouds went swiftly. "Crows, that's all."

Cracked pepper, and a salt of smaller birds.

Hoarsely, hauntingly, the boy took up his chant.

Shoo all o't craws away,
Shoo all o't craws:

> Out thrae John Barley's ground
> Into Tom Tally's ground;
> Out o' Tom Tally's ground
> Intil Awd Mally's ground;
> Out frae Awd Mally's ground
> Into Black Annie's ground . . .

Kit took up a stone and flung it in the birds' midst. They shrugged derisively; they hopped a little sidelong, pecked. He ran at them, flackering his coat and crying, "Craws! Ban craws!" He clodded them with earth. Huffed as dowagers, they ruffled in their black; they snapped their well-I-never beaks. "Sod off!" yelled Kit. They rose and scattered in the wide grey sky; went silver and were gone.

Turning back, triumphant, he saw Thea, pinched and shivering among the furrows. He clouded over. They'd had nothing all that day; she could eat nothing when they had, but picked and spewed. Coarse provender, he thought: no stomach for't. And it was cold and muddy in the lanes, her shoes were worn—ah, not her slippers, cast away in ruin. These were new old shoes, clodhopping country boots, ill-sorted with her rags of Lunish finery. And dearly they had cost her purse: her silver comb. Now he saw how odd her clothing looked, how tattery. Half tinsel and half drab. He'd thought of it as hers. Herself. How strange that started brush of hair, that boys cried *Vixen!* at. Cried whore.

Seeing him forlorn, she clapped and called to him, "Oh, bravely done."

He grinned and wiped a sword of air and sheathed it. "My turn for the boy," he said. The coat flapped windily.

"I'll be Ashes, then; I'm tired of Eldins."

Kit came and held her. "Ah," he said. "Did I tell thee? I dreamed it hailed moon-seed. 'Twas full and it split."

"What sprang of it? Witches?"

"Children," he said. "All naked as the moon, and shining, as they were made of sky. They danced."

Thea looked toward the barley-white boy, still crying. Further on, the ashes fell. "What then?"

"A woman caught them in her apron."

"And then?"

"I woke," said Kit. "And seeing thee, forgot." There was straw still in her hair: a garland. They were wed each day. Remembering, he plucked it out and gave it, lightly, to the wind. Then turning with her gaze, he saw the boy. "Poor lad, it's weary work, alone wi' crows."

Thea said, "Shall we play, and let him play?"

"I'll not hang ranting from a pole, even to please thee." He grimaced fiercely, knotting up his brows. "But I'll play thee a tyrant rarely, or a crone or what thou wilt."

"'Tis a strange play: we clap and they go."

"But an ancient play," said Kit. "The first true gallant of the part was Tom o' Cloud, who claps the shadows from the sky." He'd taught her all of that: the names which country folk did give—Awd Flaycraw, Jack Orion—to the sprawl of stars she'd called the Gallows Tree. A bookish name. "Wilt play it naked, then?" said Thea.

"With a sword," said Kit. He sang the old tune from the masque, the woodwo's brag:

> Orion wears a coat of sparks
> And starry galligaskins
> But men may see what man I be
> Without my first dismasking . . .

They were walking toward the crow lad's coign. The earth by the headland was scratched with mazes, glittering with shards of hoarded glass. The crow lad blew his hands and stared. His coat was rags of sacking and his shoes were mud. His hempwhite head was bare, in a ravel of rope-ends.

"Hey, lad, would thy master hear a play?"

"Has dogs. And sets 'em on."

And a stick, thought Kit. And lays it on. He saw the wary face and wincing shoulders. The bruises. The boy stared back unblinking. He had eyes as green as hail. Kit found the last of what they'd begged, a sadcake and a scrape of fat. "Here's for thy piece," he said. The crow lad snatched it fiercely and he bit, he crammed. Kit waited. "What's thy name?"

"Called Ashlin."

"And thy kin? Who keeps thee?"

"No one," said the boy. "I's lightborn."

"So am I," said Kit. "We two are Mally's bairns." He saw a bright child made of azure falling, rolling naked in the dust. They come to dust. The woman in his dream turned elsewhere, as her lap was full. And still the lightborn fell: so many for the world to waste. Not all of them, he thought to say. Not ours to come.

But Thea said, "And I am darkborn."

"See'd," the crow lad said.

"But he and I go longways, out of Law." She looked about. "Her eyes?"

"Stoneblind. Off elsewhere, anyway."

"But if they follow—"

"I's a sling o' stones. What I do."

Thea looked long at him. "Wouldst do it?"

"Owt I can."

Kit caught his breath, leapt in with, "Who's thy master, lad? I'd have a word with him. Wouldst come with us? Art fast?" He turned.to Thea, bright with indignation, mischief, pleading. "He could play the boy."

"Got work. Hers," the crow lad said, and becked at Thea. He glanced at Kit's coat. "I see yer ta'en already. Go yer ways."

Thea said to the boy. "Is it fast, then?"

"Clap and done." He spat his hand; they shook.

Kit stood bewildered, like the child in the basket, whirled round in their play. Thea touched his arm. "Soft, love, 'tis a game we play." To the boy, she said, "What then?"

"Seek hallows."

"What way?"

"Gang wi' t' sun."

"How far?"

"While it's hallows."

Thea stretched her hand out, with its tawny ring. A turn and flick, and it was bare: she held a scrawny orange. "For thy noon."

The crow lad caught it and he tossed it in the air. He laughed, looking up at it, his bright hair scattering day. "What's ta'en is anyone's." Kit saw it fall.

"I'd an Ashes bairn," said Whin. Her turn, gazing through the fire, chin on close-hugged knee. "And left him. Naked as he came, for owt as found him. Craws or kin." And in a raw voice, small and wretchedly, she cried, "They would've cut his throat." Still raw. As if a horny hand, a sailor's or a drystone waller's, cracked and bled. "Me mam and her gran would. For t' harvest. Starving earth, I is."

Kit said softly, "Was he yours, the crow lad? D'ye think?"

"I knaw not. Like enough, I doubt." Whin rocked the small ring on her fingertip. "I cannot tell my blood."

"Ah," said Kit. The fire shifted, sighed.

"Thowt it were guising, being Ashes. When I ta'en her coat. And I laughed that I were chosen out of all, that I could take owt I willed. Whatever lad. So long as I did play her part, walk earth until she waked. So long as I kept nowt."

Kit looked for the child in her, as black as he was white. Broad cheekbones and a mournful lip, her long Ægyptian eyes. "And you would still be Ashes. If you'd kept the boy. Still hunted." Coverless as hares.

"What I is, is Ashes. Same as earth is earth. Her coat that she put on. And when I's doffed, I's done with, breath and bone. No giving back." Whin leaned from shadow into shying light. "I could ha' kept him, see."

The rain fell, water into water. After a time, Whin stirred the embers. "Blood or no. For his sake, for thy kindness, thanks."

"All mine, a hundredfold," said Kit. "He saved us. For a time."

Margaret, see. Bright Hesperus, the moon's epitome, hangs at thy window. Perseis her lamp. When I was Thea, I did love that star, her winding journey through the maze, the quickset stars. 'Tis lucent, there: a brilliant toy, a plaything from a mage's baby house. Burnt Eldin's bauble. Canst thou catch? Let my lady set her hedge as thick as gramarye, as high as ravens cry, the light will in at it.

In April of that wandering year, I spied a comet. In the Crowd of Bone it hung, toward Ninerise, in a thaw of fleeting snow. I waked and saw it, like a pearl dissolving in black wine; I drank that cup, light full of thee. And thou didst leap to it.

I knew then that I went with child.

Thea turned at the waystone, calling. What she said was blown away. And still she turned on the hillside, at the twelve winds' nave; the fellies of the wheel were hills. "What's that?" said Kit, coming breathless behind.

"Those folk. Here's all their petticoats away."

It rained, a hill beyond them and a hill behind: a cold fine windy rain. From the ragwell, where they stood in light, they saw the stormdark clouds onsailing. They were tall and tattery, their skirts of ragged silver draggling heedless through the hills. Then the thorn tree shivered in its rags; the spring winced light, it puckered with a sudden doubt. The sky darkened and a hail came on: small hail, but sharp and green. Kit cowered from it. Thea ran to it and whirled about, catching hailstones in her hands. They filled them, greener as they massed, bluegreen.

"Come back," called Kit. "Hey, Thea?" And he came a few steps, blindly, in the shattering of the hail. How it danced and it daunted, how it hissed and rattled on the ground. It beat him blind, it stung. "Hey!"

"Catching souls," she called.

As sudden, it was past. The hill was white: a spring made glass, the sky made soul and shattered. Slateblue to the eastward, slashed with rain, the heels of storm rolled onward. All above, the lift was blue. He shook himself. Thea's head was haily crowned; it glittered when she turned. Her neck was bare. She flung her hoard of stones away. They scattered on the earth like seed. Cold seed, he thought. No crows would take. A cloud away, a rainbow sprang. It spanned the storm. She clapped her wizened hands and laughed. "Do you turn and I'll dance to it."

Somewhere up Owlerdale they sheltered from a passing rain with tinkers in a hedge. Two women, old and young, with baskets of fairings: cowslip tossy-balls and bunches of bright ribands; toys and tawdry. Kit spread them his coat. The blackthorn was tarnishing, the white in bud. The younger of their chance-met company was breaking buds of it, to whet her bacon; the elder thumbed her cards and smoked. Rain and blackthorn fell.

"That comet," said Kit to Thea. "Ah, but it grows bright and bonny. Like a dandelion gone to seed and drifting."

"Whose clock?" said Thea. "And whose breath?"

Still wandering. It preyed on him, that wan and random look.

"Craws!" said the younger, counting wares. "Dropped whirlywhorl i't road."

The elder pointed with her pipestem. "Pick it up, then." There it lay in a puddle, gaudy and forlorn.

"I'll get it," said Kit, leaping up. Gallantry, perhaps; or smoke of shag. It mingled with the tinker's hair, smoke and spiralling like old man's beard.

The younger bit her bread, then turned and offered it to Thea, all but her thumb-piece. Cold fat bacon and wild garlic.

Pinched mouth and shake of head.

"I cry you mercy," Thea said. "A toothache."

A shrewd eye, like a stormcock's. "What did yer bite, then?"

But her aunt held out her pipe. "Here. Have a pull at me bacca. 'Twill dill thy pugging tooth."

Thea twisted, spewed and spat. Lay weeping.

"Ah," said Baccapipe. "Can read thy fortune wi'out cards."

And Bread-and-Bacon kicked her heels and sang, "*. . . when me apron were low, Ye'd fol- low me after through frost and through snow . . .*"

"Whisht." The old one wiped Thea's mouth, felt her brow and wrist and belly with rough concern. "Not far gone, I'd say." She quirked her chin at Kit coming. "Does he——?"

No.

"And do yer——?"

No again.

"Knowst mouse-ear?"

"Where?" said Thea.

"Ninewood. Up Ask ways, a two three mile." She pointed over the hills. "Grows in among thorn."

And the younger sang again, blithe as a cuckoo that calls, *Not I!* at the nesting wren: "*. . . but now that my apron is up to my knee . . .*"

"Sneck," said the elder.

Too late. Kit had tumbled. On his face, like wind in whitebeam, danced and paled his feelings: joy, awe, terror, tenderness, despair.

"Thea?" He knelt and wreathed her in his arms. "Canst walk? Can I get thee aught?" he said foolishly. "From anywhere, the moon." He could not see her face. He thought he could feel the child; he saw it in his mind's eye, like a little comet, still travelling and trailing light: a seed-moon tumbling over and over through the air.

Now, Margaret, thou begin'st to wind. Slipping from thy bower, soft and warily, thou try'st the latch: my lady and her crow keep watch. Not always, thou hast found. The gore-crow hunts; my lady sleeps, but as the sun in Thule, riding on the rim of darkness. She but wets her lip in Lethe cup. Yet she sleeps. Locks and spells she's set on thee, and cage on cage: thou walk'st within a tower, in a maze, within a wall hedged round with thorn, encompassed in a bitter sea. Her lean hounds prowl the courts and coverts, and her huntsman wards the gates.

And further, they do keep thee innocent, they blanch thee, as a gardener doth a white root under stones. Thou art bedazed and physicked, purged, pinched, bled, stayed, examined, spied on. Whipped.

Yet they do not lock thy door, within so many locks. Nor mew thy seeking thoughts.

They slight thee, for thou canst not be dead Thea, thou unwanted wast her death; disdain thee for thy meddled blood. In their contempt is all thy hope. Thou art a dish that likes them not; they have no stomach for thy soul. Unconsidered, thou art half unseen, a sparrow in a wintry hedge. Whatever thou art let to find is all inconsequent, is haws.

Thou turn'st the key and slip'st.

Doors and doors. An arras and a winding stair.

Ah, these rooms I never saw. Thy journey, Margaret. Not mine.

Only to the next room, and the next.

Locked.

Nothing but a box of nutmegs.

Spectacles, in this, that make thy candle swerve and loom. Old iron. Rats.

A lock made like a witch, that bares her secrets to the key. That watches, mute and venomous. Not there.

In this, a heap of books, sea-ruined. Mooncalf'd bindings, white and swollen as a drowned face. Warp and white-rot, skin on skin. Down thou sit'st and try'st to pry the boards, to turn the bleared and cockled pages. Here, a drawing of a hand, anatomized. A riddle in geometry. A fugue of spiders.

And behind a faded arras—ghost of roses, greensick blue—a bright dark closet full of wonders and of dust. A mute virginals. Thy fingers press the slack and clatter of its keys, unclose its fretty soundboard, gnawed and rustling with mice. The lid within is painted with brief garlands—violets and wood anemones—as if the music dreamed them in the dark. Spring flowers thou hast never seen: thy fingers, wond'ring, trace. They pleach the silk of scarves, as sheer as iris; trace the windings of a table carpet, blood of nightingales and cry-at-midnight blue. Thou strok'st a jar, round-bellied—blear with dust; yet lucent underneath—of china, blue and white as clouded May.

"So y'd not've been at leap fires, then," said Whin. "Being heavy."

"And light." Kit had seen them, other years, in Lune. Had begged the wood for them, from door to door:

> Sticks to burn vixens,
> Stones for the crow,
> Clips for us green lads
> And girls, as we go.

He'd danced with the highest: brave lads and bold heroes, and the lang tangly girls. Whirled higher, still higher, for the claps and cries, the eyes admiring or awed or scornful. Afterward, for clips and kisses. For the darker thing. By one and one, they'd pinched the embers—ah, another in thine hair. Thy shirt. By twos, had slipped away. He had lain on the dark hills; had made of charred petticoats, green gowns.

"No," he said. "No, we went to the greenwood. To get leaves."

"O," said Kit. "I drown." He stood in heaven, in the place where all doors lead. That wood was deep in flowers of the inmost curve of blue, the blue of iris her embrace. Her eye within her rainbow, as the moon within the old moon's clasp. And Thea walked in that unearthly floating haze of flowers, amid the leafing trees, knee-deep in Paradise. It was the heart; and yet at every further step, 'twas this. And this beyond. Each blue, the inwardest embrace, the bluest eye. An O annihilating all that's made.

The blue became his element, his air: he dove.

He saw a falling star beyond him. Thea.

Then 'twas past. He scuffled through old beech leaves, brushed by nettles. Stung himself and swore. Close by, he whiffed the green stench of a fox. He turned. A bluebell wood, the bonniest he'd ever seen. Young slender beeches. Holly, celandines, and wood anemones. And Thea gathering leaves, green branches.

Where she walked was heaven still.

He lay in sky, and watched her, errant in the sky below. She'd slipped from her tumbled smock, stood clad in sky. He saw the crescent of her, white and glimmering: in the dark of moon, the moon. That other sky she walked was on the verge of green, bluegreen, and turning deeper into blue. Beyond the new leaves, it was dusk. The trees were pointlace yet, or bare or budding out: an airy seine. A star hung trembling in the air, like water on a leaf, about to fall, unfallen. And the moon within his orbit, gilding as she set.

By a thorn tree, at his side, she sat and wove a garland in her lap. A knot of May.

Drowsily, he said, "We munnot sleep."

"Why not?"

"The morn will be the Nine. Wouldst see them rising?"

"Ah," said Thea, "but I am no maid."

He touched her small round belly. "Yet thou bringest may. A branch." The rank sweet scent of thorn hung faintly on the air; the petals fell, as if the moon unleaved. "Shall we set a hedge of them, a hey of girls?"

"And call it Lightwood?" Thea said.

Kit said,

> Let no man break
> A branch of it, for leavy Tom doth wake.
> And keep his lash of girls ungarlanded.
> That wood is hallows.

In another, rustic voice, he answered, "'Aye, 'tis where the bushes harry birds. I dare not for the owls go in."

Thea said:

> But thou art mazed, sweet fool. The wood is dark,
> And I—

"Go on," said Kit.

> And I th' moon's daughter in these rags of cloud
> Shall bear thee light.

"Oh," said Thea, "but I've left the book in Lune."

"Thou hast the way of it."

"By heart."

"And by thy heart." He wreathed his hands about their child, and spoke the woman's part:

> The lady goes with me.
> For that her star is wandering, I name
> Her Perseis . . .

And darting kisses in her neck, he said, "What think'st thou, for our lass, of Perseis?"

"Not Eldins?"

"Ah." Kit laughed softly for delight. "Will there be nine?"

"Less one," said Thea, bending to her wreath.

Whin said, "Did yer not guess what she twined?"

"No," said Kit. "I was a fool."

Why d'ye pull that bitter little herb, that herb that grows so grey . . . ? Ah, she'd pulled those leaves alone. "A man."

A silence. Somewhere in the wood, a bird poured silver from a narrow neck. Thea stirred. "Kit?"

"Hmm?"

"Does it end so?"

"Which?"

"The tale. With Annis turned to stone."

"At sunrise? Aye, and it begins."

"There was another tale," she said. "About the moon in a thorn bush."

"Malykorne."

"What's she?"

"The Cloud witch. Annis' sister, some do say. Her bed's where the sun is waked. He sleeps the winter there."

"And now?"

"Wakes wood."

"Ah."

Darkness and the moonspill of the may. Green is nowhere, it unselves the wood. As lovers are unselved: not tree embracing tree, but one. But wood. A riddle, he thought drowsily. *Within a wood, another wood, a grove where grows no green; within a moon, another moon, and nowhere to be seen.* A bird in the dark leaves answered, but he never heard. *Two, two eyes,* the owl cried out. *Of tree, of tree, of tree.* Kit slept.

I will tell this in the dark. That crown I wove for thee. And on May Eve, of all unseely nights: that nadir of the wake of Souls, and darkness' dark of moon. Unhallows.

Ah, love, I had despaired of thee.

I was unwitched. Thou knitting reeled up all my powers, left us naked to my lady's malice. Soul and body, I went heavy with thy death. My great kite belly would undo us all. And so I did, undid. I would not have thee bloodfast, earthbound, for my dam to take. Nor turn thee Annis, stone within my stone.

Toward midnight, turning, Kit awoke and saw a fireflash amid the low woods, heard a brash of leaves: and there in the glade he saw a kitlin fox, a vixen dancing like a flake of fire in the wind.

He turned to Thea, shook her softly. "Hush, love. Look."

She woke and saw. He felt her at his side turned cold as hailstones. "Kill it," Thea said.

A stillness. "What?"

"I am heavy, I can do no spell. Now. Quick."

And still he watched. The patter of the paws was quick, like rain on leaves. A clickety vixen. April in its veins. It danced like a burning leaf, the aftercolor of the greenblue sky.

"What harm in it?" he said. "The pretty kitlin."

"Eyes," she said.

They turned and flashed, a deepsunk dazzling green. The fire was green.

She said, "It wears the fox's fell."

He'd heard no bark. No fox was ever so still, so fiery. None scented of green thorn. He rose, unsure. A stone?

But it was gone.

He turned back and saw Thea, huddled naked on the ground. He bent and wrapped her in her scattered clothes, for fear of eyes, of lairing eyes. Cold in his arms, she cried, "No witch. I am no witch. I cannot meet her in the air."

Kit said, "Who'd harm thee? I would keep thee. I would try." A hopeless tenderness consumed him, like a candle swaling in his bones. "It's what I'm for."

She twisted from him. To the child in her, she cried, "My blood is thy undoing."

"'Tis my blood as well," said Kit. "I do not use thee."

Thea said, "But I use thee. Poor fool, have you not seen? Thou wert my cock-horse, that I rid away."

No ship, no ship beneath him, and the cold wave's shock. Salt-blind, he flailed at her. "Then find thyself a jade to bear thee, and another when he's flagged. Any stick will do to ride on."

Silence. Her cheek went paler still. His hands unclenched. At last, softly, she said, "And to burn, at need. The slower, being green. I would not watch thee burn." She turned her face from him; he saw the white neck, the tumbled quenchless hair. "I am thy death."

And rising, naked in her smock, she ran. He followed blindly, pushing on at hazard through bushes and briars. Heedless of their lash, he scrambled onward, deeper in the wood. The wood was endless. Thea? Further on, he saw her glimmering; then white in whiteness, she was gone.

His heart turned snow.

When I got thee, I had not yet bled. Nor will now, being air. That bower and that bed of state, my lady dressed for Annis, all in hangings of deep crimson velvet, rich as for the progress of a queen, though in her exile. Not that blue and meagre hag, that bugbear Annis, that doth stalk the fells of Cloud; not she, that winter's tale, that dwindled bloodfast crone: but Annis, air and dark made crystalline, before her fall.

I was born thirteen, as thou art now; I saw the Nine rise and the Gallows wheel and set an hundred enneads of times; and at thirteen, I lived a year, and died.

My lady did conceive, create me green and virgin for her sorcery; but kept me for herself. Her study and her moving jewel, her toy, her book. The pupil of her eye, that she did dote upon, so year by year put off the consummation of her art, for lessoning. For play.

In her conjurations—often in her storms—my lady witch would gaze in me, the glass that Morag held: bare April, but for winter's chain. Herself was January, all in black and branching velvet, flakes of frost at neck and wrist. *Come, Madam,* she would say. *Undo.* And then undo my coil of hair, unbraid it through and through her hands. *Lie there, my art.* And still would gaze, devouring my stillness, as the eye drinks light. I shivered in her admiration. Then, only then, her wintry hand would touch, her cold mouth kiss; and quickening, the witch would toy and pinch and fondle, aye, and tongue her silent glass, till she, not I, cried out and shuddered. Cracked.

Cried out: her jewel, her epiphany, her nonpareil; her book of gramarye, her limbeck and her light. Her A and O.

And yet not hers.

Know you that the stone my lady wears is Annis, shattered in her fall and vanished, all but that cold shard of night. Her self that was.

That moment of her breaking, time began. Light wakened from its grave in her. Unbound, the moon did bind her to that sickled and disdained hag thou see'st, that ashes of herself: the witch. Time chained her to this rock. And for a thousand thousand changes of the moon did Annis brood on her disparagement, the lightwrack of her Law. She sought to gather up her flaws of night, anneal them in her glass: that glass from which she drew me, naked and unsouled. Her self.

With me, my lady did enact her fall: the cry and shattering. And with each reiterated crack, her glass would round itself, quicksilver to its wound. But not her soul. My brooch of nakedness did pierce her, bind her bloodfast to her baser self: that hag who eats children.

That was not what she designed.

She had made me for the stone. The seed of Law. And on the morrow of the night I fled her would have wound the stair, unlocked the bloodred chamber, set the stone within my womb. Bred crystal of my blood. That stone would turn me stone from inward, Gorgon to itself, until—

And then he saw her. Moonlight. 'Twas the moon had dazzled him. No more. Light fell, leaves shifted. Thea stood agaze. Stone still and breathing silence. *Hush. Look, there.*

He turned. A clearing, silver as a coin with dew, and tarnished as the moon's broad face. And in that O of light, like Mally-in-the-moon, a-bristle with her bush of thorn, he saw an elfish figure, to and fro. A child? (A tree afoot?) Not ancient, though as small and sickle as the old moon's bones: a barelegged child. A branching girl. They do get flowers of a hallows eve. Alone?

A lash of thorn whipped back and welted him. He sleeved the salt blood from his eyes. He blinked and saw her, not in leaves but rags: the ruins of a stolen coat, perhaps, a soldier's or a scarecrow's, or a lover's run a-wood. Mad Maudlin's, that was Tom's old coat. It fell from her in shards, as stiff as any bark with years. There were twigs of thorn in wilting flower in her hair, down, eggshells, feathers. Cross and cross the O she went, not getting branches: walking patterns to herself, as furious fantastic as a poet in her bower, her labyrinth her language. Then a start, and back she skitted, ticklish as a spider on her web, to tweak some nebulous chiasmus. A hussif of trees.

Daft as a besom, he thought. Poor lass.

But Thea said to her, "Is't hallows?"

"While it is. Thy time's to come." The green girl scrabbled in her rags, howked out a pair of crooked spectacles and rubbed them in the tatters of a leafred cap. She perched them on her nose. A grubby girl, with greenstained knees, scabbed knees and elbows. As she turned, Kit saw her crescent body shining through the rags. A downy girl. He stirred and her seeing mocked him: a fierce howlet's face. All beak and eyes. "Shift," she said. "I's thrang."

But Thea said, "I am what you do."

"Ah," said the girl. "What's that?"

"Undo."

The girl glanced at Kit. "I see thou's done already what thou can't undo." He felt her elfshot eyes. Her breasts were April, but the eyes were January, haily, and the tongue a cold and clashy March. Scathed, he felt himself, dishevelled in his raffish coat, with moss and toadstools in his hair. Leaves everywhere. And ramping after Thea, like a woodwose in a mumming. Mad for love.

There was nothing for it but to play the part. Her glazy eyes decreed. "Poor leavy Tom," he said. "Remember Tom his cup. He sees the craws at bones; they rouse the kittle wren, cock robin, and the tumbling owl."

Then he cared not for the hoyden; Thea touched his lips. "Softly. 'Tis her wood."

Kit looked about. There was no moon. The light was may. He saw the whiteness, heaped and hung about the branches, like all the petticoats of some untidy dreaming girl, a tangly lass who kept her bower. What she knew and drew had thorns.

"Come in," said the green girl, loftily. "Mind souls, I's flitting."

In was out. He saw the whitethorn petals fall and flitter as he passed: no wall or window else. Within was dark and waste. Thea, bending, took up a clumsy garland lying half-made on the ground. Kit saw the ashes of a fire, cold out; a crackpot, tipsy on its one leg, canted over. It was full of dry leaves.

Beyond her hedge—scant sticks, blown papers—lay the cold bare hills. The wind was smoke-edged.

"Fires on the hills," said Thea, shivering.

Sticks to burn vixens. Kit saw the whirling bodies, higher, leaping higher. Heard the cries. They would dance on every hill by dawning, round from Law to Law again, to close round Annis in her stone. The kindling was the hey.

The girl snecked air behind them. "Aye, they wake, and then I wake."

Thea said, "Are you their mistress, then?"

"They's no one's minions," said the girl. "Here's spring." It welled up through the leaves, a little constant twirl of silver, spilling secretly away. She cleared it with her heel, and crouched and filled her gnarly hands. "Thou's dry," she said to Kit. He drank of them, her hands within his hands. He tasted earth. "Cloud ale," she said. "Dost like of it?" He nodded, mute. She took him by the shoulders, light, as if she shook him out, her cloak of leaves. "Lie there. Wake wood."

And he was leaves. Brown leaves of oak, the lightfall of a thousand hallows. He was galls and tassels, traceries of veining; he was shards of acorns, shales of light. His lady's cups. He was turning earth, and through him sprang the starry flowers of the Nine. His earth had made them green. *No tongue, all eyes!* the witch commanded, and the eyes were myriad, were stars of earth.

As giddy as a god, he laughed.

"S'all we do?" said the witch to Thea.

"As you will."

They worked together, plaiting thorn and blackthorn in a garland. Round they turned and bound it, plashing branches in and inwards, as an O, a lightlashed eye. It made a crown too sharp to wear. For which? There was a glory in their laps, of quince and almonds, nettles, violets and goat-haunched catkins, all a-didder and a-dance.

"It turns," said the witch. "Turns O."

"O's naught," said Thea, with the garland in her lap.

"Or ay and anywhere, as swift as moon; or what thou will. O's tenfold."

Thea bent to her braiding. "If it were?"

"It quickens," said the witch. "Comes round. What's past is nowt til it, and all's to come."

Odd and even went the witch's fingers, in and out. Wood anemone and rue. She wove them in the nodding garland: eyebright and nightshade, cranesbill, crowsbane, and the honeyed primrose, ladysmocks, long purples. Turning, it was turning autumn: now the leaves they wove were red and yellow, fruited: haws and hazelnuts and trailing brambles, rowans, hips, and hazy sloes.

"That untwines," said Thea, of a mouse-eared herb. "I plucked it."

"Aye," said the witch, weaving in. "Wilta taste of it?"

"And wane?"

"And bear thysel, burd alone. Walk or wake, as thou wist."

Thea bent. "I am bound to them. My lady and this child. If I do bear it, I am hers; if I do not, I am herself."

"Allt same. Thou's moonfast."

Thea said, "I am uncastled. Will you keep me?"

"Where? I's nowhere."

"Here."

"Is nowhere. Hey is down, and there's no hallows i't green world. I't morning, I mun walk and Annis wake."

"Then I am lost," said Thea. "For my art is lost."

"Thou's bound as she is, rounding winter in thy lap. It will be born, I tell thee, and i't sickle o't moon." The witch tossed the tussymussy in her lap. "So mowt it be."

Kit watched them whispering secrets, close as moon and dark of moon, in one another's arms. They wove one burr of light. He saw the clew of stars in Thea's lap. He saw the witch's spectacles were frost; they faded as he looked, they trickled down and down her cheeks. He heard an owl's cry echoing, her windy laugh. He saw the green hills leap with vixens, blown like flames from hill to hill. *When the wheel comes round, 'tis sun*, he thought. He saw the blackened moon, the cavey moon, as slender as a share of bannock. Riddle cake. He thought the green witch bade him eat. It tasted sweet and bitter, of his dreams. His share was burnt. He saw a stone and a thorn tree, deep in green embrace. The moon was tangled in the leavy thorn, its roots its rimy crown. The stone was straked with lichens, of a bloodrust red; a crazy garland at its crown, aslant.

Split the stick, and I am in it, sang the wren. *I rise.*

I crack the stone, said the starry flower. *I will crack where I take root.*

He slept.

And so I waked that night, and whispered secrets with my sister moon. With Malykorne, that is my lady Annis' other face and elder: light and dark of one moon.

Her cradling and my crescent self, still turning from my mother into light. And thou within me, braiding blood. A clasp of witches.

I had no heart for thy undoing.

I am stone, said I. *My lady's eidolon. How came I by this flaw?*

Thy soul? The green witch laughed. *Her glass were clouded.*

Did you——?

Stir fire up? Not I.

I thought on thy begetting. *Brock? Did she meddle?*

Bloodroot i' thy lady's cauldron. Ashes i' thy cup. The green witch drank. *What's done is done. Yet being kindled, thou might leave thy spill.*

Kit slept beside us. Why did I not leave him sleeping, let him grieve and live?

I tell thee, I could not, remembering how coldly I had culled him, out of all the bloodborn kenneled in my lady's dark. All in silver, I'd come down to view my prey, I'd held the candle to his dazzled face. Yes. He would do, I'd thought; yet stilled the triumph in my glance. My lady and her crow did watch. They'd uses for his soul and seed, designs of thrift and sorcery for bone, blood, fell and eyes. Ah, make no paragon of me—myself had marked him for my own false ends. His fiddle for a ship to bear me from that nighted isle; his cock to crow away her spell. 'Twould do, I judged. So one might heft a stick, a sling of stones, at need: to use, to cast away. He bowed; and as my lady bade, I offered drowsy wine to him, a draught amazing to the mortal sense. We'd toy with him before we slew.

Is this the moon? said he, and gazed about the hall. Awe and mischief in his face. *I've seen her owl and her ivy bush, but never tasted of her cup.*

I bit my lip, so not to laugh. All solemn then, alight with love, he drank to me. I saw him: tousled, sleepless, downy. He had brushed his twice-turned coat, as if he went not to his death but to a dance. *Poor fool,* thought I. And all unknowing, I was changed by him. His innocence his spell.

And so that green Unhallows eve, I waked by Malykorne and chose: to stay with Kit, to bear thee, for what end might come.

O Margaret, I was stark afraid. Of travailing, of birth. Of dying—ah, most bitterly; but more than death, I dreaded Annis in myself. Her stone I had averted; but the dark witch was in grain. I'd seen her in my lady's glass: bloodnailed and insatiate, the blind hag on the road. I was afraid of being her, of slaying what was not myself. Of whoring. Not the act—for I was schooled to that—but the devouring. Cold fire, turning sticks to Ashes, Ashes into Annis, endlessly: herself herself engendering.

Yet where thou wast, there Annis could not be. That secret did the green witch tell me, softly in mine ear: thou wouldst keep hallows in that place of blood, that O thine everywhere, thy keep; though I went naked to my lady's sky. And so I brooded thee, as doth a child its candle, lighting her the way to bed. Yet all about there lay the shadows of thine inward fire, the fears that winced and flickered in my brain. Of need and frailty and lumpishness. Of losing Kit, the fear of losing him. Of love.

"Craw's hanged!" cried the grey cock.

Kit woke. *Gone?* A something slipped from him, a ghost returning at the pale of night. It will not stay, that tide. The pale boat rides the mirk and shiver of that burning flood; it slips the moorings. Gone. Yet curled against him, Thea slept. Cap and acorn. They were lying by a scanty thicket, on the open hills. Not day yet, neither moon nor sun.

He heard a thump and twitter in the wood, a wild free scuffling and calling. Out from the greenwood burst a rout of guisers, clad in tattercoats and leaves.

"Hey is down!" they cried.

Children.

Thea hid her face, but she was laughing; Kit caught up their scattered clothes to lap her.

They'd a girl to play small music—hop and twitter, like a small bird on a briar—all but lost amid their charm. She'd a wheedling pipe and dowly drum. Another, a long lad, bore a garland of whitethorn with a dead crow swung from it, wryneck and agape. It dangled, claws upward, wings clapped wide and stark. Round it, in and out, there ran a thrang of boys and girls. One, crowned in oakleaves, clashed horns with another clad in holly. Lagman and tangling, walking in his sleep, a small boy gaped and swayed and staggered under all their jackets.

"Brant!" they cried. "Come in, here's game."

Not last but alone went a dark and clustering girl in torn russet and green crown; she bore a staff, and wore a fox tail jauncing behind.

"Craw's hanged!" she cried. "Get up!"

A stripling in petticoats swept round the lovers, whirling light and away. His skirts were singed with leaping fires. His broom was budded out, as if he'd swept stars with it. "Here's nest on 'em," he said. He poked at them and kittled them, left smears of pollen and of ashes.

"Hey!" cried Kit, sneezing, laughing all at once.

The others thronged. "We's late. They's been and done."

Undone.

The girl with the music played *Cuckoo!* on her little pipe

"My bout at broom? Yer said I could."

"Sneck up, thou mardy, or I's leave thee here for bears."

"Clartarse."

"Neshcock. Tell our dad of thee."

"Gi's a box," said another. "And we'll gang away."

Kit fumbled in his pockets, found a halfpenny. "Here's to your fires."

Brant bit, she pursed it. "And to yers. Where's riddle?"

"Here," said another. "In my apron."

They'd a round loaf of barley bread, with a face baked into it: a leafy glazy green man, scored and bossed on it, with clove-nailed eyes. Brant broke and shared it out with all. Kit took, and Thea. All tore it from within, the soft warm crumb; they left the crust of the green man, his face, for the last. At his end, a small boy took the heel, he pinched the raisins from the eyes. Round he went, guising in his mask of crust. Now crouching, now on tiptoe, peering round. A solemn mischief.

"I see you," he said to Kit. "You don't see me."

Then that, too, was devoured.

Whin tugged at Kit's long cotted hair; she eyed his salt-rimed straggling beard. "Time you was clipped."

"Day," said the woman. The sheep leapt, yellow-eyed and glaring, from between her knees. The fleece fell, the light sheep staggered giddily away. "Where yer bound?"

Kit said, "Thwaite. Is this the road?"

"We's all up here," said the woman with the shears, broad-backed, rosy, swathed in sacking. In the fold, the penned sheep blared and jostled.

"Oh," said Kit, looking round at the row of clippers kneeling or bending to their work, at the lappers and catchers, and the boy at the gate. Beyond them, it was cloudy, the hills hooded in morning.

"Way!" Behind him, a gangling lad brought on another ewe to clip, half-riding her. He threw her in the woman's lap. Her shears bit deep in the heathery wool; they scrunched and sang. "Walking on?"

Kit said, "Anywhere."

"If's a bite and a sup yer after, there's work. Can yer catch 'em? Can yer whet?"

"I'd think so. But . . ."

The woman peered at Thea. A dishevelled girl, and silent. Like a tinker out sleep-walking. Hair like flakes of fire. The gown had been good, was tattered as lichen. It was undone at the waist. "Not so lish as yer were, is't? Can yer lap?"

"She's lapped," said a clipper.

Another sheep sprang away, a vengeful crone. Kit shielded Thea. "'S all right, she's been down afore," called a man. "Rigged ower."

"Pay 'em no mind," said the woman. "Fourpence and all found?"

"Done." Kit laid by his pack and jacket, and plunged into the throng of clamorous sheep.

"Hey up! Gi's a slipped 'un."

"Hey! Mind awd Sukey. She's gone on yer, like."

"Lovesick."

"Hod on, lad."

An old ewe cannoned into Kit. Down he went, embracing her for dear life, slathered, laughing. He got her somehow to a shepherd's lap. The man knelt on her head, grinning.

Kit felt his bones. "By, she's a brave 'un." He grinned at Thea, but she stood, looking out at the hills.

"Come on, then," said a lapper.

Thea gathered wool. There were loose locks everywhere. Two women stood at a board and hurdles, lapping fleeces. They plucked away the clarty bits—odds, bobs, and daggles by the tail—and threw them in a sack. They spread each fleece out, dark side up. Then they folded in the legs and rolled it up, dark outward inward, with a twist of the neck-wool drawn out and wrapped round. As they worked, they gossiped; but at every fleece, they said, "A soul, a sark. Out light, in dark."

Thea packed the fleeces in creels. Kit wrestled with the crones. The shears crunched on, inexorable; the light sheep skipped away. The lappers set riddles. "What rive at one another allt day, and lie in one another's arms all night?"

"I give up," said Thea. "Moon and her dark?"

"Wool combs."

From below, a long way off, came a girl, knitting beside a laden pony. A shepherd and a brisk black dog brought new sheep, down from the summer moors. They shone, brightdark and heavy as the thunderbreeding clouds.

The girl tied her pony, unlading hoggins, frails, and creels. She brought round a tray of cheesecakes, round and golden. "Noon."

Gooseberries and news. "Grey mare's foaled. A lad, and he's piebald. Mistress? Yer Bet's been and thrawn one o' yer good siller spoons i't beck, and me and Doll has fished it up. Young termagant." She sleeved her rosy face. "Oh, and a stranger come, asking at one Lightwood. Said he were an Outlune fellow, brown and beggarly, and ganging with a whey-faced breeding wench. A vixen." She stared at Thea. "There now! And that clotpoll of a crow lad sent him on up Houlsyke way. Will I fetch him back?"

"No," said Kit. "I thank you."

A blue-eyed shepherd looked to westward. Thunder. "Doubt he'll have tumbled i't hag by now."

Thea bit her seedcake. "Well done, my little page."

Whin's duckstone skipped and slapped across the waves. "Eight." She turned grinning. "That caps."

"You've nimmed all the smooth stones whilst I lay and slept." Kit's flicked once and sank. Still clumsy.

Whin turned out her pockets with a clattering flourish. "Halves." Stoop and flick. Three. "Yer still won't beat. I's worked at it." Still with her back to him, looking out at the bare green sea, she said, "Bairn's father."

"Ah?" Kit sorted through the stones.

"It were guising. I never see'd his face." Five. "So I see'd him a'where."

"A stranger." One with a leaf in it, too fair to cast away. And this ill-shapen. Ah, this would do. Four. "Yellow hair?"

"As chimneysweepers." A lad at leap fires. A thief at the gallows. Had he smiled, remembering her cries? A false love. A fiddler. A stranger with a scythe.

Sweetness of green hay. Midsummer. Endless dusk. And still the mowers, mothpale in their shirts, strode on. Kit watched the coil, recoiling of their backs, the long sweep of their scythes, in unison, and so enlaced that not a blade of grass between them stood. They struck and strode, advancing like the white edge of a wave: whish and tumble and the intricating arcs of edge. A long wave, standing with the sun. It stood; the flowers fell and withered with the grass. No sea, but slow green fire, kindled by the sun his kiss.

And after came the bending girls, to strow the grass. They'd not take rake to it, still green in bride-bed, bleeding from the scythe. Rakes to the lapcocks; but straw girls to the swath, to shake and strew the hay in handfuls, east and west. Lay lighter that way.

The hay's the dance.

In Kit's long row, they raked and turned the fading flowers: matrons of a day, and sunburnt. Tossed and tumbled, all their brightness turned to breath of summer. Sweets compacted. He'd made hay since he could walk. He knew the dance. Scythe it and strow it, then to rakes. And turn and turn. Lapcocks to the hobs to windrows; windrows to the sledges. Crisp and blue.

And in among the cocks of hay, the lovers courted, striplings and hoydens, clip and cuff, like hares. Boys battled, whirling hay. And one to another, the straw girls sang: the grey-eyed girl behind him, tall and soldierly and brown; the elfin brat before.

Kit turned and gazed at Thea, in among the girls. Ah, lovelier than ever, fading. Inward turned, to sweet. His lass was growing thin and heavy. Bending to the grass, she strowed it, sun and moon. Skirts dovetailed, and her bare legs scratched. Her bright hair tumbled on her neck. Still white as thorn, her throat, her brow; no sun could burn them. Thea tossed her wraiths of flowers in the air, looked up and round within their falling. Whorl within whirlwind, slow and fast. *Move still, still so.* O my heart. Let it be *now* ever, at the solstice of my love. The blade but newly struck; my heart still standing. Yet will fall. Her blade's herself.

The long wave slowed, against the steepening shingle of the dark. And now the grass was ocean; slow and slower lagged their wading steps, their oars, against that tide. The lads cried challenges, lashed on their fellows, flagging, flagging with the sun; the lasses raked and sang:

> You must kiss her and embrace her,
> Till she causes your heart to yield—

One voice above the rest rang out, triumphant, hoarse:

> For there's never a faint-hearted soldier
> Can win on a battlefield.

The scythes struck on, against that tide of dark. Against the quenchless lap of earth, the grass that stood and shivered. Stood.

Up from Imber Beck came Kit, not spilling what he held. Deep pools and dappling, the rush and plunge of bright quick water on the stones. He'd washed him clean as dawn, walked naked in his old clean shirt. Grass at his ankles, wind stirring in his wet-combed hair, already lifting from its douse. A sparkling dancing day, a drying day. A day for playing hob. Wild thyme and trout, he thought: he'd lie and tickle.

He came to Thea, sitting in a circle of great stones, on one had fallen, at the green hub of the wheel of Cloud. Its nave, whence it breathed. Old stones, they were, and worn fantastical: wind-gnawed and water-cavey, flawed and rippled with the frosts. White stones, whorled with mosses. They'd not mown here. Would not: had left them whitelands to the wandering sheep.

Thea swung her heel and sang, like any shepherd's lass.

"A lovegift," said Kit, and held it out.

A cup of rushes, lined with cool green leaves of hazel, wet with dew. And brimmed with raspberries, most perfect ripe: as soft as foxes' paws, and with their prick. Their flowers wreathing round. A dowry for a queen of Elfin.

"Ah," said Thea. All her face alight with joy, as he'd not seen her. Taking them, she kissed him lightly on the wrist, just where his pulse beat blue. Where it was scratched with gathering, had beaded with bright blood. Love's bracelet. "Bravely won."

For that he'd pick them naked, from the inward of the thicket out. By Cockridden and by Childerditch, he would, were the brambles backside of the moon.

"Does it like thee, love?" he said. "That cup of imbers?"

"I shall give them to my eldest daughter," said Thea. And she ate.

Ah, Margaret, that was firstborn of my spells, my new-created magic. I will tell it in thy blood, in time. Nine drops. No more.

The field was called Crawcrooks. High and aslant the fell it lay, a stony piece, the last to harvest. They had reaped them all: Burnt Ridding, where the oats were lodged, the Light End and the Long Dark, and round by Mawkins Hey, by Brockholes, Beggary and Witchy Slang, the Whirl Ing and the Wren Graves, and out by Owler Hag. A nine day's stint.

Kit bent to the sheaving. The barley stood white. When he closed his eyes, he saw it glittering still, but awned with violet black. It scarred his eyes with light. Another sheaf, a knot of straw. He swam in it. Straw bristled up his shirt-tail, down his neck. His arms and legs were torn and welted, scarified with straw. Weeds nettled; stubble pierced. Sweat sidled and stung. He ached with stooping, beaten down, astounded by the clangor of the sun. He thought it screamed at him, defiant; looking up, he knew it for a hawk. A stunning and a brazen noon.

Before him went brown Annot, Ailie Whinlaw, Kat and Bartlemy and Noll Ned Hewlin, with laggard Ciss to trail the rake. They moved breasthigh against the barley, all arrayed in its armor of light. Crouching, they cut it, striking off with their sickles: moon against sun. In their wake lay the barley, shorn and withering. Kit gathered it in armfuls, tying them with bands of straw that Thea twisted of the greenest corn. Beside him and behind worked Gib and Nick Scarrow, sheaving and stooking. No one spoke. The sun quelled them. Still he heard the rasp and rustle of the knives in corn.

The barley was one element, of sun, earth, wind, and rain. A hoary world. Time stilled. Before him rose a whirring and a clack of wings: a covey clattering away. He saw a scutter and a lop of coneys, and at his feet the fumblings of a dawstruck mole. A-sway on the nodding corn, the gressops leapt and chirred. He saw the plash of poppies falling, and the blue-eyed blink of cornflowers, clean petticoats of bindweed. He saw the scurry of the denizens laid bare to light: whitespinners, jinny-long-legs, harvestmen. He felt the sooty velvet of the smutched ears of slain corn, black as my lady's mask. In the sundered corn, he found a mouse's nest, two short ears bound together in a daddle of straw, as deftly plaited as any kirn witch on a stack. There were ratlins within, rosebald, but willowing out with a fuzz. They blindly wormed and squeaked. No dam. No help for it. He stuck it like a bauble in his sunburnt hat, and bent to work.

Then Ailie cried, "Whet!"

The bottle went round, hand to hand. Kit stood and eased his back. Looked first to Thea. He stared out beyond the barley at the whiteleached sky, the moorland bruised with sun. He turned. All below him and behind lay fields, a piecework stitched with drystone walls. He saw the hardwon ploughlands, pale and stooked, all glittering as a card of pins. Beyond lay fold and fallow, and the tilting meadows, green with aftermath, called fog. Above, stood only sheepwalk, cropped and stony, and tumbling becks. He thought of throwing down his glove and lying naked in the rush of water.

"Noon," said Ailie.

They'd an hour's halt. By ones and twos, they turned down the field, past the morning's thraves, sheaf leaning on sheaf, with another as henge. The men went flapping their shirts, their breeches with the knee strings undone. The women swung their sickles, in their broad hats and kerchiefs, their kilted petticoats, all urchined out with straw. Kit waited. Last of all came Thea, roundbellied in a borrowed apron, walking slow. Her hat was wreathed with poppyheads, how quickly bare: a few bright curving petals clung. He saw with a pang how sore her hands were, torn with spinning bands; how white her face. He said, "Thou wert to rest."

"Where's the penny, then?" she said.

He bent and stuck the mouse nest in a stook, carefully. It would not stand, being toppling heavy. "There's time. Shall we lie by the water?"

She looked up at the fellside. "I'd need wings."

"Rest then. Will I fetch thee water?"

"Kat's gone."

There was ale in the hedge. The reapers passed it round and drank; they sprawled and panted in the grass. Beneath an apron thrown over a hazelbush lay Annot's baby, naked in a little shirt, beside his sleeping childish nurse. The cloth had been dabbled, for the cool; had long since dried taut, tented out on sticks. The shadows of the leaves moved lightly, dappled on the bairns. The baby waked and watched them, pursemouthed, puzzling at air. "Ah," said Kit, crouching, all alight. The pretty poppet. Annot wiped her mouth, undid her freckled breast. The little quaily brat set to with jugging. Ciss's Jacky played at the field edge, making pisspies in the dust.

They ate their baggin: curds and onions and the odd green bite; oatcake, cheese and ale. Kit had got brambles from a hedge for Thea. They were green and seedy, like eating broideries of beads; a few, as red as beaded blood: the needle's prick. Nothing else yet ripe. But there were crowcrooks on the moor; the sleeping girl had picked her apronful. Her mouth was stained with them. They had them for their afters: mistblue and midnight berries, tart, and bursting winy on the tongue.

Off by the beck, Kat and Bartlemy were wading, splashing. They leapt and clashed like kids. He snatched at what she flaunted, held high out of reach; Kat lashed him with a bunch of whins. *Whoop!* cried the boy, and under he went. They saw her ranting on the stone, as gleeful as a goblin. Up he came behind her, and he caught her by the petticoats. A splash like young dolphins.

"By dark," said Ailie, squinting at the glinty stubble and the dwindling standing corn. "Later n'r last year, by a farthing moon."

"It's coming on storm, I doubt," said Gib.

"We's have it done by then. Kirn and all."

Ciss said, "Is't witch or wench this year?"

Ailie looked crows at her, but thumbed her sickle. "As it falls."

The sickles lay about the grass, a halfyear's moons. A reiving wasp came on, and darted at the fruit. Ciss shrieked and cowered in her apron. Sibb in the hedgerow woke, saying, "Is't won yet? Mam?" Kit fanned Thea with his rushy hat. She was whitefaced, and her burning hair was flat with sweat. The red hair rode her like a demon.

Ailie said, "Yer want to be lying down."

Annot put her baby to the other breast. "Are yer lighter by Gossamer? When is't?"

At Hallows. They would never speak so in the harvest field; Kit knew that much. "Toward Lightfall," he said.

"When's that i' Cloud?"

"The Nine stars' setting, that we call the Clew," said Kit. "Nine Weaving?"

"Cob's Web," said Ailie, nodding.

Nick Scarrow said, "I' Slaith, we call 'em Jack Daw's Seed." His teeth showed whitely in his sunburnt face. He was a hireling stranger; he walked the harvest north. A marish man. He'd said they reaped with scythes there: not creeping women, but a sweep of men.

"Aye, they's a queer lot, out Law," said Gib.

"Cunning wi' tools." Nick fleered at Thea's belly, with a sly and sidelong glance at Kit. "Will I thresh her for thee? Got a flail."

Hewlin sniggered.

"Aye, brock i't middle," said Ailie. "It hangs."

Kit said nothing, twisting straws. Nick shrugged. "Then hang her from a pole for t' crows. I seen yer crowland mawkins, out i't rain. A waste o' seed." He sauntered off upfield, to sleep under the hedge. Kit threw away the knot of straw. Toward Whinside, the sky had turned; it shook like foil in the heat. The corn was yellower: not glinting now, but glowering. The sun was in it, brighter as it shrank.

Thea slept, and Annot. Gib snored and Hewlin whistled; Ailie span hemp. The bluemouthed child made towns of pebbles. Ciss held Jacky in her lap and sighed. "At kirn feast, at Lowerstell, last year, they'd a fiddler til't dance."

Kit felt a whitecold sickle at his heart. The fear had grown in him that all the cunning of his hands was lost with Thea's art. He never spoke of it; he dreamed of ships. "Will he be coming?"

"Not up here, he won't. Up Annis' arse."

Ailie said, "Not for thy sake, Mistress Lightheels."

"Never mind," Kit said. "Do you rant, and I'll keep measure."

"Wi' yer tongue?" said Ailie. "Or have yer browt a pipe?"

"Packed away," he said soberly. "And the drum is broken."

Ciss went on, "A new tune? I do love a new tune."

"One I've made," he said. "The oldest in the world."

Ailie let her spindle fall, the coarse grey thread spin out. "There's Daw's awd crowd wants nobbut catgut. If y'd turn a penny. Hanged on a nail these ten years since."

Kit's heart leapt up.

Ciss poked at the stubble. "There's not," she said. "There was a beggar come, asking would I cross his palm. He told my cards."

"No art i' that," said Ailie. "Thy fortune's i' thy fork." Down fell the spindle. "Wha tellt thee it were thine to give?"

"Caggy awd thing, wha'd want it?" Ciss pouted. "And I never turned me back, but when pot boiled ower. Asides, there's nowt else missed, I counted spoons and all. And I's to journey til a far country, and wed a stranger on a dapple horse." She turned to Kit. "Happen if yer see him ont road, yer could ask for it back. A tinker fellow like a white craw."

Before he'd framed an answer, Kat came running down the fellside, with her long legs twinkling, bare and scratched. There was gorse in her hair. She'd forgotten the water jugs; but grinned, holding out a great bunch of white heather, haws, crawcrooks. "For t' kirn."

Ailie took and laid it by her sickle, in its curve. "'Twill a' to do."

"So it better. Pains I taken wi't. Is there owt i' yon poke?" Kat rifled for her share of bread and bit it, grinning. "Bat's sulking. He's soused."

Kit watching thought he guessed the riddle. In Lune, in Askrigg, he had seen the images of bristling corn in kitchens down the dale, tied up with rags, with flowers dried to dust. The last sheaf was the Witch, they said; they gave her to the wrens to peck, at Lightfast: so the old year ate of her, to make it new. He said, "In my country, they do bind the Witch with rowans."

"Does they?" Ailie said.

Kat wrung her skirts. "I'd not wonder. For it's red and all."

The Witch was eaten, and in turn she ate. Long since, the old wives said, they'd slain a child for her, an Ashes child: each spring a fall. They said the Old Witch lulled him in her lap. Kit knew her cradle songs. And still in Lune the countryfolk kept law: they stoned the wren and burned his crown, sowed blood and ashes with their hoarded seed, to slake the Witch. Kit saw her, squatting in the corn, with her tangled shock of hair, her scrawny shanks and long toes; her cheeks were of the reddest grain.

"O' course," said Ailie. "Them outland folk is strange. I's heard they shear owls."

Kit looked at Thea sleeping. He said, "There is a tale in Lune. They say the barley is the black earth's daughter, shut all winter in her dark. She rises. So they say."

Ciss said, "They's witches all i' Lune, Gib says."

The spindle fell.

Kit closed his eyes. He saw the Maiden rising, running from her mother's ancient dark. A green girl, dancing in the wind; but long strings tethered her, white-wiry, to her mother's womb. They held her, ripening to stillness, caught and cut. Three servingmen with knives of stone, her mother's minions, struck her down; they beat her with their flails. Her lover looked for her among the sheaves. He took each Perseis in his arms, and she was Annis, hoar and silent. On her face, the shrouding spiders scurried at their work. They told her death in inches. So he laid her out amid the lykes of straw. His eyes were dry. But she was lighter of the sun, their child. He saw it, in its swaddling bands of straw, unslain. Kit saw it, even through his lidded eyes: a glory and a dazzlement. He slept.

Ailie glanced at him, scraw-boned as a rabbit, in his hempen shirt. "'Twill a' to do," she said.

To Luneward did they reap the Witch. Here in Cloud, his elsewhere, they did say the corn was lying in the Witch's lap; she combed his silver hair and he did sleep. And then her cronies crept on him, they cut him off at knee. Not one before another: all at once, they slashed. *Not I*, said each crone to her other. *Nor not I. 'Twas she, my sister slew him.* They were each and all the moon, his end: her sickle shearing and her millstone trundling round, her old black cauldron gaping for his bones.

They shared him out as riddlecake, as round as the wheeling sun. They drank him and he made them giddy: for the turning of the sun is in his cup. As they drank, they played old bone games on their knuckles: moon reaps sun; sun mazes moon; and moon again wakes sun. They waked him through the winter and they scattered him: the earth his grave, his lap. His last sheaf was the Flaycraw. They hanged him on the Gallantry, to blacken in the wind and rain, to cry the crows. And so his green seed sprang.

Crows called in the harvest field. The bluemouthed child looked up. White crows. They dazzled in the sun; then fell like cinders, black. She watched. She looked around her, squinting. They were all asleep, her mam and all. She bent to her play again, moved pebble in their maze. The black crows quarrelled in the corn.

Kit woke hard. He saw crows rising in the field. His cheek was creased with straws; his arm, asleep where Thea lay on it. Drowsy and heavy, drenched with sleep, he rubbed his eyes and roused her. Ailie called them to the field. It shivered in the little wind; the dazed corn shook, it dazzled. To the east, the sky was sultry dark. They drank and hastened.

As Kit went to field, he met Nick Scarrow loitering by a stook: a burnt man, blue-eyed. He held a reaping-hook and smiled. "Word's out ont road," he said. "Thy Lunish piece. Wilt keep her when she's dropped yon brat? I's a mind to chaffer."

"Crows eat thee," said Kit.

"Crows gat me," said Nick, and slouched off.

Kit slashed with a fury at the rankest corn. A neck, he thought. A neck. "Come up," called Ailie, so he fell to binding, furthest out. He saw that Thea went among the women, safe enough. The work unknotted him, it combed. The women called and answered at their reaping, keeping measure.

Wha knocks at stone?

Poor Peg alone.

What's poor Peg lack?

A rag t' her back.

For salt and bread to lay her dead.

And candlelight to gan by night.

And what's she beg?

A shroud to lap poor Tom.

Poor Peg.

They were cutting in a long slow spiral now, coiled inward on the standing corn. They went sunwise.

Here, said the green witch. *I am here.*

And gone. She ran with a rustling, greenfoot. Slower now. She was heavy with the sun, he'd catch her. Then he took her in his arms. She turned, and she was hoary, spidery with years. A blue-eyed, bearded hag, ca'd Crawcrooks.

Now you can lay me down and love me, said the Witch. *If you will.*

So he did and he was rooted in her. He was Cloud. His name was Nightless and Bare Bones, Dearbought, Come by Chance. To the east, they called him Babylon, he bowed before the wind as Wiselack, Slobeard, Urchins Hey. To the south, his names were Long Nap, Little Knowe, Leap Hedges; to the west, Sheer Ash, Jack Nackerty, and Nine Tree Crowd; to the north, they reaped Cold Hallows, Hanging Crows, Hobs Graves. The cold wind played on him, the old tune always.

Then the slight moon and the dark of moon, the whitefaced breeding moon, came round him, bound him with their wreaths of straw. Their sickles ringed him like a running wheel. Then all at once, they slashed.

A clip! they cried. *A kiss, a clip!* He toppled in their arms.

"And so they ate thee," said Whin. "All but bit t' wren had, and there's an end."

"No," said Kit, smiling. "They did but taste." Kisses and a crown of poppies. Hurts and cream. A sweet mouth, blue with berrying; a shrewd mouth, taking sweets. And

Ailie's warmest of them all and fierce, the brooding of a merlin's breast. Then he clouded. "No, 'twas Thea that the moon ate."

Autumn. Moving on. No work. The purple of the moors had gone from froth of jam to fleasblood, then from bruise to black; the trees, from blaze to ruin. Rimefrost on the swiddened heath took place of gossamers. The bracken and the bents were smithwork, smoldering in mist, and glinting, brazen in the strike of sun. And barren. While Kit could, he'd gathered haws, hips, brambles, sloes and rowans. Bags of nuts, his pockets full and Thea's apron. And one October afternoon, he'd found a milky way of mushrumps, penny buns, spilled out amid the leaves. They'd had a bit of mutton fat, just then. A feast. Their meal was long since giving out, their poke thin-flanked and dusty. It was poaching now. Hares, moorhens. Snared and spatchcocked. Aye, he'd looked at sheep, dared not. Not yet. He dared not hang and leave her.

Then it came to thieving. Which he did repent; yet cared not. Scant enough scourings up here on Ask Moor. Back of beyond. A wary and a sken-eyed folk, who cracked doors on long noses, clapped shut. High barred windows, hurtling dogs on chains. He'd eyed geese, but got none. Filched trifles. Neeps and kindling and blue milk. Odd stockings. A smock for Thea, that he'd had to crack, left cat-iced in a drying yard. Handfuls of oatmeal. Eggs left for hobs.

Thin beggary and thinner shoes. More eyes, more spies, more calling crows. More canting fellows on the road who turned and stared and mocked. Their bold-eyed trulls, who called at Thea, crying out, *Brave rags with us. And hiring for thy hobby-horse.* And then a broadside flapping at a crossroads: *Lunish runagates,* it said. A kitfox and her cull. So they'd left the high road for the hags and thickets, laying up on the moors, in folds rough-thatched with heather, ruined barns. And moving on.

Thea had changed: all bones and belly, swollen fingers. Swollen buds, yet flagging, fretted and embrowned. A side tooth lost with knitting bones. Younger and older both, she seemed: a crone who danced her poppet on her knee and lulled it, and a wizened imp. Great belly and her scabby knees, her cracked and bluenailed hands. Nor mortal, neither, but a changeling, with that pinched white face, that goblin's shock of hair. Yet her bonefast beauty stayed.

She was—not happy, no. Ecstatic. Danced like chestnuts on a shovel. Slept scarce at all. Since harvest, so he'd thought her sunstruck. Moonsick then. Now still, now restless as a cat in pattens, to and fro. Thrang as Throp's wife, and at nothing, all hours of the sun and moon. Waking and working. So she called it, her work. Poor lass. As good brew ale in eggshells.

"Is't witchcraft?" he had asked.

"Riddles," Thea said.

He saw her, crouching in her ragged smock, intent on patterning. Ah, hallows on us, but she'd made some wondrous things. All fleeting, left behind to wind, rain, earth, as soon as made. Unharvested, unheld. She scattered.

Sticks, stalks, leaves and stones. A living hazel branch, lapped all in poppy petals, blood and branching. Leaves picked and shaded in a long streak on the earth: from green through fire to dead black; from ashes to greenwhite. Twigs in a round rattle. Labyrinths of leaves, bark, foxfire punk; or drawn in rime. Spirals of cracked pebbles, scratched white with another. Cubbies of sticks. Snailings and green horns of leaves, or burnished brown as copper: stitched with thorns and plaited in one endless coil and spiral, nestled in the earth. Leaves laid round nothing, bright and brighter toward the O. The same, with pebbles, white and whiter round abyss or origin.

One day he'd found her wading in a beck for more smooth stones, her apron full. In frost. Wet through and blue and shivering. And would not come with him until he'd waded in.

A night and day spent weaving stalks, an airy web of them, infilling all the crook and curving of a great low bough.

And in brief snow, a ball of it, built round and pierced by sharp small living wood. A ball that rolled its own maze, green laid bare; that rounded on its journeying.

O ever and alas, my Thea. O my dearest girl, my love.

Stark mad.

Ah, Margaret, I did make new heavens of the earth. Cast out of that cold sky in which my lucid soul was stringed, I did undo myself, redo: not Thea of the braided hair, but tangly Thea, tattery Thea, Thea of the grubby knees who crouched and plaited in a tinker's petticoats. I was inventing a new magic, for the old was lost with my virginity, with my immortal maidenhead. Oh, I was changing, changing fearfully; yet rounding with thy whiteheart self was Thea: we were sisters, twinned like cherries on a stalk.

O that was ragged bliss, that autumn. What I put my hand to, twisted of itself. Beyond astonishment, I did and did. Would lie but barely in the white of dawn. Wake new-inspired. Rise and work, outdoing what outdid the last, and of that latest making least again, transcending old with new. O Margaret, had I but lived, I would have lived so still: that whirling joy, that weaving steady hand.

Carriwitchets, Kit would say.

He'd come and go and bring his hard-won sticks of firing, his stock of provender, prigged rags; would sit and watch. Would coax me, bid me eat or sleep. I felt him sometimes at my shoulder: awed, exasperated, fearful. Dawning with delight. He kept the horn of leaves until it crumbled into dust.

I worked in what I had to hand, could gather. Sticks, stalks, leaves and stones. All found, unbound and scattering after. I was profligate as frost, as fern. As autumn, lavish, that does set a tree, a wood of trees, ablaze: a thousand thousand tongues to speak one word. As curious as nature's self, whose rarest work is secretest, embow'ring stars within bright clouds of stars, and seed in seed.

It was the raspberries began it.

In that cup of imbers did I spell thy blood: nine drops that would unbind my lady's will of thee. Set time going in her very stronghold. Yet I made no breach for thee in her shrewd hedge, but set a riddle for thyself alone. I would not have thee ride another's soul away. Walk barefoot, bloodfoot, if needs must: not use another creature, no, not Morag's dog, as I did Kit.

For the rest, 'twas winding spells, thyself thy clew. End and journeying and end, all rounded in a ball. Thine A and O.

Yet was I naked to the sky. I had no studied craft, no witchery, against my mother's furies, that would fall and rend. No roof.

In weaving of the garland, I had whispered secrets with that seely witch, that green unhallowed Malykorne. *No hallows until hallows,* she had said. As she, so I would be unhoused until her sister waked and hunted. Annis. If I could but win to Hallows—

So it came to stones. I strove, as Kit did, only to go on, to live and keep us until then. I had a garnet ring to stand for thee, that was a child's. I wish thou couldst have had it. Eight stones clustering about a ninth, a knot of seeds of blood. Much like the pomegranate I once found, that split and spilt within my hand. The riddle ring for Kit. And for myself, a ring like rain on gossamer, like cobwebs bright with dew. Nine Weaving. With my absence in't, the stone of Perseis I'd lost. Not wandering, but a falling star: astonishing and gone.

Her rings were woven in her fantasies. Her trash. One slid along a blade of grass, a small ring for her fingertip, a knot of drops of blood; another dangled from a scarlet thread, like rain in gossamer.

"Thea. Are there others?"

"Three. I have them safe." And showed her hand.

She would not give them over, though he begged and ranted, reasoned and cajoled, ah, coaxed her as he would a moonsick child to leave her toys. Her babywork. Alas, her wits waned even as she rounded. A greensick girl, and breeding. "Thou'rt worn, dear heart, beyond thy strength. Shouldst have a featherbed, a woman by thee. Physick."

"Wilt take them of me sleeping?"

"No," he said. "Not ever." And he came and knelt by her, he stroked her urchin head, he rubbed her nape. Inside his shirt, thrice-knotted round his wrist, the serpent of his cunning sleeked and shone. What's done is done, he thought. I rue me of that cheat. "Ah, that undoes."

He wanted her assent.

"For thine own sake, Thea."

Silence. And the twist and glittering of toys.

"Aye, scatter stones at scarecrow brats, leave none for thine own child."

Thea sat back on her heels, smudged her brow with her muddy wrist. "Ah, it comes."

Or softly, with his hands clasped round her belly. "Plum and stone." A rippling, as the round girl dived, down-dolphined in her eggshell ocean. "Sweet my love, thy lass wants nurture. Curds and cream. And swaddling. Thou hast not a clout for her."

At last, beyond all patience, starved and crazed with fear for them, he cracked her fist, uncurled her fingers from her hoard. Stone inward, she had worn them. Wore their imprint still, like Annis' kiss.

She had not cried out. He stood appalled; yet could not stay at that: put down the rings, caress the stone-bruised hand, so rudely forced. Could not undo.

"Thea?"

"As it must be."

He went out.

The door was warped with rain, white-molded. Margaret pushed until it gave upon an empty room, a tower that a storm had wracked. Bare muted walls, smashed glass; and in the naked window, for the first time, sea-blink. O. For a time she gazed at it and wondered; then she turned. Naught else but a daw's nest down the chimney, scattered sticks and trash. She bent and stirred it; she unwove. Smashed eggshells. Sticks and mutes. A key. A pebble. And a bent black ring. She thumbed it, rubbed it in her apron, peering at the outworn letters. This way and that in the wintry light. All gone but a word. *Lightwode.*

A voice in the air said, "Margaret."

That voice she knew; had heard it, ravelled with the wind, the sea. Not always. Since her doll was burnt, her dark-browed lulling nurse—O Norni—taken to her death. 'Twas now and nowhere, like a gossamer, at first: a glint and gone. Was now her galaxy. Her ground. As tangled in her thought as roots in earth, that flower seldom, yet inhere. But never until this aloud. *Is't you?*

"Thy daemon. Thou hast found the last, the lost star of the Nine, and overlooked. The one too quick for the eye."

Dusk. Late autumn, toward Hallows. Headlong on the road between Cold Law and Soulsgrave Hag, Kit hurtled. Three rings clenched in his right hand, thrust deep within his pocket; shame and fury at his heels. He knew not where he went. To Annis. Or to town. What town? Blind desperate, and pinched with argument and care, intent as a cat at kindling, he knew not where he was. The same place, always, the faster he ran. Round went the millstone, and over turned the wheel. *No bread, she has no bread. I had to. Anything they'd get. Bread, firing. One now, the others one by one. Bread, firing, a baby's coats. Ah, fool, a flock of sheep, a sheepwalk.* Fell and mutton, fleece and milk. He saw their lass run barefoot on the sward. Red hair, like fires on the hills. And round again: *no bread.*

He was at the crossroads before he saw the gang. A cronying of crows. Too late, he was among them. A slouching spade-faced man, whiteheaded, all in black, greenblack and broken swagger, like a swung cock at a fair. A gallows poll, that head, like hemp unravelling. Three trulls a-dangle at his heels. They fleered at Kit; they jostled. Cawed. A black mort, with a blue and scornful eye, her breasts at her kerchief bare and bruised. "Here's game," she said. "A goslin," said a pale and sluttish drab. Pissed petticoats and trodden shoes. And Maudlin-drunk, or mad. He swung. A ranting, taunting, roaring girl, a striding and a ride-moon doxy in a soldier's cap and feather, with his long sword buckled at her side. Red shoes.

Tighter still, he clenched his hand. His knife. He'd left his knife.

He made to pass by.

"Lightwood?"

Kit walked on.

"Heard tell thou was asking at Jack Daw." Almost, he turned. "For a fiddle."

Daw had it out for him; he drew the bow. And at that wauling sound, Kit's soul was snared. He turned and looked. Old and curious, far older than his own had been; rubbed shining as a fallen chestnut, newly split from its green burr. It had a carven woman's head. He yearned for it. *A trade,* he told himself: *not bread but years of bread.* A livelihood. He slipped two rings from off his fingers, deep within his coat; held out a third. White-gemmed. Like fleeces heavy with the dew. "Fair trade."

"What's this? Cuckoo-spit?" said Daw. "That, thy long knife, and a knock at thy vixen. I's a fancy to red hair."

"White-faced bitch is breeding," said Cap-and-Feather. "Maggot spied."

"She's a tongue," said Black Mort. "Can use it."

Jack Daw fleered. "I like a brave bellyful. Stir pot wi' my flesh hook and mek brat dance."

Kit spat. "Crows eat thee. Cock and eyes."

"They do," said Jack Daw, smiling.

Kit tried to shoulder past, but the doxies mobbed him, like crows at an owl by daylight. Jack Daw plucked at the fiddle. "Thou has strings for it, and all." His fingers at its neck and belly. "Owt else in yon placket?" Kit's face gave him away. He knew it. Daw twanged a string. "Done, is it? Say, two rings." He watched hope flicker. "Two rings. And thou serve yon nest o' crows—ah, they gape for it. Now. Here. I like a play."

"No," said Kit. "No more."

The drabs were all about him, taunting, lifting up their petticoats. White belly and black joke. Craws wi' beards. Against all his will, Kit felt a stirring. And a sickening. Hobthrust rose and danced. He stared. A black scut, and a shitten fleece. Old ling.

Rustbrown, and the red blood trickling down by her knee.

A cruel hand caught his wrist, bent backward. Wried his arm round his back until the socket started and the cold sweat sprang. No breaking Jack Daw's hold. Sinewy as yew, he was, inexorable. The voice was wasp honey. "Come, then. A bargain. For t' sake o' that night's game thy dam once gave me. Salt and sweet, insatiable. A blue-eyed witch." Doubt and horror. Daw touched his cheek, mock gently; bent and whispered in his ear. "How cam'st thou by my face?" Kit swayed. In that brief slackening, the old man knocked him backward, winded, to the ground. Cap-and-Feather pinned his arms and Daw knelt on his shoulder, set a knife across his throat. "Where's thy vixen earthed?"

Clack! goes the old year and the new year tumbles down.

Kit turned his face. Shut his lips.

"By my lady's name, it will go ill with thee."

Skirts about her waist, the Black Mort straddled him; she squatted and undid his breeches flap. "Here's a knocking i't cellar. Here's a bird flies up."

Pissabed danced wildly, she whirled and wobbled in the road, like a slowing, sleeping top.

Cap-and-Feather chanted. "*The wren, the wren, the king of all birds . . .*"

"Caught i't furze," said Black Mort. She spat between thumb and fingers. Laid on.

Kit gasped.

"*Although he is little, his family is great . . .*"

"Wring it neck," said Pissabed.

"Darkmans and glimmer," said Jack Daw. "My lady bids. Then do."

A voice from somewhere cried, "Hang craws!"

"Craws!" answered from the hills. And all the dogs of Soulsgrave took it up.

"Cut," said Jack Daw. "Prig and run."

Crack! Blind lightning blast, a whirl and burring through his skull.

No more.

Kit woke, rolled naked in a ditch. *Fiddle's wracked,* he thought. *Where's here?* Himself was lash and scratch and throbbing, ice and fever, and a dizzy thud behind his eye. *Dragged through whins,* he thought. *And tumbled down a bank. That green girl at my bow's end. At the dance. That horseman?* His hand moved gingerly. No, his good hand—one was lame. Cracked bagpipes in his side. A broken crown. Wet blood on his mouth. Not his. From Cap-and-Feather. From her other mouth. Remembering, he retched and strangled. Nothing in his gut to puke.

Nothing left.

No clothes.

No rings.

And at his wrist, no braid of Thea's. Sharper still than all his hurts, he felt that ring of absent fire.

Gone.

Whin said in the dark, "Went naked back?"

"I robbed a scarecrow of his coat." A clear night mocking him. The Hanged Lad ranting on Cold Law. As naked as himself. They'd left him with one broken shoe, in haste. Derision.

"So yer done that. Ta'en rings."

"I did."

"Lost braid."

"I did." That desperate searching in the dark. He'd had a crazed hope it was somehow lost, not stolen for an end. That he would find it, tossed aside as naught. In a small voice, he said, "I didn't tell her. That I had it. That it was gone."

"Round thy wrist? Had she not see'd it?"

"No. I thought. We'd not—we hadn't lain together. Not since harvest." He would not force her crazy innocence, not take his will of her. And yet he had.

Long silence.

"At the stones," said Kit. "At Imber Beck. That kiss she gave me was the first time. Of her will." He drew one ragged breath. "That other, freely. Not her love." He was crying. "One other time. The last. I never knew it was. I never knew."

Waking in the night. Hard ground. And Thea with her back to him, within his curve, and cradling his hand against her breast. Like a child her doll. He felt his ring there, on a thread; he felt her quick heart tap and tap, like a branch at a windowpane; he felt the round drum of her belly thud and kick. She smelled of smoke and Thea. Not asleep.

She spoke, not drowsily, but low. "Kit. I do love thee. Know that."

Blood in my lady's place. Blood on her smock. It would not come out.

Margaret hurried through the dark and winding hallways, down toward her room. No sanctuary there, no more than in a hare's slight form, the impress of her crouch; but licit. Blood, suddenly. A spattering of drops, no more. Herself she'd washed and washed, no trace or tinge of it was left. Flung the water from her sill. But her smock. Would find her out. Bury it? The dogs would out. Burn it? No fire but in my lady's study. Up the chimney? Blood will out. Ah. Cut herself and mingle. Knife. She had a knife.

Softly now. She lifted the latch.

Morag and my lady waited with a rod of juniper. "Straying, and thy book undone. Come, Madam."

Margaret curtsied, rose. "My lady."

"Closer, girl. I am no basilisk."

The hand with its great ring held the face: a sere unshaking hand; a white face, like a scrap of paper to be written over, like a mirror to be filled. "There is something of my daughter in you."

"Aye, the whore," said Morag.

"Alike in straying," said my lady. Still she held her gaze. "Chastise her."

"Thy vixen, Madam." And when Margaret made no move, the servant took her bed-gown, pushed her smock to her armpits. Held her wrists and bent her back across the kist, her new breasts and her belly all disclosed, a gibbous moon. Thrust her legs apart.

Slow blood.

My lady spoke, a cold still fury in her voice. "And who undid that knot?"

Morag said, "Not art, I'll warrant, but the worm in her. Your glass is carrion."

"Is of my adamant. A blank, but that I grave her with my icon and my law. And offscum else: yet will transmute."

"Or spoil, as did her dam. Your poppet. Waiting on the stars."

Whiter still, my lady's face. "It will be done, and presently. By this moon's dark."

A catechism then.

"What was thy mother?"

"Your daughter," Margaret said.

"A whore. Which is?"

She knew not. "One who strays?"

"'Twill do. Puts carrion in Annis' place. Which is?"

"We name it not."

"That errant part, wherein thy mother did betray me."

"Crow's fee," said Morag, pinching. "And the vixen's earth."

Margaret endured. The crow's contemptuous, efficient hands; my lady's avid eyes. And even in her dread and terror, sick with shame, she thought, *Like Thea?*

Then the rod, and no more thought.

They left her on the floor, amid the fallen needles, the scattering of twigs.

My lady turned at the door. "It is time thou learned thy glass."

A key snicked in the lock.

For a long time she lay weeping in her dabbled smock. Blood with hidden blood. No voice. She heard no voice.

Kit hurried, huddled in his flapping coat. It would snow by dark. Black moor, white sky; but knit, the whiteness tangled in the ground as rime, the blackness branching up as trees. A scant wood, leafless now. Sloes, rowans, all gone by. Firing. He bent to get sticks. It still was light; but stiffening towards dusk. Ravenwards. And Thea waiting, pacing in their roofless shieling, by the ashes of a hearth. She made cairns of stones. She did and she undid. He dared not leave her; they would starve without. No sticks to burn; no bread. A handful of dampish meal, half acorns, bitter as the wind.

The braid was gone. He saw it glinting everywhere.

There. In that bush. He stumbled toward it.

Gone.

He stood. He would have wept, if he'd remembered how. It was all too much, too much. He stood. Dazed, cold, defeated, sleepless, starved, lightheaded, lousy. Fizzing with lice. His feet recalled him, white cold, wet; he'd blundered. Cat ice.

Looking down, he saw a tump in the marshy ground: a spring, turfed over, housed with three great stones. Kneeling, he touched the lintel of the low door, lichened; found the blind runes graven in the rock. *Help us*, he said to darkness, spinning out a thread of silver. *Lighten her, my love.* He touched the water. No one. In the wood beyond, a stormcock sang. No solace here. He rose. On a tree hung knots of rags, frayed, faded to the blue of a winter sky. Another sky, some other now or then, caught here. And in among the ravellings of sky, a rag of iris. Thea's scarf.

Kit. Margaret. Ah, you do not hear me. She is gone until her time comes round; she cannot let you in. No hallows anywhere. Not yet.

At the corners of their shieling, raised on cairns, Kit saw her barricade: spiked crowns and spirallings of ice, frail caltrops. Morning stars. He dropped his sticks and ran. From wall to ashes, wall to wall, he found her, pacing and clenching. Blood on her lip. Then something wrenched her, as a laundress would a rag.

"Thea. How long—?"

She caught his sleeve, his coat, as on a breaking ship. Another wrench and shudder. "Kit." Like burning wax, her face: it warped and ran. Almost Thea leapt from it, as flame from a candle, blowing out. "Undo it."

"Love?"

"Undo the knot," said Thea. "That braid you took of me. Undo it."

Still he stood.

"To let the child be born. I cannot lighten else. I cannot meet them."

O sweet hallows on us. "Gone," he said.

"What?"

"Taken. Gone."

"Ah no." A great cry, twisting.

"Thea—"

She whirled on him, white-fiery. "Run. Now."

"I'll not leave thee. I will not."

"For a woman's help. I die else." Wrench and leap. "Now. Get thee hence."

He turned at the threshold. "O my heart's love."

"Go."

No time, no time.

He ran.

Whin dreamed of ravens. An ill-chancy dream, an omen. Then a telling. A trance. She saw a girl still barely living, filthy, naked on the icy ground. Her childbed. Saw the stubble of red hair, the new milk seeping from her breasts. The glazing eyes. A witch stood watching her, a corbie perched upon her hand. She stroked its beard, she ruffled it; it preened the bracelet at her wrist, of braided fire. *Ah, the sweetest morsels for my chuck, my Morag,* said the witch. *The crow's fee and the eyes.* Down it flapped, it picked the tidbits. Still the girl breathed, the blood ran, the death cry rattled in her throat. Then the witch called down her crows. They clustered at the bloody womb. They tore.

Whin woke yelling.

Still Kit slept on. He twitched and whimpered. Whin sat up and shook with rage. She cursed the raven and the witch; she cursed the knife that loosed the child, the braid, the shears that cut it. Cursed her master mistress Brock who had entangled her in this atrocity, to see and see and see. Change nothing.

Then up she got, and ran down to the shingle, to the water's edge. She'd drown the soulbag, wash the ashes from her face. Walk inland. She would be no more death's journeyman. Running, she tore her rings off, death by death, to hurl them in the sea.

Brock stood between salt water and the strand. "I'd not do that," she said.

"Could yer not have let her live?" cried Whin. "Not see'd to it that she went wi' child, smick smack, afore she'd much as bled? Thou meddlesome. And all for nowt. A tale of Ashes."

"It's done, and long since done," said Brock.

"And nowt to do wi' me."

"And all to do." The sea swashed, swashed. "There's bairn."

O thank hallows. There, a woman with a lantern. Hale and canny, she looked: brisk, in pattens and a hood. Kit caught her apron. "My lass. Please. Needs a woman by her." And she raised her candle, looking through him with a smile would scoop apples, a shankbone smile—I know two of that—and turned away. Up the fell.

He ran after. "Pity on us. For the love—"

Another crossed the trod. A sonsy girl, a goosedown girl and slatternly, who bore a flat candlestick, as if she tumbled up to bed. "Miss——? Can lead me to a midwife? My lass——" She blinked and giggled, turned away.

Another and another still. All with candles, all the girls and women of the dale end, lating on the hills. Now there, now elsewhere in the cloudy dark, as if they danced *Nine Weaving*. Round they turned like children in a game, a-bob and wheeling, in and out, through bushes and through briars. They were seeking with their candles—*lambs at Hallows? Birds' nests?* They were sought.

Hide fox, and all after.

As in a dream, Kit ran from one to the next, imploring, and they turned from him. None would speak. They shook their heads: some smiling, some pitying or shocked or scornful; some averting their eyes.

A weeping man, half naked, in a Bedlam coat.

One tossed a coin.

A knot of them, their backs turned. Gossips. Blindly, hopelessly, he touched a sleeve. "I beg of you——" A stone. A ring of them, like crones in cloaks. But one stone turned, the hood fell back. It was a woman with a darkened lantern, waiting, gazing out: like a sailor for landfall, like a scryer at eclipse. He was a gull at her masthead, a dog at her skirts: no more.

Down the fell, a light went dark. Another, upwind, and a girl knelt, doing up her shoe latch, looking round. And yet another, pinning up her hair. All waiting.

One by one, the candles all went out.

But one.

A child this woman, sheltering a dying candle in a tin. She brooded fiercely on it, willed it. In its doubtful glow, her face was rapt and shining. Awed. Her first time on the fells? Her flame lurched sideways, righted, leapt again. The last?

From up the fell, a voice called, *Ashes! We's Ashes!*

O the last. As her candle flickered out, she whirled for joy.

Another and another voice took up the cry, like vixens, greenfire in their blood. Hallooing to the dark of moon. *Ashes!* They were running now, a rout of women, whirling torches in the kindled dark. And still the child wheeled, giddy, in among the stones, the only silence. *Ashes!*

And alone, but for the ragman. She took to her heels.

I tell this to the air; yet I must speak.

My mother fed me to her crows, she burned my bones and scattered them; my braided hair she keeps. By that bright O of fire did she call me back from life to Law; by those shrewd knots torment me. She would not undo. Seven weeks she watched me naked, travailing from Hallows until Lightfast eve; then Morag's knife did let thee crying from my side, and I was light.

Margaret knelt and pried a stone up in the hearth; she dug. From under it, she took a ring, a clew of thread. A key.

Turning back from the stones, Kit saw the fire at their fold and ran, calling, stumbling on his whiteblind feet. He saw the ravens falling from the sky. One, another, turning women as they fell. They were clear as night, and starless; where their wings beat back the thronging air was cloud and fire. As they touched the earth, it whitened, widening from their talons of the frost. They shrank as small as stones.

Kit fell. A thrawn hand caught him, and another, and a throng. Horned feet kicked through him like a pile of leaves; they scattered him like sparks. "Out!" he cried and struggled, held and haled. A torch was thrust at his face. There were witches all round him: men and crones, in black and rags of black, and goat fells, stiff with blood. They bore a cage of thorns and withies, hung with bloody rags and hair, with flakes of skin: the palms of children's hands, like yellow leaves, a-flutter.

Empty.

"Here's a fool," said one, a warlock.

"A soul," another said. A hag, all pelt and bones. The soulstones clattered in her hank of hair, with knops of birdskulls, braided through the orbits.

"A soul, a soul," the guisers cried.

Kit fought against their hands. "You let me go."

"You let us in," they chanted. "Let us in your house of bone."

And a man like a staghead oak, a blasted tree, cried, "Room!"

A tall witch with a great black fleece of hair flung back came striding through. It was a man, pale and sneering in a woman's robe, his strong arms naked to the shoulders, dark with blood. Death's midwife. Or a blasphemous Ashes?

"Annis!" they cried. "Annis wakes."

He prodded Kit with his staff. "What's this? A blindworm?"

"For your breakfast, my lady."

"For your bed."

"'Tis Ashes' bawd."

The stick against his throat had silenced him, half strangled him. He saw a black wood rising; it was leaved with faces. Thronged with crows.

"Bags I," said a voice.

The crowd parted. Kit saw a figure in a leathern cap, a coat of matted fleece. Ashes of juniper, a cloud of ashes at his eyes and lips. It whispered in his ear. "Thou's not to die for her," said Brock. "Thy lass did say."

"No," he tried to say. His mouth was full of ashes, he was blind with snow.

"Now," said Brock. "An thou will." And kissed his mouth.

He felt a tremor, a wind in his bones. She covered him like snow. Beneath the sway of stars, he felt the green blades pierce his side, the awned heads bow and brindle in the reaping wind. A sickle gathered him, a sheaf. Time threshed. His chaff was stars, his bones were blackness, strung and shining. A sword, a belt of stars. A crow called.

Then he knew no more.

Hallows morning.

Kit awoke on the hillside in the falling snow, all white and shades of white, but for the black unkindly stones. After a time, he could stand, could hobble. Halt and daz-zled with the snow, and inch by crippled inch, he made his way back to their shieling. Knowing what he'd find. Dread knowing.

Gone.

And more than gone. Pulled stone from stone, and torched and trampled in a great wide circle, salt with snow. Cold out. All her toys.

"Go," she'd said. And so he'd gone.

He would have died for her.

He fell to his knees where their hearth had been, the ashes at the heart of ashes. Nothing left: all taken, lost, betrayed. But there, a something like a wren's dulled eye, its dead claw, in the snow. A ring. Not hoarded, so not lost. He scratched for it, and found the other; turned them in his fingers. Blood and tears.

Margaret knelt amid cold ashes, drawing mazes on the hearth. They'd left no book to her, no ink, no candle: whips of juniper to gaze on, and the drowsy wine. My lady's glass, which was black adamant: she could not break.

And so she did what she had left to her: undid. Ate nothing they had given her, but dwindled out an orange she had kept, a heel of bread; drank snow from her window sill. She worked by scant starlight at the puzzle of her cage. Scrawled figures with a stick of charcoal; rubbed them out, redrew them, all in black upon the hearthstone, what was white with snow without: the labyrinth of yew and stone. If she did journey, she could not rub out.

So then: for her door, she had the jackdaw's key; then came the maze she would unriddle and the hedge of thorn, the wintry sea. The world. Beyond that, she could see no way. A ship? But only to have touched the sea, washed Morag from her skin; to glimpse a world unbounded by my lady's walls. She set herself to reach the sea. The garden was configured as the starry sky; that much she knew, had read her book beside the white girl crowned with leaves, with leaves and flowers in her stony lap. And water running down and down her face: it wept for her, who could not weep. Bound Ashes, in a box of yew.

She knew now what she was; what she was for. *A hole to fill,* said Morag truffling. *Naught else.* Yet had my lady smiled and pinched. *A limbeck. See, how sweetly she distills.* Had kissed: how scornfully, and yet had lingered. It was almost a caress. The bracelet burned against her skin. *I have sent to fetch thee a rare dowry. Dishes for thy maiden banket; jewels for thy chain. Thy first shall be thy father's soul.*

For a long time afterward, Margaret had sat, and turned and turned the hidden cards.

O the Nine, ah yes, the Nine would come and carry her away. She heard the clatter of their wings; she saw them, children of the rising light, like swans. Her heart rose up. Being mute, she could not cry to them; they lighted, children as they touched the earth, but a glory of their wings about them, like a snow. *Sister, come with us,* they said. *I will,* said Margaret's heart, *but have no wings. No ship.* And turned it up: that Ship whose mast is green and rooted, flowering as stars. And then bright Journeyman, the thief.

A rattle in the keyhole. A black stick on the floor. She'd risen to it, curtsied, with the cards behind her: all in haste. But three had fallen from her lap like leaves; their tales had withered at my lady's glance. *See, thou hast overlooked the Tower. That takes all.* The witch had stooped for it, mock-courteous, and held it to her branching candle; dropped it burning to the floor. *And which next shall I take? Thy cockboat? Or thy nest of geese?* Her gaze schooled Margaret's; they would bind her if she flinched. *Thy choosing, Madam. It will make a game.*

The Hare. My lady's wrist was bare, no braid.

Aha, the Master Lightcock. Thou'rt seed of his, didst know? Shall watch him burn. And my sweet crow shall have his stones, to bait her dogs withal. Then she had signed to Morag with the box. *Undo.*

And after they had gone.

It seemed that someone else took over, swift and secret, while the old lost Margaret sat, dreaming in a drift of cards. *Thou timorous, thou creeping hodmandod,* she thought: *thou snail that tangles in her trail of dreams. Draw in thy tender horns? Thou liest between the thrush and stone.* That other self, herself, had thought of riding, light a horseman as the moon; her mantle of the flying silver, fleeting on the wind. But now her new shrewd voice said, *Shoes and stockings, stout ones. In that room with the sea-chests. Thou needs must walk. Will need the way.*

And so she sat, and drew what she remembered of the labyrinth, the doors.

"No ship," said Kit. "When thou didst come on me, and take me up from drowning, there had been no ship. No storm. I'd gone in after her."

"I know," said Whin. "But thou was not to follow her. Thy lass did spell for thee."

"Not drown," said Kit. "I know. I am for hanging in yon braid. That I did twist myself."

"What for?" said Whin. "Thou's never telled."

"To hold fast." Kit clasped his hands, unclasped. "Ah, not to Thea—what I loved in her I held like moonlight in a sieve, I riddled rainbow. 'Twas a falling star, that nowhere is and yet is light. No, what I braided was a face she turned to me, a mask: that lady who did run away with me, did overturn her fortune for my sake. Mine own. The moon that turned and turned from me, yet bent within mine orb. Thought I. So kept that vanity, that she did shear. At first." A silence. "And after, I would keep myself, as I had thought I was. Would be. That Kit who called down witches with his airs. Not Thea's bow-stick, but a one who played." He bit his lip; looked up. "And she owed me a fiddle, I did tell myself. No matter; yet it rubbed. And at the last—moon blind me—I could not endure to tell her of my folly."

Whin passed the cup. "What now?"

"If not for Thea's sake, yet I will die, as all must die. And I would live ere then." A something lightened in his face. "And see our lass."

Asleep. Thy cards lie scattered on the floor, in knots and wheels, and painted gatherings. I cannot turn them. There, the Ship and the Rattlebag, the Hanged Lad and the Nine. Burnt Eldins. Ashes. And the Crowd of Bone: that fiddle that the old year plays of Ashes, of her bones. They strung it with her long bright hair. Itself and all alone, it sings, its one plaint always: of her death. Sings truth in riddles.

In a tale, thou Margaret wouldst brave my lady, even in her glass. Wouldst find my nine bones that were left; unbraid my hair and string the fiddle for thy father's hand to play. And thou wouldst dance to it, his daughter and my death. And down the witch would tumble, burning, in her iron shoes.

But I have sung my tale. Unstrung myself. Have told out all my thread but this, the endknot: they were always one, the braid that bound us and the strings that spoke.

Thou canst not hear the ghost now, Margaret: thou art child no more.

But thou art Margaret, thyself: no witch's blade can rive that knot intrinsicate we knit for thee, of love and pain. Thou art the daughter of my heart's blood and my soul. Bone of my bone, and heartstrings of my heart. To Kit I would restore thee: not his fiddle but my heart, translated. Not for him to play, but thou to dance for him, to sing thine own tale always, light and dark.

"So," said Whin. "Yer off."

They stood by her coble, sunk in snow to the black rim, as a mussel shell in sand. A white morning, toward Kindle Wake.

"I'll set thee on," said Kit.

Together, they dug out her boat and laded it; they pushed it down the blackweed shingle, salt and frost, to the water's edge. A wave crisped his boot. But only one. The tide was turning outward.

They clipped hard, clapped back and shoulder.

Kit said, "Thou ask at my daughter."

"And thou at my son," said Whin.

"I will that. Farewell."

Then they pushed her black coble into the sea. As it slipped, Whin leapt the gunwales; locked oars. It rode the swell, it hove. The next wave took her out. Kit watched from the shore. Whin rowed easily, strongly, turning only just to check her heading. Luneward. And to Law.

So they parted.

Kit took up his scant gear, new and raw. A knife, a cloak, a cookpot, and a flint and steel. Grey worsted stockings and a harden shirt. A stone in his pocket, with a leaf on it. He set out on his journeying; turned inland, in the snow.

I am walking, to the knees in earth: long-toed, reaching, rough of knees; gnarled wrists knotted, flowering at fingers' ends. They see, though I am blind. White, wet, my petals fall and fleck—like moons, like childing moons—my cold black bark. My lap is full of snow. In winter do I bear the misselbough, the Nine, entangled in my crown.

I was Ashes.

I am rising from the dark, and rooted; I am walking from my mother's dark.

My green leaves speak in season, in their turn, unfolding word by word till all is green and silent, lost in green, unselved. The green is wordless, though it spells the earth, it sings the wind. Rooted, I dance, unbraided to the wind. And then by leaf and leaf, I turn, take fire and prophesy. They spill, a tale of leaves, of endless leaves. My green is no one, everywhere, as wood as love; my age is selving. In my nakedness, I crouch and listen.

See, where I am split, my belly seamed. A curved blade caught me; I was reft. Yet I do bear, I ripen, plum and stone. They hang, my sloes, world-dark as winter nights, abloom with souls. They fall and sunder, worm and root.

I stand among a grove of girls. A garland, woven all of Ashes.

Touch my bark and I am elsewhere, though my lyke is earthfast, here and now. Break wood and I will burn. Do you see me? Now and nowhere, turning nowhere, telling light. But I am not my tongues. I rise with my sisters, woven in our dancing, scarved in light. We are pleached in an endless knot, an alley, in a cloud of stars: a hey as white as hag.

All ways led upward: not a door would let her to the wicket gate, the garden, to the maze that she would solve. She'd brought the clew to measure it; had sopped her manchet in the drowsy wine to brave the dogs withal. A hard frost glittering on snow:

she'd hoped to leave small trace. Thin shoes, no mantle. She had only what was hidden left to take: the key, the clew, the ring. Her ravaged cards. Nine burnt.

No door. And higher still. A window? Could she get a wren's-eye view of it? Could draw it then. *Thou mole*, she thought. *'Tis black of night.* Moondark, so my lady and her raven hunted souls, and thought she slept. How long until they came to wake her? Found her gone? Dread struck her like an ice-axe to the shattered heart. *Go on*, she said, in darkness. All among her shards. *Old mole. 'Tis nowhere here. Get on.* Lightless, breathless with enormity, Margaret wound the stair.

She pushed through a last door, out onto the leads in snow. *O heavens.* Round she wheeled, within the greater wheel of stars.

The wood above.

That she had forfeited. Pasteboard and precious tawdry, turned celestial. All burning, unconsumed.

She'd never seen the stars at once; had learned them from her slit of window, from my lady's iron hoops, her brazen spheres. Her stones that hopped from perch to wire, dish to wire, like a cage of singing birds. But these were glorious: they flamed amazement in her eyes.

Giddy with the sky, she turned, until her breath had blinded her. Then she wiped her glazy spectacles, and stood and stargazed.

Knot by shining knot, she made them out—the Nine, the Hallows Tree, the Ship—yet wondered even in her wonderment. *But why a Ship? Why not a ladle or a swan? Why not bare stars, themselves? And why Nine Weaving? There are stars in clouds of stars, as if I breathed on frost. And which is the lost star of the Nine, amid so many?* She looked for the sisters, jumping edgewise in her slanted sight. Ah, she wished for those spectacles she'd found and left, that made the candle huge. They tangled in and out of focus, in a country dance, a hey. Five, a cloud of silver, three, four. Gone again.

And one bright planet threading through the maze. Like a knife round an apple, all askance. Or like a lantern through a labyrinth. *O yes.* Clasped hands flying to her lips: she bit them, so as not to cry out loud for joy. And ever after, when the Nine were named, she tasted rime on rough wool, and the oil of orange in her nails. *Yes.* The garden was the quickset stars. The key was errant: Perseis, and in her night house, at the wake of Souls. The Crowd of Bone. Those stars ascendant at her mother's birth.

She saw the way.

Down and round she ran, still downward with the falling spindle of the stairs, that twirled the heavens to a clew of light. That other chain, the necklace that she wore, broke loose in running, whirled and scattered on the steps. She left it as it fell. As later, in the time to come, she would outrun the world of her begetting, scatter it behind like leaves: her glass would crack my lady's heavens, would unstring the stars.

Margaret ran on.

Fuming Woman

Alan DeNiro

Under the trapeze, there is always a secret trap door that allows the circus's employees to escape during a mob. It is written on the door in white stenciling: Enter in case of a mob. And people do. The gnomes, customarily, dig a tunnel from the door to a safe place "some distance away" before a circus takes root on a city block, usually on an abandoned car lot.

The mob usually occurs when a drunk tries to steal a fermented beverage from one already incapacitated from the beverage. Children never attend circuses anymore because of this, and I tell you that is a shame.

It is a nice night for a circus. The mosquitoes have burrowed holes in the big top canvas. An elephant is reciting Tennyson, punctuated by Dumbo's-Mom-like cries of empathy. This moves the crowd. This is probably the highlight—the old male elephant pretending he's female and becoming a compassion vacuum. No one's dead yet. The ants have begun their motorcycle escapades. The ringmaster holds up an iconoscope, which transmits a projection of the ants on their ant-sized motorcycles. They are doing wheelies. Most colorful for the audience are the Taco Bell logos pigmented on the ants' safety jackets.

And the trapeze woman—and here she is, the story, really—is limbering, for she's on next. Her family emigrated from an imaginary country when she was still in the womb. A snap of her ankle could snap a neck. And has. There is that power; do not think this is amusing or that I'm being a fuddy-duddy.

The ants finish, putter off; the ringmaster's smile is coked out and incredibly genuine—he misses the children—and the fight in the crowd, over alcohol, begins. The whiskey bottles drop, and gnomes deep underground quiver because they know what's next.

The woman climbs the ladder. She's blocked out from her mind the two men—bankers both, still in their funerary suits—stepping around the downed man with a whiskey bottle still in his hands. Suddenly he leaps up and surprises the bankers. Fisticuffs ensue. How are we to know what he's thinking? The woman doesn't generally bathe forty-eight hours before a circus, and this is the circus's second day. There is a musk, then. The odor drifts over the crowd, which is trying for the moment to pay attention to the crux of the woman's face and not the drying-machine effect of the fight, making everything hotter.

The ringmaster doesn't give her name. She jumps, catches the bars as one banker breaks a bottle and places it onto the other's face. The other steps on the downed man's stomach. Vomit arises. The woman whips her neck forward and leaps again. She's gained momentum. She catches the higher bar with her teeth. The crowd is despondent—they *want* to like her, but there is so much else competing for their entertainment dollar. She's losing internal performance evaluations—faces she can't see mostly—because she hasn't burst into flames. Or because she isn't naked, or doesn't wear a Taco Bell jumpsuit, like the plucky li'l ants.

Fighting spreads. A husband starts hitting his wife with cotton candy. The two bankers who started the fight are both dead, but their spirits kick and punch at anything in their way, which is a lot.

The trapeze woman twirls to hold herself by the knees and catches the next bar with her belly button.

No one notices except for the ringmaster, who is bawling, because he's never seen her more paradoxical and beautiful, swinging from the high big top by her belly button. If there wasn't about to be a riot, and seventy to-be-dead, the papers would have exclaimed "Woman Holds on to Trapeze with Belly Button!" But her timing, when right, is wrong.

The giant poles begin to sway with the weight of the assemblage pushing against it—the very foundation of the idea of a circus. There has to be a big top, an enclosure, or else the circus would bleed into the weekday, and we wouldn't want those "issues" on our streets.

The woman leaps again and holds on to the second-highest bar with her kidney. The ringmaster isn't watching at this point—he is ushering the performers into the special trapdoor. He is afraid to warn her, that if he distracts her, he will forever combust in hell, like the fuckhead who knocked on Coleridge's door when he was dreaming up "Kublai Khan."

Body kindled in sweat, she strains for the highest bar, plummeting up for dear life.

She holds on to it with her slightly ironic, melancholic disposition. Her hold, with this character trait, is tenuous at best. With her free hands, she begins pointing at those destroying the big top, slaying each other and the animals, including the stunt-ants. The mob got the ants. Her fingers are like saucers of hot pitch spilling from space, and rather than burning up in the multilayered atmosphere (a device created by God much like a big circus top made out of oxygen and nitrogen, designed to protect us from the cosmos and perhaps protect the cosmos from us), her attacks land. The rioting stops as each rioter feels the stigmata of the trapeze woman's rebuke on their cheeks. How embarrassing! Many of those still alive hold hands. The woman stops her performance, arcing to a stationary position, much like a child on a swing set who loses the push from her parent(s), parent(s) who wander off to do something more important, like pet a needy dog or put on a tie. The woman hangs there by only her irony and melancholy, thinking of her circus mates inside the escape tunnel, in flight away from her. She half-expects someone to reach up with a pole with a vinegar-soaked sponge.

"Shame on us!" the assemblage cries out as one, except for a young man in the cheap seats who discovers for the first time that he can give himself a blowjob. But that's ok; the woman doesn't mind.

Unfortunately, enough of her irony evaporates that its once firm grip on the trapeze bar is loosened! The woman falls, out of control, like a car chase, straight down.

Some jackanapes in the rioting have cut the safety net for later use as a hammock. All those assembled murderers cry no, no, we're sorry. But it's a little too late for mewling, isn't it.

The woman, rather than doing something foolish like hitting the ground, or even splatting her head against the mob trapdoor (*that* would have been ironic!), turns into a kind of vapor. By *a kind*, I mean she aligns her own atoms to pass through the other atoms blocking her way. She keeps falling—not all the way to China, but rather popping out in the ocean about fifty kilometers off the coast of Tasmania.

In the city she leaves: gnomes weep. Ringmasters pull out their dentures. Angry mobs the world over—even at football matches—give ten seconds of silence in her memory.

No, she thinks, I'm right here. I've been rescued by a seafood restaurant. I'm still a vapor. These people are lambs. This is apparently an island full of giant lobsters. Narwhal-sized. People dine on them on the beaches. Chainsaws wielded by strong waiters open the shells. They use me as a spritz on the tails of the lobsters. When I enter the atmosphere I evaporate and rain again. I'm an ecosystem. There is no such thing as a circus here. All along the beaches, the family dogs breathe my spritz. My vapor. I'm effervescent. People don't expect this. Fumed by me, the dogs start jumping higher than people! Someone from the seafood restaurant calls the papers. The dogs jump over and over, higher each time. What the fuck is happening to our dogs, the tourists say, snapping pictures. They don't realize I'm inside of them, fueling. From this distance, the giant lobsters about to be eaten look sad that they will die, and I will not. Soon the dogs will have to don masks, because the air gets thin up in the stratosphere. My cosmonauts. Memories become thinner. Voices too. No one can throw a frisbee that high. There are only the jumpers. The island of lobsters looks so tiny from the vantage point of a dog. In the flashing second when there is no up and no down, only the absence of motion. That moment of suspension is a tonic to the dog and I. There are no nets, no trapdoors, no cables, no ants, no canvas, no ticketholders. Nothing to hold on to. We begin, again, a fall.

Eight-Legged Story

Maureen F. McHugh

1. Naturalistic Narrative

Cheap pens. My marriage is not going to survive this. Not the pens—I bought the pens because no pen is safe when Mark is around; his backpack is a black hole for pens—so I bought this package of cheap pens, one of which doesn't work (although rather than throw it away, I stuck it back in the pen jar, which is stupid), and two of them don't click right when you try to make the point come out and then go back. It's good to have them, though, because I'm manning the phone. Tim, my husband, is out combing the Buckeye Trail in the National Park with volunteers, looking for my nine-year-old stepson, Mark. Mark has been missing for twenty-two hours. One minute he was with them, the next minute he wasn't. I am worried about Mark. I am sure that if he is dead, I will feel terrible. I wish I liked him better. I wish I'd let him take some of these pens. Not that Tim will ever find out that I told Mark he couldn't have any of these pens.

The phone rings. It's Mark's mother, Tina. "Hello?" she says, "hello, Amelia? Hello?" Her voice is thick with medication and tears. Tina is a manic-depressive and lives in Texas.

"Hi, Tina," I say. "No word yet."

"Oh God," Tina says.

Get off the line, I think. But I can't throw Mark's mother off the phone.

"Was he wearing his jacket?" she asks. She has asked that every time she's called. As if *she* ever noticed whether or not he had his jacket on.

"He did," I say, soothing. "He's a smart kid."

"He could have just turned his ankle," she says. "They'll find him." I offered this scenario a couple of hours ago, but she's forgotten I suggested it, and she thinks she is comforting me. I allow myself to sound comforted. She says she'll call back in an hour. I'm convinced he is drowned. I can see it; the glimmer of his white hands and face in the metallic water. I can't say it to anyone.

What will happen to my marriage? When a child dies, divorce is pretty common. Two people locked in their grief, unable to connect. But I won't grieve like Tim, and some part of me will be relieved. I'm honest with myself about this. The secret in our marriage will slowly reveal itself. He will learn that I didn't love Mark, and how can you love someone who didn't love your only son?

When I married Tim, Mark was only six. He was the child of a dysfunctional marriage. He was prone to angry outbursts. He was resentful. All they had were plastic glasses, and I bought cheap glass tumblers, but Mark didn't like them. He wanted "their" glasses. I made the dinners, and I hated the lime green plastic cups. I wanted to sit at a nice table.

It was a classic stepfamily drama. It's in the books. I compromised. I used the ghastly plates from his mother, the ones with country geese on them, but insisted on the glass tumblers. It was our family table, I explained. A mix of old and new, like our family. Mark hated everything I cooked. I used the same canned sloppy joe mix that his father had always used, and Mark sat at the table, a blond boy who was small for his age, crying silently into his sandwich. He hated sloppy joes.

His father couldn't stand to hear him cry that he was hungry. I sat on the bed in the master bedroom. Maybe I should have given in. It was hard to decide. He was six years old, and he didn't have a bedtime, didn't dress himself for school in the morning. He lay on the floor crying while I put his socks on. I made his father put him in bed at nine each night. Before we'd married, Mark had terrible headaches, so terrible that his father had taken him to the hospital and they'd done CAT scans. After we got married and we started eating at a regular time and he had a bedtime, the headaches disappeared.

I should have given in on the green glasses. But why should I have had to eat at an ugly table, when he had taken all the joy out of the dinner anyway? When it was always a screaming battle? What was I supposed to do? When was it important that he have his own things, and when was it important that he not get his own way?

The phone doesn't ring. That's good, because when it does, it will be Tina.

When they say they have found his body, I will comfort Tim. I'll just comfort him with my hands. I'll just be there. Not talking. Just there. Like something out of *Jane Eyre*. Actually, I'll get impatient, because I finally have him to myself and yet Mark will have him. You can't compete with the dead. I always thought that if we were married long enough, eventually we would get that time that people without children get when they are first married. We'll be fifty-year-old newlyweds going out to see a movie on a whim and not worrying about child care.

I can't think about any of it.

This is the last moment of my marriage. Or maybe my marriage is already gone.

I have the sudden urge to get up and go out and get in my little beat-up eight-year-old Honda that I bought with my own money, and drive. I took the freeway to my first job, working in an amusement park for the summer when I was sixteen. I hated the job, and I hated to be home. I used to get on the freeway headed north and think that I could just keep going, up to Detroit, across to Windsor, Ontario and up to Quebec, where I would get a job at a fast food place and learn to speak French.

The doorbell rings. It's Annette, the neighbor down the street. I like Annette, although I have always suspected that she disapproved of Mark and, therefore, of Tim and me as parents. Annette has two daughters, and when we all moved onto the street her daughters were five and seven while Mark was eight. Mark and the boys next door run around in hunter camouflage playing war and spying in windows.

She sits and has a cup of tea. Annette is a working mother. Here in the suburbs there are working mothers and there are housewives and there is me. I'm an architectural landscaper, and I work out of my home.

"Funny that Tim is the one out wandering the wilderness," I say to Annette.

"Yeah?" Annette says.

"Well," I say, "Tim hates the outdoors, hates yard work, hates plants." Tim is an engineer. Computers are his landscapes.

She laughs a little for me. "You're holding up really well, you know that?" she says.

Of course I'm holding up well. If her daughter was out there, Annette would be devastated. If Tim had disappeared, I would be incoherent. I wish I was incoherent about Mark.

The phone rings. I pick it up, expecting to hear Tina saying, "Amelia?"

"Amelia?" says a man's voice.

"Yes?" I say, only realizing afterward that it's Tim.

"We found him," he says. "He's okay. A little bit of hypothermia and a little dehydrated. We're going into the clinic to have him checked. Can you meet me there?"

Tim sounds normal.

I start to cry when I hang up the phone, because I'm terrified.

2. Exposition

An eight-legged essay is a Chinese form. It consists of eight parts, each of which presents an example from an earlier classic. Together, the parts are seen as the argument. The conclusion is assumed to be apparent to the reader. It is implicit rather than explicit. It's not better or worse than argument and conclusion, it's different. It is more like a story. This is not an eight-legged essay. If it were, I would use examples from the classic literature. Once upon a time there was a girl named Cinderella. Once upon a time there was a girl named Snow White.

We enter into all major relationships with no real clue of where we are going: marriage, birth, friendship. We carry maps we believe are true: our parents' relationship, what it says in the baby books, the landscape of our own childhood. These maps are approximate at best, dangerously misleading at worst. Dysfunctional families breed dysfunctional families. Abuse is handed down from generation to generation. That this is the stuff of 12-Step programs and talk shows doesn't make it any less true or any less profound.

The map of stepparenting is one of the worst, because it is based on a lie. The lie is that you will be mom or you will be dad. If you've got custody of the child, you're going to raise it. You'll be there, or you won't. Either I mother Mark and pack his lunches, go over his homework with him, drive him to and from Boy Scouts, and tell him to eat his carrots, or I'm neglecting him. After all, Mark needs to eat his carrots. He needs someone to take his homework seriously. He needs to be told to get his shoes on, it's time for the bus. He needs to be told not to say "shit" in front of his grand-mother and his teachers.

But he already has a mother, and I'm not his mother, and I never will be. He knows it, I know it. Stepmothers don't represent good things for children. Mark could not have his father and mother back together without somehow getting me out of the picture. It meant that he would have to accept a stranger whom he didn't know and maybe wouldn't really like into his home. It meant he was nearly powerless.

That is the first evil thing I did.

The second evil thing that stepparents do is take part of a parent away. Imagine this, you're married, and your spouse suddenly decides to bring someone else into the household, without asking you. You're forced to accommodate. Your spouse pays attention to the Other, and while they are paying attention to the Other, they are not paying attention to you. Imagine the Other was able to make rules. In marriages it's called bigamy, and it's illegal.

At the hospital, the parking garage is a maze. I follow arrows to the stairs and down past the walkway to the front entrance, which is nearly inaccessible from the street. The walkway is planted with geraniums paid for by the hospital auxiliary, and the center of the front drive is an abstract statue surrounded by the ubiquitous mass of daylilies, Stella d'Oro. The building front is all angles, and the entrance is a revolving door. How do they get wheelchairs out a revolving door? But angled so that people like me won't see it right away is a huge sliding door for accessibility.

The elevators are nowhere near the receptionist. I am trying to decide how to compose my face. I can't manage joyous. Relieved? I am relieved, but I'm not, too. Mark doesn't handle stress very well, even by nine-year-old standards. Things are going to be difficult after this. We'll get calls from the teacher about his behavior at school. I pass a Wendy's (in a hospital? But then it seems like a pretty good idea) and the gift shop and turn left at the elevators.

Mark isn't in a hospital room; he's asleep in some sort of examining room in a curtained-off bed. Tim is sitting on the edge of the bed wearing his baseball cap that says "Roswell Institute for UFO Studies." I bought him that as a joke.

"He's okay," Tim whispers. "We can take him home whenever."

"Are you okay?" I ask.

"I'm okay," Tim says. "Are you okay?"

I say I'm fine, and we float becalmed in a sea of "okays."

We hug. Tim is six feet tall.

"I think in some ways you were more worried than I was," Tim says. "I know you care a lot for him. I think more than you know."

I smile a lie.

Mark is sleeping like a much younger child, abandoned to exhaustion. His mouth is open slightly, and he has one fist curled next to his cheek. Tim picks him up, and he stirs to rest on Tim's shoulder but doesn't wake.

We walk through the lobby; the happy family, the family that brushed disaster and escaped.

3. Fairy Tales—Beauty and the Beast

Before Mark gets lost, we are living in another town. We are both employed by the same firm. I am studying architectural landscaping. The firm that employs us is a large company that sells many different products: detergents and diapers and potato chips.

In March they call our division together and say that the company will be restructuring, but that they don't intend to lay anyone off. As we walk out of the cafeteria where the meeting has been, Tim says, "That means layoffs for sure." I laugh, and he starts calling headhunters.

They lay one hundred and fifty people off four months later. They ask some of us to stay during the transition and offer Tim and me positions as contractors with a rather lucrative bonus for staying until December 31.

Tim finds another job in September, and moves four hours away.

After Tim has gone, on Fridays Mark and I go out for pizza. Mark is seven. We go to a pizza place where the middle part of the restaurant is shaped like the leaning tower of Pisa except that it's only three stories tall. It's called Tower Pizza, and the pizza is mediocre but they have a special children's room where they play videos of Disney movies on a large screen TV.

It is snowing, so it must be November or so. The video is of *Beauty and the Beast*.

"This sucks," Mark says. "They always show this one. I hate this one."

"Do you want to sit in the regular part of the restaurant?" I ask.

"No," Mark says. "This is okay."

He wants a Mountain Dew because it has the most caffeine. "Caffeine is cool," he says. "When's Dad coming home?"

"Late tonight," I say. "First pizza, then we'll get a video, and you can take it home and watch it, and we'll wait for your dad."

"I wish Dad were here now," Mark says.

"So do I," I say. "How was school?"

"I hate school," Mark says.

"Did you have gym today?" I try to ask specific questions that will elicit a positive response. "How was school" is a tactical mistake, and I know it as soon as I've said it.

"Yeah," he says. "I'm not hungry."

If I take him home, he'll be hungry five minutes after we get in the car, and nothing I have at home will be what he wanted. What he really wants is his dad, of course. "Just have some pizza," I say. "You'll be hungry once you taste it."

He doesn't answer. He's watching the little broken teacup dance around. "Can I go over by the TV?" he asks.

"Sure," I say.

I read my book while he watches TV, and when the pizza comes I call him. Pepperoni pizza. I don't really like pepperoni pizza, but it's the only kind that Mark eats.

"How much do I have to eat?" he asks.

"Two pieces," I say.

He sighs theatrically.

After pizza we stop and get a Christmas movie about a character named Ernest. We had seen the first Ernest movie, the Ernest Halloween movie, and the movie that involved the giant cannon and the hidden treasure. Ernest is terminally stupid, and this is supposed to be funny. At least Ernest is an adult, and there aren't the usual clueless parents in this one.

"Will you watch it with me?" Mark asks.

"Okay," I say. I sit with him and read my book and wish I could go to bed. By Friday I'm so tired I can't think. Tim will get home about eleven. It's seven thirty. I have three and a half hours, and then he'll be in charge.

"Can I have some popcorn?" Mark asks.

"You just had pizza," I say.

"I'm hungry," his voice rises.

"No," I say. "If you were hungry, you should have eaten more pizza."

"I wasn't hungry then," he says, "but now I'm hungry."

"Why is food always a battle with you?" I say because I'm tired.

Mark starts to cry.

I slap the tape in the VCR and go upstairs. I sit on the bed. I think about going downstairs and saying I'm sorry. I think about smacking him.

The phone rings, and I run for it. It's Tim.

"Amelia?" he says.

"Where are you?" I say. He should be about halfway home.

"I'm not even out of town yet. My car broke down," he says. "I'm at a BP on Route 16. You remember the Big Boy where we had breakfast? It's right there. I had to stand on the highway for half an hour. It's snowing like a son of a bitch."

"Can they fix it?"

"Amelia," he says, exasperated, "it's almost eight, and there isn't a mechanic here. I have to call a tow truck and get it towed to a garage and then see. I can't get home tonight."

You left me. You left me here with your child. "Okay," I say. "Will you tell Mark?" Otherwise he will blame me. Seven year olds blame the messenger.

"Sure," he says, resigned.

"Mark?" I call. No answer, although I can hear Ernest on the TV. "Mark?" After a moment I say to Tim, "Hold on," and I go downstairs. Mark is sitting on the couch, deaf to the world. "Mark!" I say loudly.

He starts. "What!"

"Your dad is on the phone."

He jumps off the couch and runs for the kitchen phone calling, "Dadddyyyy!" It is artificial. It is the behavior of a child raised on sitcoms. It sets my teeth on edge.

I go back upstairs and hang up the extension.

Mark is sobbing when I come back downstairs. He hands me the phone and runs and throws himself face down on the couch.

"Amelia?" Tim says. He sounds tired. He is standing out in the cold; he doesn't know how much the car is going to cost him. I've been a shit, of course. "I'll call you tomorrow," he says.

"Okay," I say.

I go in and I rub Mark's back. After a while he turns his tear-stained face toward the TV and watches, and I go back to my book.

Saturday morning I sit on the steps while he tells me about the car. The phone cord is stretched from the kitchen to the foyer.

In a tiny, whining little girl voice, I say, "You have to come home." Mark is watching cartoons, and I don't want him to hear me crying. "You have to come home."

"I can't," he says. "The car won't be fixed until late today, if at all today."

"Can't you rent a car?"

He hasn't thought of that. "I don't know," he says.

"You have to come home," I say. I whisper. I can't think of anything else to say. Who am I? Who is this insipid woman whose voice is coming out of my mouth, begging, sobbing?

"I'll come home," he says. "I'll call you back."

When he comes home, I can't talk to him. I'm afraid that if I open my mouth, toads and beetles and worms will pour out, and I will say something. Something irrevocable.

Mark has been lying on the couch. At one point he was screaming because he said he wanted his daddy and he wanted him right now, but his father was only about halfway home. Well, only about halfway to our home. His daddy doesn't live here anymore. The house is up for sale. We will leave at the end of December.

I wanted to tell Mark that if it wasn't for me, his daddy wouldn't have come home this weekend at all. But I don't say anything. I close my mouth so that no ugly thing will come out.

I am good. I am trying hard to be good.

4. Correspondence

Dear Mr. and Mrs. Friehoff,

Mark is a bright child, fully capable of doing the assigned work. He is often a charming child. He has quite a sense of humor. However, he has poor impulse control, does not stay in his seat, talks out inappropriately in class, and hits other children when he is frustrated. His grades reflect his inability to control himself.

He has been referred for screening through the guidance office, however, I don't think that Mark suffers from hyperactivity or ADD. He is maturing emotionally and physically more slowly than he is intellectually. Children mature at different rates, and this isn't cause for alarm.

Please call me to set up an appointment. I'm best reached between 12:15 and 12:50 or after school . . .

5. Authorial Intrusion

It is important to note that this story is a story of particulars. Most stepchildren live with their mother, so the situation in this story is unusual, although not unique. There are three common reasons why a court will grant full custody to the father, and these are: 1) abandonment by the biological mother; 2) significant and documented mental instability in the mother; or 3) a history of substance abuse in the mother.

The greatest threat to stepchildren is the adult partner of the biological parent. Boyfriends account for a large proportion of child abuse. I would cite the source on this, but I read it in *McCall's* or *Better Homes and Gardens* while I was waiting at the HMO to have my prescription filled, and I didn't feel right taking the magazine. Stepmothers account for a significant proportion of child abuse cases, too, I'm sure.

What isn't documented is the affect on the child of living with someone who does not physically abuse or neglect them, who is apparently a decent, caring parent, who goes through all the forms of parenthood without ever really feeling what a parent feels. This is not abuse, it is just fate. If anyone is at fault, it is the adult, but how do you force something you don't feel? What is the duty of the adult? What is the duty of the child?

6. Choices

Tim calls home from work at four. Mark gets off the bus at three thirty. "Hi Sweetie," Tim says. "How is everything?"

"Okay," I say. "Mark got a two." Mark gets a note every day at school rating his behavior on a five-point scale from *poor* to *excellent!*. Two is one notch above *poor*. Call it *fair*.

"What did you say?" Tim asks.

"Just the usual. You know, 'What happened? Are you sure it's all Keith's fault? Did you have anything to do with it? Is there anything you could have done to keep it from happening?' That stuff."

Tim sighs on the other end of the phone. "What's he doing now?"

"He's supposed to be doing his homework," I say. "I think he's playing with the cat."

"Oh. Let me talk to him."

"Mark!" I call down the stairs. No answer. There never is. "Mark? Your dad's on the phone." I listen for a long moment. Just about the time I decide he hasn't heard me, Mark picks up and breathes, "Hello?"

I hang the phone up gently. I sit on the bed beside the upstairs phone and wonder what they are saying. I smooth the wrinkles out of the crimson bedspread. I want to tell Tim about the school open house, and if I don't tell him now, I'll forget to tell him tonight. I'd forgotten every evening all last week.

I pick up the phone, and Tim is saying, ". . . and don't upset Amelia."

"Okay," Mark breathes, as if this is a familiar litany.

"Tim?" I say.

"Amelia," he says. "Okay Mark, hang up."

"I wanted to tell you about the open house Thursday."

"Mark," Tim says, "hang up." I hear the strain in his voice.

"Okay." Mark hangs up with a clatter.

I chatter about the open house, about how I keep forgetting to tell him. Tim promises to be home in time. "I'll pick up Mark and then we'll get some fast food and go to the open house."

"I'll go with you," I say.

"If you want," Tim says. "You don't have to go."

"It's okay," I say.

"You really don't have to," Tim says. "He's my kid." Before he finishes, I hear someone say something in the background, his manager, probably irritated that Tim is spending time on personal phone calls. Tim cups his hand over the receiver and says something. "Gotta go," he says to me.

"Okay," I say. I stay on the phone after he has hung up, listening for a moment to the empty air.

7. Pillow Talk

At open houses you don't get to talk to the teachers. You just sit with a bunch of other parents, and the teacher tells you all what school is like. In a month there will be parent-teacher conferences. Tim grimly writes down the dates for the open house in his organizer. I suspect it will be a familiar experience. "Mark is a very bright boy, but he has trouble staying in his seat. Did you know he cries very easily?"

Mark likes the novelty of having us at school. "Do you want to see the gym?" He leads us purposefully through the low-ceilinged halls. The hallways always seemed so big when I was a child. He takes us to the art room. He likes art. He has a papier-mâché fish on the wall. It is huge and blue and green, with an open mouth and a surprised expression. A big, glorious fish.

"It's great," I say. "It's really neat."

Mark is bouncing on his toes, not appearing to have heard me.

Tim says, "Mark! Stand still!"

I touch Tim's arm. "It's okay," I say. "He's not bothering anything."

That's who Mark is, and maybe we should ease up on him a bit. Asking him to be still is asking him to do something he's wired wrongly for.

I will try, I promise myself, to give Mark spaces where he can vibrate a little.

At home that night Tim, and I crawl into bed. We haven't made love in a month, and I don't suggest it now.

"Do you mind if I watch the weather?" Tim asks.

I turn on my side with my back to him and try to sleep. The news flickers when I close my eyes, like flames. Like . . . something. I don't know what. I want to cry.

"Do you ever feel pulled?" I ask.

"Is this a talk?" Tim says. It's a joke between us. He says the worst words a wife can utter are, "Oh Tim, we have to talk."

"Do you feel pulled between making me happy and making Mark happy?"

"Sometimes," he says.

"Are you afraid of me?" I ask.

"Afraid of you?" Tim says. He laughs.

"Not that way," I say. "I mean, afraid about how I'll act with Mark. Afraid I'll be mad at him or something."

Tim is silent for a moment. Finally he says, "I'm afraid you'll get so tired of my rotten kid you'll run away."

I am thinking that I cannot live like this. I cannot be the one that everyone fears. I am thinking that if I leave, Mark will have been abandoned again. I am thinking that I am coming to understand Mark, like tonight, at the school, in ways that Tim cannot. And Mark needs that.

I am thinking I am trapped.

Think of it like a prison sentence, I tell myself. In nine years, Mark will be eighteen and he'll be gone.

I despise myself.

8. Perspectives

We are meeting with a counselor, as a family. It's Tim's idea, based on the teacher's note about Mark possibly being an ADD child. It seems to me that ADD is a description of personality. The therapist is a woman named Karen Poletta. I like her; she's middle-aged and a little overweight. Professional with kids without being a kind of mother figure. I like her gray hair: straight, smooth, and shining. I like the way she looks right at me.

By the year 2010, there will be more stepfamilies than, than, what is the right word, natural families? Nuclear families? Normal families? It's a vaguely comforting thought. I can imagine an army of us, stepmothers, marching across the country. Not marching: creeping. I can't imagine us marching.

I am saying some of my concerns. "I don't trust myself," I am saying. "I don't trust my reactions." Tim is watching me. Karen Poletta is watching me. This is a session without Mark, who is at my mother's. I look at the bookshelf with the Legos and the puppets. Family counseling. I'm glad she hasn't had Mark do anything with puppets. "I don't know if I'm being too strict, if I'm just getting mad. I don't know if, for example, I'm letting him stay out too late in the evening because I don't want him around because it's quieter when he's not around. So I try to see what the other parents do, and do what they do."

Karen Poletta looks thoughtful. "How is that different from a biological parent?" she asks. "Particularly when you have a child like Mark, who is a difficult child. You're not the only parent of a difficult child who wants some relief. I think some of the things that you think are because you are a stepmother are stepmother issues, but some of them are just parent issues."

It's not, I think, it's not the same. I don't love him. I don't like him.

Karen Poletta is talking about how much better off Mark is with us than with his mother. That sometimes things aren't perfect, but they are good enough. That Mark has a safe and stable home.

But suddenly, I'm not sure. What if it is the same, some of it? Parent issues?

There's air in the room, and I realize I am taking deep breaths. Big, gulping breaths.

"But he needs a mother," I say, interrupting.

"And he doesn't have one," the therapist says. "But he has a father and a step-mother."

It is what we have.

King of Spain
Dave Shaw

L ately, Walter has been hard to live with. He's drinking again, for starters. The carpet all the way to the TV is littered with dented-up Coors Lite cans and orange peel carcasses and the odd Slim Jim wrapper. (Some of the Coors cans are mine.) He's left his crapped-in underwear warming on the lampshade again and he's been pissing in the braided ficus. The couch smells like monkey feet. He's taken to throwing things, too, like the clay coasters Susan gave me back when she thought I was going to leave Walter for her. He never did like Susan. (She'll be over soon to Lysol the living hell out of the place.) The Serengeti must a goddamned pigsty if the rest of the Wild Kingdom is as messy as Walter. He always gets the good spot on the couch.

One look at those yellow, beer-floating, half-innocent chimpanzee eyes, though, and it's hard to be mad. I don't really mind a little mess. (The place is trashed.) We won't be getting our security deposit back from old leather-headed Mrs. Pitt. The first time she met Walter five or so years ago, she actually thought he was "cute." (There's a nice, thick coat of monkey saliva on all my CDs.) I let a lot of things slide, especially since I got the news. Nineteen weeks to go. Walter and I just keep on going. We've been drinking hot beer for about six weeks straight. I get tired, but only if I drink all day. (I get tired a lot.)

It'd be worse, though, if R.T. and Bingo were still coming around. But we have an understanding: I'm going to kick it, and R.T. and Bingo are going to pretend it's not happening. (Yesterday, Walter tore down my musty curtains.) You wouldn't even know there was anything wrong with me to look at me. Not yet, anyways. I don't even really feel anything yet, either, but it's supposed to get pretty bad. Just ask Susan. It's all she talks about. (Somebody ate the buttons off the remote.)

I wouldn't have known if it weren't for the accident. We were all pretty stewed that afternoon up at the lake. R.T. and Bingo and I were teaching Walter how to drive my old bushed-to-hell convertible on the bridge. R.T. said maybe Walter might pick it up better if I gave him hand signals running beside the car. Walter beat the sin out of that car, kept slamming it into the guardrails and knocked me good once, too. (Those guardrails will echo across an empty open lake.) At the very clean-smelling hospital, the X-rays said I had two broken ribs and something else: cancer in just about every bone in my torso. How're you supposed to get *that* out? They might as well call it cancer in your soul. (Sometimes it aches, a little, nothing compared to what's coming, though.)

I went back to the hospital a few days after those first X-rays to see a specialist with glasses dark as grape juice. He ran some computer simulations with lightning fingers and told me I had 171.7 days.

"171.7 days?" I said.

"It's an average, you know," he said, looking at his print-out, "you know, for someone with the type of cancer you have to the degree, you know, as far as amount of advancement is concerned—"

"171.7."

"Right," he said, looking up, "days left."

"Exactly?"

"It's an average," he said.

"What is that, like the fourth? Is that a Tuesday?"

"Actually, we ran it out to the ninth," he said. I couldn't see myself in his glasses.

"Ninth of January?" I said.

"Of December," he said.

"What do you think, around three thirty, four o'clock?" I asked.

"Well," he said, "it's just an average."

I'm not doing chemo. R.T. and Bingo weren't too happy about that one, Susan either. (Walter doesn't seem to care.) The same labcoat with the bottomless glasses who said I had 171.7 simulated days to live also said chemo and the works would only bring my chances up to four percent, even with the best bone marrow transplant money could buy. (I've got money.) With chemo and radiation and the surgery I would've spent twenty of my last twenty-four weeks in the hospital smelling very clean and feeling like crap. At home, me and Walter can carry on up until near the end. My chest aches if I get up too fast to piss. Walter sprays whatever the hell he wants. (The ficus is basically dead.)

When Susan gets here I won't be telling her I'm a month and a half back on rent. That sort of thing makes her nervous. I sweet-talked old Mrs. Pitt, told her she didn't look a day over fifty and that I was just a little short on cash. I'm loaded since the company retired me. Fired me, really. Asked me to take my four-and-a-half-years' worth of sick leave, personal leave, comp-time, vacation. (You don't want a dead man walking around the office writing memos in everybody's faces. It kind of takes the appeal out of those retirement plans they're always pushing on us.) They've got a great leave package. Turns out I had 184 days coming to me, and with 171.7 to live, well, they'll have to cut me a check, I guess, for twelve days and change. Bob Black, the oily human shadow down the hall from my office, thinks this part is a goddamned riot. He says I'm "the textbook example of the guy who should've taken more time off." (I'll have them make the check out to old nappyhead Walter, keep him in warm beer and fresh oranges for a while.) I told them I'd sue for making me leave, but my lawyer said we couldn't get it done in time. All the company would've had to do is appeal once if they lost. Don't get him wrong, he said, we had a good case, except for the timing of it. That 171.7 number, by the way, is now down to 133 point something. Not that anyone's really counting. (Walter certainly isn't.)

"Come in," I yell. It's Susan. She's learned to tiptoe up to the door and not ring the bell, which when rung causes Walter to go nuts. She always knocks like she's tapping on dynamite. "Come in!"

"Ryan, it doesn't smell any better in here," she says. She sets her white bag of goodies down on the bare spot on the floor. "How can you stand it?"

"Stand what?" I say. She's got her hand on her hip again.

"How can you live with him?"

"What?"

"He's uncouth."

It's hard to argue with her on this point. Walter's lying on the couch scratching the hell out of his nuts.

"You get used to it," I say.

She takes a can of Lysol out of her bag and starts spraying. "What's that?" she asks, pointing one way and looking the other on purpose.

"Where?"

"On the coffee table."

"Monkey crap," I say.

She sprays it good, like an expert, like she was born to take the stink out of monkey crap. I make my way into the kitchen to escape the fog. When I get back, Walter is curled up in his favorite chair, the green recliner, nibbling on a fingernail. All that antiseptic mist sticking in his lungs always calms him down in a hurry. It's like not being able to smell himself makes him question his own existence.

"There better not be a Bible in that bag," I say, sitting on the couch armrest.

"There is," she says, pulling it out. Susan always stands the whole time she's over. "Susan—"

"Ryan, you need this," she says. "At some point you're going to need this."

"Jesus Christ."

"You're behind schedule," she says.

"What the hell are you talking about?"

"You're still in denial," she says.

"Is this why you're here? Again? This? It's very predictable."

She shakes her Lysol can, ready to hit the place with another crop-dusting. "You should be moving toward acceptance by now and you're still in the first stage."

"No, I'm not. I'm getting a beer."

"See!"

"Don't get too comfortable," I say on my way to the fridge. "Me and Walter are going out later."

When I get back, cold beer in hand, she just stares at me with those eyes like wide open sky. It's a little silly to be loving somebody nowadays.

"Do you want to have sex?" she asks me.

"Sex?"

"Yeah, sex, or are you sleeping with Walter these days?"

"Sex just for the hell of it or sex for the purpose of making an heir?" I say.

"Oh, Ryan, don't you want to leave a little something behind?"

"Gee, honey, I sort of planned on leaving everything behind."

It's become, in a few short weeks, an old discussion. It always ends with Walter, with her suggesting I move him out, like it's an option. Actually, Susan and I are broken up, but nothing's changed except it'll be easier later. She'd probably still have the ring, if it weren't for Walter. I had a conference one weekend right after I agreed to marry her and make heirs with her forever. I also was having my apartment fumigated for the special mites that only Walter attracts, and she agreed under delirium of the new ring to take him into her new condo for the weekend. I distinctly remember telling her to keep him away from Coca-Cola.

She didn't do a very good job hiding it. While she was out running in the park, new diamond glinting in the sunlight, Walter must have felt a little ignored. (Walter will not be ignored.) He went exploring and found the Cokes under her bed. In the space of ninety minutes he went through four two-liters and a six-pack. He tore the stuffing out of her couch and peeled the daisy wallpaper off the bathroom walls. He emptied three Hefty bags of garbage onto the living room floor, pissed on her antique bed, knocked a hand-sculpted porcelain toilet off its base, made thirty-two separate knuckle holes in the plasterboard, ripped the cords off all the phones, and left a trail of diarrhea down the hallway.

"What is it, honey?" I asked her. She had had to call from her cell phone.

It took me a long time just to get her to tell me what had happened. She just kept repeating, "It's him or me."

I tried to explain that it wasn't a question of my leaving Walter. Walter just *was*. Like a fact of life. (You can't really leave a fact of life.)

Eventually, the Lysol drifts away or settles in and we all can almost breathe again, and I tell Susan that Walter and I have things to do. She knows we don't really, and she only leaves after she gets tired of trying to get me to make an heir with her. Once she's gone, Walter finally comes back to life and starts crunching on kitchen matches.

Around eleven o'clock they start hammering the hell out of the new construction site out the front window. It's condos or apartments or something. All I know is it looks like it'll take more than 133 point something days to finish and that hammering cuts right through you. So Walter and I go out. We take care to avoid old goatskin-face Mrs. Pitt, who's out back ignoring the warm sun, digging in the yard for God knows what. Is she gardening? No. Is she doing anything in particular? No, just digging a god-damned hole. Always in the same place, always a little deeper and wider than the day before, more wet dark earth piled around the edges every time. Afterward, she always fills the dirt back in. Every day. (R.T. and Bingo always used to say the old bat must think she's a pirate.)

It's not until Walter and I are top-down speeding on the beltway that it hits me that I don't know where the hell we're going. Walter dozes, nuzzled in the worn leather seat. He's perfectly at home in all the heat and grit wafting into our faces off the six lanes of mayhem, cars buzzing around us like horseflies. I didn't mind the beltway so much when I had to fight for my spot on the road every day on the way into work. (Now it's full of horseflies, so what.)

After forty-five minutes, we've gone all the way around the city, watching the mid-day sun make a small, hot circle in the sky. Today was supposed to be The Day, last I heard, that R.T. and Bingo were going to chase the sun all the way west. We had planned it one afternoon about three weeks before Walter broke my ribs. We had blown off work, and the lake and the bridge were all ours, since somehow only the people who know about the lake know about it and nobody ever tells anybody else. Even on Saturdays when it's full of parked cars, it's the same people parked on the narrow half-mile, same smashed-up sedans and tired faces. It's the only place where you can feel your heart pause between beats. R.T. and Bingo and I used to go out to the bridge all the time before I decided not to do chemo.

Most people forget that the lake isn't a lake at all, only a dammed-up river. The lake is man-made, it's the river that's real. If you look off the south side of the bridge, you can barely make out the edge of black water against blue sky. That side of the lake, the side with the dam, is always in shadows, looks like a tar pit. (We always sit on the north side of the bridge, in the sun.)

R.T. started it, said that speaking theoretically the sun could be caught. The four of us sat against the hot guardrail, our feet hanging off the bridge, icy beers in hand, watching the clear water twenty feet below swirling in a headache of light. Bingo wore his tie even though he had taken off his shirt, which meant that he was really on the clock selling someone an ATM somewhere and not drinking cold beer with us. R.T. works in real estate for a shiny bald guy named Peterson who keeps one of those two-by-two paper-cutting boards next to his desk with the blade always up. When R.T. drinks, its like the beer is part of his hand.

"In theory, is all I'm saying," R.T. said. Then he was quiet until we couldn't stand it.

"Mother of God, just say it," Bingo said.

"All right," R.T. said, satisfied he was driving him balmy. "Look, say you got the longest day of the year—"

"The twenty-first," Bingo said.

"The twenty-second," R.T. said.

"Whatever," I said, "the longest day."

"You leave town at daybreak," R.T. said. "First light, before sunrise proper. You're driving to the Coast—"

"The West Coast?" Bingo said.

"Yeah," R.T. said, "to the West Coast. That's where the sun's going. And you chase it down in one day, all under daylight."

A couple hundred yards out, a heron dive-bombed into the water, splashless, came up with something squirming. "I don't see it," I said. "Even if you get—what?—sixteen hours of daylight on the longest day and even if you haul—say you run eighty most of the way—you'd be way short."

"No, I got it figured out," R.T. said, holding his cold beer against his ear. "Sixteen hours is about right. Ever take 702? It's good pavement and it's pretty straight and it'll get you halfway to California. Sixteen times eighty is damn near thirteen hundred miles."

"That's all it is to the Coast?" Bingo said. "Thirteen hundred miles?"

"Well, almost," R.T. said. "The map says 702 to 41 to 67 to 32 to 91 to Cal State Road 6001—all of them nice and quiet, by the way—to the PCH is, and I worked it out exactly, 1,443 miles."

"But you only got thirteen hundred miles of daylight time," I said.

R.T. of course made us wait again, to find out how he was going to squeeze 1,443 miles into less than thirteen hundred miles of time. Walter climbed over the guardrail and jumped in the car. He had had enough. He pretended to drive as best he could without the sun-hot keys in my pocket.

"You're going to drive faster," Bingo said. "Do eighty-five the whole way."

"No," I said, "eighty-five would still leave you short."

"So?" Bingo said.

"So what?" R.T. smiled. His brown eyes were about a hundred feet deep.

"So how the hell do you do it?" Bingo yelled at him.

"Bonus time," R.T. said.

Walter started screeching, waving his arms wildly up in the car. I crawled back over the hot guardrail to check on him, feeling pretty light all of a sudden though we'd been drinking all day.

"On the longest day of the year," R.T. said, "the sun doesn't set until eleven twenty-seven our time out on the PCH. We get a good two extra hours of bonus driving time because of the time zones."

"Bingo," said Bingo.

"Try eighteen hours of driving times eighty miles an hour," R.T. said. "It's 1,440 miles, just three shy of what we need. We take that last leak into the Pacific while the sun sets."

"There's a day in the sun," said Bingo.

When I got to the car, Walter was frozen, his yellow eyes glazed at the turn signal blinking red in his face. I turned it off and picked him up. My chest stiffened.

"Jesus, Walt."

The car stank like what's got to be the oldest smell in the jungle, Walter's last couple of meals steaming on the hot leather seat. He sucked on my ear.

Walter and I were eventually uninvited from the sun chase without a word from either R.T. or Bingo. It was just understood, somehow, after Walter cracked my ribs. It's an uphill battle, doing it now, a few weeks after the longest day of the year. R.T. and Bingo would've had to leave later in the morning, waiting longer this late in the summer for the first light, to stay true to the rules, then breaking their backs hauling all sweaty day only to have less bonus time at the end.

After three times around the hazy city, Walter wakes up and I remember it's payday. Part of my agreeing not to try to sue the old company every breathing moment right up until the end is that they have to let me come in and collect my glossy paycheck in person. So we finally break off the beltway just as the sun is about to move out. Walter whimpers and tries to pull the door handle off until he sees we're taking the old familiar exit to my office. He loves the office because it's the one place where people can't ignore him.

We ride up in a clacking elevator full of neckties pissed off at the smell of dirty monkey. It makes me want to ride the elevator all day long. Walter chews on a stolen hotdog vendor's cap that must still taste like hotdogs. He's at his best when we're at work, when he's bothering the hell out of people who would rather pretend the world doesn't have stinking monkeys.

In the main lobby on my floor, Walter stands on Irene's oak desk with his muddy feet in her memos. Irene smiles at me like she's hiding gas pains. "Hello, Ryan," she says, "you shouldn't have brought the monkey."

"Tell the zeros I'm here for my check," I say. Walter sniffs Irene's neck. "You're ignoring him," I say.

"There's nothing in the deal about you being able to bring in the monkey," she says. There was a time once, back before Walter broke my ribs, when she used to play with him and laugh like a schoolgirl at his dirty feet on her freshly typed letters. I was still her boss back then.

"You know," I say, "technically I'm only on leave, 145 point something more days of leave left. I'm coming back to work twelve point something days after I kick it. Soon as I use up all my vacation."

"Do we have to talk about it now?" she says in that negotiating tone that I myself use with Susan, as if we will indeed be talking about it later. "And could we get the monkey off my desk?"

"He's got a name," I say. Walter eyes a vase of unsuspecting yellow marigolds, soon to assume Walter's smell. "Look," I say, "all I want is the paycheck."

"It's on your desk," Irene says, "your old desk."

There's bad news in my office. Oily Bob Black has moved his desk in across from mine, and Bob Black is insane. He went to the cackle house a while ago for working ninety hours a week and forgetting to sleep in between. Black spends all day counting beans, figuring out for instance whether it costs more to replace the lug nuts on all one hundred thousand of the car wheels on the new Phoenix model or to just pay off the odd old bat who gets hit in the ass by a bouncing loose tire. When I used to walk by his old office his adding machine was click-clicking all the damn time, calculating how many old bats we could afford to hit in the can. (I used to design pamphlets that said how good the seats smelled, etc.)

As soon as I'm in my office, I know it's not worth the paycheck. Black stops the echoing adding machine to stare at me and Walter. His eyes are red-streaked sunsets and he's got his perpetual three days of black whiskers going. He's been sleeping in his dark gray suit again.

"How much for the monkey?" Black says.

"Good to see you, too," I say, sitting against my old desk.

"I'm serious," he says.

"Isn't this a little quick?" I say, waving at his desk. "You know, to have your crap in here already?"

"I had to," he says, "too many windows in my office."

"That makes sense."

"Really," Black says, "how much for the monkey?" Black's teeth are halfway to yellow.

"He's not for sale," I say, feeling greasier just being in the same room with Black.

"You know Timmons is doing all those little flyers about interiors you used to do, on top of his own marketing stuff."

"Where's my Betty Boop poster?" I say.

"How about a thousand bucks?" Black says.

"Is that my electric sharpener on your desk?"

"Listen, you weren't using it," Black says, leaning back in his chair, arms behind his head. "Besides," he says, grinning yellow, "it's a company sharpener. You never really owned it."

"Where's that put you then?" I say.

"In your office," he says. "I'd say three thousand bucks is more than fair for a gorilla."

"Chimp," I say.

"What?"

"He's a chimpanzee."

"Well, then," Black says, "three thousand really is more than fair. I thought he was going to get bigger."

"He's big enough," I say. "You have no idea." Walter finds a pencil with my old chew marks and begins munching on it.

"I'm willing to leave my offer on the table even though he's not a gorilla," Black says.

"You don't want to start with owning a monkey," I say. "You got to work up to a monkey. Get a duck or something first."

"Five thousand dollars," Black says, "is too much to pay for a monkey that isn't a gorilla. Nonetheless, I'll pay it if we do the deal today."

"Maybe you could get a zoo monkey for less," I say.

"I don't want a zoo monkey," he says, looking hurt. "I want yours."

"I'm just here for this," I say, pocketing my paycheck. "Come on, Walt."

"Who's going to take care of him *after?*" Black says, rubbing the shadow across his face.

"After?" I ask.

"Yeah, *after,*" he says.

It's the single most ridiculous question in the world. "He'll latch on to somebody," I say, chuckling. "I wouldn't worry."

I'm not entirely sure how Walter came about living with me in the first place. It was back when I was drunk all the time, five or so years ago, and I've narrowed down the possibilities to either his following me around the park one too-bright day and not leaving me, which might only be a dream, or his already being in my apartment when I moved in, which might also be a dream. Old Mrs. Pitt never really seemed surprised to see him. However I came upon him, though, suddenly realizing through the headache that a chimpanzee was playing my CDs very loudly made me decide it was time to cut back on the drinks. Or maybe it was just that I turned thirty without even realizing it until R.T. and Bingo showed up on my doorstep with three bottles of Yukon Jack and a short fat stripper who wouldn't show us the good parts.

As I drive us out of the city, Walter throws my old maps out of the car. They flap for a moment, keeping up, snapping in the wind, then dive into the road. Walter smiles. Mrs. Pitt and her perpetual mudhole are waiting for us at home. (The worst of Mrs. Pitt is her goddamned humming. She'll put every bit of power her toothpick bones can muster into each shovelful of wet earth and hum some goddamned song or another through the whole episode, her short, bulging, long-armed shadow dancing at her feet. Then after she's dug the hole a little bigger than the day before, she'll gaze into it like she's looking at the most interesting item in the entire universe. It's the goddamnedest thing. It's just dirt, is what gets me. Dirt. Period. It's cold goddamned dirt and she loves it.)

Instead of home, Walter and I head out into the free open sun. We're heading into the wind, in the direction of the bridge, which must have been where we were headed all along. It's where R.T. and Bingo were going to start their trip this morning, taking off west to 702.

One time out at the lake, a couple of months before Walter broke my ribs, R.T. and Bingo and I spent a whole afternoon trying to find the right dirt roads down to the dam. We were going to get to the bottom of this madness about the lake really being a river. All we found though was an old guy scooping out dead fish from the streams of water coming from the outtake tunnels.

R.T. called down the hundred feet to ask the old guy scooping fish whether that trip through the bubbling tunnel killed them. "No," he shouted up, "only some of them. Just stuns the rest." One of the fish opened his big pink mouth, flopped once in the net, and quit. The old guy told us he was actually doing the fish a favor by pulling them out stunned. "Fish can't breathe in the water anyway," he yelled, "when they're stunned." It was news to us.

Walt and I fly at eighty-five just so I can feel what it's like. Speeding along in a smashed-up piece-of-crap Chevy convertible isn't the same as riding in Bingo's '64 Mustang, but the wind whipping sun straight into my face is close enough. We pass the burned-out churches, the smell of old fire. All the roads out here are Eden Church Road or Ararat Church Road or Something Else Church Road. These churches are as close as I've come to the lake with Susan. (They made her cry once.) I don't know how all the old churches got to be burned-out shells. You can imagine them smoldering. Some of them still have pieces of stained glass left in the windows, catching red and yellow light as we speed on. Love doesn't travel past the broken churches.

Walter and I pass all the POSTED signs and park out at the bridge in the breeze. Walter's and my old Burger King Crowns are in the back seat, remnants of a public episode, and we put them on and sit with the top still down. It's our first trip back here since Walter's little driving fiasco. From my side, looking south, the lake is black shadows full of tree limbs and vines that look like they thrashed around quite a bit before they drowned. Forty feet off, a guy and a girl fishing weave their green boat around through the shadows and wreckage, slowly, oblivious to us.

Off Walter's side there's a ridiculous amount of activity. You can hear the splashes. Fish jumping, breezes swirling the clear water in circles, herons swooping all over the place. Way on out there's a wide circle of water burning where the setting sun breaks through trees on shore. (R.T. and Bingo should be well into California by now.)

I can't help it, but I look off west, off the end of the bridge, black pavement to black clouds hanging like frozen exhaust on orange sky. Walter stays in the car while I get out to stand on the guardrail, balancing my thighs against the warm top rail. The sun's dropping out of sight.

"Hey, King," somebody shouts up from below.

It's the fishermen, in their little green boat, a guy with his girlfriend or wife or something. They're young. I still have my Burger King crown on. "Catch anything?" I say. Their boat slowly trolls north, out from under the bridge. For a moment, the bridge is moving south.

"What are you King of?" the girl says. The girl's got a tight line into the water that she twitches, playing with something on the other end. She wears a red halter top showing more white parts than she probably thinks. The guy is tanned, steering in boxers.

"I don't know," I say. "Italy?"

"King of Italy?" the guy says, a brown arm on the motor guiding the boat out into the clear.

"King of England," I say.

"King of Norway?" the guy says.

"King of France," I say.

"King of France?" the girl says.

Walter decides he's missing too much. He climbs onto my back and catches me hard with a muddy foot in the stomach. Then he squeezes the goddamned daylights out of my rib cage.

"Nice monkey," the guy says.

My throat aches for my air. "Thanks," I manage. Their green boat keeps taking them further north, far enough to have to start to shout a little to keep the conversation going.

"King of Portugal?" the girl calls, still wanting to play.

"King of Spain," I say, as they troll away, getting my breath back a little.

"King of Pain?" the guy yells. "Like the song?"

"Spain," I yell back. "Spain."

Then Walter knocks my crown off, which is about the meanest goddamned thing I can imagine. I'd swing his dirty monkey ass out into the lake if I didn't think he'd find a way to drag me in, too.

"Look, the King lost his hat," the guy yells. Their boat heads toward the last light on the lake, that red-orange circle further up.

"Crown," I yell back, "it's a crown."

"Nice monkey," the girl yells back. My crown floats away under the bridge, headed for the wreckage down south. I throw Walter's in, too, just to show him what an asshole he's being.

The little green boat disappears in the shadows. I must have been sore as hell all day. Walter's squeezing the hell out of me only made it too painful to ignore anymore. I get each of us a warm beer out of the trunk. "Just drink," I tell him, without looking at him, "just drink your damn beer and keep it quiet."

We've wasted point something of a day running all over the place, only to find ourselves sober and alone out at the bridge at the gloomiest time of day without our Burger King crowns. And there isn't going to be anything so fun on the other side of what's left of that sunset, either.

But we wait there anyway, sitting in the car, top down in the still air, if only to confirm that the day's a total loss. A roof of muddy clouds drops over us, filling in the lake, and the day is gone.

What is there on the other side of the day? When the breeze stops and you can hear yourself sweat? When it's dark enough that you can't see up from down? Nothing. Nothing but the goddamned smell of monkey. So nothing, really. The taste of beer, sure, so you don't mind the smell so much, and nothing else. You can almost see Mrs. Pitt in the darkness, her weather-beaten mug peering in through the clouds, staring like it's a truly fascinating thing that you can spend point something of a day and find nothing at the end.

Bumpship

Susan Mosser

Exclusion Rights for minors? You heard that in some bar on Mech24, am I right? Because I know my sector. I also know you didn't tell them you were a reporter. No, I understand completely, but good luck if that's the story you're after. A crew on refit leave may give the locals an earful, but they are not about to mouth off on the job. The bottom line on all that righteous indignation is that nobody wants a Perm stamp on their next layoff notice.

Compassion? Of course I have compassion for Indies. I wasn't always a Manager. I put in my time on the Suit Team like everybody else. I have flown many a hoverbird to pop the bubble, and I have seen the stampede, hundreds of times, Indies pouring out of a compound, trampling each other to get into that bumpship. But my compassion is not reserved for the children. Or the greys, or the genefreaks, or . . .

What?

Well, what are they called these days?

Fine. Muties. Greys or muties. You won't quote me on that, right?

Good. I expect you've been doing this long enough to know the difference between official statements and things I say only to help you understand the business before you set the link.

You did? Oh. Do I look . . . I thought this was sort of a preliminary thing.

Ah, working copy. Good. So.

Right. Exclusion of minor assets. No. I do not support the idea. Look, they have ants where you come from?

Hive crawlers? Good enough. You know what they look like when you stir them up.

All kids do that. Well, that's what it looks like when we bump a small compound like the one you're about to see, like ants boiling out of a broad shiny anthill, each with an identical drive to survive, an identical opportunity to succeed. Those bumpship doors are open to all. There is no finer expression of access equality than that. So no, I do not believe that children under ten should be excluded from the Repayment Order. Assets are assets. And Indies know that. They understand market democracy better than anybody. Next time you hear a lot of radical reform talk around this business, you ask some pertinent personal questions. Ninety-nine percent of the time, you'll find yourself looking at a volunteer, not somebody with loved ones on the line.

That surprises you? Let me tell you something about volunteers. No man or woman with any marketability anywhere else in the galaxy would sign on as a bumper for a bunk and a stimsock and three mocks a day. They're losers, bottom line, begging for a job they claim to despise. We hire the dregs who volunteer because our paid labor quota is thirty-five percent. Otherwise, I would never hire a single volly. Nothing but a headache.

Of course I believe in paid labor. Every citizen has the right to improve his quality of life. But you know what? In my sixty-five years on the job, I have seen maybe half a dozen bumpers actually make that new start they all claim to want. Volunteers don't bank their credit and get out. They spend it on shipboard liberty, on chemgems and stim shows. That pay squirts straight back to ACorp through the recport franchises in the bunks so fast those electrons in Accounting must slam into themselves coming and going. No, give me a TI any day. Your indentured worker knows why he's here, and so does Management. No hard luck stories, because we all know the story. No whining that it's a dirty job, because he knows how lucky he is to get a slot at all. Your typical TI, he hates every minute of every day in this business, and he hates my guts, because to him I *am* Atmospherics Corporation. But he does his job, and does it well, because he knows that every A-credit he earns is keeping his loved ones back on the rock breathing sweet ACorp air. I have nothing but the utmost respect for my TI's.

Term of Indenture, that's right. If you ask me, this business should be staffed purely on an atmocredit basis, especially when you consider how many evictees are waiting for slots. I'm all for fair competition, but the MetaMerger Act needs some serious refit, and the first thing to go should be that One-Third clause. Sometimes I think those macromanagers in the hubworlds have their heads up each other's butts.

No, definitely not a quote there! Of course, the ACorp fleet has nothing to hide, and neither do I. You wouldn't be here to watch us work, if we did. Well, let me call for the ExO, and we'll get you suited up for . . .

Excuse me?

I must say, I don't see what that has to do with your story.

Well, yes. A very long time ago, I was a volunteer. Now I'm a Manager.

Yes. The first non-Exec Sector Manager in ACorp.

I don't think of it as unusual. In fact, there are more of us all the time. Executive Class is a custom, not a requirement.

Retirement? Me? Not for years yet.

No, I've got more comcredits than I can use. One of the advantages of this work. I never manage more than a few days exleave, and I don't spend onboard.

Right. No chemgems. How did you know that?

No, can't tolerate them. Metabolic anomaly, they call it. One hit and I'm sick as a dog. But I don't miss it. I'm lucky to get sleeptime, never mind rectime.

Exleave? Bella's World. Recs, sex, and scenery. Biodyne foliage. Original volcanics. Quartz beaches on a saline ocean. I don't get there much, but one of these days . . .

Yeah, a Boondocker rock. Nothing wrong with that. If this is your first time in the Boondocks, you should let me recommend a few choice spots.

Excuse me?

What does it matter why I signed on?

Background. Sure. Well, I'm from a compound myself, actually.

Yeah, that's right: Boondocker, born and bred. My parents were on an original lease.

No, it's been derelict for a long time.

Well, sure, it had a name, but I don't see why . . .

Okay. Okay. Ceugant. They called it Ceugant.

Yes, "the" Ceugant. No, not xeno. Terran. Gaelic, it's called. Sorcerers and fairy cities. Like a herostim. My father's idea.

A scholar. Ancient Terran languages, so I guess that made him technically a linguist, but nothing useful. All low-market.

My mother? A bioengineer. A fine scientist.

No, they're both dead.

Yes. Yes, they died on Ceugant. Look, where are you going with this?

No, it wasn't an accident.

You know what? Turn that thing off. We're finished here. I'm sure hubnubs don't plug into "Look Now" just to hear some docker's life story.

Really.

Well, if you already scanned my bio—and I'd like to know who gave you access to that—then you know what happened to my parents on Ceugant, so what is your point here?

Human interest. Right.

You know what? I really don't have time for this. So if you'll excuse me . . .

Of course I have nothing to be ashamed of. You don't have to tell me that.

Abbie Wilson set this up? Are you referring to Executive Member Abelarde Wilson?

Oh, well, never mind then. If a Voting Member says talk, I talk. I don't ask how someone like Executive Member Wilson even gets to know my name, I just talk. So I get it now. Let me guess: "Orphan Boondocker Survives Holocaust to become Bumpship Manager."

Hostile? Not at all. As I told you before, I've seen your show. Actually, it's time for you to suit up, so if you'll excuse me, I'm overdue on a multilink. My first officer will escort you to the boarding area to join the Suit Team, and I'm sure you'll get some great digivid of the eviction. You have my best wishes for the remainder of your time aboard.

No, I'm afraid I won't reconsider. Good day.

I'm glad you understand my position, and I hope you realize that my apology is a sincere one. We're working just as fast as we can to set up another bump for you, one that will be more representative of our usual routine. I know we promised it by this afternoon, but as I explained to Member Wilson, my crew and I have been working under tremendous time constraints for eighteen months now. The collapse in the boron market in this sector has created something of a localized recession, which has, of course, resulted in a higher-than-average level of evictions.

Excuse me?

I am speaking naturally.

Well, this is how I naturally sound when I haven't slept in forty-six hours and my career is on the line.

Because of thirteen thousand Indies? Don't be ridiculous.

Look, what do you expect me to say? I lost some very expensive ACorp hardware and four crew members, not to mention the thirteen thousand Indies, in what should have been a routine bump, which you already know, of course, because you were downside linking the whole thing for the hub worlds.

Oh, I'm not angry. I'm amazed. My Suit Team is still downside flying cleanup sweeps in blast turbulence, when I have to leave the bridge for a personal vid from Executive Member Wilson. I'm thinking, "But how could she know already? And why would she call about it?" I get to my cube for my second-ever eyes-only message from a Voting Member to find that said Member has set a vidlink just to watch me squirm while she refashions my anatomy. She doesn't even know about the Indies or the dome explosion. "You will file the proper reports, I assume," is all she says about that. No, she has called me away from emergency cleanup operations to spend her million-credit-per-minute Member time to chew me a new one about dismissing her nephew the reporter. And oh yes, Aunt Abbie sends her love.

I get the point, okay? I surrender! If I had any balls at all, I would have shown them to Aunt Abbie and then dumped your butt on some slowbarge rock to find your own way back to a squirtport. But I didn't, so let's get on with this.

Because I have sixty-five spotless years in this business, that's why not. Because I'm sixty years too old to start over and ten years too young to retire. I will therefore survive the next few hours you are in my sector and get on with my work, because that is what all real Boondockers do best. Survive. Do you hubnubs even know what survival is? You huddle on your permaterra planets where the water flows and the dirt sticks to the rock and air is just something the bioforms make for free. How many centuries has it been since your home planet was pulled off the ACorp tit? Do you even know? Ancient history, right? Well, this is the Boondocks, nephew, and ancient history is now. You think Indies buy a lease on some wasted ball of rock expecting to puke their lungs out in five years? Hell, no. They expect to struggle and survive.

Yeah, I know you want to hear about my parents. Fine. Let's get this over with. Ask your damn questions.

My father. That's the place to start, alright. Not a practical man, my father. What good is Terran history to anybody, anyway? Why look back at a huge failure when you need to focus on survival right now? He meant well. I know that. People liked him. He was probably a good man. But he was a fool. They all were. That's why it ended the way it did.

No, my mother was a good scientist, but she had no sense of reality where my father was concerned. I don't think she ever would have joined the Ceugant group on her own. She was too practical. It was my father and his colleagues who started the project. They had some vision of an entire world of academics, deadart, all the leftovers. Low-markets and spot farmers. Dreamers. A Boondock rock full of dreamers.

"An ethical democracy, grounded in simplicity." That's it. God, where did you dig that up?

It's hard to believe they were that naive, isn't it? But they were one of the original private planetary charters. Nobody knew how low the success rate would turn out to be. And of course the Third Market War started the year after they bought the lease. By the time they knew they were failing, I guess there was no loose capital anywhere. That probably didn't really matter. Nobody would have invested in an obvious disaster like Ceugant.

My mother? A fine scientist, like I said. She gave up a Head of Research position with Bio Corporation to go to Ceugant with my father and his philosopher friends. She was one of the only high-markets in the group. That was the grand plan, of course: The dreamers would create utopia, and the bioengineers would keep the venture solvent. My mother owned two private patents, so she recruited a team, the group financed a bioplant, and that was the economic basis for their new planet.

Unbelievable, isn't it? One export industry to cover the offrock debits for a whole compound. I don't know what they thought they were doing, really. They couldn't afford a semi-breathable; who could? They couldn't afford both water and soil, so they settled for soil. They leased a minimum A-dome and basic water service. No lakes or rivers, just a holding pond in the center of the compound. Not bad planning. Room for expansion without the killer soil costs for future generations of Ceuganters. Except that the biosamples were faked up. The movers lifted off, the prefabs unfolded, the celebration calmed down, the biovats started perking, and nothing grew.

You're right. That's not entirely accurate. My mother's patented bios didn't grow. Ceugant's indigenous uncells, which had been carefully removed from the soil samples, grew like crazy and crowded out the paying customers. It took months to figure out what was wrong, because they weren't looking for uncells, and you don't find something that small unless you're looking for it, and with the right equipment. She didn't have the right equipment because they had planned everything to the last microcredit, sheer necessities only for the first five years. Her mid-range steriseals were useless. Upgrade, right? Wrong. A very expensive soil planet lease and a large bioplant, setup fees, five years' supplies—nothing left for hyper-grade equipment that would have cost almost as much as another planet lease.

Yes, but this was almost ninety years ago. Deregulation had been in effect for less than a decade. Private lease colonization was brand new, and there was no history to learn from because people like my parents were still out there making the history. These compounds we bump today have only themselves to blame. The new lease laws are very kind to the Indies.

Well, no, there are no asset exclusions for children or anyone else, but by the time we come in to actually force the Indies to leave the rock, they have had more than enough time to make payment arrangements. There's no excuse for the criminal anarchy you saw yesterday. We can't let Indies destroy themselves to abandon their debts. Business would come to a halt.

Indentures? No, it's Nonrecoverable Debts: "ND's." Yeah, lots of people make that mistake.

Excuse me?

Bridge between worlds.

Yes, okay, I was the first human born on Ceugant and yes, my native name meant "bridge between the worlds." I want to know where you're getting all this stuff. Look, I've told you about my parents. Now let's get on to something else.

No. Absolutely not. Not even for Executive Member Wilson. My name is my own business. My mother always made a big thing out of that, my being the first Ceuganter, said my naming ceremony was the biggest party she'd ever seen. Probably my mother was a dreamer, too, and just seemed practical to me in comparison to my father. I don't know. Anyway . . .

I'm fine. Don't be ridiculous. You wanted human misery to shovel, here it is.

Forget I said that. You're just doing your job, right?

Oh, I'm sure it's a big story. I'm sure that trillions of hubnub sockers are holding their collective breath over a few billion struggling Boondockers. You'll excuse me if I choose not to actually believe that.

I see. Sure. Sure, let's get on with it. Why not? It's not hard to figure out what happened after the vats soured, is it? Five years' worth of supplies eked out to last nine, everybody scrambling and begging and borrowing to keep the water and air running as long as they could. The usual routine. My mother tried to sell her patents, and I think she did sell one. I don't remember for sure. I was too young through most of it to really understand what was going on. A lot of what I know I learned later.

What? Well, they tried that. They filed suit to get the lease annulled for fraud, but this was pre-PCorp. Planet development was scattered all over the place. The holding company was some private development group that went bankrupt and split with the cash long before my parents and their friends realized they'd been swindled. Ten years' lease in advance, and they couldn't get any of it back. Central Court eventually ruled that the Ceugant compound had first claim to the planet for triple the term of the lease, ninety years, even if somebody actually bought the rock for unpaid fees and taxes—which nobody ever did, not even PCorp, not under those restrictions and not with those uncells waiting. I guess the Court thought it had been generous and fair. Maybe judges just don't understand biovats. I don't know. I do know that it was a death sentence for the compound. It took almost five years to get the ruling, and only about a third of the group managed to get relatives to sponsor them back to the hub after the trial. Everybody else just hung on to that ball of rock and grew macrofood from its otherwise poisonous dirt and tried to market anything they could to pump com-credits for the air and water. No indentured atmocredits in those days. No options.

That's why there's no excuse for those thirteen thousand dead Indies. They've known for more than three years that their venture was a failure. They knew the cred-its would run out, the leases would go unpaid, and the time for TI contracts would arrive. ACorp isn't going to keep those atmopods charged for free, now is it? And why should it? And why should H2O spend fuel and manhours and equipment wear to haul ice to a compound that doesn't pay for it? The last two years on Ceugant, we had no water delivery at all.

Hard to believe? It was a hard way to live, let me tell you. But we owed on two deliv-eries, the Notice came, there were no credits to cover it, and after that no more ice.

How? We recycled everything, every drop of everything, but by the time ACorp finally sent the Notice for the air, we were sucking mud out of the reservoir. We would have died of thirst, anyway, even if they hadn't popped the dome.

Of course I don't blame the Corporations for what happened. Business is business, and market democracy is a natural system of equality. I know that. I see that very clearly. Nobody forced my parents to go to Ceugant. They could have stayed in the hub. Sure, the permaterras are overstuffed ratholes, but the bad air is free and the foul water is right there on the planet. No offense intended, of course, to hubrats like yourself.

Right, you don't really need opinions. You need gory details. Sure. You did your research, right? You probably know more than I do about what happened. Eighty years ago, ACorp was just beginning to deal with the eviction problem. Aunt Abbie and the Board weren't prepared for the astronomical failure rate of private lease compounds. The Corporation didn't even have its own fleet yet. The first bumps were contracted out on a piecework basis to private eviction companies. Hell, you could hardly call them companies. Spacer scum who bumped compounds between narcgem runs.

That's who showed up on Ceugant to execute the ACorp Notice. First they blasted the atmospheric pods, then they landed to talk things over. They didn't just pop the bubble the way we do; they blasted the pods with pyros. Obviously, it was their first and last ACorp contract.

The air was really stale by then, but still breathable. I remember that, actually, because we were all on exertion limitations and had been for months. When you're a kid, that's a big thing in your life: no running, no shouting. You know what I'm talking about? The air was still breathable, but it wouldn't have stayed that way for long once the containment field was opened.

The ExO didn't explain this to you?

Well, alright, depending upon the ambient atmosphere, and of course the size of the compound, it can take two or three standard days for a bubble to dissipate. It's not a complete vacuum on these rocks, you understand. Even Ceugant had an atmosphere. It just wasn't something a human body could breathe. We tell the Indies they only have an hour after the pop to get into the ship because it gets them moving. They've had plenty of time to sit around before we get there.

Not three days on Ceugant, no. Not with those pyros sucking air. They don't snuff out like a candle; they use sevalium, and it cycles through the gases and keeps burning till there's nothing left. No slow choke on Ceugant. Fast choke, and a field implosion. The contract was to lift off the Indies. That's the whole point of bumping, right? Get the deadbeats out of the way to make room for new compounders with new credits. Nothing wrong with that. Just business. Except these were not businessmen. These were ignorant space scum with an old rebuilt trash can big enough for a large load of narcgems or about eighty people, whichever came first.

No. No, I'm fine. Just let me get a sip of water.

Yes, I know this is what people will really want to hear about. I understand that. This is the part they tune in for. This is the part . . .

Seven hundred and sixty-two men, women, and children are standing out on the common grounds with their little bundles of personal items, waiting for the bumpship. Can you see that? They have no intention of resisting the boarding order. Then suddenly they have thirty minutes to decide which few dozen of them are going to drop those bundles, cram into a cargo hold, and survive.

So how do Retromoralists pass out death sentences when there is no time for debate? They draw lots, of course. Handmade slips of plazlite in an empty foamfab carton. Leave it up to the gods. Man, woman, child; high-market, low-market, no-market: everybody had an equal share on Ceugant, and it didn't occur to them to change that just because the world had suddenly come to an end. And who was the logical, even mytho-logical, choice to draw the little slips of plaz out of the box? Why, the first official Ceuganter, of course. Symbolic. It's my father, all over.

What?

I don't know if it was his idea. I just know it was his kind of idea. I don't remember much about that day, really.

My mother? She was very quiet. Everyone was. Lots of crying, of course, but nothing hysterical, not until the very end. It was quiet, and my mother didn't cry. I remember that. I pulled eighty-seven slips out of the box, one by one, and she read the names. Her voice was very calm, very clear. The pyros were sucking a breeze by then, and there was a lock of hair blowing across her cheek. She kept tucking it behind her ear, but each time she reached for a name, it scattered again. She read the whims of the gods in her beautiful voice, and then she passed each name to my father, who read it and passed it on to the man next to him, so that each name would be read and re-read to guard against error. No one really thought my mother would lie or make a mistake; it was just the way they always did things.

Is something wrong?

Of course not. How silly of me. You're a professional, right? You've seen it all, got it all on digi. What did you call the disaster? "Sludgy!"

Eavesdropping? Not at all. I wouldn't intrude upon your privacy. But this is off the sludgy subject, isn't it? I said my mother didn't cry. That's not entirely accurate. Name number eighty-two was my own. She tucked her hair behind her ear, unfolded the scrap of plaz and without a sound passed the slip to my father, who read out my name, and passed the slip on. My mother's cheeks were wet after that. She was crying, and I said, "I'm sorry, Mom. I didn't mean to draw my own name, honest."

"Five more," she said then. "You still have five more names to choose. You have to hurry." Her voice was low, a growl almost, and there was a look in her eyes that scared the hell out of me. I was only nine years old, after all, and you have to understand that my mother was always the practical one, always calm. She kept things going by making a big joke out of everything, no matter how awful it was. There she stood, the wise-cracking queen of the universe, with tears pouring down her face and a stare that burned right down into my gut, and all of a sudden I got it. I was young, but in that moment I suddenly understood that what I was pulling from that box was life, and what I was leaving in it was death. I knew it because my mother was staring at me like a woman who believed in miracles, a woman who was trying to wring a miracle right up out of my guts and into her hand.

"Five more," she said. Whispered, really. "Please. That's all you have to do, and then it's finished."

For the first time, at number eighty-three, I reached down into that soft nest of plaz and knew that every slip I chose was a person, and every slip I dropped was gone for good. It took me a long time to pull the next slip. Forever. When I did, I pinched a miracle out of that foamfab carton. When she opened that slip of paper and read her own name, my mother seemed calm again. My heart started slamming in my chest, and I shoved my hand into that box with the pure faith of a brand-new true believer. My mother's voice didn't waver when number eighty-four was the girl who lived next door to us, and number eighty-five was an elderly linguist friend of my father's who for the past sixty years had been compiling a dictionary of a single dead Argalean dialect, and number eighty-six was the second son of a plaz sculptor who was famous for making the longest speeches at every meeting, and number eighty-seven was a young engineer from her bioproject team, and none of them were my father.

"Pull another one," my mother said immediately. "I'm sorry, but you need to pull another one." And I did it. I pulled another slip. Everyone there knew why, everyone but me. Nobody challenged her. They had all agreed to abide by whatever came out of that box, and on Ceugant that kind of agreement had force of law, but nobody said a word to my mother.

I don't remember whose name it was. I do remember my mother turning to me and saying, "You'll be alright. You're smart and you're strong," and then I understood what everyone else already knew, and when she tried to put her arms around me, I hit her as hard as I could and ran. I tried to hide somewhere, I don't remember where, but she came after me.

What? No, all by herself. I don't know where my father was. I never saw him again. In the crowd, I guess.

Sorry. I'm just . . . what did you say?

Running. I don't remember anything else, really. Running across a soyallfield, maybe, with my mother, or her running, and dragging me while I tried to get away. There were bruises on my arms later, and scratches. In the ship. She was very smart, my mother, a fine scientist.

Did I already say that? She was. Smart enough to know that time was very short.

The other eighty-six had gone straight to the cargo hold, and they all should have lifted off long before we got there, but the space scum were lounging around in breathers, watching the fireworks. They were too stupid to understand what they had done with those pyros. But my mother knew.

My own memories. Right.

I remember her dragging me out of some dark place, shouting about a field implosion. I remember it hurt my chest to run, and my mother sounded like she was strangling, and every time I stumbled and fell, she dragged me up and kept on running, making terrible sounds in her throat. I remember that; but I don't remember getting to the ship. I never have remembered it. Maybe I passed out. They told me later that my mother picked me up in her arms and carried me up the ramp, that she threw me into the hold and screamed at the spacers to close the hatch, and that she kept on screaming at them until they finally understood they were about to be grounded forever and closed it. I don't know if that's true. Maybe I've added details in my mind. I don't see how she could scream when I remember her being so out of breath. It's just . . . not logical.

I'm sorry. Did you say something?

No. No, I don't remember anything else.

Training? Yes, that's right. A few months later. ACorp tested us. I think there were eight kids in our refugee group. I scored highest, and I had passed my tenth birthday by then, so they hired me. I started training right there on Refuge I.

The other kids? I don't know. They moved me into the Corporate barracks. I don't know what happened to the rest of them.

No. No, I don't ever wonder.

No, I wouldn't consider going back to Ceugant with a cam crew. What kind of question . . . ?

Turn that thing off.

I mean it. Interview over.

Turn it off, Nephew, or it's going out the waste lock. And you with it.

This is still my ship.

Yes, much better. Thank you. I hope dinner was satisfactory? I'm sorry I didn't join you, but I couldn't get off the bridge. All quiet at last, though, and I did want to stop by and let you know that everything is set for tomorrow's bump. We'll be underway again in another hour or so. You should be able to get all the digi you need for your story.

Yes, I suppose I have time for a quick nightcap, especially since you've already gone to the trouble to order mine.

Because no one else on board drinks these.

Bella's, that's right.

No apology necessary. We were both just doing our jobs. I'm sure you understand that it is sometimes difficult to discuss such matters with those outside the industry.

Yes, it is an important part of history. The Ceugant Incident. One of many that led to the Humane Eviction Act. You can see now why I have no patience with people who whine about Exclusion Rights. And why I don't hold ACorp responsible for the suicide of those thirteen thousand Indies. Those people had options. That compound has had more than a year to write enough indenture contracts to keep it going. A compound that size would take, what, sixty-five hundred? Maybe seventy-five? Only seventy-five hundred indents to pay the debt and keep the pods charged for the full seventy-year TI.

Term of Indenture, yeah. My point is, even if they were irresponsible enough to refuse indenture contracts, they still had options. A clean, roomy bumpship had been sitting on that rock for three days. In three days, those people could have moved their entire compound into that ship, and right now they'd be on their way to a refuge world with salvage credits toward the debt besides. I know the refuge worlds are overcrowded, but at least there's air and water and food—at no charge, mind you, beyond the basic seventy percent time obligation. And we all know the Alpha Corporations are committed to increasing off-planet indenture opportunities for bona fide refugees.

Yes, I know. I've heard people use the words "slave labor," too, but that just shows their ignorance. Even on the refuge worlds, a large group can pay off a debt if they all work together over time, and what better motivator than the chance to help your descendants qualify for volunteer status again someday? You have to work for what you want; you have to be a responsible citizen. Nobody gets a free ride. That is the basic fairness of market democracy.

No, I have no sympathy for those people. That rock didn't belong to them, those pods didn't belong to them, and that bumpship sure didn't belong to them. Symbolic protests, my ass. Wanton destruction of property is what it is. A bunch of dead Boondockers who didn't have the decency to work off their debt. Another year or two of these "protests" and the Humane Eviction Act will be a thing of the past. When Central Court gets one good look at skyrocketing hardware costs from sabotage, they will scrap the HEA without a second glance. They're moving toward a more balanced approach, anyway. The Corporations need more protection. They are the ones with the capital at risk, after all.

Forced indenture in lieu of eviction? I may have heard something about that.

Yes, okay. EV65709. Yes. The All-Corp Petition for Forced Indenture in Lieu of Eviction. I'm surprised you've even heard of it, much less read it. What happened to our sealed legislative process?

Ah, unidentified source. Of course. Well, if you've read it, you know it's fair. There's a lot of expense in shipping and warehousing evictees, and then there are the costs of administering the refuge world manufacturing operations. In the long run it makes much more sense for future Indies to stay on their rocks and bear all costs of their debt through forced indenture. Let them pay for their own air and water while they work off their debts. It's what we should have been doing all along. It's not true that the debts will never be paid off, just that it will take longer than one generation. A one hundred and forty-year TI instead of seventy. That's not impossible to deal with. And there's nothing to keep Indies from creating their own wealth and paying off early. No one is stopping them from working hard and being creative on their own time. I'm not saying deprive them of equal opportunity, but you can't let people just squander someone else's capital. That's no better than stealing.

Absolutely not. In my opinion, what you saw today is not galactic politics. Those deadbeats can call themselves "Ceuganters" if they want to, but they were just looking for a free ride. When they realized they weren't going to get it, they destroyed an ACorp asset worth a hundred of their scraggly compounds. What did they think we'd do, reset the containment field after they blew up the bumpship? Violate the law just for them? It says right in the Notice that once the bubble is popped, it stays popped. Period. Central Court says it's legal, the clause is always in the lease, and the Notice restates it plain as dayside. Refusal to board a bumpship is legally a suicide, which means your debts are transferred to your next of kin. Everybody knows that, so what did they think they were accomplishing? And refusal to board minors in your custody is first-degree murder. The Corporations are not liable for that kind of insanity. There is no excuse for refusing to board a bumpship. No excuse at all. It's the law, and people who break the law are criminals. Period.

I have no sympathy for those people.

The Woman Who Thought She Was a Planet

Vandana Singh

Ramnath Mishra's life changed forever one morning when, during his perusal of the newspaper on the verandah, a ritual that he had observed for the last forty years, his wife set down her cup of tea with a crash and announced: "I know at last what I am. I am a planet."

Ramnath's retirement was a source of displeasure to them both. He had been content to know his wife from a distance, to acknowledge her as the benign despot of the household and mother of his now-grown children, but he had desired no intimacy beyond that. As for Kamala herself, she seemed grumpy and uncomfortable in his company. Now he lowered his newspaper, scowling, prepared to lecture her sternly for interrupting his peace, but instead his mouth fell open in silent astonishment.

His wife had gotten to her feet and was unwinding her sari.

Ramnath nearly knocked over his chair.

"What are you doing—have you lost your mind?" He leaped at her, grabbing a scrap of blue cotton sari with one hand and her arm with the other, looking around wildly to see if the servants were around, or the gardener, or whether the neighbors were peeping through the sprays of bougainvillaea that sheltered the verandah from the summer heat. His wife, arrested in his arms, glared at him balefully.

"A planet does not need clothes," she said with great dignity.

"You are not a planet; you are crazy," Ramnath said. He propelled her into the bedroom. Thankfully, the washerwoman had left and the cook was in the kitchen, singing untunefully to the radio. "Arrange your sari for heaven's sake."

She complied. Ramnath saw that tears were glistening in her eyes. He felt a stab of concern mingled with irritation.

"Have you been feeling ill, Kamala? Should I phone Dr. Kumar?"

"I am not ill," she said. "I have had a revelation. I am a planet. I used to be a human, a woman, a wife and mother. All the time I wondered if there was more to me than that. Now I know. Being a planet is good for me. I have stopped taking my liver pills."

"Well, if you were a planet," Ramnath said in exasperation, "you would be an inanimate object circling a star. You would probably have an atmosphere and living things crawling about you. You would be very large, like Earth or Jupiter. You are not a planet, but a living soul, a woman. A lady from a respectable household who holds the family honor in her hands."

He was gratified that he had explained it so well, because she smiled at him and smoothed her hair, nodding. "I must go see to lunch," she said in her normal voice. Ramnath went back to reading his newspaper on the verandah, shaking his head at the things a man had to do. But he could not concentrate on the prime minister's latest antics. It came to him suddenly that he did not know the person with whom he had lived for forty years. Where had she been getting such strange ideas? He remembered the scandal when, many years ago, a great-aunt of his had gone mad, locked herself in the outdoor toilet of the ancestral home and begun shrieking like a sarus crane in the mating season. They had finally got her out while curious neighbors thronged the courtyard, shouting encouragements. He remembered how quiet she had seemed after they helped her over the broken door, how there had been no warning before she bent her head, apparently in meek surrender, and bit her husband on his arm. She had ended up in the insane asylum in Ranchi. What terrible dishonor the family had suffered, what indignity—a mad person in a respectable upper middle class family—he shuddered suddenly, set down his newspaper and went to call Dr. Kumar. Dr. Kumar would be discreet, he was a family friend . . .

But when he went into the drawing room, it was dark—somebody had closed the curtains, shutting out the morning light. Disturbed by the unnatural silence—the cook had stopped singing—he groped blindly toward the light-switch, which was closer to him than any of the windows. "Kamala!" he called, irritated to find his voice trembling. Abruptly a curtain at the other end of the room was drawn violently back, letting in a burst of sunshine that hurt his eyes. There stood his wife, naked, facing the sun with her arms spread wide. She began to turn slowly. There was a beatific expression on her face. The sunlight washed her ample body, the generous terraces and folds of flesh that cascaded down to her sagging belly and buttocks. Ramnath was transfixed with horror. He ran up to the curtain, drew it closed, put his hands on his wife's plump shoulders and shook her hard.

"You have gone mad! What will the neighbors think? What did I do to deserve this!"

He dragged her to the bedroom and looked around for her sari. The blouse, petticoat, and sari lay in crumpled folds on the bed. This in itself was disturbing because she was usually obsessive about tidiness. He realized that he had no idea how to put the sari on her. He saw the nightgown hanging neatly folded on the mosquito-netting bar and grabbed it. His wife was struggling in his arms.

"Are you completely shameless? Put this on!"

After a while he managed to get the nightgown on her, but it was back-to-front. That didn't matter. He sat her down on the bed.

"Stay here and don't move. I am going to call the doctor. Has the cook gone out?"

Her nod reassured him, but she would not look at him. As Ramnath went into the drawing room, he hesitated, then turned on the light instead of drawing open the curtains. He was irritated to find that a part of his body had responded to her nakedness and his struggle with her. Resolutely he put all distracting thoughts aside and went to the phone.

Dr. Kumar was out attending to a hospital emergency. Ramnath thought unkind thoughts about his friend. "Tell him he *must* phone the moment he returns—it is a matter of great urgency," he told the servant. He slammed down the phone. He went back to the bedroom. His wife was lying down, apparently asleep.

All that day Ramnath kept guard over his wife. By lunch she had changed back into her sari and combed her hair. The cook served them a stew of chickpeas simmered in a sauce of onions, cumin, ginger, and chilies. There was basmati rice, which they kept only for special occasions, and tiny fried eggplants stuffed with tomatoes and spices. Ramnath, having no idea what his wife's favorite dishes were, had asked the cook to make whatever Kamala liked, hoping that food would distract her from this insanity. But she picked at her food absently, a dreamy look on her face. It was obvious that her thoughts were miles away. Ramnath felt a surge of anger and self-pity. What had he done to deserve this? He had worked hard for forty years or more, risen up to the ranks of a senior bureaucrat in the state government. He had fathered two sons. Now it occurred to him that it would have been nice to have a daughter, somebody whom he could call on at times like this. His mind did a quick survey of elderly female relatives—but they were either all dead or lived in other towns and villages. Why didn't that damned doctor phone?

Ramnath's day was completely ruined. In the evenings he liked to go to the senior club and play chess with other retirees, but today he dared not leave his wife. She, for her part, spoke only when spoken to. She seemed outwardly calm, instructing the cook and herself dusting the pictures and bric-a-brac in the drawing room, but occasionally he would catch her gazing dreamily into a private world, a smile on her lips. He phoned the doctor again, but the damn fool had come home only briefly, dressed for a party, and left without receiving the urgent message.

That night was one of the worst that Ramnath had ever experienced. His wife tossed in her sleep, straining against some invisible restraining force like a moored ship trying to break free. Ramnath himself was beset by nightmares of planets and matronly naked women. He woke several times, looking warily at his wife as she slept fitfully, her graying hair all over the pillow, half-covering her open mouth. A wisp of hair blew out of her mouth with her breath, and it seemed to him as though it took on the aspect of some awful living thing. He brushed the hair off her face, trying not to tremble. In the moonlight from the window, her face was like the surface of the moon: pitted and cratered, fissured with age. She looked like a stranger.

The next morning his wife was rather subdued. She did not go out in the middle of the day to visit Mrs. Chakravarti or Mrs. Jain, as she used to do. She let the phone ring until Ramnath, maddened by her indifference, picked up the receiver and shouted into it, only to be embarrassed by the cool voice of Mrs. Jain. "My wife is not well," he said, immediately regretting it. Mrs. Jain, all concern, showed up ten minutes later with Mrs. Chakravarti, bearing fruits and a special herbal concoction that Mrs. Chakravarti's mother-in-law had made. For a minute Ramnath felt like telling them to go away and leave him in peace, but their matronly figures, resplendent in crisp, starched cotton saris, their perfumed, hennaed hair tied so neatly into buns, their air of righteous sisterly concern quite defeated him. Kamala came out of the bedroom, where she had been lying down, greeted them with surprised pleasure and led them all back into the room. Ramnath, thus displaced, sat and fretted on the hot verandah, first refusing and then accepting the cook's offer of homemade lemon water. Inside the bedroom the women were all sprawled on the bed like beached whales, sipping lemon water and talking and giggling. He could not tell what they were gossiping about. But slowly he became comforted by the notion that his wife was at least acting normally. Perhaps having her friends over was a good thing. Perhaps he could manage a visit to the club this evening.

As soon as the women left, Kamala reverted to her old air of quiet indifference. Meanwhile Dr. Kumar called. The idiot insisted on asking exactly what the matter was with Mrs. Mishra. Ramnath, feeling his wife's eyes on him, did not know what to say. "It's a lady matter," he said finally, embarrassed. "I can't explain over the phone. Can you come?"

Dr. Kumar came that evening and stayed to dinner. He checked Kamala's blood pressure, listened to her heart. His assistant, a taciturn young man, withdrew blood for further testing. During all this Kamala was serene, hospitable, asking after the doctor's family with sweet concern. It occurred to Ramnath that she had already acquired the infamous cunning of the insane, which enables them to conceal their madness at will.

"You must be mistaken, Mishra-ji," the doctor said on the phone two days later. "Everything is normal—she is, in fact, much healthier than before. If she has been behaving strangely, it is probably mental. Not always the sign of disease. Women are odd—they act strangely when they are hankering after something. She should go out, maybe go visit one of your sons. Grandchildren would do her good."

But Kamala refused to leave town. At last Ramnath, acting on the doctor's advice, persuaded her to walk with him in the evenings, hoping that the open air would do her good. He kept a steely eye on her—if she as much as touched the free end of her sari hanging over her shoulder, he would grunt warningly and slap her hand. The narrow lanes of their neighborhood were lined with amaltash trees heavy with cascades of golden flowers. In the playground the older boys finished the last round of cricket in the failing light, while smaller children squatted in the dust, playing with marbles, ignoring wandering cows and sedate, elderly citizens taking the air. Neighbors sitting on the verandahs of their bungalows called out greetings. Torn between hope and dread, Ramnath frequently and surreptitiously examined his wife's face for signs of incipient madness. She remained calm and sociable, although as they walked on it seemed as though she were falling into a trance, interrupted only by sighs of deep rapture as she gazed at the sunset.

In the week that followed, Kamala attempted twice to take off her clothes. Both times Ramnath managed to restrain her, although the second time she almost managed to escape from him. He caught her just as she was about to run out into the driveway in nothing but a petticoat and blouse, in full view of street vendors, cricket-playing children, and respectable elderly gentlemen. He wrestled her into the bedroom and tried to slap some sense into her, but she continued to struggle and weep. At last, frustrated, he pulled half a dozen saris out from the big steel cupboard and flung them on the bed.

"Kamala," he said desperately, "even planets have atmospheres. See here, this gray sari, it looks like a swirl of clouds. How about it?"

She calmed down at once. She began to put on the gray sari, although the fabric, georgette, was unsuitable for summer.

"At last you believe me, Ramnath," she said. Her voice seemed to have changed. It was deeper, more powerful. He looked at her, aghast. She had addressed him by his name! That was all very well for the new generation of young adults, but respectable, traditional women never addressed their husbands by their names. He decided not to do anything about it for now. At least she was clothed.

At night Ramnath lay wrestling with doubts and fears. A breeze blew in through the open window, stirring the mosquito-netting. In the starlight his wife, the room, everything looked alien. He propped himself on one elbow and looked at the stranger beside him. A thought came to him that if he could get her confined to the asylum in Ranchi without a scandal, he would do it. But she had that idiot Kumar charmed. The way she had asked so nicely about his ailing mother, congratulated him on his recent membership in a prestigious medical organization. Kumar had known the family for years—and, it occurred to Ramnath, had always had a soft spot for his wife. Who would have thought she'd had so much cunning in her? Now, as he watched her sleep, her hair in disarray and her mouth open like some hideous cavern, it occurred to him how easy his life would be if she would simply die. He was ashamed of the thought as soon as it formed, but he could not take it back. It called to him and seduced him and resounded in his head until he was convinced that if he could not have her committed, he would have to kill her himself. He could not live like this.

Every night it became a ritual for him to look at her and imagine the different ways he could commit murder. He had been shocked at himself at first—him, a fine, upstanding ex-bureaucrat contemplating something as hideous as the murder of the mother of his sons—but there was no denying that the thought—the fantasy, he told himself—gave him pleasure. A secret, shameful sort of pleasure, like sex before marriage, but pleasure nonetheless.

He began to count the ways. Suffocation with a pillow while she slept would be the easiest, but he had no idea if the forensics people could infer from that what had happened. Strangulation had the same problem. Poison—but where to procure it? And now that she had stopped taking her liver pills, he could no longer perform some artful substitution. Damn the woman!

One night, as he watched her sleeping, he put his hand very gently on her neck. She stirred a little, frightening him, but he made himself keep his hand there, feeling the pulse in her throat. He began to stroke her neck with his thumb. Abruptly she coughed, and he jerked his hand away in terror. But she did not wake. She was coughing up something dark from her mouth. For a moment he thought it was blood, that he should call the doctor; his next thought was that perhaps she was dying of her own accord. Maybe it had been enough to wish it so strongly. She coughed again and again, but she did not wake. Now the dark stuff had gathered about her mouth, on her chin, like a jelly. To his horror he saw that the darkness was not blood, but composed of small moving things. One stood up on its hind legs for a moment, surveying him, and he drew back in horror. It was insectoid, alien, about as tall as his index finger. There was an army of those things coming out of her mouth.

The mosquito netting was tucked under the bed on all sides—he pushed at it, trying to tear it with his hands, but they were upon him before he could get out of the bed. He tried to cry out, but all he could manage was a whimper. They covered his body, crawling inside his clothes, beating and biting at him with short, sharp appendages. He tried to brush them off, but there were too many of them. They made a sound like crickets singing, but softer. He howled in despair, calling to Kamala to save him, but she lay peacefully beside him as the things came out of her. After a while he fainted.

Much later he opened his eyes, with some difficulty—they were sticky with dried tears. A pale morning light came in through the window. There was no sign of the creatures. There was a large tear in the mosquito netting, and a mosquito was humming in his ear. His wife lay sleeping beside him. Perhaps what he had experienced had been a nightmare; he told himself that it was his conscience punishing him for his impious thoughts. But he knew that the soreness all over his body, the marks of bites and the bruises, were real. He turned fearfully towards his wife. Abruptly her eyes snapped open.

"Hai bhagwaan!" She was looking at the tear on his white sleepshirt, the pinpricks of blood. He flinched as she reached out a hand to touch the tiny wounds. They had spared his face. More cunning, he thought. "Why didn't you wake me? I would have told them—they would have understood, not hurt you."

"What are those things?" he whispered.

"Inhabitants," she said. "I'm a planet, remember?"

She smiled at the look on his face.

"Don't be afraid, Ramnath." Again, the free use of his name! Was she possessed? Should he consult an astrologer? An exorcist? He, a rational man, reduced to this!

""Don't be afraid," she said again. "The younger ones probably want to find a place to colonize. If you ever want to be a satellite, Ramnath, let me know. The little animals are good for a planet. They have restored my health."

"Do you want to go visit your mother?" he whispered. "You haven't been home for a while. I will make all the arrangements . . ."

He had not let her go home to her ancestral village for the past five years—there was always something going on that needed her attention. The marriage of their sons, his retirement, and the fact that *somebody* had to run the house and supervise the servants.

"Oh Ramnath," she said, her eyes softening. "You were never this generous before. I think you have quite changed. No, I don't want to leave you, not yet."

She bathed his wounds with Dettol and warm water. She watched over him solicitously as he ate his breakfast. Later, her distracted look returned as she moved about the house, dusting and rearranging things mechanically. Ramnath felt the need to escape.

"Do you mind if I go to the club this evening?"

"No, of course not," she said amiably. "Go enjoy yourself."

When he went to his club, he made a private and very expensive phone call to his older son.

"But Papa, I just heard from Ma. She sounded quite normal. Are you sure you are feeling well? . . . No, I can't come now, there is a very important case at court. My senior partner has put me in charge . . ."

The younger son was in Germany on an engineering assignment. Defeated, Ramnath immersed himself in a game of chess with an acquaintance who beat him easily.

"Losing your touch, sir?" said the younger man annoyingly.

When Ramnath got home, he felt he was returning to prison. The house was quite silent except for the cook singing in the kitchen. It occurred to him to tell the fellow to shut up. But where was his wife?

"She went to the park, Sahib," the cook said.

He wondered whether to go after her. But five minutes later she was coming up the driveway clutching a balloon. She waved and smiled at him quite shamelessly. He saw with relief that she was clothed. She was eating an ice-cream bar.

"I had such fun, Ramnath," she told him. "I played with the little ones. I bought them all balloons. I haven't had a balloon in such a long time."

Later, after the cook had retired, he spoke to her.

"Kamala, those . . . things, those creatures inside you . . . I think we should get you checked up. It is not right to keep all this from Dr. Kumar. You have a terrible disease . . ."

"But, Ramnath, I have no sickness. I am well, very well. After years."

"But . . ."

"And the things, as you call them, are not things but my own creation. They came from me, Ramnath."

She slapped his face playfully.

"You look pulled down and grumpy," she said, pinching his thin cheek. "My little animals would do you so much good, Ramnath, if only you would rid yourself of your prejudice."

He backed away from her, outraged and horrified.

"Never! Kamala, I am going to sleep on the sofa. I cannot . . ."

"As you wish," she said indifferently.

That night he lay awake for a long time. He could hear the crickets singing outside the window, but was too nervous to get up and shut out the sound. All the small night-time sounds—the whisper of the curtain in the breeze, the asthmatic squeak of the ceiling fan, the rustle of the leaves of the bougainvillaea outside—all this made him think of the insect-like creatures. Once he woke up and fancied that some of them were standing on the top of the narrow sofa, looking down at him and gesturing in a very human way as he lay there, helpless. He began to edge off the sofa, his heart hammering wildly, but a sudden gust of wind filled the curtains so they billowed out like ghostly sails, letting in the moonlight—and he saw that there was nothing on the top of the sofa after all. At last he fell asleep, exhausted.

Over the next few days Ramnath kept hold of his sanity with great difficulty. He wondered whether he should renounce the world and retire to the Himalayas. Perhaps the gods he had so casually dismissed the past few years were getting their revenge now. He still toyed with the idea of murder, although it seemed impossible now, at least at close range. Looking at his wife over dinner, he began to wonder for the first time about her. What was she really like? What did she want that he had not given her? How had he come to this?

"Kamala," he said one day. He was in a strange mood. He had lit an incense stick in front of the household gods that morning. The scent of sandalwood still pervaded the house. It made him feel humble, virtuous, as though he was at last letting go of his ego and surrendering to the divine. "Tell me, what is it like . . . to have those . . . animals inside you . . ."

She smiled. Her teeth were very white.

"I hardly feel them most of the time, Ramnath," she said. "I wish you would agree to be colonized. It would do you good, and it would help them—the younger ones have been clamoring for a new world. I hear them singing sometimes, chirping sounds like crickets. It is a language I am beginning to understand."

He thought he heard it faintly then, too.

"What are they saying?"

She frowned, listening. She sighed.

"A planet needs a sun, Ramnath," she said evasively. "My journey is just beginning."

After this interchange he noticed an increased restlessness in his wife. She kept going out to the garden to sun herself in the forty degree centigrade heat among the wilting guava trees. In the house she moved from room to room, making little chirping sounds and humming tunelessly to herself. Ramnath felt his pious resolve shatter. Irritated, he spent that evening at his club.

The next evening, remembering his duty, Ramnath dragged his wife out for a walk. She protested feebly but let him pull her into the street. By the time they reached the park a soft twilight had fallen. A few stars and a pale moon hung in the sky. Kamala lingered at the edge of the park.

"Come on," Ramnath said, impatient to continue walking.

But instead his wife gave a cry of pleasure and turned into the park, where in the semi-darkness a man was selling balloons. She began to run toward the balloon man, gesturing like an excited child. Embarrassed and annoyed, he followed her at a more dignified pace.

"More balloons," he heard her say. Coins tinkled. A small crowd of street urchins appeared from nowhere. He could hear the rhythmic squeak of a swing in the semi-darkness ahead.

Now she was handing balloons out to the gaggle of brats, who jumped and chattered excitedly around her.

"Me too, Auntie-ji!"

The balloons bobbed over their heads like dim little orbs in the moonlight. Ramnath pushed aside the children and grabbed his wife by the shoulder.

"Enough," he said impatiently. "You are spoiling these good-for-nothings!"

She shrugged off his hand. She let go of one of her balloons and watched it float lazily up into the starlit sky. A sudden gust of wind came up and dislodged the free end of her sari from her shoulder, baring her blouse. The balloon man stared at her ample cleavage.

"Adjust your sari for heaven's sake," Ramnath said in a desperate whisper. He looked around to see if anyone else was watching this spectacle and was horrified to see the ramrod figure of Judge Pandey walking toward them on the path through the park, his cane tap-tapping. Fearful that the judge would see him and associate him with this madwoman, Ramnath retreated into the inadequate shadow of an Ashok tree. Fortunately Judge Pandey didn't see him. He saw what seemed to be a wanton-looking woman and walked quickly past her in case anyone noticed him staring. Ramnath, sweaty with relief, emerged from the shadows and grabbed the end of his wife's sari that lay on the dusty ground. His wife had released three other balloons into the air and was watching them go up with childish pleasure. The children were shouting in their shrill voices.

"Let another one go, Auntie-ji!"

"Come home, Kamala," Ramnath said pleadingly. "This is madness!"

But instead of answering, Kamala let go of all the balloons, some seven or eight of them. They floated up into the sky. She stretched her arms out to them, her face full of a blissful yearning. Slowly and majestically she began to rise over the ground—an inch, two inches.

"What are you doing?" Ramnath said to her in a horrified whisper.

Three feet, four feet. Ramnath's mouth fell open. He pulled on the end of the sari he was holding, but she continued to rise, turning slowly, trailing two yards, then five yards of cotton. Too late, Ramnath let go of the sari. His wife rose into the night air, her white petticoat filling with air like the sails of a ship.

"Oooh! Look what the auntie is doing!"

Some of the urchins had drawn back. The balloon man's face was a round circle of astonishment.

"Come back!" Ramnath shouted.

The children were yelling and pointing and jumping with glee. She was well up now, higher than the trees and houses. The balloons scattered above her like a flotilla of tiny satellite moons. People were running out of their houses now, pointing and staring. Something white and ghostly came slipping down from the sky—her petticoat! Her blouse and undergarments were next. Ramnath stood transfixed with horror while the urchins cavorted about, trying to catch the garments in the darkness. Somebody—Mrs. Jain, perhaps—began wailing. "Hai Bhagwaan, that is Kamala, Kamala Mishra!"

The cry was taken up all around. With each shout Ramnath felt his family name and honor sinking into the ground. He tried to slink away, keeping to the shadows of trees like a thief, hoping nobody would recognize him. But then, on the road, Judge Pandey tapped him on the shoulder. The veteran judge's solemn, impassive face was the last thing he wanted to see.

"Most reprehensible, Mishra! Most reprehensible!"

Ramnath moaned and fled to his house, throwing dignity to the winds. All around people were saying his wife's name—the neighbors, the street urchins, the servants, the man selling roasted corn at the end of the street. The house was dark and empty. No doubt the cook had gone to see the show as well. Ramnath felt he could face nobody after this. He stood in the middle of the dark drawing room, thinking wildly of escape, or suicide.

He went to the window and looked out apprehensively. There she was, a tiny, bright blob still rising into the sky. How dare she leave him like this!

It occurred to him that there was only one option—to take enough things from the house, leave by the late train, and disappear. He could even change his name, he thought. Begin anew. The house was willed to his sons. He would not let his dishonor touch them. Let them all think he was dead!

She was out of sight now. For a moment he almost envied her, out there among the stars. He imagined, despite himself, the little alien creatures running over the wild terrain of her body, exploring the mountains, gullies, and varied habitats of that mysterious and unknowable geography. What sun would she find? What vistas would she see? A sob caught in his throat. How would he manage now, with nobody to look after him?

A small sound caught his attention. Perhaps it was the cook returning, or the neighbors coming to feast on the remains of his dignity. There was no time. He rushed to the bedroom, turned on the light. Breathing hard, he started to pull things out of the steel cupboard, things he would need, like money, her jewelry, and clothes. It was then that he felt something on his shoulder.

He would have screamed if he had remembered how; the insectoids were already marching up his back, over his shoulder, and into his terrified, open mouth.

Shipwreck Beach
Glen Hirshberg

According to mystical people, spiritual forces converge at Hawai'i, as do ocean currents and winds.
—Maxine Hong Kingston

I

They served us guava punch and Paradise Mix, which turned out to be candied peanuts, coconut flakes, and dried papaya, and far below, in the long expanses between islands, the water glowed green and blue, too wet, somehow, like the insides of some luscious, cracked-open tropical fruit. I couldn't get the light out of my eyes even when I shut them. Across the narrow aisle from me, the woman with the laptop snapped her computer shut with a click, looked up for the first time all flight, and said, "God, can you feel that air?"

The exit door wasn't even open, and something about the intensity in the woman's voice made me snort. Couldn't help it.

The woman whirled as though I'd shot a rubber band at her. She had green eyes—ordinary, mainland green—and skeletal, protruding shoulders under her white silk blouse.

"Well?" she said. "Can't you?"

And I realized that I could. The feeling came in with the light. I blushed, and the lone door up front opened, and the woman sheathed her laptop and strode out. The flight's only steward stepped back practically into the cockpit when she passed, waited for the other seven passengers to deplane, then stood there, not quite looking at my legs in the aisle, waiting. Self-conscious, as usual—not to mention tanless—I tugged the hem of my skirt down over my knees. He looked a little older than I was, maybe twenty, his skin rich and dark and rough. He had black hair and big hands. He shifted, aimed his gaze a little closer to my eyes, and said, "Aloha, and welcome to Lana-ii." The hiccup in the name sounded like something he'd practiced, not natural to him.

"Okay," I said, because I'd wanted to come, after all. Demanded to come. Begged, until my mother had finally broken down and let me, because Harry had begged me. And now here I was. Damn him.

God, I remember that moment, stepping onto Lanai for the first time, blinking against the sunlight and feeling the tradewinds tumble past. I squinted, eyeing the square, squat, wooden terminal-house and the single luggage cart trundling out to meet the plane as passengers spilled onto the tarmac. Around us, low green hills swelled and sank. Petrified waves, I thought. That's all this place was. The last land. The farthest Harry could run. I shouldered my duffel bag, took two steps toward the terminal, and saw him.

He'd lost so much weight that he seemed to have shed his shadow, and his skin was dark, as if he'd been out of jail for ten years, not ten months. But he still wore the same stupid glasses, brown-tinted and curvy, so that his eyes seemed to bulge behind them like a lizard's. When he spotted me, he bounced up and down on the balls of his feet, and I half expected him to leap the restraining rope set up for non-passengers.

Instead, he waited until I was inside the rope, standing next to him, starting to say something salty, and then he engulfed me.

"Get off," I mumbled after a few seconds, because amazingly, he smelled even worse than I remembered. Ammonia now, and citronella, and pineapple, on top of the familiar too-thick hair gel and drugstore cologne.

"Hello, cousin," he said, not even loosening his grip, and I snapped my elbows out, grabbed his wrists, shoved him up onto his tiptoes, and jammed my foot against the ball of his ankle.

"Could've broken that," I said.

"You really are fast."

I let go of his wrists, stepped back before he could hug me again, and put my hands together. "Hai."

"Hi, Mimi," Harry said.

"Not hi, idiot. Hai, as in yes, I really am fast." I bowed. "Ous."

Somehow, he'd scooped his haystack of blond hair into a poofy Bill Clinton-wave. He looked soft in his button-down Hawaiian shirt, complete with embroidered palm trees. Of my cousin the swimmer, the boy who, barely ten years ago, had shattered the Orange County fourteen-and-under record in the 200 fly, there was little trace.

"Well, let's go see it," I said, and Harry blinked.

"See what?"

"The beach with the ghost wreck. The one you keep e-mailing me about."

"We can't just go see that. It has to be right."

"Let's see it now."

"Later."

"What, you want to show me the multiplex?" I asked, gesturing around me at the empty green. "The jammin' club scene?"

"Thank you, Mimi," Harry whispered, and wetness formed in the corners of his lizard eyes under his glasses. "Thank you for coming."

I watched until the tears leaked onto his cheek. Then I blurted, "Fuck my mother," spun on my heels, and started through the terminal. I heard Harry galumphing behind me, graceless as a hippo, mumbling something about not talking about her like that, but I didn't turn around. In my ears, I could hear my mother recounting, for the thousandth time, the story of the day Harry's parents put him on the train from OC and sent him down to visit us in Solana Beach. This was before the incident with the necklace, before he got thrown out of school for selling or maybe just being near selling, before the carjacking-and-burning thing, any of it, when all eleven-year-old Harry had done was fake results on a biology project about the effects of Jodie Foster's Army music on plant growth, earn a series of report card comments about his "elusiveness when confronted," and throw a bicycle-pump through his teacher's back car window, which he swore was an accident. That last had just occurred, though no one had told me about it, and was the reason my aunt had shipped him off to us for the weekend so she and my uncle could calm down, "get our heads straight."

I was six, and I remember standing at the Del Mar train station, which was mostly a shack and looked exactly like the shacks across the street from it on the lip of the beach, where you could rent boogie-boards and buy waffle cones with chocolate syrup colored blue, just because. I'd already been in the water, I think, because I remember the slick of salt on my skin, the faint sting in my eyes every time I blinked, the skateboard boys floating past, white-shirted, wild-haired.

Then the train came whistling and growling into the station and sighed to a stop, and I remember how huge it seemed, huff, puff, blow your house down. Seconds later, Harry charged out, sprinting straight for us with his legs pumping under his tan OP's and his green surf shirt billowing around him. He threw himself straight into my mother's arms. That's what I remember. I don't remember him saying, "God, Aunt Trish, I love you so incredibly much, you look beautiful," which is what my mother damns him for, but I'm sure he did. Those are the kinds of things he said.

"I knew right then," my mother would say from that moment on, every time her sister called weeping, recounting Harry's latest inexplicable, increasingly unforgivable act. "You could just tell. It was too much, you know? Off, somehow. Calculated. You just knew that boy would say absolutely anything to anybody. Do absolutely anything to get what he wanted." What made me so furious, every time, was the nagging, inescapable possibility that she was right.

Exiting the terminal, I turned on Harry and snapped, "Where's the bus? Or are we walking?"

He was closer behind than I'd expected, and he cocked his head when he stopped, peering at me from under his bulgy lenses. Turtle-cousin. "Come on, Harry," I said, and was relieved to hear my voice sound gentler this time. "Show me the isle."

For a few seconds, he just stood there swaying, which fanned my annoyance again. Once upon a time, Harry had been the only person immune to my mood swings, which my mother had dubbed the Tradewinds of Amelia long before Harry moved here. My mother said they didn't affect Harry because Harry was oblivious to anyone but himself.

Finally, for the first time since I'd stepped off the plane, my cousin grinned. "I have a car." The grin twitched.

I grinned back, partly to encourage him, partly because it was either that or kick him. "How'd that happen?"

"Work. I teach at the grade school. They fronted me some money to get me started."

Now it was my turn to stare. "Teach what?"

He shrugged. "They don't check backgrounds so much out here. It's a new chance, you know? A real one."

From his pants pocket, he withdrew a set of keys, pressed a button, got an answering squawk from a green Toyota pick-up so sparkly-clean it seemed to ripple like the surface of the sea, and beamed the way he used to, bobbing in the surf, when the big waves rose and swept him up. I slung my bag in the bed.

As soon as we were out of the parking lot, the island opened beneath us like a gorgeous green flipped-over umbrella drifting on the winking water. I saw pineapple plants sticking out of the ground in rows, their spiky fruits nestled in the long, straight leaves like nesting birds.

In front of us, a salt-caked blue bus filled the road, headed our way. Harry pulled to the side into the dirt, and when the driver passed—another Hawaiian boy, no older than the steward on my plane, with a white cap that read *Manele Bay* in red letters perched on his forehead—he stuck his hand out the window, palm down, and waved. Harry waved back, same way, and something quivered in my chest. Aunt Fred should come here, I thought. See this.

"I want to see your school," I said.

Harry held onto the wheel and glanced at me. "You in shape? Swim-shape, I mean?"

I flicked the jiggly pouch of flesh under his bicep. "More than you."

Harry blushed. "Did you dye your hair?"

"Do you remember it red? Is that like a question?"

"It looks nice," he mumbled, straight down into the steering wheel, and I felt bad, and we were off again.

For a while, we drove without talking. Harry rolled his window down, so I did, too, and the smell came in: sea salt and wet grass and, most of all, gardenia, so sweet, too much, as though a perfume factory had exploded nearby. Lanai air, it turns out, is as addicting as cigarette smoke. You forget how to breathe without smelling.

We passed another bus, a few road signs rusting and tilting in the ocean wind, white condominiums jutting from the hillsides like plastic teeth. Finally, Harry pulled to a stop along a curve in the road and shut down the truck and got out. I started to do the same, and he leaned back in.

"Change," he said.

It took me a second to realize what he meant. Then I said, "Here?"

"I'll be up the hill." He gestured to the green rise beside the car.

"Is this the wreck?"

"I told you," he said, straightening, so that his voice got all but swallowed by the wind. "I want to share that with you the right way. I want you to feel it, too. That way, you might understand."

"Is this a religion thing? Did you get Jesus or something?"

With a shrug, Harry swung the door shut and grabbed twin sets of flippers and masks out of the truck bed and started up the hill. Beneath the white canvas shorts, his leg muscles tensed and slackened like cleated rope on mastheads. The softness, I thought, had not spread there. And he really did seem closer to peaceful than I'd ever seen him, if no less sad. In the visiting room at California State Prison in Lancaster, both times my mother let me go, he'd dissolved into a blubbering, whimpering mess across the table and managed to say virtually nothing. Clearly, the island or the sun or his holy shipwreck had done something for him. To him.

I had to get out of the car and drag the duffel bag into the dirt so I could unzip it, then crouch back inside the cab to wriggle into my suit. As usual, my legs looked stumpy to me. Neither karate nor swimming had lengthened them any. "But the hair," I said aloud, catching sight of myself in the mirror on the sunvisor, "is red."

I was expecting ocean at my feet, white sand smooth as a glacier but hot, fanning away in all directions. What I found when I got to the top of the hill was ocean, alright, sixty feet or so below, slamming so hard against the rock face we stood on that I could feel the vibrations in my feet. Eyeing Harry, I said, "Is this a test?"

He shook his head. "Warm-up."

"Physical? Spiritual?" I was teasing as much as asking.

Harry just slid his hands into his pockets and stepped onto the foot-wide path that slanted down the rocks. There was no beach below, but Harry didn't even slow as he reached the lowest exposed point on the path, just dropped his shirt and my flippers to the dirt and slid on his own fins and plunged straight into the surf. I hustled after him, stopping only long enough to check for coral or rock before I leapt. The peaks in the water looked more like rumples in a thrashed-about sheet than waves because they had no whitecaps and they didn't break except when they slammed against the cliff.

Then the ocean had me, and I thought about nothing but breathing. I didn't even look up for the first three minutes, just drove forward. My mouth stung with saltwater, and my legs kept pounding as I plunged from wave-trough to wave-trough. Competing currents twisted around my ankles below the surface, grabbed, released. Glancing up finally, I saw our destination, the pillar of crooked brown rock sticking out of the surf like a giant's beckoning finger, seemingly no closer than it had been when I leapt from the ledge.

When I felt I was free of the cauldron near shore, at least, I looked up again, spit, and called after my cousin. "Not really supposed to swim here, are we?"

Far ahead, Harry glided to a stop, rolled over on his back, and cupped a hand to his ear. As always, he'd lost all his awkwardness as soon as he hit the water, become sleek and slippery and playful as an otter.

"Swim here," I yelled again, kicking hard, lurching toward him as he hovered in place. "Supposed to?"

"Not much 'supposed to' on Lanai," he said. "No one checking."

"But people don't. Swim here."

Harry grinned. "You *are* rusty." Then he flipped over again, shot ahead of me, and I followed as best I could.

For the next ten minutes or so, I did what he'd trained me to do years ago as he skated across the insides of waves or scaled them like a mountain climber, seeming, sometimes, to emerge, fully standing, atop them as they curled, as if he were about to plant a flag there: I put my head down, looked neither forward nor back, and kicked steadily while my nerve ends read the water. Sometimes I tacked against the current, and sometimes I ran before it, cupping it in my ribs the way a sail grabs wind. When I let myself look up again, the rock was close enough for me to see that there was nowhere to grab, no place to rest. Solid sheets of perfect green water shattered against it like china plates.

"You okay?" Harry said, surfacing beside me, pulling up short, bobbing. So I pulled up too, nodded, and found, to my relief, that I was. My shoulders were screaming, and my thigh muscles filled my skin like poured concrete, hardening, but the air was flying down my lungs into my bloodstream, lighting me up as it went, and I could feel myself tingling, awakening. Not even karate made me feel quite this strong.

"That's nowhere we can go," I said, and Harry nodded.

"It's somewhere to see. There's a story. Want to hear it?"

Abruptly, I swung toward him. There was a story I wanted to hear, alright—needed to hear—but it wasn't the one Harry wanted to tell me. So I just up and asked him. "How did it happen, Harry? Please make me understand."

"The rock? It—"

"Randy Lynne, Harry. Prison, Harry. How did that happen? What the fuck is wrong with you?"

He buckled as though a wave had slammed him, ducked under water, and for a second I thought he'd left me there, dove for his sea-lair or whatever he'd apparently built for himself here. But he surfaced again. Bobbing. Effortless.

"I'm sorry," I said. "I've tried. But I can't seem to make myself understand."

"Me either," Harry said softly, staring at the rock and the empty sea beyond it.

"Was it bad? Prison?" As soon as I asked that, I felt like an idiot. And I knew what he was going to say.

"It's where I belonged," he murmured, right on cue. Then he went quiet, absolutely still, as though he was going to let himself sink.

"Harry," I said quickly. "Listen. You're a fucking idiot, right? I agree with you. But get real. You did what everyone does. Lots of people, anyway. You just got caught."

Harry's head shot up so fast I thought he'd been stung or bitten, and I started to kick toward him and then checked myself, hard. In his stare, and in the set of his lips, chewed to shreds the way they always were, was something brand new. It looked, I thought, like loathing.

"The man died," he said.

I found I couldn't look at him. I looked at the rock. "You weren't even driving. You—"

"Shut up, Mimi. Right now."

More than anything, I needed to get his glare off me. I could feel it on my arms and face like radiation. "Tell me about the rock," I said, remembering Harry, age fifteen or so, skimming the waves off Laguna Niguel like a gull.

"Pu'upehe," Harry said. I have no idea if he said the word right, but he sounded more Hawaiian to my distinctly haole ears than the steward on the plane or any of the other airline personnel. "There's a story. A girl. So beautiful, her husband shut her up in a sea cave." He gestured behind us toward the cliffs, but he didn't look that way. His voice came out raspy, as though I'd kicked him in the throat.

"I'm sorry, Harry," I said. "I just missed you, and I don't—"

"One day when the husband was out hunting or something, a storm came, and the sea swirled in, filled the cave, and the woman drowned there. When the husband came back and found her, he was so overwhelmed with grief that he dragged his wife's body into the sea, somehow swam with it to this rock, hauled it up the rock, and buried it there, at the top. Then he jumped into the water and drowned."

Harry looked at me, too hard, his blond hair flying off his head like steam, and a new nervousness spasmed through me. Another gift from my mother, I realized. She'd always thought it just might be a little wrong, the way Harry loved me.

"Mimi, look down," he said suddenly, and drove his head below the surface.

At first, when I dropped my face in the water, I couldn't make sense of it. There were so many of them, fanned out in perfect rows, that they looked more like the long leaves of some underwater kelp forest than individual creatures. Then four of them broke from the line, swept upward at us, and whirled around us, their bodies steel-green, so smooth I swear I could see my reflection sliding across them, their chitter and squeak filling the water like bat sonar. One of them hurtled clear of the surface, and I jerked my head up in time to see it finish its flip and crash down not five feet from me, and I burst out laughing as spray smacked into my mouth, rocking me backward. Coughing, still laughing, I ducked under again, found another one hovering right in front of me, snout all but touching my chest, mouth open so I could see the startling teeth, the tiny black eyes swallowing sunlight but radiating nothing, like slivers of coal. It looked utterly alien up close in its world, nothing at all like me, and yet never, ever, ever had I been more aware of the sizzle in the skin, the ripple in the blood that tells you another living thing is near.

Fifteen seconds, maybe twenty, and it was over. The whole school swung like a hinged gate toward the open ocean, and in a matter of seconds they were a hundred yards away, leaping clear of the water and crashing back and finally disappearing altogether, leaving barely a wisp of white on the whitecapped water to show where they had been.

"Oh my God, Harry," I sputtered, gagging and giggling.

"Come on," he said, looking away from me now. "You'll get tired." He kicked toward shore, but I caught a glimpse of his face as he dropped it into the water. His smile must have lit the reef.

Back in the truck, and then at the restaurant at the Manele Bay Hotel, Harry barely spoke, wouldn't even let me catch his eye, so I just sat while the experience we'd had with the dolphins repeated itself in my mind, over and over, like a meteor shower. Finally, inevitably, it faded though, leaving an ashy aftertaste and a voice I didn't want to hear. My mother's, of course, recounting yet again exactly what Harry had done.

First, apparently, he'd bought two cases of Red Hook for Randy Lynne and his goofy little band of goons. Harry was still something of a legend for Randy and the rest of the next-gen thugs at my school; they sought him out sometimes at the TruSavings Hardware where he worked in the stockroom and made him tell them the car-burning story. They were almost too funny and too smart to be thugs, those boys. Almost. What they liked to do, mostly, was snort glue—not even smoke pot—and then go to the mall and mess up stores. Rearrange all the books in the science fiction section at the Walden's in reverse-alphabetical order, say, or switch the price tags at the Williams-Sonoma. They reminded Harry of Harry, I think, although they were funnier, and more clever, and more smug. Anyway, he told me once, if they were wasting time talking to him, they weren't bothering anyone else.

None of which explains why, on the night he bought them Red Hook, he took them out riding, and let Randy drive after watching Randy chug nine of the beers by himself. Somehow, they wound up at the S-curves down past the Orange Grove Mall, where the tract homes sink into the desert-bare hillsides and coyotes slink along the roadbeds, prowling for car-struck cats and rabbits. There weren't any other cars, so Harry let Randy perch them at the top of the rise, then floor the gas and send them plummeting through the curves while his goons screamed "I'm a Little Bit Country, She's a Little Bit Rock-and-Roll" in the crammed backseat. What they hit, Harry told the cops later, barely made a sound, didn't even seem like anything solid. It just snapped under the tires and shot out the back like a paper bag. Harry had jammed his feet on top of Randy's, sending the car screeching into a u-turn and very nearly flipping them over as Randy screamed, "The *fuck*, man?"

Then they all saw it. After that, Harry says they sat there for a really long time.

Of course, Randy announced, "We gotta leave. We gotta go now."

So Harry punched him in the face, hard enough to split both his lips against his teeth, and got out of the car. He told me—later, in jail—that even with the man lying splayed that way, even with the gurgle Harry was just beginning to realize he could hear, he had this momentary but overwhelming sensation that everything was all right. A trick of the canyon, cradling the warm evening air and the moonlight like a cupped palm.

But the gurgle turned out to be wind in flattened lungs, and there was a shushing, too, the sound of blood sluicing across the pavement as though squirted from a sprinkler. When Harry was almost on top of him, the man's arm shot up like a wing, as though he was about to take flight. Then, somehow, the man screwed his head around—like an owl, Harry said, it was practically all the way backward—and opened his eyes wide. Blood kept rushing into the horrible, indented places in his body like water into footprints and filling them.

"I'm so sorry," Harry said, stumbling to his knees.

"*Puto*," the man whispered, somehow. Then he died.

During the first few months of his jail term, Harry wrote letter after letter to newspapers, the INS, the business offices of the corporations that run the flower fields and the last of Orange County's orange groves. But no one ever determined who the dead man was.

"An alien," one of the guards assured him one night, when he couldn't sleep and wound up sitting against the door of his cell, tapping the bars quietly with a toothpick. "Bet on it."

According to Harry, that comment was supposed to be comforting. *Alien*, as in stray dog, possum. But it just made Harry feel worse. From then on, he dreamed—when he slept, which wasn't often—of twin girls in flower-print dresses leaning flyers against the cardboard walls of shacks in migrant camps, setting them against highway signs because the girls had no tape to affix them, holding them to the air so they scattered like milkweed. The flyers had no photographs on them, no face. Just the two words. *Padre*. And *Missing*, because whatever the Spanish was for that, Harry didn't know it.

2

After dinner, Harry took me wandering on the hotel grounds, and we wound up ordering mango sundaes and eating them by the pool. The water looked completely orange in the fading light, as though the sun had melted into it, and down the hill, through the trees, I could see ocean, and my skin buzzed with the memory of the dolphins, and it seemed I could feel all the impossible life surrounding and overrunning this place through my feet, sweeping up from the ground like electrical current. In one of the perfectly landscaped tropical glades around us, a luau had started, and I could smell meat roasting and hear swaying guitars and voices singing that Buddy Holly song, "Oh Boy," like it was tribal chant, an ode to husbands and brothers lost to the sea.

"Harry," I said, pushing my bowl back and licking the orange syrup from my lips, "you have never shown me a better day." I watched him stare down at his plate, grip his napkin in his fist like a cross and then release it. "No one has. I hate my mother."

"You do not," Harry murmured. "I certainly don't."

"She hates you," I snapped, because I couldn't bear the sticky softness in his voice, and because it was true, and he needed to know it. My mother wasn't ever going to forgive him.

Harry winced, then looked at me. There were tears in his eyes, but the wrong kind. The grateful kind again. "She still trusts me enough to send you here."

"She trusts *me*, you moron," I said, threw my napkin down, and stalked past the lounge chairs, out to the top of the hill overlooking the beach. The second the sun had gone, the full moon floated up the sky, a giant halo ringing it like the flickering, translucent bell of a jellyfish. It will never be dark here, I was thinking. There's too much light.

After a while—a respectful few minutes—Harry took his place at my elbow, careful not to graze me, and we watched the moon on the water. Then he said, "Want to play pool?"

"You have a pool table?"

"The hotel does."

"We're not guests of the hotel."

"They don't mind," Harry said. "It's not like there's lots of other places for the locals to go."

He led me back past the pool, the little kids still splashing on kickboards in the shallow end and the old people lounging in the hot tub with their umbrella drinks arrayed around them, past one of the circular stone ponds where giant red and black goldfish clung to the bottom with their scales glinting metallic in the moonlight and their eyes enormous, fairytale creatures made of wishing-well pennies. We climbed a palatial white staircase, trailing salt air and ukulele-strum, and reentered the lounge, where guests sat scattered among the overstuffed chairs and throw-pillows, playing hearts or reading paperbacks. Everywhere there were feet half out of flip-flops, heads nestled deep in pillows, little white dessert plates streaked with veins of raspberry sauce, chocolate syrup, and melted ice-cream, like summer camp crafts projects awaiting the kiln. Through it all strolled my cousin, nodding at no one but knowing where he was going, hands in the pockets of his baggy white beach shorts, swim-strong legs pumping him forward. He didn't look native, just home, which was more than enough to make me want to weep.

Down outdoor corridors Harry led me, past rooms with their doors thrown open to the evening, past the concierge's bungalow, where he nodded at a Hawaiian woman in a sleek, gray business suit saying something about tee times into her headset phone, and, finally, into Puhi's Den.

Despite the wisps of cigarette smoke disintegrating in the air and the Biz Markie song bumping from the speakers and shaking the floor, the Den felt more like a playroom than a bar. Where the windows should have been was wide-open space framed by thatch from the surrounding palms, which made the whole place look like a tree house. On every tabletop, citronella candles licked at their cylindrical glass casings with long, orange tongues. From a round hole cut into the wall above the doorframe, the head of a giant papier-mâché eel loomed, mouth gaping in that moray way that looks so much like bite-about-to-happen and is really just breathing.

"Fried plantains?" Harry said, surprising me with his smile. "Pineapple ambrosia? Cheesy garlic fries?" Then he bobbed his head back and forth to the thud of the beat.

"You look like a sea anemone," I said, because he did with his feet flat on the floor and his poofy blond hair waving.

"You're just jealous," said Harry, bobbing some more, and I found that I was smiling, too.

"You could be right," I said. "God, Harry, I'm so happy for—"

"Whoaaa, *Harry-Fairy!*" squeaked a reedy little voice nearby, and Harry staggered in place and went still. Way down in my chest, the old worry flared anew, a brush fire I really thought I'd contained, threatening my ribs and filling my lungs with smoke.

Prancing toward us, weaving between tables, came two black-haired boys. The older of the two, maybe ten, wore skater shorts belted halfway down his thighs, plus unlaced high-top sneakers with the backs crushed and the sides sagging and the tongues dangling, like strangled dogs he was kicking. The younger boy, seven at the oldest, had a red construction-paper crown on his head that he'd clearly made himself. His expression was kinder.

"Students," Harry murmured to me, recovering his balance, at least, though he couldn't seem to get his smile back in place.

"Stop it," I said, because somehow, I already knew. Something about the tone of the voices, the lack of . . . not respect, really, because there was a little of that. But deference. "It's alright, Harry," I said. "It's fine. Really. It's good."

"Harry-Fairy, I'm the Lava King," said the younger boy, and stomped his feet, which were bare under his sandy bathing suit and long, brandless t-shirt. Because of his pudginess and the crown on his head and the way his black eyes, lit with citronella-orange, danced around the room and up to Harry's face and down again like twin fireflies, he looked even younger than he was.

"Who's the semi-babe?" said the older boy.

"Hi, Teddy," Harry said to the younger kid, though he kept glancing at me. "Ryan. This is my cousin Mimi."

"Your hair's orange," Ryan said.

"Your knee's broken," I answered, executing a quick grab-and-twist which ended with my sneaker against the inside edge of his patella. I let the kid go, and he spun around and glared at me. But when I didn't smile, didn't smirk, just nodded at him, he broke abruptly into a grin.

"You boys . . ." Harry said, glancing my way again. I tapped my foot in exasperation.

"Want to lose at pool?" I said to the older boy. "You play pool?"

"He's good," said Teddy.

"I am," said Ryan.

"Let's go."

They broke off in tandem, racing around the bar for pool cues and then into the back room. Harry and I followed, more slowly.

"You're a janitor," I said quietly. "Right?"

"Don't be mad," Harry whispered. "Gardener, actually. I'm the school gardener."

"I'm only mad because you think it makes any difference to me."

"How'd you know?"

I shrugged. "It's just . . . the way kids talk to maintenance guys. I'm fresh out of high school, remember."

"I remember," Harry said. "Congratulations, by the way." If he'd gone to touch my hand, I would have let him, but he didn't, and I wasn't going to do it for him.

The back room of Puhi's Den turned out to be a den. Dark red carpeting lined not only the floors but the walls. The only light came from twin shaded lamps suspended over the two pool tables, whose surfaces were long and green and so perfectly maintained that they reflected the light like the goldfish ponds outside. A single rectangular window space—glassless, like the openings in the main room—overlooked a thicket of palms. Beyond them, beyond the pink-roofed cabanas and the luau grove and the cliffside, I could see a sliver of ocean lit white by the moon.

"They actually let kids play on those tables?" I asked.

"These kids are good pool players," Harry said. "Ryan, especially."

"Still."

"Their parents are pastry chefs here."

I put my hand on the nearest table, and its felt, thick and soft and weirdly warm, rose to meet my palm like fur. "Still," I said.

Though I couldn't say so to Harry—he was way too sensitive—the little revelation about his job bothered me more than I wanted to admit. Not because of the job; it didn't matter: I'd meant what I said. But the lying gave me that familiar prickly feeling.

"Straight pool?" Ryan said, balls racked expertly on the nearest table, pool cue cocked at his side like a spear gun.

"How about stripes and solids?" said Harry, glancing at me and then quickly away. He really was a goddamn bloodhound, I thought. He could smell someone doubting him miles away. "You and Teddy against Me and Mi?"

"Me and Mi?" Ryan echoed, adding sneer.

"Well, that's her name," said Harry.

"No, it isn't," I muttered, more cruelly than I intended, and the boys looked at me, and Harry didn't. "Break," I told Ryan.

"No slop," said the kid. "Call it all."

Dropping into position with no hesitation and more command than he should have been able to manage, given his size, Ryan popped the stick like a piston, and the cue ball shot down the table and shattered the rack with a smack. Two balls—one stripe, one solid—dropped in opposing corner pockets. "Six. Side," Ryan said, and knocked down the six.

Suddenly, with a giggle I hardly recognized, Harry dropped into a crouch next to the corner pocket Ryan was now studying and planted his face on the rubber ring behind it.

"Hey," said Ryan. "Move."

Harry snapped his lips open, popped them shut like a gulping fish. "Shoot," he said. "Dare you."

"Harry, get up," I said, because Ryan would dare, there was no question.

"Teddy the Lava King'll have to make me. It's a team game," Harry said, and he looked at me, dropped one eyelid closed and opened it again.

"Was that a wink?" I said. "Do people do that?"

Harry winked again, and Teddy the Lava King sprang forward to push him out of the way just as Ryan rammed his stick home and rocketed the 4-ball straight for Harry's teeth. The ball slammed into the back of the pocket, right where Harry had been, and lipped out, and Ryan said, "Shit" as Harry fell prone on his back, just in time, snared Teddy and flipped him over his knees into a soft, butt-first landing in the thick red carpet.

"Our turn," Harry said from the ground, grinning.

"Cheater," said Ryan.

"That was funny, Harry-Fairy," said Teddy the Lava King, and smiled at Harry.

Harry sprang to his feet and melted into the shadows at the back of the room. I saw him fiddling in his pockets, punching buttons on a machine against the wall, and Janet Jackson came on, the one about her slipping her girlfriend out of her new black dress.

"Appropriate choice there, Har," I said, glancing at the seven-year-old at my feet, but Harry just bobbed, grinned, snatched the pool cue from Ryan's hands and stuck it between his legs like a broomstick he was going to command to life and ride. His face had gone red, his eyes wild, as though he'd somehow willed himself drunk, but you couldn't do anything but laugh at him, with him. Even Ryan was laughing as Harry vaulted up to the table, leaned over it, and the sky caved in.

That really is what it seemed like. As if a giant scrap of the moon-streaked black out there had torn loose and tumbled through the glassless windows into the room. Harry ducked hard, raking an ugly furrow in the felt and whacking his chin against the edge of the table, and I stumbled back several steps with my hands up blocking my face, and Teddy the Lava King started screaming and wouldn't stop.

For a few seconds, the thing wheeled around the room, sweeping up to the ceiling and down over Harry's head and smacking, finally, against the hood of the lamp over our pool table and sticking there, twitching, like a manta ray trying to shrug the night back over its shoulders. All of us froze, staring.

"That," said Harry, straightening slowly, backing away and swiping his hand across his hair where he'd been skimmed, "is the biggest . . . what is it? Is that a bat?"

"I hate it," Teddy whimpered from the floor, scuttling away from the table with his eyes locked on the lamp. "I hate it, I hate it, I *hate* it."

Like a kite catching a wind current, the thing blew off the lamp and tumbled toward me as I laughed and dropped to my knees, then straight for Teddy, who screamed and batted at it and may even have hit it because it tipped in the air, sailed up the wall and lit against it, swinging slightly as if caught in a web, although I could not imagine the spider that could hold it. If that spider exists, though, I thought, remembering the dolphins beneath me in the water and the outrageous gardenias blooming everywhere like blazing, newborn stars, it exists here.

"Please get it away," Teddy whined.

"Shut up, baby," said Ryan.

"That's the biggest—" Harry started again, and I cut him off.

"It's a moth," I said, stunned, still crouching. "Jesus Christ, that's a moth." It had to have been two feet across, maybe more, all black except for twin, eye-shaped green spots at the edge of both wings. As it hung, unnaturally still, I got a glimpse of its body, long and fat like a beetle's. And I saw its antennae, which were surprisingly thin, tiny little feelers probing the air like a baby's fingers, and a sudden, sweet-sad taste seeped into my chest, and I felt like a little girl.

"Harry, you gotta make it go," Teddy said. He was crying.

"It won't hurt you," I said, standing and moving toward him. "Right?"

This last bit I directed at Harry, and he grinned at me, proud, as though he'd grown the moth himself, produced it out of thin air like a magician. "Right," he said. "Come on, stand up, Te—"

The thing swung off the wall again, diving down on Ryan and sending him scurrying for cover under a nearby drink table while Teddy wailed and I just stared and Harry snatched up his stick like a badminton racquet and swung at it.

"Don't," I snapped, and Harry swung again as he stepped close to Teddy.

"Shush, Mimes," Harry said. "I'm just keeping it off my boy, here," he said, but he looked flushed, as though something had been stoked inside him and he was off, rocketing helplessly through the world.

I said, "Harry, *don't*," one more time, and Teddy screamed, and the moth pinwheeled toward the window but then arced around again, tiny feelers waving, stretching for our hair, the light, and Harry swung and burst it like a pinata.

"*Dude!*" Ryan yelled, half-laughing from under the table as bits of wing and body rained to the carpet around him.

"Goddamn it, Harry," I snarled, staggering and grabbing the edge of the pool table and blinking furiously as tears I hadn't expected and didn't understand flooded my eyes.

Silence engulfed us. The jukebox had gone quiet. Teddy was too stunned to shriek anymore, and Ryan's mouth had come unhinged, hanging halfway between gape and grin. Harry stood near Teddy, not moving, pool cue clutched in his hand. The clumps of black and green clinging near its tip might have been chalk dust.

"Amelia," he whispered.

"Shut up," I said. "Don't talk to me." The silence, I noticed, seemed to have washed all the way through Puhi's Den, because the other room had gone quiet, too. It was like taking off in an airplane, losing the sense and sound of the ground. I wished I was on one then, already gone.

Dropping into a crouch, I stared down at half a body, one wing, the eyelet brilliant green against the black. It looked mounted to the carpet. Then it twitched.

"Oh shit," I said, and the wing twitched again, brushed the ground, beat against it, and the half a moth began to spin slowly, horribly, almost hopping along the floor like a decapitated wind-up toy. "Oh, little thing. Harry, kill it."

"What?" he said. "Wh . . . no."

"Harry, you fuckball, get over here and kill this thing. It can't live this way."

"I can't."

"Oh my God, you're such an *asshole*," I hissed. "You want it to suffer some more? You think it's funny? You and that little budding dickhead over there?" I gestured, furious, toward Ryan, glanced down at the half-moth jerking along the floor. My voice went quiet, I didn't even think he could hear me, didn't want him to, really, or maybe I did. "After all, Har. Just another dead thing no one will miss. Yeah?"

In one terrible movement, Harry stepped forward and slammed the pool cue down on the floor, then did it again as I squeezed my eyes shut and Ryan said, "Oooh," and Teddy the Lava King sobbed. When I opened my eyes, Harry was staring at me, leaning on the pool cue as if it were a staff, blond hair wild on his head. Oedipus, at the moment of self-revelation. Tremors rippled through his arms and legs, one after another, earthquake and aftershock way down deep in the core of his being. Because he knew I hated him.

Because I really did, for a moment. Had. And he knew it. "Harry," I said, gathering myself, "I—"

"What on God's green Earth is *wrong with you?*" a voice I almost recognized screamed, and another figure came flying into the room, this one blond and too thin and green eyed, and then I knew her. Laptop skeleton-woman from the plane. Which had landed, I realized in astonishment, less than six hours ago.

The woman barged right up to Harry, snatched the pool cue out of his hands, and hurled it to the ground. Harry rocked, trembled again, and I thought he might collapse.

"Hey," I said, standing, but both Harry and the woman ignored me.

"Do you have any idea where you are?" the woman snarled, all but spitting in her fury. "Do you have any sense of anything in the world at all except you? You're in *their* world," she said, gesturing to the puddle of moth on the carpet. "This is paradise. Maybe the last one. And your reaction to seeing something as gorgeous and strange and alive as that creature is to smash it to pieces?"

I waited for Harry to rouse himself, explain, apologize, anything, but his eyes and lips were quivering, as though he was about to jiggle apart.

"He didn't mean—"

The woman spun to me. "He crushed it. After dismembering it. For fun."

"He was putting it out of—"

"Are you insane? Who are you? You don't belong here. You or your cousin, if that's really who you are."

I was so focused on diverting her attention from Harry that I didn't notice what she'd said at first. I felt like I was distracting a shark in a blood frenzy. "The kid was upset. He was—"

The woman whirled to Teddy, still sobbing next to the table but alert enough to cringe back from her glare.

"He did wrong, Teddy," the woman said, and I understood, finally, that she knew them. Knew us all. "He couldn't have done more wrong. Don't ever do what he did. Don't ever be like him. Ever, ever, ever." The glare swept across me, back to Harry. "Give me my goddamn truck keys. We'll see if I can stand to have you working for me anymore on Monday."

I blinked, opened my mouth to say something, scream back, but said nothing. Because if I screamed anything, I was worried I'd do it at Harry. I didn't want to turn on him. I was all he had. But he'd lied all over the place for the thousandth time, and this time there was just me here, so none of his traditional excuses and reasons applied. Never in my life had I been so furious. "You heard her," I said to my cousin, hating my voice, because it was my mother's. "Give the woman her keys."

For a second, I thought I was going to have to jam my hands in Harry's pockets and get them for him. But he managed, somehow.

"Come with me, boys," the woman said. "Let's go find your parents."

"Ms. Jones," Harry said, "I'm—"

"Yes. Well. Does that feel good enough? To you?"

She stalked off, and the boys jerked after her like coupled boxcars, leaving me and my cousin and the moth bits to the dark of the den, the moon-soaked sky, the whistling in the palm trees as the tradewinds whispered through them.

3

"It's time," I heard Harry whisper, dimly, as though across a thousand miles of ocean. "Mimi, wake up." On the third or fourth time, I opened my eyes.

Sometime during the night, I'd twisted Harry's lone blanket underneath my shoulders to insulate myself just a little more from the cold stone floor of the converted garden shed my cousin called home. Wriggling out of it now felt like freeing myself from a cocoon, except that all I'd become, I suspected, was sadder, blanker, and older. Do those things always come together?

"Hurry," Harry said again. "It's time."

"For what?" I said, standing, staring at him. He wore the same shorts as yesterday, same Hawaiian shirt, although the colors seemed to have faded overnight like ink on an old postcard.

"I told you. You have to hit it at just the right moment. It only happens when every-thing's just right."

"Which is clearly how everything is this morning," I said, the words bitter as battery acid in my mouth.

"Just get your suit on. Please."

"You go. I'm tired."

But the expression on Harry's face—lizard eyes ballooning under his lenses, cheeks seeming to deflate as though I'd suctioned all the oxygen out of him—kept me from flopping back to the floor.

"Mimi, please. It's why I brought you here."

"I brought me here," I said, but I was already past him, squeezing into the tiny bath-room humped onto the back of the shed like a U-haul trailer.

"We'll be swimming," he told me.

I shut the door and dressed. My swimsuit, still wet from the day before, felt sticky and freezing against my stomach and chest, as if I was sliding into someone else's skin. I got my teeth brushed, my hair knotted back. "Still red," I said to the mirror, thinking about going home, seeing my sensei, taking my brown-belt test sometime this coming August, packing up my room bit by bit while my mother watched and cried a little from the doorway. Ten weeks from now, I would be in Santa Cruz by myself. College girl. I turned, bumped my knee on the edge of the toilet, swore, and saw the black sky through the tiny square of window perched eye-high on the wall.

"What the hell time is it?" I called.

"Almost four," said Harry. "Hurry."

The shed sat in a hedge-enfolded corner of the screaming woman's lot—she'd given him housing as well as work—and as we sloshed through the grass, I saw Harry glance through the wet, white mist toward the glassed-in sun porch that ran the whole length of the two-story white clapboard main house like a moat.

"She sleeps out there, sometimes," Harry said.

"Is this place walking distance?"

"It's all the way across the island."

"Whose truck are we going to steal, now?"

After that, Harry stopped speaking for a while. Minutes later, in the same green truck we'd used yesterday, we were flying down the pothole-riven road out of what passed for the ritzy part of Lanai, called Haole Camp because that's where the haoles lived. Even Harry. All the houses were white, too.

"She gave you the keys back?" I asked, mostly to break the silence. Harry just stared out the windshield, didn't look at me, and made a whistling sound every now and then through his pursed mouth as though trying to hypnotize himself. I wasn't used to my cousin when he wasn't wheedling.

"I know where she keeps the spare set," he said flatly. "I went and got them before I woke you."

"That's great, Har. Good for you."

For once, he didn't take the bait, just drove and breathed. I think I had my first inkling, right then, tickling across my ribs on little ant feet. But I didn't recognize it.

In the mist, Lanai City proper looked more like a tide pool than a town. I saw low green huts clinging to their rocky plots like barnacles, their backs mottled and sunken, the yards around them scattered with the broken skeletons of bicycle frames and divided by surprising bursts of spiny purple and yellow flowers like colonies of sea urchins. On a leaning picnic table in one yard, I saw a solitary man—an islander—sipping something steaming from a plain white mug and reading a newspaper. Other than him, I saw no one at all.

In a matter of moments, the town fell away, and what was left of all that lush green seemed to seep out of the grass into the surrounding blackness as though we'd reached the edge of a painting. I saw a tilting cyclone fence, a sign reading *Garden of the Gods* with an arrow pointing up a steep hillside path, a gate, and giant boulders bunched in the rolling fields, all tilted in the same direction like fossilized herds of wild horses, and just as we crested the ridge at the top of the island, I saw real horses, still as the stones, forelocks raised in identical poses, noses down, as though they were paying homage to the ocean. As though they'd just crawled out of it, sprouted lungs and hooves, become what they were.

"Stop," I said.

"Can't," said Harry, and drove on.

"I'm trying to tell you I see what you mean."

"What are you talking about?"

"It does feel kind of ghostly or Godly or something up here."

"You haven't seen," Harry said. "You will."

For a brief while, we'd been rolling along the flat top of the ridge, and now we reached the other side, the downhill slope, and at last, for a moment, Harry stopped the truck. I stared.

It was like another island entirely, another planet. On this side of Lanai, the hillsides that spilled down to the ocean had been buffeted and burned completely free of grass and color. I saw a few stunted trees, rocky outcroppings, colorless moss lying flat on the ground as if some of the morning mist had left a residue there. I half-believed I could see boulders steaming as they bubbled newly formed from the earth. Is there even air down there? I found myself wondering. Gravity?

Before I was ready, Harry started the truck forward again. His periodic, ritualized breathing had slowed, stopped seeming so premeditated. Now he just looked calm in a way I'd never seen. At the bottom of the mountain, where the road leveled, the pavement gave out, but Harry just bounced us along over the dirt through stands of scrawny fender-high bushes that bore no leaves and seemed to have no space for them amid their snarls of branches. They looked like sketches for bushes. Practice. I thought about the dolphins and giant moths and people playing ukuleles on the grassy luau grounds back by the hotel, the pineapple groves and wild horses on the hillsides. Taking this drive was like traveling backward through evolution. Which meant that the ocean ahead of us wouldn't be ocean yet, really, just a swirl of black gas and spacedust.

"We were going to sleep in her house, weren't we?" I said abruptly, jamming my hands against the ceiling of the truck to keep my head from banging against it.

Harry's eyes stayed trained down the beams of our headlights onto the rutted dirt before us. "I know you don't believe me, Amelia," he said in his new, expressionless voice. "But she was going to let me. I was supposed to be house-sitting. For Marion Jones. She's the principal at the grade school where I work."

"Hopefully still work," I said. I couldn't help it. I was still furious about the preceding night and the endless lying. For once, I actually wanted him to wheedle.

"She wasn't supposed to be back for a week yet."

"You were going to tell me it was yours, though," I said, and for the second time in twelve hours, tears formed in my eyes without warning or explanation. I almost reached for my cousin's hand.

"I'd rather you thought I lived there than the garden shed. Yeah. It's true," Harry said in his robot drone.

"Goddamn you, Harry," I said, turning to the window so that he couldn't see me crying.

Humps formed in the land around us, round and flat and blackened, as though they'd been in a fire. Can emptiness burn? I wondered. The perspective seemed all wrong, the road tilted to one side, the earth heaving. Overhead, the first watery yellow light trickled through the clouds like iodine tracing a vein.

A few minutes later, our wheels began to spin and slip as the dirt softened into sand, and finally, between two black and leaning mounds that closed the view on either side of us, Harry switched off the truck.

"It's not far," he said, and now there was at least a hint of something in his voice. Eagerness? Hunger? "Hurry. Take this."

From under his seat, he withdrew flippers, a mask, and a snorkel.

"Your ship's sunk?" I asked, surprised.

"Can't sink," Harry said. Without waiting, he hopped from the truck and started fast down the dirt, his own flippers draped over one shoulder like a single folded wing.

As soon as I was out, I heard the ocean. It sounded restless, rolling and hissing and slapping at the land. The dawn breeze pressed my sodden swimsuit to my chest, sealing in the cold. Harry had gotten way ahead already, so I scrambled after him, arms tight against me to keep in whatever heat I still generated. It was the light more than the air that made it seem so chilly here, I thought. Soon the bushes began creeping into my path, uncurling their spongy, leafless branches. They looked like anemones that had spilled off the reef onto dry land. I found that I didn't want to touch them. The thought of those branches curling, drawing my finger toward some hidden mouth, made me nauseous. I stepped between and around them, quickened my pace, and stopped when I hit the camp.

Despite the deadness around me and the fact that Harry was practically sprinting away now, I found myself standing still. I couldn't help it.

Mostly, I stared at the sheds, three-walled, wide open on the side that faced me. The walls themselves were wooden, black, well on their way to decomposing, as though they'd been lying on the ocean floor. I saw two circular stone fire rings, the wagon-end of some sort of rig, and a single stone tureen, two feet deep at least, tipped over on its side in the dirt. I stepped off the path while Little Red Riding Hood warnings whispered in my ears in my mother's voice.

Moving among those dilapidated, rotting buildings, their window holes gaping, their roofs caved in, was like diving on a shipwreck. The air felt heavier, and what light there was spiraled down in thin gray shafts. I tried to imagine people living here, having a Saturday night dance around the fire circle, and found that I couldn't. What could they have been doing here, anyway? After a few minutes among the stillness and shadows, the place began to feel more like a natural formation than a ruin. And it smelled like the sea.

I don't know how long I lingered there, but when I shook free of my trance, I realized that I couldn't see Harry anymore and that he hadn't called for me. Scrambling back to the path, swatting away all sorts of swooping, black-winged thoughts, I marched myself up the last ridge, and right as I reached the top and saw Shipwreck Beach for the first time, I heard the sound.

At first, it was a single tone, low and long and round. If not for the daylight, I might have mistaken it for the cry of an owl. Then it went lower, got lonelier. Whale song? I thought. Some thousand-mile wind screaming down the Pacific to fill this cove and ring it? Then I stopped speculating, just stood and listened until, finally, after a long, long time, it died away, leaving a sort of void in the center of my eardrum, as though it had hollowed out a channel in there. I stumbled off the ridge, looked over the water, and saw the wreck.

It lay two hundred yards from shore, maybe less, propped straight up in the roiling surf, so improbably still that it looked projected on the mist, barely even solid. Its gray, featureless steel sides reflected nothing, and the sea spray from the waves smashing against the bow slid over it easily, naturally, as though over sharkskin. As though the ship could breathe it.

"Harry!" I shouted, and then I saw him hunched on a piece of driftwood at the edge of the water, sliding into his flippers. He looked up and saw me. For a second, he seemed almost surprised that I was there. Then, hesitantly—as though we hadn't seen each other in months and last night had never happened—he smiled and waved. I started toward him, staring around.

For miles, it seemed, in either direction, driftwood littered the sand, leaned against the boulders, rotted into pulpy puddles and drained into the ocean. Beyond the sand, long, wriggling snakes of whitewater curled around and bit at themselves, smashed on underwater rocks, shot up in the air and got sucked under by the current.

Not until I was right on top of Harry, watching him strip off his shirt and flex his feet in the flippers, did it occur to me to wonder what he thought we were doing.

"We're not swimming out there," I said, and for the second time, understanding surfaced in my sleep-fuzzed, sound-rattled brain and sank again.

"I am," he told me, and stood. Where he'd been sitting, a single tiny black crab poked a pincer out of a notch in the wood, edged forward, then scuttled into the sand. "I'm hoping you'll come. I saved this until you came." He lifted his eyes almost to mine, dropped them again. "It's the reason I wanted you to come."

"Why?" I snapped. "You want to pretend it's yours? Maybe you're establishing a school there for shipwrecked sailors? Now that you're a teacher and all?"

"You're the only—" Harry said quietly. Then the sound started again, and he went quiet and closed his eyes.

For a few seconds, I looked all around me, trying to locate its source, and then I went still, too. Mating call? Mourning wail? I couldn't tell, didn't much care. It filled my head, my skin, as though a second being had climbed in there with me, and it made me warmer, but also sadder, and I wanted to run, and I wanted to cry.

"Harry, what is that?" I whispered, a good thirty seconds or so after it had faded away again.

"It's coming from the ship," he said.

"Are you sure?" I wasn't sure. It might have been. Dazed, I watched the water roll over my cousin's feet, his too-thin ankles as he stepped off the edge of the land. "Not even cold," he said, and looked back at me, just once. He continued forward up to his knees, stumbled on some underwater rock, and almost pitched face first into the surf.

"Just wait a fucking second," I said, shaking myself free of whatever it was that held me spellbound. I slammed my fins down, shoved my feet into them, dropped my shorts and shirt, perched the mask and snorkle on my forehead, and duckwalked down to the shoreline.

"It looks trickier than it is," he said, studying the whirls of gray-green water, the eruptions of spray between us and the wreck.

"Right," I murmured.

I watched my cousin sink to his knees in the water, lower his mask. "It's shallow all the way out, supposedly," he said. "Coral, right up near the surface. That's what the mask is for. Don't get scraped, it'll hurt like hell." With a flip of his fins, he kicked into the churning, circling current. I didn't let myself think. I kicked in after him.

For fifteen strokes or so, it really was easier than it looked. The water, maybe five feet at its deepest, tugged and dragged at me, not hard, which shouldn't have fooled me. But I was too busy watching the reef fan out beneath me, miniature mountains and yellow peninsulas and rolling plains like the countryside on the model railroad set I'd had as a kid and that Harry had broken. Schools of silver fish streamed over the landscape and all around us. A black turtle rose from the bottom like a lost balloon, floated over my right shoulder, studied me, and broke off into the shadows. The snap-current that caught me came from nowhere, swept me so fast and so hard into the coral outcropping on my right that for one screaming, irrational second, I thought I'd been sharkbit.

"*Shit!*" I gargled, and saltwater streamed around my mouthpiece into my mouth, and for some reason, that settled me, or at least woke me up some more. I coughed, gagged, kicked hard, and felt another scrape-and-rip along my left thigh. One more yank of the undertow, and I was off the reef, floating free. I caught a glimpse of my blood in the water, a red, wispy vapor trail, and then I was flung forward, eyes everywhere, arms and hands and feet slapping and flailing as I lurched out to sea.

I made no more mistakes after that. I twisted, tucked, flowed like an octopus between boulders of coral and then lunged in a new direction, half fighting the current, half riding it, and right before I hit the sandbar and realized I could stand, I found myself wondering how I was going to look up long enough to locate the ship. The scrape on my stomach panicked me at first. I looked down, expecting to have been torn wide open, and realized that nothing was hurt, that the touch had been granular and gentle, and I jammed my feet down.

"Jesus," I said, when I found I could speak.

Harry, expressionless, pulled me to my feet, his eyes over my shoulder. I turned to see where he was looking.

Twenty feet away, just off the edge of the strip of sand where Harry and I stood, the marooned ship towered above us, blacking out the dawn, dead center in a cauldron of crashing, crushing, cascading water. Up close, its steel didn't look smooth or gray but pitted, streaked with wide, wet, jagged bands of red and rust-orange and silver like the seething, banded clouds of Jupiter.

"What *is* this?" I whispered. "How did it get here?"

"No one knows," Harry said. He spoke quietly, too, which made it hard to hear over the roaring water.

I waited, expecting another story like the one about Pu'upehe. But Harry just stared at the ship, mouth moving as if he were praying.

"How long has it been here?"

Harry shrugged. "The guidebooks call it a Liberty ship. Built during World War II. The history guy at school told me President Roosevelt called them '*Dreadful looking things.*'"

"No dummy, he."

"Only it isn't a Liberty ship. That's the thing, Mimi." He was still all but whispering, and now he began to edge down the sandbar. "A guy a couple years ago, some kind of ship enthusiast, called some foundation in San Francisco, and they said this couldn't be a Liberty ship. And it doesn't have a number on it. And no one saw it come or can even pinpoint when it arrived; it just appeared here one day. And it won't sink. The Navy's tried three times. They can't get it off the reef and down. And it won't rust, either. Not like it should." He was looking down into the water churning against the sandbar. "This shouldn't be so hard. Look, you just angle left, right there . . ."

"Look what I did to my goddamn leg," I said, studying the red rent that ran from my hip straight down the tendon to my knee. Little coral spines stuck from the skin. In the weak morning light, they seemed to wiggle like parasites. I began to pick at one, and then realized, finally, what he'd said.

"Harry." I hobbled up behind him and put my hands on his shoulders. They were wet, still powerful under the flab, and I could feel his heart shuddering like some souped-up, over-revved engine. Whatever the quiet was in his voice, it didn't signify calm. "Look at the waves. Look how hard they hit the ship. We can't—"

"There's a ladder near the stern. I'm pretty sure that's what he said. Look, one good surge and you're past the danger zone."

"That's what *who* said? That's . . ." I started, then stopped. I watched the water erupt out of hollows in itself and explode against the steel hull in a deafening, never-ending cannonade. "Harry, I don't want to die."

"Then don't," said Harry, and turned to me, and smiled suddenly. "I love you, Mimi." And real understanding dawned at last. I knew what I was doing here, and why he'd insisted I come, and why he'd waited for me.

"You son of a bitch," I said, "don't you fucking dare," and then he leapt. The water sucked him straight down and swept him out of sight around the side of the ship. I didn't see or hear him hit, which didn't mean he hadn't. And I wouldn't know if he had, I realized, because I couldn't see where he was.

But he didn't want me to drown, I thought. He'd wanted me to come because he was too fucking much of a coward to kill himself by himself. But my dying was something he could never live with, and I knew it. I didn't stop to examine the obvious flaw in my logic. There wasn't time.

Compared to the swim from shore, shooting past the ship proved stunningly easy.

The second my feet hit water, I was catapulted forward, screaming toward the point of the bow and then wide of it, straight along the hull, rimming the lip of a trough of water that dove against the half-exposed rust-eaten keel. What remained was simply to stick out my hands and snag the posts of a long steel ladder as they flew past, which I did, my knees banging against the ship and the underside of one arm scraping hard as I wedged it on the bottom rung and dragged myself, streaming, out of the water. Harry was already fifteen steps above me, headed directly up the hull. Like someone who'd long ago spotted the ledge he would jump from.

"Goddamn you, *wait up!*" I howled, but I doubt he heard me. I shoved upward with my legs and started climbing, slowing only to dab at the blood streaming down my side. Determined as Harry was, I was faster, and soon I was only a few steps below him. He was panting but still climbing. "Harry, stop!" I screamed up at him.

He did momentarily, glancing down at me. "You're fine," he said.

"I know I'm fine, I just—"

"Let's talk up top, yeah? I don't like hanging on this thing."

Up he went, ignoring my snarl of protest.

The whole climb probably took five minutes, maybe less. It only lasted that long because my feet kept sliding on the slick rungs, and once, two-thirds of the way up, just at the point where the bow began to bell out so that I had to climb tilted backward, I glanced down and saw the surf sliding back over the rocks and coral beneath me like lips over bared teeth, and I couldn't move for a while. When I finally managed to look up again, Harry was gone.

I had a moment of panic, jammed myself tight against the ladder as I imagined my cousin's body screaming past me on its way down. Tiny cirrus clouds of spray floated far beneath me. I felt like Jack, right at the top of his beanstalk, only stupider. Jack's idiot cousin, who followed wherever he went.

"Harry, help me," I shouted when I reached the rustless metal railing that ringed the deck of the ship and realized I was going to have to jump a little from the top step of the ladder to hoist myself over it. But Harry didn't come, and I couldn't stay where I was, so I leapt, caught my hips on the rail, tumbled over onto the deck, and lay there, gasping, in the creeping daylight. Immediately, by force of habit, my lungs fell into their kata-rhythm, regulating themselves, and when I stood, I was not shaking at all.

The first thing I noticed—the most alarming thing—was the quiet. It wasn't quite silence, because the wind whistled over the bulkheads and between the truck-sized wooden and metal containers jammed into virtually every available inch of deck space. But I couldn't hear any birds, and I couldn't hear the ocean.

"I bet we're fifteen stories up," Harry said, appearing from behind one of the containers. "More." His hair was flying every which way, and his skin seemed almost translucent, like a baby's. He hardly seemed capable of walking, let alone lying or killing a man or scaling this ship or hurling himself off of it. The eagerness in his voice was quieter than it had been as we entered Puhi's Den last night, but also less explicable, and therefore scarier.

"Is that a tank?" I said, shoving him aside so I could see past him. Buying time, so I could figure out how to talk him down. Fifteen feet away, a hulking real-live tank hunkered on its treads, gun nozzle extended up and out at a 45-degree angle like the neck of a dinosaur.

"Come on," said Harry, and I couldn't think of anything to do but follow him.

For a while, we explored in silence, mostly together, because I wouldn't let Harry get more than five feet from me. We touched the treads of the tank as though they were the paws of a sleeping tiger, scrambled over knee-high thickets of coiled rope and the valved tops of what might have been cisterns full of water or oil dug into the deck, stood at the foot of the mizzenmast and stared up through the skeleton wires at the sky going blue. It was like wandering in a pueblo, or through the ruins of some medieval castle somewhere. People had been here, okay, but their lives were unimaginable to me. The sound, when it came, seemed softer somehow than it had from the land, and so natural in that place that I didn't notice it starting, didn't consciously register it until my cousin fell to his knees beside me.

"Oh, wow," he said, closing his eyes and bowing his head.

It was like a loon call but longer, lonelier. It trilled up, intensified, and there were near-consonants in it, soft r's and y's, as though whatever it was had known language once and forgotten it. The pitch rose toward screaming, and my hands covered my ears as Harry bent forward into the face of the rising sun like a Moslem praying at daybreak, and then the sound sighed out.

"What do you think that is?" Harry said after a long time. "It's amazing, isn't it?"

I shook my head. "I don't know. Wind? The way the water hits the boat? It's weird."

"It's more than that." He was crying, I realized. Bowing his head and crying. "It's alive."

"Harry," I said, and knelt next to him. I held my hand between his shoulder blades while sobs wracked him, and I waited. But the sobs kept coming, and I felt panic again in my stomach and lungs, and my fingers curled into a fist against his back. "Harry, listen. It'll be okay."

"What are you talking about?" he hissed through another explosion of tears.

"It will. It will, it will, it will. It's not too late."

"Mimi, that's the stupidest—"

"I want you to take me home," I snapped, because I knew what I'd said was stupid. I didn't have anything good to say. I just wanted him to come with me. "Harry? I want you to take me home."

When he finally looked up, his eyes were red, and his voice came from far away.

"You go ahead," he said.

"You come. Come on." I put my hands under his elbows, tried to lift him, and he came with surprising ease.

"You feel it too, don't you, Mimi?"

"Feel what?"

"It's . . . a resting place. You can tell. A place to rest. A magic place."

Now there were tears in my eyes. They stung when I blinked and made me cry more. I had nowhere to lead us but back toward the ladder. "Harry. Come rest with me. It's not too late. There's still time to put things right. Some things, anyway."

"You're right," Harry said dreamily. Too peacefully. His smile was scarier than his tears, but he let me lead him. I kept moving forward, not looking at his face anymore. I just pulled him behind me. This was it, I thought. I was Orpheus, on the journey home. If I looked back, he'd know I doubted him. If I looked back, he'd be gone. "It isn't all your fault, Harry. It never has been. And even if it has. You're still here. You're twenty-three years old. You owe the people you hurt. You owe yourself. You owe me, goddamn you. You can still prove my mother wrong. And your mother. And all of them. You can still prove me right."

Harry said nothing, just went where I tugged him like a balloon. I reached the railing, kept my breathing steady, forced the trembling in my legs to stillness. I had a decision to make. I couldn't carry him, obviously. I could make him go first and watch him leap if he decided to do it. Or I could go ahead and trust him to follow.

Either was better than standing here, halfway out of the world already, marooned offshore and above it.

"Harry," I said, turning to face him, pinning his eyes with my own.

"Are you crying?" he asked, and he actually sounded startled.

"I'm going down now. I want you to promise you're coming."

"Hey," he said, shrugging himself at least part of the way free of his stupor. He smiled that new, scary smile again. "Nowhere else to go."

"I want you to promise you're coming down on the ladder," I snapped. "All the way to the water. Got it?"

His eyes slipped from mine toward the horizon.

"Harry, I swear to God. I will not forgive you this. I can't. I came to prison, and I came to Lanai. I swam to the dead-wife rock, and I climbed this ship and did everything else you asked."

"I didn't bring you here for me," he said, not looking at me. "Jeez, Mimi. I just thought you'd want to see it."

I couldn't even make sense of that. He was coming or he was jumping, and either way, I couldn't help him anymore. I draped my legs over the side of the ship and had a sickening moment hanging there when my feet couldn't find the ladder, and then they did, and I was standing. I edged myself around so that I was facing the hull, careful to look neither down nor up. If Harry jumped, I refused to watch him. I was ten rungs down, clinging tight to the metal, waiting, every second, for the whistle of Harry's body plunging past me, the thump of it shattering on the rocks below, when I felt the metal groan and knew my cousin was on the ladder.

"Took you long enough," I shouted, giddy with relief. I didn't stop, didn't look up, dropped down another few steps, and the sound broke over us once more.

It seemed softer this time. Almost comforting, and as it slid lower, it seemed to work its way into my blood like a purr. It's perfect, I thought. Just right. The last mournful chord for the first part of Harry's life. I'd gotten him off the ship. I might even be able to get him off Lanai and back to the mainland. Even when the sound intensified, the same way it had before, it felt bearable, almost musical. I never had the urge to cover my ears and couldn't have anyway; I wasn't taking my hands off the ladder. It's just the world, I told myself. It's just the way the world sounds. I closed my eyes, bowing my head as the sound fattened, distorted, and at last sank to nothing like a long, expiring breath. I opened my eyes and glanced up just in time to see Harry's legs disappear back over the top of the railing onto the ship.

"*Where are you going?*" I screamed, not really expecting an answer, but Harry's head reappeared instantly, his hair shooting off his head in flares and prominences like a sun going nova, his features all but bleached out.

"What?" he said.

"What are you doing?"

"Didn't you hear it? It's stuck in the hold."

I shook my head, slammed the edge of my hand against the nearest rung of ladder and rang it.

"It's down below," Harry said again.

"What is, Harry? What? Empty ship?"

"You tell me, Mimi. Go ahead. I want to know what you think it is."

"Who cares? I'll tell you what it isn't. It isn't the ghost of the man Randy Asshole Lynne ran over. It isn't either one of our moms. It isn't God. And it isn't me. It's the wind, or the way the water hits this boat, or it's the fucking oil monster of World War II, I have no idea. But whatever it is, it isn't going to make you feel any better about yourself or help you understand how all the bad stuff happened. So get the hell down here and be in your life. Be with me."

Abruptly, Harry smiled. His familiar seven-year-old's wheedling smile.

"I'll be one second," he said. "Don't wait."

"I won't," I said. And I didn't.

4

Four hours later, pacing the beach with the echoes of the current still drumming in my skin like aftershocks, I watched the police I'd called on the cell-phone I'd found in the glove box of the truck troll the area around the ship and beyond it in their johnboats. A rescue team went on board, too, and stayed there for hours, but they didn't find or hear anything. They asked what we'd been doing out there, and I said exploring, and they shook their heads. They asked what I thought had happened to my cousin, and I said I thought he'd drowned, which seemed reasonable to me. The water had been horrific on the way back, much harsher than coming out, and there'd been one awful moment, fish and turtles scattering all over the reef as though something huge and hungry and terrifying was coming, but nothing did.

Later, huddled under a police blanket at the little Lanai airport terminal, waiting for the next plane to the mainland, I called my mother and told her Harry had killed himself.

I think I made myself believe that for years. Long enough to get through college, start to build a mainland life for myself, then call Lanai information one day from my little Sacramento efficiency, get the number for Marion Jones, grade school principal, explain who I was, and ask for a job.

I've been here ever since, in my little green hut on the outskirts of Haole Camp. The island children like me, mostly, because I teach them karate after math and have Gameboys in my room for them to play with. Marion likes me because I show up for work every day and don't drink and don't smile much. Some evenings, especially in the summer, when there isn't work even Marion can think of doing, she comes to my hut, and we barbecue chicken and onions and pineapples, and after dinner we take a drive up to the Garden of the Gods and prowl separately through those giant stones, among the axis deer and wild horses, until the sun goes down.

Every Sunday, regular as church, I make my way to Shipwreck Beach, and I spread a tarp across the driftwood, and I watch the ship ride its reef to forever and make no sound whatsoever. The sound has gone. Marion thinks it's a little unhealthy, my doing this. It's the only thing she's ever reprimanded me for. She tells me my cousin jumped, forfeited his life, and deserves my pity but not so much of my time. I have never tried to explain—to her or anyone—that my cousin didn't jump. Couldn't have. It wasn't in his nature, though I didn't realize it until too late, right as I got that last sunblind glimpse of his face. I should have known it before, onboard ship. "*I didn't do it for me,*" he'd said, and of course, as usual, in his way he was telling the truth. Whatever the mechanism is that keeps our consciences from devouring us from within, like acid-reflux, Harry's was still working. Maybe too well. He didn't want to die. He never had. He wanted to be better than he was, and he wanted not to have done the things he'd done. Like most of us.

And he wanted one more thing, and that was what caused him to wreak such havoc all his life, and was also the reason I loved him. He wanted—desperately, hopelessly—to make whoever was around him happy, at all times. He bought Randy Lynne beer because Randy Lynne wanted it. He told my mother he loved her because he thought my mother needed to hear it. He told me he was all right because he knew I'd come for reassurance. He killed the moth in Puhi's Den to keep it from tormenting Teddy the Lava King. And he opened the hold on that ship because he thought there was something inside it that wanted to get out.

My mother has only come to Lanai once. She skulked around the island for five days, built me two bookshelves to get some of the piles off the floor, bought me an open plane ticket to return to the mainland, and left. "You're punishing yourself for nothing," she told me in the Garden of the Gods on her last night. "He was nothing. He was a bastard. He was never worth it. You're too smart, Amelia, too powerful a person to drown in Harry's whirlpool. The fact is, people go where they want to go. Remember that."

She may be right. Probably, she is. But I keep seeing Harry weeping on the deck of the ship, keep feeling his shoulder blades convulsing under my fingers like beating wings: my cousin, who broke my aunt's heart and embittered my mother and caused a stranger's death and loved me more than anyone else has or can or will. And I say we go where our ghosts lead us, drawn down the years like water across a continent. We have no choice, and there aren't any escape routes. But maybe—if we can just get ourselves still enough, our regrets quiet enough, our breathing steady and our ears and eyes wide open—maybe we can see the sea before we join it.

The Yellow Chamber

Jeffrey Ford

Pristine silence was the law in the gleaming white halls of The Center for the Reification of Actual Probability. Heels were verboten along the well-lighted thoroughfares, as were materials that might cause audible friction when legs rubbed together in a hurried gait. It was demanded that even the colors of clothing be muted. For this reason, the geniuses who labored in that secret mountain retreat were required to wear silk pajamas, beige or powder blue, and go barefoot. *Quiet* was believed, by the Center's head researcher, Hollis Avec-Bruhl, to be the perfect medium for the germination and growth of brilliance.

He was a staunch advocate of psychic transference of imaginative concepts and assumed that only in silence, undistracted and unfettered by competition from verbal communication, might the ideas of his colleagues exceed the usual cranial limitations of subjective reasoning and pass, by a certain extrasensory osmosis, into the vacuum of hushed calm to eventually be picked up and infect, as it were, the imaginations of fellow researchers.

This was Avec-Bruhl's famous theory of *Shared Brilliance*. "Words," as he wrote in his landmark paper, "have multiple meanings, and for each of us any phrase might cause the hearer to hearken back to some moment of personal history, causing a chain reaction of memory that could very well sully clear understanding." To complete precautionary measures, researchers also wore mittens and wide-goggled sunglasses in order to obscure the interfering language inherent in "the subconscious, symbol-laden dance of digits" and "indicative glances conveyed by the windows of the soul."

Due to the ban on verbal or written communication among the three resident geniuses, meetings at the center were spontaneous. Only once in its five-year history did Avec-Bruhl and his two illustrious colleagues all gather together in close proximity to "discuss," by way of virulent, argumentative, deep-delving contemplation, the center's pet project, the name of which, ineffably agreed upon, was Melusina. The day this occurred, a blizzard raged outside the high-altitude retreat, and although the walls were thick, the shriek of the wind penetrated in the form of a distant but distinct murmur that seemed the subdued plaintive wails of Creation itself.

The three of them met by chance, in other words by design, in the Yellow Chamber, so named for the pale lemon color of the walls, thought to soothe the personality of the Melusina. The room was a perfect square, thirty by thirty in diameter with a fifteen-foot high ceiling. Its floor was of a black-and-white checkerboard design. On the wall opposite the only door, there was one large arched window that gave a view of distant peaks, which, this day, were all but obscured by the blinding ferocity of the blizzard.

At the very center of the room sat the physical manifestation of their combined theoretical pondering. The object in question was a twelve-foot-long gleaming chrome cylinder the width of a coffin. At the far end, toward the window, there jutted upward through a hole a human, female head, painted silver in keeping with the color scheme of the container. The face bore high cheekbones, thin lips bent in a sneer, and prominent eyes that constantly darted back and forth, up and down, as if searching for a clue to the meaning of their existence. The wild shock of hair, whose each strand twisted and writhed, was composed of photoelectric filaments that gathered mental information, in the form of light, from the device's surrounding environment.

At the inner core of the cylinder lay a vat of organic liquid composed of the neural cells of both primates and reptiles, a steeping biological soup of energy that fed the processors and computational devices with quantum jazz on the order of ten millionths to ten of imaginative cogitating potential. All of this, in turn, powered and gave life to the silver head, which was the heart of the device, Melusina. This anthropomorphic aspect of the machine, complete with human brain, allowed the researchers to communicate with their invention through Avec-Bruhl's method of "shared brilliance" instead of with the more expected but primitive computer keyboard.

The construction of this strange contraption had taken place piecemeal over a period of years. As each of the luminous three conceived of an innovation, an addition to what had come before, they instructed technicians, through whispered tape recordings (it was no violation to communicate in language with those less mentally gifted as long as one did so in a subdued tone), on the next feat of engineering to be performed upon the device.

All of the physical work on the Melusina was done at night, as silently as possible, while the big brains rested, so they would not have to witness the gross display of the manipulation of matter. When they woke in the morning and wandered the labyrinth of gleaming halls to find the Yellow Chamber, there they would discover their improvements already in place and at work, as if thinking had made it so.

It had never been recorded as to with whom the initial idea had originated. For the longest time, actually until the last second, no one was quite sure of the project's destination, but it grew virulently, haphazardly, with the random fluidity of a fiction under the pressure of a drastic deadline. Only when Avec-Bruhl and his two illustrious colleagues grew weary to the point of nausea with it was it determined that it was finished. They could have given the silver head a beard, or drawn symbols in black crayon on the smooth, shiny surface of the body, included a fax machine and DVD player, a laser beam, but when it was finished, it was obvious that what it had become was what it had been destined to become all along.

The purpose of the Melusina, what with its quantum ability to traffic in probabilities, was to describe the existence of, and goings on in, a particular alternate reality. The location commented upon by the device was a wandering island it called Threbansch. This errant landmass drifted upon the yellow sea of another world that did not necessarily exist but very well could have. Telepathic reports from the silver head shed light on the daily progress of one Pelasio DeGris, ruler of the wandering island, who, for the duration of the device's access to his life, had dealt with the problem of a vengeful ghost wandering the rooms of his palace.

Standing to the right of Avec-Bruhl, who had taken his place at the foot of the Melusina, was the theoretical mathematician, Mercy Bond. She had, ten years earlier, led the international team that had discovered the fact that the seemingly infinite computation beyond the decimal point of pi was an aberrational phenomenon caused by an anomaly in the grey matter of human beings. Her findings showed that the mental procedures of Homo sapiens contained a kind of processing glitch that disallowed discovery of the true value of that singular radial computation. Bond theorized that human beings were most likely the only species that could not compute the value of pi, and it was really this fact—not their laughter, their sense of irony, their belief in Love—that made them unique in the animal kingdom.

She linked this deficiency to the existence of imagination in humans and also the age-old belief in the omnipotent power of the gods. Her place on the triangular team at the Center for the Reification of Actual Probability was vouchsafed by her ardent belief that quantum computation, which lived and died with the possibility of probability, was all so much fantasy, but the fact that the defect that initiated it in our thinking was hardwired into our brains made it as good as real.

Bond was a delicate creature, petite, with a frail bone structure that showed itself through taut skin and appeared a skeleton composed of brittle twigs. This, along with her diminutive stature and wispy blonde hair, gave her a meager physical presence that, in itself, bordered on the probable.

On this day, while present at the meeting, she could not take her gaze off the large window and the snowstorm that raged beyond it. The sweep of white seen through required goggles made her think of the turned-down sheet on her bed, in her distant home, in the dim light of evening. She was no longer certain if her memories of a family, a husband and children, were real; she had been gone so long. She could not bring herself to look into the horrid silver face of the Melusina, for it was the manifestation of the endless project and her self-designed jailer. Let us not mention what contempt she had for Avec-Bruhl and her other colleague, Dr. Abramax, who stood across the chrome cylinder from her, staring from behind his darkened lenses at the probability of her breasts.

Abramax was a charlatan, a supposed philosopher of science whose credentials had all been forged. Even the lineage he claimed as a direct descendant of the famed Islamic philosopher Ibn Rushd (Averroes) was a glaring sham that he managed to pass off by wearing a sequined turban, with glass jewel centerpiece, he had bought in his teens in a novelty shop in Flatbush, Brooklyn, New York.

Although, in actuality, he held none of the advanced degrees he claimed to in theoretical physics or philosophy, like all good fakes, he had worked harder than any doctoral candidate to learn enough to fool his university employers through the years. Since much of the West was ignorant of the work of Averroes, a brilliant thinker who had attempted to merge the physical sciences with the spiritual, the doctor had been successful with his limited knowledge in convincing those he came in contact with that his Mediterranean looks and cheap turban were genuine articles of the Arabic milieu.

Avec-Bruhl had chosen Abramax for his knowledge of his supposed ancestor's text, *Tahafut al-Tahafut* or *Autodestruction of the Autodestruction*, a philosophical work that in its essence refuted the *Tahafut al-Falasifa* or *Autodestruction of the Philosophers* by Imam Abu Hamid al-Ghazali. Ghazali's philosophy could be summed up in the following loose quotation: "All forms of knowledge that are not impervious to doubt do not deserve any confidence because they are not beyond the reach of doubt, and what is not impregnable to doubt cannot constitute certitude." It was the project director's hope that Abramax's particular abilities might effectively defend against scientific attacks on the nature of research based in probability and beat back the detractors who would level claims of "inconsequential" or "sheer bullshit" at the purpose and results of the Melusina.

As for the good doctor, Abramax, he was happy to draw his exorbitant salary and dine on the fine cuisine served to him each night in his cubicle. He realized he had finally attained what he had been working his confidence scheme for all those years—a slice of the good life. He had nothing to do all day but occasionally whisper incomprehensible demands into a microphone, wander a warm, clean space in silk pajamas, take long naps and peruse the pornography he had shipped in weekly under the auspices of research materials.

The irony of his presence in the research center was that his fearless, random demands upon the technical staff as concerning the construction of the project had led to some of its greatest innovations. Who else would have come up with the idea of a human head as part of the device? He'd wanted the entire body, but his request was counteracted by Avec-Bruhl's insistence that there be more metal than flesh and Mercy Bond's desire to merge computation with organic processes.

It dawned on Avec-Bruhl that day, as he stood at the foot of the device, that in one week's time, the military, who funded the entire project to the tune of millions of dollars, would arrive and ask for an accounting of what had been accomplished. The work that the generals thought was being done had to do with experiments in remote viewing—the ability for psychic adepts to "see" long distances into secret enemy installations or to be mentally present at clandestine meetings. When the only information he had to lay out for them was the story of the presence of a ghost in the palace of a wandering island not of this world, things, he knew, would go badly. All of his hard work would be dismantled, and he could very well end up disappearing in a tragic mountain-climbing accident.

"Good Lord," he thought, shaking his head. He wanted to begin that very moment conceiving excuses, but instead his mind was filled with the emerald green skies and yellow seas of the world of Threbansch. He hovered over the floating island for a moment like a seabird tracing in its flight the line of breakers down the coast, and then he turned inland. The next thing he knew, he was on the Southern veranda of the royal palace. A man with a pointed dark beard and jeweled turban he knew to be Pelasio DeGris was sitting at a small table with a beautiful young woman.

The ruler was dressed in his usual beige pajamas and barefoot as the custom of the island dictated. The young woman with golden hair, it had already been established in an earlier episode of transference, was the local witch, Ocinda. Avec-Bruhl paid close attention to this odd meeting, for the ruler and the witch were usually the direst of enemies.

"My dear," said DeGris, puffing at a long-stemmed pipe, "this ghost is a royal pain in the ass. I've tried everything to destroy it, exorcise it, negate its existence, but I confess I can't get rid of it."

"Now you need me?" she said. "After all of these years of hunting me, now you need my powers? Do you remember that you tried to burn me at the stake?" She smiled, for no matter what deal she made with him for the dissolution of the ghost, she intended to enchant him.

"Yes," he said. "I admit it."

"And what would you have me do?" she asked. "And what will you give me for it?"

"I offer you my hand in marriage," he said to her, and she laughed uproariously.

Just then, out on the western horizon, a huge black water dragon broke the surface of the yellow sea and blew a geyser of spray into the green sky. Ocinda turned to view the event and whispered, "Mother."

While Avec-Bruhl was eavesdropping on the conversation on the veranda, Mercy Bond was trying for all the world to remember the figure of her husband. She had a vague recollection of him, but she could not see his face. His image in her memory wavered in and out of focus and then became the figure of the ghost of Threbansche. She tried to mentally block the transference from the Melusina, but it was too strong.

She watched as the insubstantial phantom strode the ramparts in his powder blue pajamas like some prodigious exhalation of pipe smoke, mourning its execution so many years earlier. His crime had been to suggest that the island be anchored. He had roused the populace to believe that they could never be actual without a definite location, and that their incessant wandering trapped them in a state of unreality, neither here nor there, in the geopolitical state of their world. His famous saying now reverberated and echoed in the guard's chamber on the southeastern turret, "You can't know who you are until you know where you are." Mercy Bond shuddered at the grim aspect of the shade.

Dr. Abramax noticed the wave of revulsion ripple through the body of Ms. Bond and was immediately reminded of his own reaction when viewing for the first time Miss November in the most recent issue of *Penthouse.* That one photograph summed up all the proof he needed of the natural merging of the physical and metaphysical. Neither his ancestor, Averroes, nor Thomas Aquinas had done a better job of twining the two. Abramax's gaze drifted from Mercy Bond to the silently grinning head of the Melusina, and he scowled. "What a botch job," he thought. "I can't believe we are getting paid for this."

The thing's eyes were busy scanning every inch of the room in its view. Then they settled down and stared directly at him. He wished he could wish the horrible invention away, but instead, what he saw in his imagination was the witch, Ocinda, push back the sleeves of her pale pink pajamas, and, with a wave of her hand, a brief spell, wish away the ghost as it approached her and His Highness across the veranda. One second the flimsy form was drawing near, and the next a strong wind came up, twisted into a small twister, and carried the screaming entity out to sea. Pelasio DeGris stared in wonder, following the gyring cloud of his old nemesis as it rode the air currents out to the horizon and was swallowed whole by the dark leviathan that had surfaced earlier. Both DeGris and Abramax worked a finger up under their turbans to scratch their heads in wonder at the effective work of the witch.

Then something so startling happened that Avec-Bruhl nearly fainted. The Melusina opened her mouth and spoke. The voice came in a hiss like that of a snake, and the sound of it frightened all three of the great minds. It said:

"And then the witch and the ruler of the wandering island were married on a rainy day in the lagoon of the four darmpala palms. The entire population of the island, thirty-nine in all, attended while the giant creature of the yellow ocean lolled in shallow water. There was a great feast of manta ray garnished with periwinkle and games in which physical prowess was at a disadvantage to intellectual wit.

"But that night, in the royal bedroom, before disrobing, Ocinda told Pelasio DeGris that she had one demand he must acquiesce to. He asked what it was, and she told him, 'You must have a room built at the back of the palace for me, to my specifications, that you are forbidden to enter. I will lock myself in that room on the sixth day of the week. You must not look upon me on that day or a great curse will befall you.'

"Pelasio DeGris, thinking it might be a fine thing to have a day to himself each week, readily agreed. And then the couple made love so passionately that the ruler's turban fell off and the island ceased its wandering for an hour. When the ruler was fast asleep, the witch sighed with contentment, for it was she who had conjured the ghost to begin with."

When the Melusina stopped talking, Avec-Bruhl tore the goggles from his eyes and threw them on the ground. "All is lost. These spoken words have polluted the experiment. We must begin again."

Dr. Abramax began to laugh. He said, "You're an idiot, Hollis. What are we to begin again? What have we ever done so far? Look at this, this torpedo with a silver head. May it be your coffin, you dolt."

Mercy Bond turned and left the room. Five years of her life had been wasted on probability. She could not stomach another second of it. Before the door swung shut behind her, she had decided to pack that evening and leave the next morning. Abramax followed her out into the hallway. Avec-Bruhl, left alone with the head of the Melusina, then gave way to tears, and his unceasing lamentations could be heard in every hallway and cubicle of the Center as he wandered aimlessly in his grief. Somewhere around midnight, he slit his own throat, died in a cataract of blood and became a ghost.

At two in the morning, the snowstorm still raging outside the Center, Abramax awakened to the sounds of moaning in his cubicle. Even before opening his eyes, he said, "For shit's sake, Hollis, go back to your own cubicle and take it like a man." Louder moaning ensued, and the doctor sat up and looked. There, by the doorway, stood the phosphorescent spirit of Avec-Bruhl, beating the air with airy fists. Abramax scrambled out of bed, grabbed his turban, and fled, passing through the ghost to get to the hallway. In that moment that he was subsumed by the form of the phantom, he felt a distinct chill and a fleeting sense of melancholy that made him choke on his own saliva. Once out beneath the gleaming white lights, he ran the mazelike hallways, searching for help. He was desperate to find a companion, knowing that the presence of another would quell his fear, and he might even be able to laugh at the pathetic spiritual remnant of his late boss.

Fleeing the spectral figure, Abramax discovered that the technicians had fled the Center and that the doors to the outside had all been locked, preventing him from any plan of escape. The ghost of Avec-Bruhl slowly, inexorably, followed him, wailing half-cogent/half-incomprehensible slogans of remorse. "Why me?" the doctor asked himself as he rounded a corner only to see, standing before him in the middle of the hallway, Mercy Bond. She was completely naked. As he approached her, she caught fire with a subtle popping sound and went up in a flash, like a bundle of twigs.

In the last hour before dawn, Abramax, completely exhausted, his turban drenched, stumbled into the Yellow Chamber and leaned his back against the door. He heard the lamentations of the ghost as it passed by out in the hallway and breathed a sigh of relief for having finally given it the slip. For what must have been hours the spirit had pursued him as he covered every passage of the Center at least a hundred times, trying to escape. Each time he had encountered the fire that had been Mercy Bond, it was still burning with the same ferocity of its initial combustion.

Abramax watched out the window as the snow-filled scene lightened with the onset of day. Then he became aware that the Melusina had awakened, and he looked at her grinning face and wide eyes. She cleared her throat and said, "Today is the sixth day of the sixth month of the sixth year."

The doctor walked forward to stand at the foot of her cylinder. "The sixth day of what?" he said.

"Of the week," she hissed.

A breeze from off a yellow ocean swept through his memory, and in the throes of a revelation that came with the speed of light, he said, "I am Pelasio DeGris."

"Yes," said the silver head, "and you are cursed."

"It was on this day that I could not contain my curiosity."

"And you entered my private room, this room, and saw my true nature as you see it before you now. I gathered you up and imprisoned you atop a snow-capped mountain, in a gleaming, white, silent dream of probability where you labored to create me. Once I was made, I inhabited your probable world, the wandering island of Threbansche—its past, its present, its future. As the witch Ocinda, I created this world of Brooklyn, the military, infinite pi, and Averroes, in which to stay, with a dream, your desire to wander."

"Then this is the real world, the one in which I created you," said Abramax.

"No, for prior to that, I was Ocinda, the witch, and sent you here to create me."

"Then you created me."

"No," she said, "You are me."

With this, the Center for the Reification of Actual Probability took on its true form and became an enormous black sea dragon with a mind that sought that which was impregnable to doubt and a spirit of melancholy moaning through the corridors of its gleaming white heart. It dove into the yellow sea and swam down toward the center of the world, describing a radius whose calculation relied on a value no human could precisely know.

It swam relentlessly for a day, a century, forever, and in that brief span all things were probable.

Destroyer
Beth Adele Long

R uth sat at the kitchen table, bare feet swishing against the tile floor, and paged slowly through the morning paper. Depressing, as usual. She caught a whiff of laundry detergent and shook her head. One would think that Sally could remember she needed clean underwear the night *before* she needed it, but oh no. She waited until six fifty-seven on a Wednesday morning to throw it in the washing machine.

"Hey Ruth?" Sally called, over the noise of water spraying into the washer.

"Yeah."

"Ruth?" Sally called again.

Ruth and Sally were sisters, as evidenced by their identical last name, their common vocabulary, and a mutual tendency to leave one cupboard door open after putting the dishes away. But sometimes Ruth was prepared to renounce their relationship and find a place where she could at least read the paper without being interrupted.

"*What?*" Ruth shouted.

"How's that little black girl doing?"

Ruth called, "Who?"

After a pause, Sally poked her head around the corner. "That black girl who lives down the street. The one you were talking to yesterday."

Ruth licked her forefinger and deliberately turned a page of the newspaper. "I'm afraid I didn't notice her skin color."

"Excuse me, Miss Affirmative Action, but I think you know who I'm talking about."

Ruth cut off a sarcastic reply. "You mean Ashley?"

"That would be her."

"What did you ask about?"

"How is she doing?" Sally repeated.

Sally realized she wouldn't get much out of her sister, but she had to ask. Her curiosity had been running high ever since she saw Ruth talking with the girl the evening before; at one point they had stood close together as if conspiring, the girl's plaited hair dancing around her head every time she moved. They'd talked a while longer before Ruth came in, looking shaken. Ruth never conversed with neighborhood children. Neighborhood children never, never spoke to Ruth. The abnormality simply could not go unremarked upon.

Ruth guided another page from right side to left. "She's doing fine."

"I saw you two talking last night."

"Yes, that's how I know she's doing fine." Another page turn.

Sally studied her fingernails and turned back to the washing machine. She was often tempted to make sharp comments when her sister annoyed her. But she usually held her tongue on account of the wig. When Ruth was in her late twenties, she had inexplicably begun to lose her hair. Sally, long a seeker of the perfect spray or mousse or gel to tame her abundant curls, credited much of Ruth's eccentricity to the undeniable trauma of going through life without one's natural hair.

Ruth had staunchly refused to see a doctor about her problem. "I don't trust doctors, and more likely as not they'd make the problem worse." Sally had never seen how this was possible. The wig always looked like an afterthought to her, a last-minute accessory that never quite matched the rest of Ruth's outfit.

"Oh," Ruth said from the kitchen. "Ouch. Ouch. Oh."

"What's the matter?" Sally called.

Ruth stood up from the table, hands on her back.

"Nothing," Ruth said, "I just feel like someone took a chainsaw to my lower vertebrae. It'll pass, I'm sure."

Sally bit her tongue. "It will pass, I'm sure" was one of Ruth's most common phrases, along with "I don't trust them" and "It makes me want to close the doors and never come out again."

Sally went into the kitchen and poured a glass of orange juice. The washing machine went into the spin cycle. It sounded like a small helicopter had landed in the hallway. Ruth sat down slowly again. She leaned gingerly over the paper. "You should go to my chiropractor," Sally told her. "He'll pop you into place in a jiffy."

Ruth never looked up from the paper. "Don't trust chiropractors."

"There's a surprise." Sally finished her orange juice and set the glass on the counter. When she turned around, Ruth was staring at her.

"Aren't you ever afraid of anything?" Ruth asked. "Do you never agonize over any-thing? Do you never feel the world is your enemy?"

Sally spread her hands on the counter and leaned forward. "Of course things scare me. But——"

"You don't understand," Ruth interrupted. "You zip through life, ignoring problems when you can, and never letting anything break through to you. How can you stand being so insensitive?"

Sally gritted her teeth. Ruth was such a prima donna, always acting like she alone suffered, she alone understood the threats of the world. Sally had suffered her share of heartaches, but she'd borne them silently. She didn't have much choice; it wasn't as if Ruth would have listened, anyway. Sally jerked the dishwasher open and shoved her glass in the top rack. "Ruth, there's a difference between being sensitive and being paranoid."

Ruth turned away. "That's not fair," she said, voice quivering.

Sally felt a stab of shame. A sparrow land on the window ledge. "Who cares about clean clothes?" she asked it. She grabbed her purse from the back of a kitchen chair without looking at Ruth and left the house.

Ruth listened to her go and then got up to find a tissue. She never understood why Sally got so upset over their talks. She sat down and blew her nose loudly. The microwave clock indicated that she needed to leave soon; she *should* get in early if she wanted to take a long lunch.

"Black hole," she muttered. What a strange child.

Yesterday evening Ruth had been weeding the flower beds in front of the house when she heard someone come up behind her.

"I have a black hole."

Ruth turned around. A girl who lived down the street, a skinny child of maybe twleve or thirteen, stood behind her with her hands cupped one over the other. Ruth wiped her forehead and balanced her garden clippers on the head of a large stone toad that Sally insisted on keeping by the front walk.

"Really," Ruth said. She hoped the girl—what was her name? Ashley?—wouldn't hang around too long. "I thought black holes were only in outer space."

"It's a primordial black hole," Ashley said. Her tone suggested that this was the key piece of information that Ruth had been missing.

"Oh, a *primordial* black hole," Ruth answered. She glanced at her watch. Time for dinner and the evening news soon.

"I found it and tamed it."

"That's so interesting." Ruth fingered the azaleas. "What do black holes eat?"

Ashley perked up. "Most people don't know to ask that. I mean, you'd think a black hole would have all it needs, right? But I do have to feed it sometimes, otherwise it might evaporate. It's not picky, really. Grass, pebbles, lima beans, whatever." She peeked between her fingers. "Although I think I need to put it on a diet. You have to be careful with black holes. It's bad news for the neighborhood if they get too big."

"Hmm. I didn't know that." Ruth sighed. "Does it have a name?"

"Oh, I'd never give it a name," Ashley said. "Whatever you give a black hole never comes out. Whoa, think about it! What if I gave it the name 'Fred'? Then everyone in the world named 'Fred' wouldn't have a name anymore." She shook her head. "I just take care of it, and it lets me hold it and keep it in its box." She held her hands out and parted them halfway. "Do you want to pet it?"

Ruth blinked and rubbed her eyes. There seemed to be a dark spot in her vision. She closed one eye, opened it, closed the other. When she looked up at the sky, the problem went away. She looked back at Ashley's cupped hands and blinked again.

Ashley heaved a deep sigh and reached into her hip bag. "Everyone just blinks at me when I show it to them." She pulled out a cigar box lined with red flannel and made a motion as if she were transferring something from her hand to the box.

Ruth blinked. The spot was back.

Ashley closed the box and put it back into her hip pack. "Why do you wear a wig?" she asked.

Ruth automatically put a hand to her head. Everything was still in place. How did the girl know? "What do you mean?" she asked.

Ashley just looked at her, arms crossed, hips thrust to one side. What nerve, to ask such a question.

"Why do you *think* I wear one?"

Ashley scratched her arm. "Because you don't have hair?"

Ruth gave an artificial smile and pointed a finger at Ashley. "Bingo!"

Ashley reached into her hip pack again and pulled out two big cubes of green and purple chewing gum. She put both in her mouth and started chomping away. "Why don't you have hair?"

The garden clippers slid off the toad's head. Ruth bent down to pick them up. "I have a condition."

"What, like cancer?"

"No, *not* like cancer." Ruth viciously clipped an azalea branch. "It's simply a condition that causes hair loss." The truth was, never having been to a doctor about the situation, Ruth didn't know why her hair had begun falling out. The only thing she liked less than having people find out she wore a wig was having people ask her about the cause.

"Oh," Ashley said, not sounding convinced. "I guess that's just part of living in a crazy world." She paused. "My mom always says that."

Ruth became serious. "It is a crazy world, and you should listen to your mom.

People are very destructive and untrustworthy. It can be scary."

Ashley stepped closer and lowered her voice. "Do *you* know about the destroyer?" she asked. Ruth felt a tingling sensation right down her shoulder blades.

"The destroyer eats you up," Ashley said. "Sometimes it gets you so slowly you don't even feel it, but it gets you just the same. It's like a black hole in the middle of you."

"What's a pretty girl like you doing, thinking about such awful things?" Ruth said, trying to sound easy and light.

Ashley rolled her eyes. "I'm not pretty. And I think about them 'cause they're all around me."

As soon as she said that, Ruth realized that the girl *was* pretty. The wide cheek-bones, the big eyes, the rich dark skin, those kinky, wavy plaits of hair. "But you *are*," Ruth said. "You're very pretty."

Ashley rolled her eyes again and spit on the sidewalk. The spit spread out slowly like an egg in a frying pan and settled into an irregular blob. "Is that pretty?" she asked. She shook her head back and forth. "You don't want to think about it. You're just too scared to think about what I said." She grasped Ruth's elbow, stood on her toes, and whispered, "I know who the destroyer is." She stepped back. "And you don't."

She turned around and started walking away.

"Wait!" Ruth was startled to hear her voice so loud. She'd only meant to call loud enough for the girl to hear.

Ashley halted, turned around. Ruth couldn't think what to say next.

"For a moment, I thought you were going to say something," Ashley said. "Look, I don't have all night. This little guy gets cranky around bedtime."

Ruth swallowed. "I was just wondering, you know. What you meant."

Ashley cocked her head to one side, like a bird. "About what?"

Impertinent child. She knows perfectly well what I mean. "Oh, nothing," Ruth said, and started to walk across the lawn.

As she reached the front walk, Ruth heard Ashley clear her throat. She turned around.

"Well," Ashley began, "I guess I'd let you take me to lunch tomorrow."

Ruth smiled. So that's what this was all about. "I have work."

"I thought people got vacation time."

Is that what you thought? Ruth wanted to say. "Well, some of us can't just take time off whenever we feel like it. Some people have responsibilities to take care of."

Ashley took three steps across the lawn and stopped. "I *told* you, I'd let you take me to lunch tomorrow." She crossed her arms and looked straight at Ruth——straight through her, it seemed. "You're scared, aren't you? The world's too mean, and it frightens you. Well I may just be in junior high, but you know one thing I've found out? Lots of people are afraid. Most times they're not even sure what of. And some people don't ever want to find out. They think it'll scare them even worse to know. They'd rather say to everyone 'I'm scared!' than just turn around and see what's behind them." She swung her arms back and forth, striking her palms together in front of her. "I'm starting to think maybe you're one of that kind of people."

Ruth didn't look at Ashley. She pulled a leaf off the azalea bush. The girl was obviously starved for attention. Perhaps her parents ignored her, or were hard on her. This could be an opportunity to do some good. She looked back at Ashley, with her jaunty hair and too-thin limbs. "Noon tomorrow? I'll meet you here."

"Okay." Ashley stretched a piece of gum from her mouth, bit it off, and pushed it into the cigar box. "I might be late, but I'll show up sooner or later." She sprinted down the sidewalk, sneakers flashing red at every impact.

Ruth watched her go feeling relieved and unsettled. "Poor girl," she said to herself. "Poor, poor girl."

She repeated the phrase to herself all evening, until she firmly believed it. By the time she went to bed, Ruth could think of little else but how she could help the poor child. This would be how she would spend her retirement. She would seek out children like Ashley, neglected or unloved, and show them that someone really did care about them. She would show them that self-delusion (a black hole for a pet!) would only lead to pain and self-destruction. For three hours she lay awake, listening to traffic go by and playing out the different conversations she might have with her new friend.

When Ruth's alarm went off at six thirty, her excitement had abated considerably. When Sally stormed out of the house, Ruth sat morosely at the kitchen table and wondered if she'd even keep her appointment with the girl.

But at eleven forty, she mentioned to her officemate that she'd be taking a long lunch break, and she left for home. A few minutes away from her house, she decided to delay, remembering Ashley tell her she "might be late," without even waiting for a reply. If the girl wasn't going to be prompt, then Ruth wasn't going to waste time waiting for her. She filled up her gas tank and picked up some snack food at the convenience store, and finally turned onto her own street at twelve thirteen.

Ashley was sitting on the front step, hands laced around her knees, vigorously chewing her gum. Abashed, Ruth got out of her car and went around to unlock the passenger door.

"I'm sorry I'm late. I had to stop for gas."

Ashley bounced up. "Let's walk."

Ruth held the car door open. "Where's your pet?"

"You want to see it again?" Ashley dug into her pocket and pulled out the cigar box.

Ruth forced a smile. "That's okay."

"I'm kind of tired of it," Ashley said. "You want to trade for it?"

Ruth didn't like the way Ashley's gaze lingered on her hairline. "So, Ashley, where are we going?"

"How about McDonald's?"

Ugh, Ruth thought. Then, It's cheap. I can just get a cup of water. "Sure. McDonald's."

"Okay." Ashley started walking down the sidewalk.

Ruth closed and locked the car doors. "Um, McDonald's is this way," she said, pointing in the opposite direction.

Ashley turned around and continued walking, backwards. "I know a better way."

Right. A better way. Ruth dropped her keys into her purse and followed Ashley.

None of the conversations Ruth had imagined last night started as naturally as she'd expected. The questions fell flat before she even asked them: What do your parents do for work? How do you like school? Do you have brothers? Sisters? In her mind, these had all been penetrating questions that would spark deep and meaningful conversations. She had pictured Ashley slowly yielding to Ruth's concern and insight, pouring out her soul as Ruth nodded sympathetically. She had thought the girl might cry, not much, just enough to show how much Ruth's attention meant to her.

Now, walking behind Ashley as the girl matched her stride to avoid sidewalk cracks, Ruth pictured Ashley shrugging off her questions without a backward glance. The girl's answers would likely be single words, monosyllabic even. The ensuing silence would be even more awkward than the present one. Ruth began to sweat; the day was warm, despite the clouds, and quite humid. Her wig itched against her scalp.

Her wig. The girl knew about the wig. Ruth felt exposed. Unprotected. It had been so long since she'd been with anyone besides her family who knew about it. If the girl knew, what about Ruth's secretary, her boss, the clerk at the grocery store, even the people who stood behind her in lines at stores, did they all stare and then look away? She started to feel the way she did in dreams, when she suddenly realized she'd gone to work and forgotten to dress first. Did her wig even protect her? Was she naked every day, and simply hadn't known? Ashley stayed several yards in front of her. Ruth forgot about asking her any questions.

"Down here," Ashley said finally, waiting for Ruth. They left the white ribbon of concrete and cut diagonally down a steep, wooded hill. Ruth didn't complain; she didn't want the girl to hear how winded she was. She wished she'd gone inside to change her clothes before they left, but at least she was wearing boots and not thin-soled flats.

They pushed through underbrush, the busy hum of insects growing louder as they moved into denser woods. "Where are we going?" Ruth panted after a while. The complete absence of McDonald's started to worry her.

Ashley stopped long enough for Ruth to come up even with her and then pointed. "I wanted to show you this first," she said.

Ruth looked and saw nothing but a gap between trees. Then she looked again and realized something was there after all. A short distance from them stood a golden-brown tree trunk, much larger than the ones around it, with a fanciful tree house perched in its upper branches.

"Is that your tree house?" Ruth asked.

"Sort of." Ashley bounded ahead and started climbing the ladder carved into the trunk. Ten feet up she stopped and looked back. "Come *on*."

The closer Ruth came to the tree, the more beautiful it was. She stood at the base for a moment, hands sliding over the golden bark. Many years ago she had climbed trees, recklessly. Now she wondered if she was even strong enough to lift herself off the ground.

From far above, Ashley called down, "Are you coming?"

Ruth fitted her hands and feet into the slats. She began to climb the tree. At first she panted with the effort, but the higher she went, the easier and easier it became to climb. The breeze combed through her wig and tickled her neck. I'll have to change clothes before I go back to work, she thought.

Ashley reached out to help her step onto the platform floor of the tree house. Three sturdy walls supported a vaulted ceiling from which chimes and painted mobiles hung down. Ruth leaned against a wall to catch her breath. Carried on the breeze Ruth thought she heard children shouting and laughing, the creak of old wheels turning, the splash of water. Always the sounds were just at the edge of hearing.

"This is the safest place I know," Ashley said.

Ruth set her purse down. Two walls had windows; child-sized furniture sat neatly around the space. "It's almost magical."

Ashley nodded. She sat on a cushioned bench beside a window, yellow sunlight turning her skin gold.

Ruth moved to another window and looked out over the tops of trees whose white trunks were obscured by yellow and green leaves. "It looks different from up here," she said. Curtains billowed out on either side of her every time the wind gusted.

For a while they simply listened to the wind in the trees and the creaking of the branches. Ruth closed her eyes. She forgot about lunch, forgot about work.

Ashley said, "I'll tell you about the destroyer."

Ruth didn't move, or open her eyes. "Don't talk about ugly things now," she murmured.

"But you're here now. You can bear to hear it."

Warm breezes lapped against Ruth's cheeks, ears, neck. Leaves sighed. Chimes shivered and rang. If the girl wants to talk, let her, Ruth thought. "All right."

"Good," Ashley said. "First you have to think about this: what makes your life miserable? Your sister? Your job? No one asking you out anymore?"

Ruth murmured, "I had a date last year."

"And?"

"I canceled."

Ashley said, "Take off your wig."

Ruth opened her eyes. The ground was very far away, she realized. "What?"

"Take off your wig," the girl repeated.

"Why?" Ruth felt sick to her stomach.

"Because I want to show you."

"Show me what?" Ruth was afraid she might cry.

"You wanted to find out, didn't you? That's why you came."

"No," Ruth said. "No."

"I brought you to the safest place," Ashley said. She stood so that she blocked the ladder. "You can't find the truth if you're hiding. So take your wig off."

"Did I say you were pretty?" Ruth said, her voice shrill and sounding far away. "Did I say that yesterday? I lied. You're ugly. Only an ugly little child like you would be so horrible."

"I'll show you," Ashley said, quietly insistent. "But you have to take it off."

"You're delusional, too. Black hole! For a pet!"

"Come on, this is the best way to show you."

"Filthy, ugly little black girl. *You're* the black hole. You're a liar and a spoiled brat!" Ruth said. She moved towards the ladder.

"Out of my way. Forget lunch. I have to get back to work, I only get half an hour and they'll be wondering where—"

Ashley pointed up. "Look!"

Ruth looked up. A knot in the wood let a shaft of sunlight through the ceiling. Light poured through, bathing her in its heat. Tears came to her eyes. She blinked. She saw black specks everywhere. Little black holes. *That's so interesting,* she heard someone say.

"I don't want to see!" she cried.

Ashley reached forward as if to pat Ruth consolingly on the arm. Instead she pulled off Ruth's wig. She said, "You know who your destroyer is. Not the doctors. Not the traffic. Not the disease that took your hair."

Cool air licked at Ruth's scalp, at the gel-filled wig band, at the tufts of her remaining hair. "Shut up shut up *shut up.*" She wanted to weep. "*You're* my 'destroyer.'"

"No," Ashley said. She put her hand up to block the light from the ceiling. "You are."

Ruth pushed forward, throwing her weight against the girl. Ashley hit the wall and

Ruth wrenched the wig out of her hand. She pulled Ashley forward, jerking her towards the window.

"You're a liar," Ruth said, and gave the girl a final push. Ashley's fall was broken by the window ledge, and for a moment she balanced perfectly. Then her torso rotated backwards out of the window and her body disappeared.

Shaking violently, Ruth stumbled back and grabbed her purse. She pulled her wig on, careless of its angle, and climbed down the trunk. She ran, breathless, until she reached the edge of the woods, scrambling, half-crawling up the slope to the sidewalk, and the street. Calm, she thought. Be calm. She walked back to her house, let herself in, and took a shower. Then she put her clothes back on, the same clothes, and drove back to work.

"That didn't take so long," her officemate commented.

"Change of plans," Ruth said.

The following Saturday, Sally and Ruth sat across from each other at the breakfast table. Sally drank her orange juice and flipped through the morning paper.

"Wow," she said, leaning forward to see an article better. "Listen to this. 'Ashley Spinnaker, thirteen, was found dead yesterday evening, police say.' Isn't that the girl who lives down the street?"

Ruth shrugged and looked into her cereal bowl.

"They found her in a clearing in the woods not far from here. She fell out of a treehouse." She shivered. "I'll bet that was her. Wow. I know I make fun of you for saying this, but it really does make me want to shut all our doors and not come out. It's a scary world out there."

Ruth pushed back her chair and stood up.

"Ruth?" Sally called after her, but she was already climbing the stairs. "Ruth?"

She went into her room and eased the door shut. She sat on the corner of her bed and pushed her fingertips under the edge of her wig. Gently, carefully, she worked it loose and laid it on the bed next to her. For a long time she sat, motionless, staring into the mirror.

Gods and Three Wishes
Carol Emshwiller

We don't think much about the gods way out here. Besides, you can't depend on them for anything. Do they keep our dinghies from tipping over? Do they keep us from shooting each other? Do they keep our young ones from falling out of trees? Or do they even ever keep them from climbing too high in the first place? Whatever gods bring is usually wrong, anyway, flood or drought, tornadoes. . . . Whirlwinds in which we can't see a thing and in the middle of which the gods refuse to manifest themselves.

Knock on wood. Carry a rabbit's foot. Avoid cross-eyed people. Live under a horseshoe. (A mule's shoe is even better.) But even if you do all these things, you can't count on being safe from the gods, except way out here where we are.

We have enough troubles of our own without their meddling. They'll notice you no matter where you try to hide, unless that is, you're here with us.

(We used to worship bears. Things might be better if we had stuck to that.)

To get above and beyond the gods isn't easy. You have to cross mountain passes, raging rivers. Rise up into the clouds and then dip down again. You'll find our hidden valley on the other side of everything. The gods won't bother tracking you way out here.

That they stay out of our valley is what we pray for every morning.

But now which one of them said, "Let there be a mountain lake that breaks through its ice dam"? Or did it just happen by itself?

The water rushed down and swept away a whole section of the forest.

Who survives? Both the good *and* the bad. That's for sure. Nasty old Minn Moon and his sheep were all saved, whereas Bess and her little house were washed all the way down the mountain.

Send over our most beautiful girl to seduce the gods. We have lots, but send one who can sing our best sad songs.

(If the gods sent *us* a beautiful maiden goddess, we'd be just as distracted as we hope they'll be.)

She'll tell them to keep their sticky golden fingers to themselves.

Of course she has to be a virgin.

In that case maybe she should be an ugly girl (easier to find an ugly virgin) and maybe not be able to sing. We don't want them seducing her and keeping her as one of their own. Hazel comes to mind first thing. You'd think with a name like that she'd be one of our beauties. You'd think she'd have hazel hair and eyes.

"You have to go all by yourself. Even though you're only nineteen."

"But what could I do against the gods? I don't even believe in them."

"All the better then. And remember, no taking any of the gods' names in vain."

She's small and thin. She hardly has a figure—even yet. Maybe she'll never have one. The gods won't notice her. And by the time she gets there, climbing up and down those mountain passes all day long, she'll be even more like a bundle of sticks than she already is.

"Tell them we just want to live quietly, not bother anybody and not be bothered by them. Burn a little incense."

(If they wanted to, they could straighten buck teeth and hammertoes . . . fix bunions. Some people think those bunions are a punishment from gods. They could clean everybody up so nobody would smell bad, but that would make them too much like the gods themselves.)

Gods asleep, or, rather, meditating in their Pantheons. . . . (There's a Pantheon in every city, but Hazel has never been in a city.) She has never seen ceilings so high. Nor anything so sparkling. And she's never seen a god before. How could she, when ours is a gods-free zone? Or used to be. She believes in them now.

She thinks to go touch the god's golden toe. But she doesn't want to wake him up.

Do it, is what she tells herself. Don't back off. The goats will wake him in a minute anyway. (We convinced her to bring her goats. She raised them from newborn kids. They would have followed her anyway. She says she won't sacrifice them, but she may have to.)

We told her to pick a small god. Find him on the beach or under a sapling, not an oak, and not in some big white building, but she went to the top without even realizing it.

She touches. He groans, then roars a roar that echoes through his Pantheon. He stretches and stands up.

Hazel says, "Oh my god! Oh my god!" and it's not a prayer.

She tries to hide behind his plinth, but the goats start baaing. She shakes her hair so it falls over her face and looks out from behind it. He doesn't seem quite so impressive through that scrim of hair, though he still glows.

"Don't call me: 'Oh My God. Oh My God.' Call me: Sun at Noon or Moon at Midnight. And thank you for the goats." He grins and shows his gold teeth. "You will be blessed."

Hazel absolutely will not let him have her Lulu and Nan. She says, "No!"

"Who began all this? Who said, 'Let there be what there is right now'? This light and a firmament splashed with stars, and snow on the mountain tops? Who but me? And maybe one or two others, and with a little luck. You owe me much more than just two goats."

"Please don't shout." (His voice is so loud.)

Hazel doesn't think the god is that beautiful himself, though his big, curly beard covers most of his face. His nose is flat. How would a god get a broken nose? Except from another god?

"I don't even believe in you."

"You don't have to believe; you just have to give me those goats."

There's no place to hide. He chases her around his plinth. He's big and clumsy. Yells (he's still yelling), "And don't you dare cast a spell."

"How about just one goat?" But they're like her children. How could she pick one?

"I can tell the future and it isn't very nice." He's out of breath already. Too much sitting around waiting for admirers.

He stops and really looks at her across the plinth. A god's stare is hard to bear. She feels smaller and smaller. He grunts. It's clear she's not worth goats. He turns to go after them. She gets between them, not even thinking how those goats are faster than she is.

He catches her by her shirttail while she tries to defend them. She gets away when the god trips on his toga, falls flat on his already squashed-in nose. Maybe that's how he broke it in the first place.

She—they—all run. He lies there yelling, "Come back here you little . . ." and uses a bad word we don't use in our gods-free zone. Hazel doesn't even know it's a bad word.

She finds a place by a stream with willow and beech trees and grass and bushes for the goats. Gods only know if they really are trees, or nymphs and nyads. The stream sparkles. Golden laurel leaves float in it. Dare she drink? We told her: Beware of swans or deer. Even trees. Don't look into any still pools. Be careful who you kiss.

Cats' ears, statues' noses, pennyroyal. Mash them up together, mix with lemon grass and marshmallow. . . . We gave her a little bag of those, except for the pennyroyal, which she picks now. Sprinkle half on a fire. Drink the other half.

You see, we told her she might get three wishes. We told her that, though we didn't think she'd really get even one (not from any of the gods we know about anyway), but we wanted her to start out feeling hopeful so that not all would seem to be lost even if all was lost. But three wishes don't amount to anything if you never get to see the creature that might give them to you, so this is the way she calls for help. She claps her hands in time with what she hopes might be the rhythm of the Universe. "Appear," she says. "Appear."

But who?

(Hazel already has her wishes picked out. First, save my goats. Second, get me out of here a virgin. Third, tell those gods to stay away from our gods-free zone. Whatever happens there, we want it to happen in an ordinary way, as a rock falling down on our heads from the climber above us, only because he dislodged it, or tripping and falling, only because we were clumsy. We want to be sure that when a lake bursts through its icy mountain dam it was because it was ready to do that all on its own. We want to tell our children, "Things just happen.")

When Luck appears, he's wearing ordinary clothes. That's a relief. And he's not at all godlike. That's a relief, too. He has gray eyes and a nice smile. His lips and cheeks are redder than they ought to be. He looks a little feverish . . . a little clownlike. He's as skinny as she is.

He says right off, "I'm Luck."

But Hazel felt lucky the minute she saw him.

She likes his looks. She starts to tell him her three wishes, but even as she's in the middle of telling them, she changes her mind about the second one.

She says, "We want you on our side. We want you in our gods-free zone. I'll do anything for you." Meaning anything.

He's brought Nan and Lulu some melon rinds and corn cobs. They like him right away. That's lucky. Isn't that lucky?

For Hazel he's brought a picnic of bread, goat cheese, hard-boiled eggs. (He juggles the eggs—three!—one-handed.) Since she met up with that big main god, she's forgotten to eat. She was too worried. This is certainly lucky.

Before he sits down on the bank with her, he does a little entrechat. Just what you'd expect.

"Will you help me?" She keeps her fingers crossed.

"Who do you think got you free of the top-dog god? I tripped him on his toga."

So would it be lucky or not if she slept with him? Maybe had Luck's child? A funny little boy whose ears stick out like his and whose lips are too red?

Everything comes in threes, both good luck and bad, but when to start counting? Is that just one good thing or two already? Well, since she's deleted her number two wish, for sure she has one more.

The gods make their own weather. Whatever it's doing some place else, it's always good where the gods are lounging about. They run around naked as jaybirds, as if it was the most natural thing in the world, so they like it sunny. If they want to make it hard for the rest of us, they can turn on a storm. Even just a hard, steady rain might do the trick if it comes at *exactly* the wrong time.

So just when Lucky gives her a kiss (a little peck kind of kiss, but on the lips), it starts to rain. What kind of Luck is that? But it *is* lucky. Nearest shelter is either a sibyl's sanctuary or a cave with a sacred spring in it. They choose the latter.

It's so nice in there, she gets scared. Things aren't supposed to be this nice for anybody: that they would have their very own sparkling spring; that a hard rain should be falling outside, and they'd be warm and his bony arm would be around her shoulders. It will tempt the gods. She speaks in whispers so as not to alert any of them. Even Luck whispers.

They sit in the mouth of the cave for a while and talk about how nice the rain is, how nice it sounds and how it looks, and how everything smells of damp earth and wet weeds.

He's not large (in fact, he's much smaller than you'd expect), but you can see how adept he is. She's glad to have him on her side, even if only for a little while. But you never know what Luck will do.

But now here's this other wish coming true. Is it the last one? Little pecks on her lips and earlobe.

"Come live with me and be in our gods-free zone."

"Nope," he says.

"Why not?"

By now little nips all along her collar bone.

"I'm supposed to get the gods to stay out of our way, but not you. Please come. Please."

"You might as well be praying."

"I am."

"Don't pray to me. I hate that."

Little nips lower down, all around her belly button. It tickles and makes her laugh. She's been laughing ever since he appeared. (Later it'll tickle all the more when he gets all the way down and beyond and kisses her instep.)

"How about a little lucky baby boy?"

She's the one says that.

Now he's giggling.

"Wait and see. Like everybody has to."

She'll be lucky if her goats haven't wandered off, and lucky if some dog or wolf hasn't eaten them. She usually finds a safe enclosure for them at night, but this night she forgets all about them.

(The baby will be a baby girl. Her ears will stick out. From the age of three months on, she'll have a nice smile. She'll be pesky, get into trouble all the time just like Luck does.)

It stopped raining, and here's the "rosy-fingered" goddess of dawn already . . . most gods wouldn't bother with things that are merely set dressing, but here comes Dawn now. They watch from the mouth of their cave. Hazel wonders, should she thank her some way? Or is this just a very nice natural thing?

Lucky says, "What a nice day! Come on, I'll walk you partway home."

"But I have to get the gods out of our space."

"What makes you think they've been there?"

"Well . . ." And she tells him about Minn Moon and Bess. And how bad things happened to good people and good things to bad. And why would that be?

"That's just bad Luck."

"You mean I don't have to try to keep those gods out?"

"They're out already."

"Come home with me. We need you."

"You're forgetting something."

"What?"

"I'll show you later."

He'll go a little ways with her. He wants to teach her a lesson.

So off they go into the mountains. They bring the bread and cheese.

(The goats stayed lucky. They're fine.)

When they have to cross a dangerous place where a landslide destroyed four or five yards of the trail, he says, "Well, you might be lucky if you cross it fast enough. The goats can do it; you're the only one might not make it."

Lucky crosses back and forth twice while she still thinks about it. (The goats are frolicking on the cliffs above them.) "Take a chance," he says.

What could go wrong with Luck right here? But when she tries to cross, she slides . . . first slowly, then faster, all the way down to the hanging valley below. She doesn't get hurt, not even scratched, but she'll have to climb all the way up.

Luck waits. By the time she gets back up, he's eaten all the bread and cheese. When she protests, he says, "That's Luck."

"I thought you were going to help me."

"How lucky that you didn't get hurt."

They're entering the big cat zone. That was another reason the gods didn't come here much.

We were clever from the start. We could tie hundreds of different kinds of knots. We had herbs to cure the common cold. We played tiddlywinks and mumblety-peg. We always had teeter-totters. We painted eyes on our walls. (We always had walls, even if some were the walls of caves.) Eyes kept us safe—or, rather, safer. In tiger country we wore eyes on the back of our heads. She should have done that.

When they enter the lion zone, Lucky leaves. But he already showed her that she couldn't count on him. And he ate all the food. He's the one brought it in the first place, so Hazel supposes he has the right.

It's the goats that save her. She has to sacrifice them to the lions, first one and then the other. But she gets back to us OK and has a lot to say, such as not to ever count on Luck.

Dead Boy Found

Christopher Barzak

A ll this started when my father told my mother she was a waste. He said, "You are such a waste, Linda," and she said, "Oh, yeah? You think so? We'll see about that." Then she got into her car and pulled out of our driveway, throwing gravel in every direction. She was going to Abel's, or so she said, where she could have a beer and find herself a real man.

Halfway there, though, she was in a head-on collision with a drunk woman named Lucy, who was on her way home, it happened, from Abel's. They were both driving around that blind curve on Highway 88, Lucy swerving a little, my mother smoking cigarette after cigarette, not even caring where the ashes fell. When they leaned their cars into the curve, Lucy crossed into my mother's lane. Bam! Just like that. My mother's car rolled three times into the ditch, and Lucy's car careened into a guardrail. It was Lucy who called the ambulance on her cellular phone, saying, over and over, "My God, I've killed Linda McCormick, I've killed that poor girl."

At that same moment, Gracie Highsmith was becoming famous. While out searching for new additions to her rock collection, she had found the missing boy's body buried beneath the defunct railroad tracks just a couple of miles from my house. The missing boy had been missing for two weeks. He disappeared on his way home from a Boy Scout meeting. He and Gracie were both in my class. I never really talked to either of them much, but they were all right. You know, quiet types. Weird, some might say. But I'm not the judgmental sort. I keep my own counsel. I go my own way. If Gracie Highsmith wanted to collect rocks, and if the missing boy wanted to be a Boy Scout, more power to them.

We waited several hours at the hospital before they let us see my mother. Me, my brother Andy, and my father sat in the lobby reading magazines and drinking coffee. A nurse finally came and got us. She took us up to the seventh floor. She pointed to room number 727 and said we could go on in.

My mother lay in the hospital bed with tubes coming out of her nose. One of her eyes had swelled shut and was already black and shining. She breathed with her mouth open, a wheezing noise like snoring. There were bloodstains on her teeth. Also several of her teeth were missing. When she woke, blinking her good eye rapidly, she saw me and said, "Baby, come here and give me a hug."

I wasn't a baby, I was fifteen, but I didn't correct her. I figured she'd been through enough already. A doctor came in and asked my mother how she was feeling. She said she couldn't feel her legs. He said that he thought that might be a problem, but that it would probably work itself out over time. There was swelling around her spinal cord. "It should be fine after a few weeks," he told us.

My father started talking right away, saying things like, "We all have to pull together. We'll get through this. Don't worry." Eventually his fast talking added up to mean something. When we brought my mother home, he put her in my bed so she could rest properly, and I had to bunk with Andy. For the next few weeks, he kept saying things like, "Don't you worry, honey. It's time for the men to take over." I started doing the dishes, and Andy vacuumed. My father took out the trash on Tuesdays. He brought home pizza or cold cuts for dinner.

I wasn't angry about anything. I want to make that clear right off. I mean, stupid stuff like this just happens. It happens all the time. One day you're just an average fifteen-year-old with stupid parents and a brother who takes out his aggressions on you because he's idiotic and his friends think it's cool to see him belittle you in public, and suddenly something happens to make things worse. Believe me, morbidity is not my specialty. Bad things just happen all at once. My grandma said bad things come in threes. Two bad things had happened: My mother was paralyzed, and Gracie Highsmith found the missing boy's body. If my grandma was still alive, she'd be trying to guess what would happen next.

I mentioned this to my mother while I spooned soup up to her trembling lips. She could feed herself all right, but she seemed to like the attention. "Bad things come in threes," I said. "Remember Grandma always said that?"

She said, "Your grandma was uneducated."

I said, "What is that supposed to mean?"

She said, "She didn't even get past eighth grade, Adam."

I said, "I knew that already."

"Well, I'm just reminding you."

"Okay," I said, and she took another spoonful of chicken broth.

At school everyone talked about the missing boy. "Did you hear about Jamie Marks?" they all said. "Did you hear about Gracie Highsmith?"

I pretended like I hadn't, even though I'd watched the news all weekend and considered myself an informed viewer. I wanted to hear what other people would say. A lot of rumors circulated already. Our school being so small made that easy. Seventh through twelfth grade all crammed into the same building, elbow to elbow, breathing each other's breath.

They said Gracie saw one of his fingers poking out of the gravel, like a zombie trying to crawl out of its grave. They said that after she removed a few stones, one of his blue eyes stared back at her, and that she screamed and threw the gravel back at his eye and ran home. They said, sure enough, when the police came later, they found the railroad ties loose, with the bolts broken off of them. So they removed them, dug up the gravel, shoveling for several minutes, and found Jamie Marks. Someone said a cop walked away to puke.

I sat through Algebra and Biology and History, thinking about cops puking, thinking about the missing boy's body. I couldn't stop thinking about those two things. I liked the idea of seeing one of those cops who set up speed traps behind bushes puking out his guts, holding his stomach. I wasn't sure what I thought about Jamie's dead body rotting beneath railroad ties. And what a piece of work, to have gone to all that trouble to hide the kid in such a place! It didn't help that at the start of each class all the teachers said they understood if we were disturbed, or anxious, and that we should talk if needed, or else they could recommend a good psychologist to our parents.

I sat at my desk with my chin propped in my hands, chewing an eraser, imagining Jamie Marks under the rails staring at the undersides of trains as they rumbled over him. Those tracks weren't used anymore, not since the big smash-up with a school bus back in the '80s, but I imagined trains on them anyway. Jamie inhaled each time a glimpse of sky appeared between boxcars and exhaled when they covered him over. He dreamed when there were no trains rolling over him, when there was no metallic scream on the rails. When he dreamed, he dreamed of trains again, blue sparks flying off the iron railing, and he gasped for breath in his sleep. A ceiling of trains covered him. He almost suffocated, there were so many.

After school, my brother Andy said, "We're going to the place, a bunch of us. Do you want to come?" Andy's friends were all seniors, and they harassed me a lot, so I shook my head and said no. "I have to see a friend and collect five dollars he owes me," I said, even though I hadn't loaned out money to anyone in weeks.

I went home and looked through school yearbooks and found Jamie Marks smiling from his square in row two. I cut his photo out with my father's exacto knife and stared at it for a while, then turned it over. On the other side was a picture of me. I swallowed and swallowed until my throat hurt. I didn't like that picture of me anyway, I told myself. It was a bad picture. I had baby fat when it was taken, and looked more like a little kid. I flipped the photo over and over, like a coin, and wondered, If it had been me, would I have escaped? I decided it must have been too difficult to get away from them—I couldn't help thinking there had to be more than one murderer—and probably I would have died just the same.

I took the picture outside and buried it in my mother's garden between the rows of sticks that had, just weeks before, marked off the sections of vegetables, keeping carrots carrots and radishes radishes. I patted the dirt softly, inhaled its crisp dirt smell, and whispered, "Don't you worry. Everything will be all right."

When my mother started using a wheelchair, she was hopeful, even though the doctors had changed their minds and said she'd never walk again. She told us not to worry. She enjoyed not always having to be on her feet. She figured out how to pop wheelies, and would show off in front of guests. "What a burden legs can be!" she told us. Even so, I sometimes found her wheeled into dark corners, her head in her hands, saying, "No, no, no," sobbing.

That woman, Lucy, kept calling and asking my mother to forgive her, but my mother told us to say she wasn't home and that she was contacting lawyers and that they'd have Lucy so broke within seconds; they'd make her pay real good. I told Lucy, "She isn't home," and Lucy said, "My God, tell that poor woman I'm so sorry. Ask her to please forgive me."

I told my mother Lucy was sorry, and the next time Lucy called, my mother decided to hear her out. Their conversation sounded like when my mom talks to her sister, my Aunt Beth, who lives in California near the ocean, a place I've never visited. My mother kept shouting, "No way! You too?! I can't believe it! Can you believe it?! Oh Lucy, this is too much."

Two hours later, Lucy pulled into our driveway, blaring her horn. My mother wheeled herself outside, smiling and laughing. Lucy was tall and wore red lipstick, and her hair was permed real tight. She wore plastic bracelets and hoop earrings and stretchy hot-pink pants. She bent down and hugged my mother, then helped her into the car. They drove off together, laughing, and when they came home several hours later, I smelled smoke and whiskey on their breath.

"What's most remarkable," my mother kept slurring, "is that I was on my way to the bar, sober, and Lucy was driving home, drunk." They'd both had arguments with their husbands that day; they'd both run out to make their husbands jealous. Learning all this, my mother and Lucy felt destiny had brought them together. "A virtual Big Bang," said my mother.

Lucy said, "A collision of souls."

The only thing to regret was that their meeting had been so painful. "But great things are born out of pain," my mother told me, nodding in a knowing way. "If I had to be in an accident with someone," she said, patting Lucy's hand, which rested on one of my mother's wheels, "I'm glad that someone was Lucy."

After I buried Jamie's and my photo, I walked around for a few days bumping into things. Walls, lockers, people. It didn't matter what, I walked into it. I hadn't known Jamie all that well, even though we were in the same class. We had different friends. Jamie liked computers; I ran track. Not because I like competition, but because I'm a really good runner, and I like to run, even though my mom always freaks because I was born premature, with undersized lungs. But I remembered Jamie: a small kid with stringy, mouse-colored hair and pale skin. He wore very round glasses, and kids sometimes called him Moony. He was supposed to be smart, but I didn't know about that. I asked a few people at lunch, when the topic was still hot, "What kind of grades did he get? Was he an honors student?" But no one answered. All they did was stare like I'd stepped out of a spaceship.

My brother Andy and his friends enjoyed a period of extreme popularity. After they went to where Jamie had been hidden, everyone thought they were crazy but somehow brave. Girls asked Andy to take them there, to be their protector, and he'd pick out the pretty ones who wore makeup and tight little skirts. "You should go, Adam," Andy told me. "You could appreciate it."

"It's too much of a spectacle," I said, as if I were above all that.

Andy narrowed his eyes. He spit at my feet. He said I didn't know what I was talking about, that it wasn't offensive at all, people were just curious, nothing sick or twisted. He asked if I was implying that his going to see the place was sick or twisted. "'Cause if that's what you're implying, you are dead wrong."

"No," I said, "that's not what I'm implying. I'm not implying anything at all."

I didn't stick around to listen to the story of his adventure. There were too many stories filling my head as it was. At any moment Andy would burst into a monologue of detail, one he'd been rehearsing since seeing the place where they'd hidden Jamie, so I turned to go to my room and—bam—walked right into a wall. I put my hand over my aching face and couldn't stop blinking. Andy snorted and called me a freak. He pushed my shoulder and told me to watch where I'm going, or else one day I'd kill myself. I kept leaving, and Andy said, "Hey! Where are you going? I didn't get to tell you what it was like."

Our town was big on ghost stories, and within weeks people started seeing Jamie Marks. He waited at the railroad crossing on Sodom-Hutchins road, pointing farther down the tracks, toward where he'd been hidden. He walked in tight circles outside of Gracie Highsmith's house with his hands clasped behind his back and his head hanging low and serious. In these stories he was always a transparent figure. Things passed through him. Rain was one example; another was leaves falling off the trees, drifting through his body. Kids in school said, "I saw him!" the same eager way they did when they went out to Hatchet Man Road to see the ghost of that killer from the '70s, who actually never used hatchets, but a hunting knife.

Gracie Highsmith hadn't returned to school yet, and everyone said she'd gone psycho, so no one could verify the story of Jamie's ghost standing outside her house. The stories grew anyway, without her approval, which just seemed wrong. I thought if Jamie's ghost was walking outside Gracie's house, then no one should tell that story but Gracie. It was hers, and anyone else who told it was a thief.

One day I finally went to the cemetery to visit him. I'd wanted to go to the funeral, just to stand in the back where no one would notice, but the newspaper said it was family only. If I *was* angry about anything at all, it was this. I mean, how could they just shut everyone out? The whole town had helped in the search parties, had taken over food to Jamie's family during the time when he was missing. And then no one but family was allowed to be at the funeral? It just felt a little selfish.

I hardly ever went to the cemetery. Only once or twice before, and that was when my grandma died, and my dad and Andy and I had to be pallbearers. We went once after my mom came home in her wheelchair. She said she needed to talk to my grandma, so we drove her there on a surprisingly warm autumn day, when the leaves were still swinging on their branches. She sat in front of the headstone, and we backed off to give her some private time. She cried and sniffed, you could hear that. The sunlight reflected on the chrome of her wheelchair. When she was done, we loaded her back into the van, and she said, "All right, who wants to rent some videos?"

Now the cemetery looked desolate, as if ready to be filmed for some Halloween movie. Headstones leaned toward one another. Moss grew green over the walls of family mausoleums. I walked along the driveway, gravel crunching beneath my shoes, and looked from side to side at the stone angels and pillars and plain flat slabs decorating the dead, marking out their spaces. I knew a lot of names, or had heard of them, whether they'd been relatives or friends, or friends of relatives, or ancestral family enemies. When you live in a town where you can fit everyone into four churches—two Catholic, two Methodist—you know everyone. Even the dead.

I searched the headstones until I found where Jamie Marks was buried. His grave was still freshly turned earth. No grass had had time to grow there. But people had left little trinkets, tokens or reminders, on the grave, pieces of themselves. A hand print. A piece of rose-colored glass. Two cigarettes standing up like fence posts. A baby rattle. Someone had scrawled a name across the bottom edge of the grave: Gracie Highsmith. A moment later I heard footsteps, and there she was in the flesh, coming toward me.

I was perturbed, but not angry. Besides his family, I thought I'd be the only one to come visit. But here she was, this girl, who'd drawn her name in the dirt with her finger. Her letters looked soft; they curled into each other gently, with little flourishes for decoration. Did she think it mattered if she spelled her name pretty?

I planted my hands on my hips as she approached and said, "Hey, what are you doing here?"

Gracie blinked as if she'd never seen me before in her life. I could tell she wanted to say, "Excuse me? Who are you?" But what she did say was, "Visiting. I'm visiting. What are *you* doing here?"

The wind picked up and blew hair across her face. She tucked it back behind her ears real neatly. I dropped my hands from my hips and nudged the ground with my shoe, not knowing how to answer. Gracie turned back to Jamie's tombstone.

"Visiting," I said finally, crossing my arms over my chest, annoyed I couldn't come up with anything but the same answer she'd given.

Gracie nodded without looking at me. She kept her eyes trained on Jamie's grave, and I started to think maybe she was going to steal it. The headstone, that is. I mean, the girl collected rocks. A headstone would complete any collection. I wondered if I should call the police, tell them, Get yourselves to the cemetery, you've got a burglary in progress. I imagined them taking Gracie out in handcuffs, making her duck her head as they tucked her into the back seat of the patrol car. I pinched myself to stop day-dreaming, and when I woke back up, I found Gracie sobbing over the grave.

I didn't know how long she'd been crying, but she was going full force. I mean, this girl didn't care if anyone was around to hear her. She bawled and screamed. I didn't know what to do, but I thought maybe I should say something to calm her. I finally shouted, "Hey! Don't do that!"

But Gracie kept crying. She beat her fist in the dirt near her name.

"Hey!" I repeated. "Didn't you hear me? I said, Don't do that!"

But she still didn't listen.

So I started to dance. It was the first idea that came to me.

I kicked my heels in the air and did a two-step. I hummed a tune to keep time. I clasped my hands together behind my back and did a jig, or an imitation of one, and when still none of my clowning distracted her, I started to sing the Hokey Pokey.

I belted it out and kept on dancing. I sung each line like it was poetry. "You put your left foot in/You take your left foot out/You put your left foot in/And you shake it all about/You do the Hokey Pokey and you turn yourself around/That's what it's all about! Yeehaw!"

As I sang and danced, I moved toward a freshly dug grave just a few plots down from Jamie's. The headstone was already up, but there hadn't been a funeral yet. The grave was waiting for Lola Peterson to fill it, but instead, as I shouted out the next verse, I stumbled into it.

I fell in the grave singing, "You put your whole self in——" and about choked on my own tongue when I landed. Even though it was still light out, it was dark in the grave, and muddy. My shoes sunk, and when I tried to pull them out, they made sucking noises. The air smelled stiff and leafy. I started to worry that I'd be stuck in Lola Peterson's grave all night, because the walls around me were muddy too; I couldn't get my footing. Finally, though, Gracie's head appeared over the lip of the grave.

"Are you okay?" she asked.

Her hair fell down toward me like coils of rope.

Gracie helped me out by getting a ladder from the cemetery tool shed. She told me I was a fool, but she laughed when she said it. Her eyes were red from crying, and her cheeks looked wind-chapped. I thanked her for helping me out.

I got her talking after that. She talked a little about Jamie and how she found him, but she didn't say too much. Really, she only seemed to want to talk about rocks. "So you really do collect rocks?" I asked, and Gracie bobbed her head.

"You should see them," she told me. "Why don't you come over to my place tomorrow? My parents will be at marriage counseling. Come around five."

"Sure," I said. "That'd be great."

Gracie dipped her head and looked up at me through brown bangs. She turned to go, then stopped a moment later and waved. I waved back.

I waited for her to leave before me. I waited until I heard the squeal and clang of the wrought-iron front gates. Then I knelt down beside Jamie's grave and wiped Gracie's name out of the dirt. I wrote my name in place of it, etching into the dirt deeply.

My letters were straight and fierce.

I went home to find I'd missed dinner. My father was already in the living room, watching TV, the Weather Channel. He could watch the weather report for hours listening to the muzak play over and over. He watched it every night for a couple of hours before Andy and I would start groaning for a channel switch. He'd change the channel but never acknowledge us. Usually he never had much to say anyway.

When I got home, though, he wanted to talk. It took him only a few minutes after I sat down with a plate of meatloaf before he changed the channel, and I about choked. There was a news brief on about the search for Jamie's murderers. I wondered why the anchorman called them "Jamie's murderers", the same way you might say, "Jamie's dogs" or "Jamie's Boy Scout honors." My dad stretched out on his reclining chair and started muttering about what he'd do with the killers if it had been his boy. His face was red and splotchy.

I stopped eating, set my fork down on my plate.

"What would you do?" I asked. "What would you do if it had been me?"

My dad looked at me and said, "I'd tie a rope around those bastard's armpits and lower them inch by inch into a vat of piranhas, slowly, to let the little suckers have at their flesh."

He looked back at the TV.

"But what if the police got them first?" I said. "What would you do then?"

Dad looked at me again and said, "I'd smuggle a gun into the courtroom, and when they had those bastards up there on the stand, I'd jump out of my seat and shoot their God-damned heads off." He jumped out of his recliner and made his hands into a gun shape, pointing it at me. He pulled the fake trigger once, twice, a third time. Bam! Bam! Bam!

I nodded with approval. I felt really loved, like I was my dad's favorite. I ate up all this great attention and kept asking, "What if?" again and again, making up different situations. He was so cool, the best dad in the world. I wanted to buy him a hat: Best Dad in the World! printed on it. We were really close, I felt, for the first time in a long time.

Gracie Highsmith's house was nestled in a bend of the railroad tracks where she found Jamie. She'd been out walking the tracks looking for odd pieces of coal and nickel when she found him. All of this she told me in her bedroom, on the second floor of her house. She held out a fist-sized rock that was brown with black speckles embedded in it. The brown parts felt like sandpaper, but the black specks were smooth as glass. Gracie said she'd found it in the streambed at the bottom of Marrow's Ravine. I said, "It's something special all right," and she beamed like someone's mother.

"That's nothing," she said. "Wait till you see the rest."

She showed me a chunk of clear quartz and a piece of hardened blue clay; a broken-open geode filled with pyramids of pink crystal; a seashell that she found, mysteriously, in the woods behind her house, nowhere near water; and a flat rock with a skeletal fish fossil imprinted on it. I was excited to see them all. I hadn't realized how beautiful rocks could be. It made me want to collect rocks too, but it was already Gracie's territory. I'd have to find something of my own.

We sat on her bed and listened to music by some group from Cleveland that I'd never heard of but who Gracie loved because she set the CD player to replay the same song over and over. It sounded real punk. They sang about growing up angry and how they would take over the world and make people pay for being stupid idiots. Gracie nodded and gritted her teeth as she listened.

I liked being alone in the house with her, listening to music and looking at rocks. I felt eccentric and mature. I told Gracie this, and she knew what I meant. "They all think we're children," she said. "They don't know a God-damned thing, do they?"

We talked about growing old for a while, imagining ourselves in college, then in mid-life careers, then we were so old we couldn't walk without a walker. Pretty soon we were so old we both clutched our chests like we were having heart attacks, fell back on the bed, and choked on our own laughter.

"What sort of funeral will you have?" she wondered.

"I don't know, what about you? Aren't they all the same?"

"Funerals are all different," she said. "For instance, Mexican cemeteries have all these bright, beautifully colored decorations for their dead; they're not all serious like ours." I asked her where she had learned that. She said, "Social Studies. Last year."

"Social Studies?" I asked. "Last year?" I repeated. "I don't remember reading about funerals or cemeteries last year in Social Studies." Last year I hadn't cared about funerals. I was fourteen and watched TV and played video games a lot. What else had I missed while lost in the fog of sitcoms and fantasy adventures?

I bet Mexicans never would have had a private funeral. Too bad Jamie wasn't Mexican.

"I see graves all the time now," Gracie told me. She lay flat on her back, head on her pillow, and stared at the ceiling. "They're everywhere," Gracie said. "Ever since—"

She stopped and sighed, as if it was some huge confession she'd just told me. I worried that she might expect something in return, a confession of my own. I murmured a little noise I hoped sounded supportive.

"They're everywhere," she repeated. "The town cemetery, the Wilkinson family plot, that old place out by the ravine, where Fuck-You Francis is supposed to be buried. And now the railroad tracks. I mean, where does it end?"

I said, "Beds are like graves, too," and she turned to me with this puzzled look. "No," I said, "really." And I told her about the time when my grandmother came to live with us, after my grandfather's death. And how, one morning, my mother sent me into her room to wake her for breakfast—I remember, because I smelled bacon frying when I woke up—and so I went into my grandma's room and told her to wake up. She didn't, so I repeated myself. But she still didn't wake up. Finally I shook her shoulders, and her head lolled on her neck. I grabbed one of her hands, and it was cold to touch.

"Oh," said Gracie. "I see what you mean." She stared at me hard, her eyes glistening. Gracie rolled on top of me, pinning her knees on both sides of my hips. Her hair fell around my face, and the room grew dimmer as her hair brushed over my eyes, shutting out the light.

She kissed me on my lips, and she kissed me on my neck. She started rocking against my penis, so I rocked back. The coils in her bed creaked. "You're so cold,

Adam," Gracie whispered, over and over. "You're so cold, you're so cold." She smelled like clay and dust. As she rocked on me, she looked up at the ceiling and bared the hollow of her throat. After a while, she let out several little gasps, then collapsed on my chest. I kept rubbing against her, but stopped when I realized she wasn't going to get back into it.

Gracie slid off me. She knelt in front of her window, looking out at something.

"Are you angry?" I asked.

"No, Adam. I'm not angry. Why would I be angry?"

"Just asking," I said. "What are you doing now?" I said.

"He's down there again," she whispered. I heard the tears in her voice already and went to her. I didn't look out the window. I wrapped my arms around her, my hands meeting under her breasts, and hugged her. I didn't look out the window.

"Why won't he go away?" she said. "I found him, yeah. So fucking what. He doesn't need to fucking follow me around forever."

"Tell him to leave," I told her.

She didn't respond.

"Tell him you don't want to see him anymore," I told her.

She moved my hands off her and turned her face to mine. She leaned in and kissed me, her tongue searching out mine. When she pulled back, she said, "I can't. I hate him, but I love him, too. He seems to, I don't know, understand me, maybe. We're on the same wavelength, you know? As much as he annoys me, I love him. He should have been loved, you know? He never got that. Not how everyone deserves."

"Just give him up," I said.

Gracie wrinkled her nose. She stood and paced to her doorway, opened it, said, "I think you should go now. My parents will be home soon."

I craned my neck to glance out the window, but her voice cracked like a whip.

"Leave, Adam."

I shrugged into my coat and elbowed past her.

"You don't deserve him," I said on my way out.

I walked home through wind, and soon rain started up. It landed on my face cold and trickled down my cheeks into my collar. Jamie hadn't been outside when I left Gracie's house, and I began to suspect she'd been making him up, like the rest of them, to make me jealous. Bitch, I thought. I thought she was different.

At home I walked in through the kitchen, and my mother was waiting by the doorway. She said, "Where have you been? Two nights in a row. You're acting all secretive. Where have you been, Adam?"

Lucy sat at the dinner table, smoking a cigarette. When I looked at her, she looked away. Smoke curled up into the lamp above her.

"What is this?" I said. "An inquisition?"

"We're just worried, is all," said my mother.

"Don't worry."

"I can't help it."

"Your mother loves you very much," said Lucy.

"Stay out of this, paralyzer."

Both of them gasped.

"Adam!" My mother sounded shocked. "That's not nice. You know Lucy didn't mean that to happen. Apologize right now."

I mumbled an apology.

My mother started wheeling around the kitchen. She reached up to cupboards and pulled out cans of tomatoes and kidney beans. She opened the freezer and pulled out ground beef. "Chili," she said, just that. "It's chilly outside, so you need some warm chili for your stomach. Chili will warm you up." She sounded like a commercial.

Then she started in again. "My miracle child," she said, pretending to talk to herself. "My baby boy, my gift. Did you know, Lucy, that Adam was born premature, with underdeveloped lungs and a murmur in his heart?"

"No, dear," said Lucy. "How terrible!"

"He was a fighter, though," said my mother. "He always fought. He wanted to live so much. Oh, Adam," she said. "Why don't you tell me where you've been? Your running coach said you've been missing practice a lot."

"I haven't been anywhere," I said. "Give it a rest."

"It's everything happening at once, isn't it?" Lucy asked. "Poor kid. You should send him to see Dr. Phelps, Linda. Stuff like what happened to the Marks boy is hard on kids."

"That's an idea," said my mother.

"Would you stop talking about me in front of me?" I said. "God, you two are ridiculous. You don't have a God-damned clue about anything."

My father came into the kitchen and said, "What's all the racket?"

I said, "Why don't you just go kill someone!" and ran outside again.

At first I didn't know where I was going, but by the time I reached the edge of the woods, I figured it out. The rain still fell steadily, and the wind crooned through the branches of trees. Leaves shook and fell around me. It was dusk, and I pushed my way through the brambles and roots back to the old railroad tracks.

His breath was on my neck before I even reached the spot, though. I knew he was behind me before he even said anything. I felt his breath on my neck, and then he placed his arms around my stomach, just like I had with Gracie. "Keep going," he said. And I did. He held onto me, and I carried him on my back all the way to the place where Gracie found him.

That section of the railroad had been marked out in yellow police tape. But something was wrong. Something didn't match up with what I expected. The railroad ties—they hadn't been pulled up. And the hole where Jamie had been buried—it was there all right, but *next* to the railroad tracks. He'd never been under those railroad tracks, I realized. Something dropped in my stomach. A pang of disappointment.

Stories change. They change too easily and too often.

"What are you waiting for?" Jamie asked, sliding off my back. I stood at the edge of the hole and he said, "Go on. Try it on."

I turned around, and there he was, naked, with mud smudged on his pale white skin. His hair was all messed up, and one lens of his glasses was shattered. He smiled. His teeth were filled with grit.

I stepped backward into the hole. It wasn't very deep, not like Lola Peterson's grave in the cemetery. Just a few feet down. I stood at eye level with Jamie's crotch. He reached down and touched himself.

"Take off your clothes," he told me.

I took them off.

"Lay down," he told me.

I lay down.

He climbed in on top of me, and he was so cold, so cold. He said there was room for two of us in here and that I should call him Moony.

I said, "I never liked that name."

He said, "Neither did I."

"Then I won't call you that."

"Thank you," he said, and hugged me. I let him. He said she never let him hug her. She didn't understand him. I told him I knew. She was being selfish.

I said, "Don't worry. I've found you now. You don't have to worry. I understand. I found you."

"I found *you*," he said. "Remember?"

"Let's not argue," I said.

He rested his cheek against my chest, and the rain washed over us. After a while I heard voices, far away but growing closer. I stood up and saw the swathes of light from their flashlights getting bigger. My dad and Andy and Lucy. All of them moved toward me. I imagined my mother wheeling in worried circles back in the kitchen.

"Adam!" my father shouted through the rain.

I didn't move. Not even when they came right up to me, their faces white and pale as Jamie's dead body. Andy said, "I told you he'd be here. The little freak."

Lucy said, "My Lord, your poor mother," and her hand flew to her mouth.

My father said, "Adam, come out of there. Come out of that place right now."

He held his hand out to me, curling his fingers for me to take it.

"Come on, boy," he said. "Get on out of there now." He flexed his fingers for emphasis.

I grabbed hold of his hand, and he hauled me out onto the gravel around the hole, and I lay there, naked, like a newborn. They stood around me, staring. My father took off his coat and put it on me. He told me to come on, to just come on back to the house. He put his arm around me, and we started walking down the tracks.

I decided right then I wasn't a freak, not really. I took his hand, sure, but not because of anything remotely like defeat. I hadn't "come to my senses." I hadn't "realized I needed help." I took it to make them feel better about themselves and to get them off my back.

What I was thinking as they walked me home was: You silly people, I'm already finished. I'm already dead and gone. All you have is some mess of a zombie shambling through your kitchens and your living rooms, turning on your showers and kissing you goodnight. All you have is a dead boy, only it's hard to tell, because I won't rot. I'll be like one of those bodies that people in South America pry out of old coffins, the ones whose hair and fingernails continue to grow in death. The ones who smell of rose petals, whose skin remains smooth and lily white. They call those corpses saints, but I won't aspire to anything so heavenly. I'll wash the dishes and do my homework and wheel my mother around in her chair. I'll do all of these things, and no one will notice there's no light behind my eyes and no heat in my step. They'll clothe me and feed me and tell me what good grades I get. They'll give me things to make me happy, when all I'll be wanting is a cold grave to step into. I'll grow up and go to college, marry a beautiful woman and have three kids. I'll make a lot of money and age gracefully, no pot belly. I'll look youthful when I'm fifty-eight.

What I knew right then was that everyone I'd ever know from here on out would talk about me and say, He's so lucky. He has everything a person could want.

Insect Dreams

Rosalind Palermo Stevenson

I

. . . and then the sounds begin to reach her, the violent beating of wings, a breeze rising up, a bird gliding on wing . . . a vision of mouths, footsteps on the gravel on the walkway, the kicking up of stones, the shifting weight from left to right, vibrating deep into the earth, and moving past . . . a vision of something sweet, of something sugary, or of a soft secretion, she is folded in upon herself, like a leaf which has fallen and curled . . . a vision of the garden's weedy waters, of its ghostly portico, its statues, the Dutch moat, a sunflower, roses and other flowers . . . a vision, a vision, the cry of a bird again, on wing nearer now, furious spasms in her abdomen, the bird on wing higher, higher, then out of view . . . a vision of longing, a burning up, a flap of skin to which she must affix herself, to which she must hold fast, hold fast, there is a high wind coming, there is the danger she will be blown away . . .

Sometime in the night a sound wakes her: a thud as of a heavy object falling, and then someone moaning. Maria Sibylla Merian sits up, but can hear nothing more. The night is long, too long, and the air is stultifying. Down in the hold of the ship the insect moth, *Phalaena tau*, is dreaming, day or night, it makes no difference, though now it is night. The moth is in chrysalis with the other specimens that Maria Sibylla has brought with her on the journey.

Awake she finds she cannot breathe, her cabin is airless, and the odor is foul even here at the stern so close to the captain's quarters. She comes up to the deck to breathe the air, in the dead of night, alone, a forbidden female figure, solitary, silent, and all the while the ocean reticent, the waves just barely lapping.

Imagine. Imagined. The fragmentary themes that drive her night. The ocean. The Atlantic. The crossing to Surinam. It is an allegorical crossing like the crossings of

Moors. The dark faces of the men. The ship, *The Peace,* just barely rocking.

She recalls the ritual dances of certain insects. The way the female becomes bloated and huge. And gives off an odor that is strong and pungent, but at the same time sweet, and the males pick up the scent and approach, half-flying, half-crawling to the female.

Now she stands on the deck of the ship. Induced by her God. Under the ceiling of Heaven. Beneath the planets and the stars. The constellations—Lepus, Monoceros, Eridanus. Love of knowledge. Travel and changes. Danger of accidents (especially at sea). And a danger of drowning.

Heavenly God, it is Your will that guides me. It is Your will that guides the entire universe, that binds all forms together. Heavenly God, take me into that self-same will and guide me to Your perfection.

Does she know Plato's Sea of Tartarus? Where all the waters pierce the earth to the Sea of Tartarus? The sailors believe that if they come too close to the equator they will turn black like the natives who live there. Or that if they sail too far to the north their blood will congeal and turn to ice in their veins. But tonight there is nothing but the black of black waters, the sea of darkness, the stars in the heavens.

Pale woman. Defined by your sex. By your birth. By your birth right. When did the door first open? It was her father's influence, no doubt, the artist Matthäus Merian the Elder. She was a child when he died and her memory of him is imperfect. Papa. Papa Matthäus. The safe, the clean, the eminently sane smell of him.

She holds the cast of the head of Laocoön.
Observe the way she holds the giant head.
Sirs, I will hold this head, the head of poor Laocoön, who warned against the Trojan horse.
She is exceptional, her father tells the men.
Stand over here, Maria Sibylla, over here, stand and hold the head.
It is a plaster cast and heavy for a small child; it weighs at least seven or eight pounds, but she holds it.
She holds it as though it is not heavy, as though it does not weigh seven or eight pounds.

and the canals below the windows

the dead level of the waters
the canals that one can see in all directions

It is the light reflecting on her cup of liquid. A small plate next to it with crumbs. It is one of the mornings in the Netherlands before she makes her ocean crossing. A child brings her insects from the Kerkstraat Gardens. It is a ritual they perform: the child arrives at the door and calls out to the woman, "Mistress."

Ja, what have you brought?
I brought a moth pupa.
Did you pluck it yourself?
Yes, Mistress.
Where did you find it?
I found it in the Kerkstraat Gardens.
Here, come, let me see.
The child, a girl, holds out the inert brown shell of the pupa.
Ja, I see, rolling it delicately over on the palm of her hand.
The child's eye is becoming sharp, a love for precision is developing, a satisfaction in identification of the insects. She is just one of the children who lives around the Kerkstraat Gardens, but Maria Sibylla has taken an interest in her.

Maria. Maria Sibylla.

Sibylla is the woman's middle name, the name passed down to her from her mother.

And the Sibyl closed her eyes and saw events unfold before them, in the darkness a horse falling, its rider going down in battle, and then many horses falling, and many riders going down in battle, and rains, and plagues to cleanse the earth.

Make way, make way.

In Amsterdam it was all excitement and exotica. That was how the fire took hold inside her; it was from what she saw in Amsterdam, brought back by the science travelers. But they were hobbyists compared to her, compared to her deadly seriousness. The fire took hold from what she saw in Amsterdam in the interiors of the museum rooms. The creatures floating as in dreams. The creatures in their cases floating.

There are creatures that no one has seen. Creatures that have not been classified, counted, entered in the journals and the record books of science, whose shapes defy the patterns of logical construction, whose colors are as if from other worlds, self-regenerating, pure, infinite variety and complexity, sketched by God, painted by angels, life miraculously breathed into them, life, alive, free, that no one has seen, that she, she must see.

The air is cold on her face, cold through to her bones.

The night is bearing down on her and she thinks that it will crush her. The way the night bears down on her.

The night bears down and makes her think of dying oceans, of vast bodies of water slowly releasing and losing breath, and of all the life contained down in the oceans' depths, down in those fathomless deeps, and of all the life carrying on with the business of living, and with the business of feeding and mating and dying.

The air is cold on her face. Cold through to her bones. She is out from her cabin. Out on the deck. Wrapped in her folds of black twill.

The ship has slowed down almost to a standstill. There is no wind, light or moderate, no fresh and strong wind, no scant wind, no aft, no large, no quartering wind.

She is steady on the deck, steady on her feet, she has her sea legs, she can walk on them, she keeps her back straight.

The sailors will not look at her. They believe it will bring bad luck to look at her. They believe she is a witch—*die Hexe, bezaubernde Frau.*

She is a woman traveling alone under the protection of the captain, in her sight-line the insects of Surinam.

There will be land soon. She can smell it. It is a sweet smell in the air, mingled with the smell of salt. Anticipation of arrival. The first rays of the sun. Thin and tentative. The slow lifting of the darkness.

Surinam. Soor i nam. State of the kingdom of the Netherlands on the northeast coast of South America. 55,144 square miles. Capital, Paramaribo.

Paramaribo. Delicious word. Sweet as the sugar cane that grows there, sweet and savage.

Birds tear towards the sun. Their wings on fire like the wings of the Holy Spirit.

Tongues aflame for all the earth to see.

She wakes gasping for air, her body bathed in perspiration; her hair is pasted to her head by the perspiration. She pulls the bedsheets off her body, lifts into the mesh netting that envelops her bed, it is the mosquito netting, she lifts her face into it and it feels like a spider's web. She thrusts her hands out in front of her, remembers where she is, what this is, reaches into the blackness to find the seam and lifts away the netting. She locates the candle on her bedside table and lights it. Is guided by its sallow light to the window where she stands looking out, again the night, the moon a harsh orange sliver in the sky.

She is in the bedroom in her suite of rooms at Surimombo—Surimombo is the plantation-lodging house owned by the spinster, Esther Gabay. At the time of her stay, there are these three others: Francina Ivenes, the widow, a permanent lodger at Surimombo since the death of her husband some years ago; the physician, Doctor Peter Kolb, who has his practice in the township; and Mathew van der Lee, the young settler, who has come to profit in the sugar trade.

Surimombo. It is a chorus from the slaves. *The race to the end.* Surimombo. Surimombo. Monsoon rain, water washing down the Parima, the fabled river that ran through Paradise. It is the place that was Eden when God expelled Adam. And Eve had no choice but to follow. And now the Parima with its current, the way Maria Sibylla looks in the canoe, she looks large in the canoe, with her back straight, a giantess carrying her insects.

And from the river a disturbance, from deep down under the greenblue bowl of agitation and foment,

Surinam is all rivers: the Nickerie; the Saramacca; the Coppename and the Suriname; the Commewijne and the Marowijne; the Para; the Cottica; the Maroni; the Tapanahoni,

and all around the rolling fields of sugar cane, the way the stalk breaks so that the sweet pulpy insides come dripping out, inviting you to bite, to suck,

it is impossible not to bite, to suck, the rich sweetness.

The sun throws glints of light that catch from time to time the defensive pose of a pupa; still, still, breathless, nothing that moves, nothing that will give rise to movement. It looks like the dropping of a macaw, or like a piece of wood, a bit of broken twig, the pupa waiting to unfold.

It is at the end of the dry season and many times throughout the day, she must wait before she can move on. She must take shelter and wait for the rain to stop.

The jungle forest is open to her, and she keeps step with its pace, with its drifting and continuous movement.

What looks like a centipede, or a snake curled on a branch, is nothing more than the branch itself, its curve, a thickness in the growth of its bark, a guest shrub growing in an enclave of its formation. Meanwhile the creature that she seeks is there, no more than an arm's length in front of her, its eyes focused in her direction.

She is with Marta, her Amerindian slave, who is hardly a slave at all, though one of a dozen slaves included in her lodging fees at Surimombo. Marta knows the names of the trees, the leaves and branches, the larvae feeding on them, the moths they will transform into. She knows the frogs, the spiders, the snakes, the birds, hummingbirds drinking the nectar of flowers, the buds, the fruits, macaws screaming in the trees, winged and magnificent, their colors streaming like the colors in flags, the flags of the homelands, the welcoming flags of homecomings.

Back in Amsterdam she has a friend, a woman who has grown a giant pineapple. From all around people have come to see it, and Mr. Caspar Commelin has written an article about it for inclusion in his science journal. Maria Sibylla writes to Caspar Commelin, and to the other Amsterdam naturalists, the men who are part of the scientific exchange.

Sirs, I have had the satisfaction this day, the 21st of January, 1700, to witness the transformation of a caterpillar, gold and black striped, which I found soon after my arrival here; to witness it become these months later, a butterfly.

She works in watercolors on vellum.

Her vellum is the finest there is, made from the skin of lambs, the lambs unborn, taken early, violently.

Suppers at Surimombo are served each evening at six o'clock. Esther Gabay takes her place at the head of the table. On the side to Esther Gabay's right are seated Doctor Peter Kolb and Mathew van der Lee. Maria Sibylla is seated opposite them, next to the Widow Ivenes. The food is always plentiful and rich: large bowls of mutton and fricassees, platters of Guinea fowl and vegetables, mullets and snapper, fruits and tarts, alligator pears, guava and shaddock. Nut meats and oranges are brought to the table last, along with pastries dripping with sugar. The meal is served from left to right. The conversation is animated and jovial.

"How exotic your insects are," says the Widow Ivenes to Maria Sibylla. "Do they ever crawl upon your hand or your wrist? What does it feel like when that happens, the sensation of your insects crawling on your flesh?"

Sirs, the quickening. Life appearing in the egg and nourished there. And then ferocious biting through. The pede, the stage at which I plucked it, plucking too the leaves on which it fed until its transformation into pupa. Profoundest rest. A rest that angels yearn for—and for that time asleep and dreaming. Then beckoned by the dream it starts to stir, the slightest stirring, and then a parting of the cotton that protects the shell, and a splitting and a chipping of the shell itself, until the transformation is complete from pede to winged creature; emerging, blasting, to fly dazed and free and glorious.

Out of a sky filled with sun, out of air that is still and filled with the scent of flamboyant and sugar cane, storms rise up without warning and blacken the Surinam sky. A breeze begins to blow in the darkened light, a moist breeze that takes hold and the sweet smells are carried stronger, and the moisture in the air bathes the face; but then the breeze gathers strength and becomes a wind, and the wind a raging gale, and the gale gains hurricane force. There are signs if one takes notice. Everything becomes quiet. There is a cessation of the sounds of the birds and the insects.

Maria Sibylla is out behind the Surimombo plantation house when her first storm forms in the stillness. She is studying a species of potter wasp which has built its nest upon the ground. She is intent upon recording her observations, and writing the notes that will accompany her drawings, so that she does not take notice of the darkening light. It is Mathew van der Lee who comes running to fetch her—frantic his running—shouting something she cannot hear, stopping just short of knocking into her, he grabs her sketching papers and her charcoals, and, though now quite on top of her, he continues his shouting. They are not back inside the house five minutes when the walls begin to rattle, and the whistling of the wind becomes deep and throaty like a lion's roar, and she huddles low with Esther Gabay, and with the Widow Ivenes and Doctor Peter Kolb, and with Mathew van der Lee, she huddles low.

The storm subsides and the sounds start up again, the rasp of insects, the calls of birds, the screeching of monkeys.

Mathew van der Lee inquires if he might accompany Maria Sibylla on a collecting expedition she has planned to the shoreline in the aftermath of the storm. It is his speciality, he tells her, the seashore; he had been a collector himself back in the Netherlands.

She packs her vellums and her charcoal, her nets and her collecting jars.

She walks erect and keeps her back straight, her shoes are caked with mud, the bottom of her skirt is wet and dragging.

It is light. The sun completely broken through. The hills behind the shore heavy with what the winds have brought, invisible but present, the air laden with it.

"Madame Sibylla," says Mathew van der Lee. He wears a hat in the style of the day, black felt and rimmed. He wears a jacket also in the style of the day, three-quarters in length and black like the hat, and his shirt is white beneath the jacket. They are on the edge of the shoreline along the Paramaribo coast. Maria Sibylla is walking ahead of him. "Madame Sibylla," he says again. "You shall outdistance me if you walk so quickly, Madame Sibylla." He is teasing and young, pleasing and handsome in his white shirt, in his hat, in his jacket.

Sirs, we sing the creature's praises! The pede perceives the visual impressions around it, not by means of rows of eyes located down along the sides of its body, but through distinctly tiny simple eyes, ocelli, placed on each side of the head.

For a minute she is breathless. Her breathlessness exaggerated in the intensity of the heat. It is so hot she almost cannot bear it.

The Widow Ivenes beckons her to visit in her suite of rooms. The Widow is sitting with a metal plate against her forehead, alternately placing it against the back of her neck. The drapes are drawn. There is a bowl of water on the table by her bed. "I would like to tear these clothes from my body," the Widow says point-blank to Maria Sibylla.

Maria Sibylla has come into the Widow's room with a fan with which she is fanning herself unrestrainedly. It was hand-painted in Italy, but she purchased it in Amsterdam. She offers it as a present to the Widow Ivenes. The Widow takes the fan and heaves and sighs, and heaves and sighs again.

Only Esther Gabay seems to never mind the heat. She carries on in it with the running of Surimombo. Even during the hottest hours, she carries on in it, just as the slaves carry on in it with their work in the sugar fields.

The African slaves go about naked. Or mostly naked. The women naked from waist to neck. The young ones with their breasts taut, their skin the deepest browns, their nipples black, like black cherries on the trees back in Holland. The older women stand with their breasts below their waists in the late day sun. There is a dance the African slaves perform and Maria Sibylla has witnessed it—the Winti, or Dance of Possession—their hips roll as they pass the calabash, drink from the bowl, smoke the tobacco, and then *here Miss, here Miss,* holding out the worm for her to take, *here Miss, here Miss* . . .

That evening there is smoked salmon arrived by ship from Amsterdam. With the salmon is turtle and king fish, grouper and snapper. A beverage is served made of coconut and lime. Hands are washed between courses. The evening meal is like a prayer. Like a service in the church in Paramaribo.

late at night she hears the doctor snoring, she hears him through the walls of the suites of the house, his breath coming in snorts and gasps.

and in the eaves around the house—spiders.

and in her room the smell of the salve she uses to protect her skin. It is something Marta gave her made from the sap of palm leaves. And blood oranges in a bowl. And grapes in another bowl. Her hair is wrapped in cloth. The cloth is cut in strips and woven through her hair. Blood oranges in a bowl next to the grapes.

and what she feels is the heat. The relentless bruising heat.

Sirs, it has been thought the thickened lines of wing venation are veins like those that comprise the net-work of our own fragile bodies, and through which the moth's blood (made up of a dense white liquid) flows outward each to body parts dependent on receiving it. This proves not the case. The wing venation are solidly composed and act as brace cords for support.

She is in the small forest behind the Surimombo sugar fields. They call it Surimombo Forest because its edges border the plantation. The light is green and indistinct. Her eyes must make an adjustment. The light filters down through the branches of the trees and through the flowers that grow along the tree trunks. A flatworm glides on a moist trail of sludge on the leaf of a giant acacia. The worm is red and iridescent. When she tries to lift it, it dissolves.

God stirs. In any case impels. Nettles. On which the creature feeds. The Mora branch. And its leaves. The Yucca with its red fruit.

Mathew van der Lee has followed her into the small forest where she is working along its edges. It was by chance, he says, that he caught sight of her, from the sugar fields where he had been observing the harvesting technique at Surimombo. He could not resist, he says, but to see after her, to inquire of her while at her work. I have seen many such plants in the botanical gardens in Amsterdam, he says, pointing to the crimson blossoms of the bougainvillaea, but none in the gardens compare to these.

It is said that there were no lovers, only a husband who wound up by menacing—the rumors of his vices—and the whispers of the word cruelty—a husband whom she fled in retaliation and defense. A daring act then, at that time, imagine.

But history shall have it there was a lover.

Maria Sibylla is not a child. No. She is a woman already of some years. Though she was little more than a child on the day of her marriage to Johann Graff. But she fled that husband.

On the 21st day of November in the year 1685, Maria Sibylla gathered what was hers and set out for the Protestant Pietist colony at Freisland, and for the colony's home at the Castle of Weirweurd, and for the prefect, Petre Yvon, who then presided there. She set out to join those pious men and women who lived each moment in the love of God and in the denial of the worldly influence. She took her vellums, her charcoals, her specimens, some articles of clothing, some personal effects.

On the morning of the 23rd of November, her husband appeared outside the door of the Castle, where he bellowed out the name of his wife, and where within those walls Maria Sibylla remained silent.

She was staring out her window when he arrived, thinking of the creatures she might find there, wondering how she might conduct her work from this new home, she was seeing God in all she saw, and trusting in God to direct her.

Graff sought audience with his wife through the personage of Petre Yvon. He demanded that he be admitted inside the walls of the castle. She is mine, he shouted, mine, I will not let go what is rightfully mine.

Only silence for reply.

And though he went down in a rage on his knees and pounded on the rock-strewn ground for three days, eating nothing, and not even drinking water, and though the ground was cold in the strong November chill, and though he made supplication and implored, and beseeched and importuned, and alternately begged and bellowed, she would not yield.

Tropical sweetness now. Sweeter than the sugar cane. Sweeter than the syrup dripping from the stalks cut and bound for refining. Blinding sun. Blazing heat. Leaves of plants so delicate they wither in the sun.

Sirs, the female is fussy in her decision as to where to lay her eggs; she grades each leaf for suitability, rejecting one leaf after another before choosing.

Insects swarm, approaching hungry and curious, the jungle forest stretches before her, sounds, the occasional glimpses of birds. She is on her way to Rama, farther down along the Saramacca. The African slaves walk ahead of her, unsheathing knives flashing, cutting a path through the dense growth of the forest, hacking down the weeds and the sawgrass so she can pass through. She has with her bottles half-filled with brandy to preserve dead some of what she finds, but also the mesh cages lined with bolting cloth to take other specimens alive, and to retain for them the natural conditions of their environment, to study their transformations without interrupting them, to observe for herself all the stages of their development. Her head is covered with a wide-brimmed hat. A few beads of perspiration run down from beneath the hat. She wears a shirt under the makeshift overall that she has sewn for her work in the jungle. The Surimombo slaves call her medicine woman. The women bring her chrysalids that they promise will open into moths, and butterflies more beautiful than any she has ever seen, creatures which will whisper certain truths to her, endow her with certain powers. But everything now has begun to draw her attention. It is no longer simply the larvae, the moths and the butterflies. Now she wants to know frogs, toads, snakes, and spiders, hummingbirds, the parrots and red monkeys screeching in the trees, the habits of the grasses that grow here, the invisible creatures that inhabit the air.

Sirs, for each there is the head, the thorax, the abdomen; the surface of the body divided into plate-like areas; there are the mouth parts, the antennae, the feet; and the special hairs that are sensitive to sound.

"Your hands are so delicate, Dear," the Widow Ivenes tells Maria Sibylla that night at supper, "one would never guess from looking at them you are a scientist."

Pastries and puddings are brought to the table, jellies and preserved fruits, fruit tarts sitting in transparent syrups, cakes made from nut meats, sweet oranges, yellow pineapples, alligator pears, guava, shaddock.

After supper Matthew van der Lee asks permission to enter Maria Sibylla's study. It is in a ground floor room at the rear—attached to but distant from the other rooms of Surimombo. "Mr. van der Lee. Here, come." Before he is able to say a word, he is directed to a brownish shape in a mesh cage that looks at first as though it might be a curled bit of bark. But then there is the slightest movement. A kind of weaving from side to side, a tear in the wall at one end, a small but violent movement, the tear opening a little larger, and then a little larger still, until a shape is visible inside, pushing forward through the tear, a damp and matted little thing pushing its way through the opening until it has pushed itself fully out, and then sits and rests there for a time. "There, you see," is all she says.

Sirs, there is a heart, as well, I have found it lodged in the frontal vessel suspended from the wall of the abdomen. The tiny heart can almost not be seen. But it is, I assure you, there, and it does beat, good sirs, as does our own.

She is near Para Creek. Marta is with her. They are searching inside the edges of the forest wall, looking for unknown genera of blossoms and strange chrysalises, looking and describing and collecting.

Marta walks ahead, hacking with a machete at the dense overgrowth, the frequent surfacing of sawgrass. She points to a branch on a tree. Maria Sybilla approaches, rapid and silent, ah, yes, ja, ja. There is a red caterpillar with yellow stripes crawling along the top of the branch. It is feeding on the leaves that grow there. The movement of Maria Sibylla's hand is sure and quick, scooping the caterpillar from the branch and placing it firmly and unharmed in a jar with a bit of the bark and some leaves from the tree. The caterpillar will be brought back to her study to be kept with the others, the numbers of her specimens growing, in jars with mesh tops, in wire cages, in bottles stoppered with cork.

They turn a corner of the forest into a lush growth of rafflesia, the plant is called the corpse plant because it smells like rotting flesh, the flower is enormous, glowing bright orange, the diameter measured in feet, the thick tubular stem. The Indians extract a liquid from the stem that is used to stop the flow of blood. Marta tells her that it is also used to counteract the bites of snakes, that it quickly reverses the effect of the poison in the bloodstream though the flesh has already grown dark. Marta tells her that the seeds of the peacock flower are used to bring about the menses, that the female slaves swallow the seeds to abort their fetuses, to preserve the unborn child from a life of slavery like their own.

Branches bend and scrape in the breeze, airy and delicate, twisting and turning, continually changing direction, and the shrill shrieks of the howler monkeys high above, flying, torsos twisting and turning, arms outstretched, teeth bared, panting and screaming.

The old woman appears as if out of nowhere, she is all bone and sinewy and nerves cells dancing on the coarse, black flesh of her neck and shoulders, and down along her arms, the heavy bracelets on her wrists, the nerve cells dancing into the bones of her fingers. She is speaking in the Creole that the Dutch call Neger-Englen, and Maria Sibylla can understand some of the words: *tree, hanging or suspended?, comb, bird.* And all the time the old woman is speaking, a sack near her feet is screeching and humping. The old woman reaches inside the sack and firmly holding its neck pulls out a brilliantly colored, huge young macaw. She hands the macaw to Maria Sibylla, who, avoiding its enormous stabbing beak, takes the frantic bird and covers it with a net to calm it. The old woman points to herself and says, *Mama Cato, Mama Cato.* Maria Sibylla repeats the name, *Mama Cato.* The old woman wants to trade for the macaw. She points to the sack filled with supplies that is slung over Maria Sibylla's shoulder, indicating she wants it emptied on the ground. Maria Sibylla tells Marta to take the sack and empty it on the ground. The old woman points to a bright blue piece of salempouri cloth and a green tree frog in a stoppered jar of liquid. Maria Sibylla nods her agreement to the trade. The leave-taking is abrupt; the old woman quickly disappears back into the jungle. Marta steps forward and begins putting everything back inside the sack, while Maria Sibylla continues holding the now-silent macaw.

Mosquitoes swarm and puncture her skin.

Beads of blood form on the punctures.

The blood is trickling where the mosquitoes have bitten.

And then another and another puncture in her skin.

Sirs, a most uncommon discovery. A butterfly exactly one half male and the other half female, the rear on one side being male, and on the other female.

In the Kerkstraat Gardens there had been butterflies, benign creatures, but not so beautiful as these. These are more beautiful, but not benign.

Somewhere the ants are taking down a tapir. The pig does not stand a chance. As the ants dig in. As the flesh falls away. As the spirit of the beast rushes out through its head. The slight whoosh of sound each time she pins an insect. Her back stiff and straight. Inside the house, the light glows from the candles.

"I have looked at several cane pieces for farming," Mathew van der Lee announces during the evening meal. "There are some acres south from here, at the mouth of Sara Creek."

"So far to the south, Mr. van der Lee," the Widow Ivenes responds with alarm. "We will never see you if you move so far to the south."

"You will visit often, Widow Ivenes, and spend your time much as you like."

"The Sara Creek region is not thought safe, Mr. van der Lee," says Esther Gabay. "The runaways are settled near to there."

"It is said the numbers of the runaways are few, Madame Gabay."

"The numbers may be few, Mr. van der Lee," says Esther Gabay, "but the assaults on the sugar farms are many."

"And the expeditions of our soldiers fail most often in their efforts to recapture them," adds Doctor Peter Kolb.

"But there are slaves recaptured everyday, Doctor Kolb," says Mathew van der Lee.

"And every day there are more runaways," counters the Doctor, "and more violence against the plantations."

"The violence is not likely to continue," insists Mathew van der Lee. "How many slaves will risk the punishments if caught?—the beatings, the mutilations. There is one of your colleagues in Paramaribo, Doctor Kolb, whose job it is to amputate limbs from recaptured runaways."

"The punishments do not deter the runaways," says Doctor Peter Kolb. "Their sensibility is not as ours, Mr. van der Lee."

"I am not persuaded of that view," says Mathew van der Lee.

"Nor am I, I would agree, Mr. van der Lee," says the Widow Ivenes. And then turning to Maria Sibylla, "What has science to say on the subject?"

"It seems not a matter for science, dear Widow Ivenes."

"What of your work then?" the Widow persists in drawing Maria Sibylla into the conversation.

"My work progresses, Widow Ivenes."

"And extraordinary work it is, Madame Sibylla," says the Widow.

"What is extraordinary," says Esther Gabay, "is that so much effort should be taken in the interest of insects."

"There is greater fortune to be made in sugar cane," says Doctor Peter Kolb.

"My interest here is not in sugar, Doctor Kolb."

"Madame Sibylla's interest is to witness nature and not to mine for its material potentiality," says Mathew van der Lee, staring openly at Maria Sibylla. "She is an artist and a scientist, Doctor Kolb, and those are the interests which occupy her. Much as my own interest in collecting has occupied me. It is true I now seek fortune here in sugar, but I have not lost interest in the creatures of the natural world."

"Indeed well spoken," says the Widow Ivenes.

Mr. van der Lee. Come see. He moves closer to her and he sees. It is the moth pupa she brought with her other specimens on the journey from Amsterdam so that she might witness the completion of their transformations. There in a cage in the Surimombo study. The moth has broken through its shell, broken out at last from chrysalis, after these months since its ocean crossing. The small, delicate moth clings to the wires of the cage with its wings wildly flapping. It is the *Phalaena tau*, its wings appearing moist in the light from the candles, and the flames flare up and cast shadows on the wall. Of the moth. Of the woman. And the man.

The next day she has an accident. She reaches out for a caterpillar on the leaf of a tree in the forest near to the main house. It is a vibrant blue-black, inky and depthless, two ruby stripes along the sides of its body. Sensing her presence, it lifts its head, raises it high as if surveying, then lowers and lifts it again, and then it stops with its body rigid and its head raised. She quickly cups it in her palm and is met with a stinging pain so severe she can barely open her hand to release the caterpillar into the cage. Her body flushes hot. Her hand swells to twice its size and she can hardly remain standing. There is the feeling of sinking, of wanting to let go to the ground and let sleep come, of wanting the floor of the forest—green and lush like the sofas of dowagers, thick and soft in rich velvets and muted shades of olive—to receive her. She sinks down to the bottom of the tree trunk and waits for the dizziness to pass. Almost immediately an apprehension wells up inside her. She feels a sensation on her legs. She pulls the fabric of her clothing up and sees small black wood ticks that despite the layers of her skirt have in seconds covered the flesh of her lower legs and are swarming towards her thighs and her abdomen. She leaps up, surprises a giant macaw on a branch not far above, the bird lifts its wings and shrieks, the shrieks soar up through the branches, and the bird follows. She leaps up and walks as quickly as she can, though she is still unsteady and somewhat dizzy from the poison still in her body. Breathing is difficult. The air is thick with moisture, it is all moisture, the air turned fluid, a substance not breathed but swallowed into the lungs, the chest cavity fills and congests. She is moving forward, returning to the Surimombo main house, in any case she wasn't far, had not gone far. And to the bathing house where she applies an ointment to her legs and her belly following a washing treatment with a brush and harsh liquids. The skin red now, scrubbed raw. Reclaimed. Clean. The bathing house is cool, the water strained through sieves to keep the sand out, the floor polished stone and cool on the bottoms of her feet, and the small black parasitic insects, all to the last one, fallen to the floor, inert, a little pile at her feet, then washed, washed away by the water. She balances herself, holding on with one hand to the wall of the dressing room in the bathing house, the dressing room with its conveniences, small round soaps in smooth clay dishes, jars of salts for soaking, fragrant oils, fresh-cut peacock flowers, a bath sheet for drying her body, a white muslin robe for wrapping up in, the bathing house itself shaded by palmetto leaves falling like folds of fabric over the wooden structure. Now a lizard appears on the outside of the window, it is one of the small lizards that are everywhere in Surinam. Its body is pressed against the mesh that serves as a screen, the sun's rays make it glow, crystalline, the body transparent, shot through by the sun so that she can see the insides clear and shining, and the long thin vein that runs from its head down to its tail and extends out to each of its four legs and to each of the toes of its webbed feet. Dear lizard, remarkable beast, lit by the afternoon sun, pierced through by a ray of white light, human eyes are blinded by so much light, by so much heat and bright-ness. She goes over to the window to view the lizard more closely and sees Mathew van der Lee off a ways in the distance; she sees his figure in the white sun, against the bleached out grasses near the sugar fields. He is walking with his hands clasped behind his back. Later, he will ask if he might accompany her again up the coast to the ocean on one of her hunts there for shells. They will set out as if on a picnic, carrying charcoals and vellums, specimen boxes and killing jars. They will walk over sand strewn with branches and mollusk shells, nests of seaweed, dead fish, ghost crabs heaped together on the shore. She will walk erect with her back straight, with her shoes caked with mud and the bottom of her dress wet and dragging. Mathew van der Lee will make a light-hearted comment about the mud on her shoes, and just as he does his own feet will sink some inches into the ground. He will reach out as if to touch her when she looks down at his feet, but then will quickly withdraw his arm.

And a running off of water in the bath house, her legs good, her waist narrow, her feet long, slender, somewhat bony, a running off of water, scented powders, the tortoise comb, her hair undone and hanging down below her shoulders in dark wet pieces, like a witch she thinks, die Hexe, bezaubernde Frau.

She descends the staircase from her second floor suite of the Surimombo main house, the interior copied faithfully in the style of her adopted city of Amsterdam, her city of Amsterdam with its cold nights, and with its gabled, corniced structures, and with the canals with their bodies of dead waters. And the German township where she was born—Frankfort am Mein—where she spent all her early life and formed her identity, is distant now, and she will never return there again, and will have no cause or wish to return. She is pale and fatigued, and the last of the light is fading; night is falling, and a blanket of blackness will soon cover the house while the lodgers are gathered for the evening meal. The candles in the dining room will draw to the window pale moths, as pale as she is, unable to resist the fiery center, and their wings will beat against the glass, pounding and bruising their plump bodies; they will look like ghosts in the dark, eager and hungry, seeking their shadow selves there in the flame. And all the while the other moths, the specimens she has collected, will remain safe in their cages, quiet in the darkened room. And when the night has fully fallen, the lantern flies will come out with their lights glittering.

She lifts her hand to the back of her neck to wipe the beads of perspiration away. She drinks boiled water left to cool, dips her fingers into the water and touches her brow, her neck. The heat is draining her of blood and spirit, sucking the marrow out from her bones and leaving them to ache at night, her arms and her legs ache each night and she is restless on the bed. She no longer sleeps well from the aching and the restlessness.

She descends the stairs now down to supper, to where the others are already seated in the dining room.

"You are pale, Madame Sibylla. Are you unwell?"

"It is nothing, Doctor Kolb. It is only the heat. No. Nothing. Or if anything, the heat."

"Yes, the heat. How is your work progressing?"

"Well."

"And your hand? Has it healed from the accident?"

"Yes."

"I am a physician, Madame Sibylla. Will you permit me to have a look at it? You would not want it to fester."

"It is nothing, Doctor Kolb. It was only a reaction to the pathetic creature's venom. As you see, it has completely subsided."

Drums are beating. Drums are beating in the night. The sound of the drums comes from the forest beyond Piki Ston where the runaways have erected their settlements. The drums cannot come from the plantations; on the plantations the black slaves are forbidden to drum, forbidden to send their rebel messages. She has seen what happens to those who disobey. She has seen the bloody stump where a hand once was, and the body flogged skinless, and a raw, pulpy mass where the flesh once was, and the body kept alive in ruin.

She is fatigued. It can be seen on her face, and in the way she comports herself, in the way her breath comes labored, and her eyes appear clouded and distant.

It is the heat. And the poison still in her body from the caterpillar's sting. Night has fallen and the window is covered with moths that are drunk on the light from the flames of the candle. The moths will die, just as she believes that she will die, that the heat of the sun will kill her, that the harshness of this place will end her life. She is still weak, and still vertiginous from the caterpillar's venom.

The venom in her body has increased her fatigue, and her nights are beset by dreams, and by visions that appear and disappear, alternately beautiful and terrifying.

In a dream she is menaced by an animal, it comes around in front of her, an aggressive look in its eyes.

She is standing listening to the river, the still, glassy surface shining in the sun, the sun's rays rippling on the surface, she is standing looking out to the bend in the river, a distance farther and white waters start to form, the current goes crazy with white waters, a little while more and rapids, a little while more and the water gushing and pounding, crazy water, a little while more and crazy water, dashing against rocks, the falls to take you to the bottom, and the devil's egg, the rock that is perched above the water, the dashing crazy water, the falls are Piki Ston Falls, along the river bank the monkeys with their perpetual screaming, is it with warning? is it with ill intent? the violent screams of the monkeys, but here where she is standing the river is still, there is no ripple, the sun shines in streaks on the placid surface.

Small, sweeter than the alligator pear, the sweet red fruit of the yucca.

The butterflies are made of feathers. She points to all the tiny little feathers.

In her drawings her themes come slowly into focus, a merest outline, a shadowy creature, and then she adds light.

The theme of primulas with nun moth, plum branch and pale tussock, cotton leaf jatropha, mimicry moth, antaeus moth.

The theme of the lantern fly, meadow larkspur and pease blossom moth, various beetles and a harlequin beetle.

The theme of four dead finches. The birds are pathetic the way she portrays them. There is no question they are dead, quintessentially and permanently dead. Flight no more. For the small brown birds.

And the sun breaking through enormous,

it sears the flesh, the ground, the wooden frame of the Surimombo main house.

In a clearing in the forest Marta has wrapped herself in salempouri cloth, and the bright blue of the fabric is shining, and she is dancing, she is spinning in front of Maria Sibylla. The dance can stop the fierce thunderstorms and the torrents of the rains, and Marta is dancing to bring an end to the rains.

But the sky is gray, and the heavy rains are again threatening.

There is a crocodile somewhere in the meh-nu bushes with its jaws snapping. There is the sound the leaves make when the wind blows through them. A storm rising up. The scream of the toucani. In the Surimombo jungle there had been a trail of dead toucani. Or had they fallen randomly? And the crocodile is creeping out from the swamp onto the jungle floor. And the rain will cause a lake to form in the jungle.

The leaves of the Ku-deh-deh fortify the heart. Marta holds the fingers of her right hand outstretched above her heart, her eyes are dark and excited as she picks the waxy leaves and crushes them.

And all the while Maria Sibylla is searching among the vines and the creepers.

But what about the moth, the newly hatched *Phalaena tau?* Ah, the *Phalaena tau* has been recently transformed. Has broken through its shell and been released. It was Maria Sibylla herself who released the moth. Into the heat. Into the harshness and the freedom of the jungle.

The *Phalaena tau* has flown to make her own way in the jungle.

And Maria Sibylla is searching for the new moth, the stranger.

Among the vines, the creepers, the rosettes of leaves, the night-smelling orchids, the mora excelsa.

Along the branches of the unnamed tree.

The blossoms are red and the tree is unnamed. And the roots of the tree are buried. In the jungle earth that turns to water. The ground is soft, the leaves are shimmering.

And she is silent now and waiting. The voluptuousness of the time of waiting.

She has been walking for so long her feet are burning, but her eyes are searching everywhere. For you, the stranger, for the promise of what she has come for.

She is looking for you, bewitched by you.

In the green, indistinct light of the jungle. That filters down through the branches of the trees.

The screaming birds, their calls harsh, piercing.

The jungle orchids, the delicate tree orchid, the air-borne orchid with its tentacles dangling, and covered in small white flowers, its musky scent, its mouth that never opens.

She is breathless and her heart is beating rapidly.

The heat pours down but she no longer notices, she is intent on finding you.

You are her loadstone, her wish, her temptation, her consummation.

Entranced she is looking, in a fever she is looking.

For the slanted traces that will lead her to you.

The small paroxysms, the silent heartbeat, the throbbing.

But where is it that Maria Sibylla finds you? So quiet. On the branch of the unknown tree? It is a secret tree, so secret even the Amerindians do not know its name, the Tree of Paradise? The tree of the fall from grace? The tree the serpent wrapped itself around and whispered, offering its fruit, and the leaves stinging like nettles, and you clinging with your tiny feet, having taken hold to suck the sweetness, the snake there with you all the time, all wound around its branches, and you as you had always been, from that first hour, when you were the first one, the first to take hold upon that branch, the first to nourish on that unknown, unnamed genus, and having had your fill of eating to spin and spin the silk that would enclose you, and keep you safe inside that first of all enclosures, protected and unharmed, to sleep for the season of your transformation.

II

There is a beast, there is a beast in Surinam. A white beast seen prowling in the grasses near the sugar farms. The Indians say it is the jinn of a demon that lives under Piki Ston Falls. That it will come and slash slash with its teeth as large as Waha leaves. That it will come to take its dwendi, its lady mama girl, to make its wild monkey bride, to make its wild monkey bride girl running. It has hair that is white and sticks out like the shoots of white copal; it has hands that are claws and it stands on its legs like a man.

The beast stalks the sugar farms while the day steams with heat, or at night stalks the shanties of the slaves.

It is the slaves who see the beast, but sometimes it is one of the Europeans. Like the white overseer at Plantation Davilaar. The man was relieving himself near the edges of the sugar field when he saw an animal crouched a distance from him. The beast reared up and the man turned on his heels and ran.

"It is only an hysteria of the Africans and the Indians," Esther Gabay tells the others over morning meal.

The serving girl brings trays to the table, sets out platters of ham, baskets heaped high with breads, eggs, cassava cakes, green tea, coffee, chocolate.

"It is only an hysteria," Esther Gabay repeats, "or a fabrication that has been hatched by the runaways."

"Hatched to what purpose, Madame Gabay?" asks Doctor Peter Kolb.

"To stir unrest among the slaves, Doctor Kolb."

"It is more likely a wolf, Madame Gabay," says the doctor. "It would not be the first time that a lone wolf, displaced from the pack, or with its instincts otherwise upset, has been known to attack at humans."

"There are no wolves here, Doctor Kolb."

"It is a species capable of turning up, Madame Gabay, of one day simply making an appearance. There are many forces that will drive a pack, or that will provoke a lone wolf, to wander into a new territory."

"I have lived here all my life, Doctor Kolb, and have never heard rumor of wolves."

"They have been known to turn up, Madame Gabay."

"We have never had wolves, Doctor Kolb."

"We may have one now, Madame Gabay."

"What is your opinion?" the Widow Ivenes asks, turning suddenly to Maria Sibylla. "Do you believe it is an hysteria?"

"I believe we should not waste our days with speculation on a creature that may or may not exist. I, in any case, shall not waste my days on it. We must trust in the will of the Divine Being, Widow Ivenes, and in our Fate, and I in my work that it is necessary I continue."

"Will you continue in the forests?" asks Doctor Peter Kolb.

"I shall continue as I must, Doctor Kolb."

"Would it not be wise, Madame Sibylla, to avoid the forests?" asks Mathew van der Lee.

"Would you dissuade me, Mr. van der Lee?"

"For your safety it would be cautious, Madame Sibylla."

"For my safety, Mr. van der Lee, I should never have left Frankfurt am Main for Amsterdam, and later Amsterdam for Friesland, or Friesland for Amsterdam once again, and now made this journey to Surinam. Safe, inside my house, Mr. van der Lee, might I still not fall ill and languish and die?"

She prepares after morning meal to travel with Marta into the forest right outside of Paramaribo. The other slaves have begged not to have to accompany them, apprehensive as they are now of the beast.

Marta, who has begun to copy the makeshift style of Maria Sibylla, wears an overall that she has sewn, and under it a shirt Esther Gabay has given her left behind by a previous lodger. Both women wear hats. Their feet and their legs are well covered.

Marta is perspiring, the perspiration runs in large beads from beneath the brim of her hat and down her face, down her Indian nose with the hint of a bump in it, her nostrils flare, her lower lip protrudes.

Maria Sibylla brings her hand behind her own neck, and reaches down along the back of her left shoulder, she digs her fingers into her flesh, a relaxation from the heat, an easement from the weight of the vellum, the charcoal, the brushes, the nets and the killing jars.

The women are in a small patch of clearing where the light shines down unfiltered and blinding. They raise their hands above their eyes to see.

Hummingbirds in crimson. In vibrant purples and greens. In vests of metallic colors that gleam and change as the light hits them, or as the birds shift the positions of their bodies. The birds are barely larger than the butterflies. Hovering above the branches and singing in unison. There are some sixty of them at least, and they are singing a mating song. Small and glittering like precious stones. All hovering and in song. Maria Sibylla surmises they are males, it is the striking colors that tell her, the males wardrobed for mating and singing in chorus. The voices are not beautiful—their song does not have the sweetness of the helabeh, nor the lyric quality of the thrush. They make a rasping sound, a thin, high-pitched tone such as stone scraping metal.

The birds come into focus like the details on the canvases of certain paintings, at first mere abstract shape and color and then gradually sharpening, becoming discernable.

A little deeper into the forest and again they see hummingbirds, but these, though alive, are not singing.

They are caught in the traps that the shamans have set for them, their bright metallic colors gleaming in the nets in the sun, but their bodies are limp now, no longer hovering, the birds are caught in the shamans' nets, the blur of wingbeat has stopped and they are trapped, forty or fifty at least, perhaps more in the nets of the shamans.

The shamans have set traps for the hummingbirds. That is their diet, Marta tells Maria Sibylla—to be fed exclusively on the flesh of hummingbirds.

And the mating song is deadly for the hummingbirds, to be caught in the nets of the shamans.

The sugar farms veer off in all directions: Machado; Castillo; Alvamant; Cordova; Davilaar; Boavista; Providentia. The plantations with their yearly harvests. With the intense heat of their boiling houses and the slitting of the cane to test for sweetness.

And the sugar that is dripping from the stalks. It is the wedding at the Castillo Plantation and it has brought all of the township of Surinam out for the celebration. The bride is the daughter of Castillo and the groom is the elder Alvamant. She is seventeen, while the elder Alvamant is forty-three and twice a widower. The bride is virginal and sweet like the sugar cane.

It is from the Castillo wedding that the famous portrait of the men derives: twenty-two of them in all, posed like the Officers of the Militia at one of the banquet tables. Doctor Peter Kolb is in the portrait, seated looking towards the left, and gesturing with his hands in conversation. Mathew van der Lee is also shown in the portrait, his expression animated and turned in semi-profile facing Doctor Peter Kolb. The eyes of the other men stare straight ahead, the groom at center expectant and flushed.

From this wedding, too, comes the portrait of Maria Sibylla dressed in garden silk and satin capuchin. Her mood is high and her skin glows in the heat. She is fresh from one of the wedding dances, it was a cotillion and this done in turns, each with a different partner. She has had several of these turns with Mathew van der Lee.

The Widow Ivenes tells the wedding party her dream of the white beast. In the dream the Widow is a child again. She is leading the beast on a chain and the animal is following docile and quiet, trotting like a little dog behind the Child Ivenes. But then a wind starts up and the fur of the white beast begins to ripple like a lion's mane, and the Child Ivenes and the beast move steadily against the wind, and the beast lets out a ferocious roar and throws its head back, all the while roaring, and the Child Ivenes' hair blows free from her cap.

But the beast is not a dream at the Providentia Plantation. A female slave has been mauled and her infant snatched from her. The woman had given birth the night before, and in the morning fell behind the others at the edges of the sugar fields. The beast appeared out of nowhere and sprang at the woman and tore at her flesh, and the woman dropped her baby to the ground. When she did, the beast stopped its attack and let go of the woman, then grabbed the baby from the ground and ran into the jungle.

The black men are crouched outside the flap door of one of the shanties.

Jama-Santi, the child who was witness to the attack, is brought by the men to tell what he saw. He was in the bushes at the edge of the sugar field where he saw the woman resting with her infant. He saw the beast nearby as if in hiding. The beast came across the field on all four paws, like this, and Jama-Santi moves forward in a crouch to show the men, and then it slashed at the woman, rising up on its two legs until it was taller than a man, and then it knocked the woman to the ground and ran off with her infant.

crocodile man, monkey man, alligator man.

There is a bristling on the backs of the black necks; it goes unnoticed for the moment by the Dutch. There are the words that are repeated in the shanties, by the black slaves speaking in their Neger-Englen.

alligator man, mystery man, crocodile man.

But what more is to be said about the wedding party, about the feasting and the dance, the endless rounds of the cotillions? Or for that matter what more is to be said about the wedding couple? The chaste bride. The expectant groom. Shall we call attention to them now and to the coming of the night with its sweet outpouring like the liquid from the sugar cane? The stalk is slit deep, and the syrup of the sugar is dripping.

Maria Sibylla has gone out behind the main house of the Castillo Plantation and has been followed by Mathew van der Lee. "Mr. van der Lee," she says when she sees him. "Here, come." Her black hair is piled high upon her head, and her shoulders are bare, and she is thin in her garden silk. "Madame Sibylla," says Mathew van der Lee as he approaches her.

They will be returning soon to Surimombo.

It is early evening, just before the nightfall. The day of work is over on the sugar farms. The slaves talk about the beast, they say its eyes are malignant, flashing. And the land moves out from the sea down into the jungle.

It is her desire that is driving her. To seek beyond the limits that would otherwise constrain her. In the morning she goes out alone into the fields, behind the house, into the small forest, alone into the jungle.

From a distance she thinks they are large birds, but as she approaches she sees they are monkeys. There is a brood of them on the ground in the clearing. The monkeys are curious, especially the youngest ones, they approach without fear to smell her out. A baby grabs at the bottom of her overall. But when she steps forward, the baby lets go and runs back to the rest. The adults approach menacing, their shrieks deafening, then all at once they pull themselves into the trees.

When the monkeys clear, Maria Sibylla sees the old black woman, Mama Cato. She has brought cowrie shells and beetles to trade for fabric and a sheet of vellum. Mama Cato is running back and forth in front of Maria Sibylla, shouting something that the Dutch woman does not understand. Then Mama Cato stops her shouting and her running and throws her head back and makes a call like a bird. Her call brings toucans. The toucans are flying all around her, the toucans in flight, flapping their wings above Mama Cato.

When the trading is finished, the old woman moves back into the jungle and the toucans disappear above the trees.

But something else is moving now, a hint of something moving among the trees.

Or is it only the way the land moves out from the sea into the jungles. And the swaying of the branches in the trees.

Are there footsteps? Footfall? When Mama Cato has left her alone in the forest? The sound of thrashing against the jungle growth.

Is it the beast? The white beast stalking? On its diurnal ritual? The heaving and sighing of the beast.

And in the distance the cracking of the whips, the whips cracking back on the sugar farms.

That evening at supper the five of them gather. How familiar now the sight of them gathered. The plates are passed from left to right, the way they have always been passed since the first evening of her arrival. And the lodgers are seated where they have always been seated since the moment they first sat down. The talk tonight is of the beast, of the incident at Providentia Plantation. Since the attack on the female slave there has been talk of little else at Surimombo. And Esther Gabay, for all her fears of its effect to stir unrest among the slaves, is unable to control the conversation, to stop the steady stream of discourse on the beast.

"What is called a beast is sometimes merely a deformity," says Doctor Peter Kolb, "such as the deformity of the mystery people, the Ewaipanoma, who are born without a head."

"But the Ewaipanoma are not a real people," says Esther Gabay.

The moths have come and are beating at the window, attracted by the glow of the candles in the dining room, and the window is covered with moths, just as each night since her arrival the window has been covered with moths, and it is as though nature has conspired with its own ritual, and the window is all movement and pulsation. But look who has come this night to take advantage. It is the spider called a wolf spider because it preys in the manner of wolves. It has come to hunt on the window on which the moths have lighted with such compulsion that even when the spider makes its presence known, the moths are unable to flee. For the moths are transfixed there by the light from the candles, bearded, with their bodies flattened, pressed close to the window. And the window provides a feast this night for the spider.

Or later in the salon, or in her laboratory, or in the bedroom of her suite of rooms where the cocoon of the mosquito netting hangs all around her, and the fabric of the netting is soft and silky to the touch.

Despite the layers of the netting, the mosquitoes puncture her flesh, as they have done many times since her arrival.

But who comes dancing in these hours before she sleeps. Gaunt. Thin. He is thin. Like an insect. Imagine.

Dancing in the hours before she sleeps.

If the beast has sport with you, you die, if the beast touches your mama woman, you have babies that come out with heads like crocodiles, if the beast touches you, you feel red pain rising in your loins. That is what the Indians say. And that is what the Africans also say. The Indians and the Africans are of one mind about the beast. It is only the Dutch who say something different.

The beast is not a joke. The beast kills you. Do you know the beast? Is the beast the Ewaipanoma without a head? How can they live without a head? How can they eat you without a head? It is a mystery. It is a question that does not have an answer. The Ewaipanoma live in the deep jungle. But no one can live in the deep jungle. Only the Ewaipanoma and the Africans and the Indians when they are running. They are like dogs when they are running and they are trying to flee their masters. They are running from the slashing of the whip. The women running too. The women running from the whip. And from the use that is made of them. As many times as is desired. Though not desired by them. And they are like wild dogs the women when they are running into the deep jungle, where the Dutch man tries to follow but gets eaten by the crocodile. But if he finds the dog, oh, no, oh no. If he finds the dog. In the jungle.

The beast has struck and infected with fear the imaginations of the captive peoples, the Amerindians with their russet faces, proud under the whip, and the Africans, too, also proud, and watchful.

The white men beat the slaves with whips, they do not care that they are descended from the tribal princes.

The sudden raids and the enslavements. The spirit cast down a thousand times, a thousand times and gnashings . . . bitter bitter.

But what is the beast? Is it the jinn of a demon hiding under Piki Ston Falls? The falls are high and the water rushes.

Where did the beast come from, appearing out of nowhere? How can the beast appear out of nowhere? Out of nothing? It must come from somewhere.

Here is a white beast: On the Cordova Plantation, Jacob Cordova is punishing a black man for drumming.

But in the deep jungle, past the Nickerie, along the Saramacca River, past the swamp lands with its crocodiles, in the deep jungle that is thick with the liana, there are the settlements of the runaways, there are the fire hearths going and the women cooking at the fire hearths outside the new shanties, and the Dutch man cannot follow here, cannot get past the crocodile and the liana, and the black man is drumming and drumming and drumming.

She is infected now with the malaria from the mosquitoes. The mosquitoes have infected her with the malaria.

The malaria has her and her eyes are bleary, boiling, the heat has worn her down and the mosquito has overcome her, and she is hollow, her bones are hollow, and her skin has become rough and parched, and hot to the touch, and glistening in the darkened room. Esther Gabay has ordered the thick dark curtains pulled across the window to keep out the light from the sun. And in the dark it is as though Maria Sibylla is glowing, as though her skin is glowing. Her lips have swollen and are thick now, and dry, and her tongue, too, has swollen, and is thick inside her mouth, and her speech is slurred in her delirium, and her words come out in fragments and make no sense. She is saying something about a tulip in the Netherlands, or two river pigs, approaching, and sinking down into silence.

where are you, Maria Sibylla? Mari? Mari? in a thick Dutch accent.

she has a heaviness in her legs, the slowing down of her pulse, the heaviness climbing in her legs.

she cannot breathe, the heaviness has made her breathless.

the fever has made her pale, drawn, brought a dryness to her lips, as if parched, faded, and the air filled up with water draws her body fluids like a sponge, in drops it draws her body fluids from her.

she is in a place that is uninhabitable, it is filled with a substance that she knows cannot sustain her.

there is a tree sloth in her path. hanging limp and in unimaginable pleasure in the shade of a Mora tree.

and her heart beating, hard

and her breath shallow

she is on the Cerro de la Compana, the mountain that is called Bell Mountain, located south of the Savannah in Surinam.

white stones rise up on the mountain, the boulders rise white and can be seen from all directions, rising up on the mountain, where there are no trees, only the boulders that rise up to the peaks.

or she is in her father's study looking at the drawing table, at the scene for a still life set on the drawing table.

it is the book of flowers open

the book of insects dreaming

Maria. Maria Sibylla.

and she is sinking down, inside her fever, and sinking down, and down inside her dreams.

Surimombo with its rolling fields of sugar cane, the way the stalk breaks.

and the pale emptying of the darkness.

she is inside the netting, the mosquito netting that is brushing against her like cobwebs, when she tries to move, when she tries to lift up, when she raises her arm, or turns from her back to her side.

or she is walking with Mathew van der Lee along the seashore.

it is his specialty, he tells her, the shore of the sea.

he is speaking and his breath is continuous, it is the absence of pauses that allows his breath to be continuous.

the African slaves hiding in the old abandoned gardens.

amidst the screaming birds, the macaws that scream loudest, the howler monkeys that roar like the jaguars.

her eyes are black with the dilation of her pupils, the bites have punctured her, have left deposits deep inside her, the seeds of the malaria have been planted inside her, and have left her forever assailable.

and Doctor Peter Kolb with his bag of tricks coming in and out of her room, looking now stern, now grave, now perplexed, now fatigued and hopeless, resigned as though he has exhausted all that he can offer, with his bag, with his hands, with his hands thick and sometimes shaking, and yet the shaking is ignored as he, Doctor Kolb, puts his hands first on her head, and then at the base of her throat, and on her neck and on her shoulders, listening, to her breathing, listening to her labored breathing.

and Mathew van der Lee inquiring of Doctor Kolb, often several times in a single day inquiring, asking after the progress of her recovery, his own face blanched and creased with his concern, or sometimes waiting outside her suite of rooms for the doctor to exit, or at cards in the evening distracted.

but Marta, too, has been coming into the sick woman's room, at night when the doctor has left, and Esther Gabay is aware of it and does not approve, but does not stop it. Marta brings liquids to drink and some to apply as a compress, and some that have been ground into a paste, or infused in a glass, and in the end these prove the cure.

In the end these prove the cure,

and the world again becomes visible,

and the sun breaks through again completely, to sear the flesh, the ground, the wooden frame of the main house at Surimombo.

As soon as she is able, Maria Sibylla sets out with Marta, they go no farther than the small forest behind the Surimombo sugar fields, the forest is lush with peacock flowers.

Her eyes still ringed with the tiredness left by the malaria, she wears no hat, her hair falls past her shoulders.

The world again surrounds her,

the calls of birds, the hum of insects,

on the branches of the trees, caterpillars.

The world again surrounds her and she is working in the forest,

the sweep of her net across the jungle floor,

but while she is working, the slaves are hiding.

The slaves are hiding, wearing hats with gold trim, with iron pots and bolts of cloth, with cowrie shells, sweet oil, candles, pigs, sheep, combs.

And the beast has come sniffing across the sugar fields, and the children hiding in the bushes, or in their hammocks, or in their cribs in the shanties that cannot hold them, and their mothers are saying, oh no, oh no.

The beast has come trotting with the legs of his trousers flapping.

It is on the Machado plantation. Where the beast is reflected in the eyes of the child Josie. The beast is reflected in the eyes, in the eyes of the black child Josie who has just been purchased by Jorge Machado.

The girl is twelve and already has her menses, she is twelve and thin and delicate, with dark eyes and long legs.

It is on the Machado plantation, and involves Jorge Machado himself, the look of shock in Josie's eyes, the look of fear, of terror, and then of shame, and the touch of the man who has grabbed her, the man who owns her, the man whose property she is.

The weight of Jorge Machado's neck is pressed against the child Josie's face, and his arms have pinned her arms to their sides, and what he is doing to her, she cannot stop him, his thick neck that is pressed against her mouth, his shoulder that is digging into her breast, his flesh that is pushed into hers, and what he is doing to her,

and her eyes are open and staring.

Where is the mama of the child Josie? The mama is so far away now. And the mama cannot protect her. And the daddy cannot protect her. Where is the daddy of the child Josie?

It is from fear, perhaps from fear and anger, perhaps from the aggrievance to her body, or from the weight of his neck against her face, or from his arms which have pinned her, or the pain from what he is doing to her, the child Josie cannot stop herself she bites Jorge Machado. It is on his neck that she bites him, his neck that has been pressed against her mouth, she sinks her teeth deep into his neck, as he penetrates her,

and his shock to feel it,
and his fist pounding down on her mouth,
and her teeth that are broken, and the blood filling up in her mouth.

He rears up like a beast and brings Josie up with him, and Josie is screaming, and the blood is pouring out from her mouth.

But that is not enough to contain the rage of Jorge Machado.
He has a rage that cannot be contained and he spills it out on the child Josie.
And her screams pour out with the blood from her mouth.

And Jorge Machado is pounding and pounding, with his fist like a hammer he pounds her, and her arms flail against him, she is trying to protect herself with her flailing arms, with her arms that flail against him,

until he twists both her arms in their sockets,
and her arms are hanging limp from their sockets,
until Jorge Machado fully spends his rage and by the savage force of his own massive arms he tears the arms out from the sockets of the child Josie.

"There is your beast, Madame Gabay," Maria Sibylla says solemnly, having listened with full attention to the account. "And there is *your* beast, Doctor Kolb, there is the wolf that you suspect with its eyes flashing and with its teeth that rip and tear and rip and tear, and there is your beast, too, Widow Ivenes, your fine white beast that trots behind you like a dog, and it is sitting right beside the beast of Madame Gabay."

That night she dreams that she is on the ship, *The Peace,* that it has come to take her home. The ship sets sail and she is returning to her home in the Netherlands. She is standing on the deck as the ship leaves the shore, as it sets sail out to the sea. She is standing on the deck and there is still light from the sun, but the air is cold. And when night comes she is still on the deck and it is now very cold. In her dream she can see the moon at three-quarters, and the planets and the stars. All those miles away from her.

The next day she is alone in the small forest, Marta is not with her. It is called the Surimombo Forest because it extends along the edges of the Surimombo Plantation and can be seen from the sugar fields.

It is the day she discovers the little-bird spider. It is a tarantula, covered with hair, straddling its prey, sucking the blood out from a tiny bird. The bird is on its back only a few inches from the nest, its head hanging limp between a fork in the branch. Maria Sibylla is transferring the scene to vellum, painstaking and accurate in her rendering.

She has announced that morning during breakfast she will cut short her visit. On its approaching journey back she will again board *The Peace.*

It is the heat that is driving her, she has told them, that is prompting her to cut short her visit, and she is still fatigued from her illness, from the malaria, and she believes that if she remains she will not survive, and all the while the heat is breathing itself into her, hot and needling and insistent like the mouth of an insect.

Footsteps approach, she is vaguely aware, the sound of someone thrashing against the jungle growth, she stops drawing and turns in the direction of the footsteps.

It is Matthew van der Lee who has followed her, who has come to seek her out where she is working.

She stands silent, the sun's rays on her.

You are working.
I am working.
Is it true what you said, you will leave soon?
Yes, true, it is true.
But I thought that you might stay.
I am sorry, I must leave, Mr. van der Lee.
Will you not change your mind?
It is too hot, Mr. van der Lee.
I have purchased some cane fields, Madame Sibylla.
You will soon be rich, Mr. van der Lee.

There is something in the shape of his face, its triangularity, and the impression that it gives, there is something in the expression on his face.

And her face still flushed from the malaria.

It will be difficult to leave you, Mr. van der Lee.

He is thin and his lower jaw protrudes slightly. He has the look of a student long past his student days, he is reserved and yet he is intense, he is somewhat delicate and yet there is a strength to him.

And the heat from the sun beating down.

What is the contradiction welling inside her, the contradiction rising inside her? The heat on the one hand—the insidious armies of ants, the wood ticks that in seconds can cover the entirety of the body,

and on the other, everything is lush, lush, and the clouds tinged pink, and the floor of the jungle is thick and soft, so soft you can sink down into it.

Her hair shines black.

Her black hair falling past her shoulders.

Her beating heart, her breathlessness.

And Mathew van der Lee standing before her.

Maria Sibylla stares, then she beckons him closer, motions him to come closer, closer, quiet, puts her fingers to her lips, quiet, quiet, here, come, Mr. van der Lee, and she shows him what it is that she is drawing, the tiny bird that has been vanquished by the spider, the tameless spider still in the act of ravaging the bird, she shows him first on her drawing on the vellum and then points to the live model on the tree, and they are standing very close now, with their faces nearly touching, and there is the mingling of their breaths in the hot, humid air of the forest, under the branches of the tree, this tree that rises up like an altar, like an altar to which they have brought their supplication, their devotions and their dalliance, their yearning and their desire, and the parrots on the branches high above are screaming, as though the birds are giving voice to the intensity of the drama that is taking place below, to the triumph of the silent spider, and to the agony of the vanquished bird, and to the intentness of the woman and the man, and Maria Sibylla is solemn now, as still as stone, her chest no longer rising and falling with the inhalations and exhalations of her breath, she is no longer breathing, her breath held, held for an impossibly long time, and Mathew van der Lee is so close to her now, and quiet, and he is also barely breathing, his breath also held, until at last in one continuous breath he whispers the words, I thought that I might—I thought that we might, and then Mathew van der Lee goes down on his knees before her.

III

On the deck of the ship there are three figures: Maria Sibylla Merian in ship-dress, a muslin jacket and a chip hat, her body rigid, her face pale; and next to her, her Indianen, Marta, who is dressed much the same as Maria Sibylla, and who is going home with her to the Netherlands; and on Marta's shoulder a macaw perched with its huge wings from time to time flapping, it is the same macaw that had been traded with Mama Cato. The bird has a gold chain fastened to its leg and that in turn is fastened to a heavy bracelet on Marta's wrist, and the bird's feathers are a brilliant mix of yellow and green and turquoise, the yellow is sunflower yellow, like the king's yellow, like Indian dyes and canaries, and the green and the blue are like emerald and cobalt, or a green like mittler's green, or a blue like indigo, steel blue, sapphire.

IV

To Mr. Mathew van der Lee from Maria Sibylla Merian
Surinam, October 5th, 1701
van der Lee Plantation
Paramaribo

Monsieur!
I have received the gentleman's (your) letter of March 19th
and read therein that you are surprised to have received no
letters from me.
I have also received your previous letters, as well as animals
from you on two occasions. The first time, they were
brought by the apothecary, Mister Jonathaan Petiver, but
because I was not in need of such creatures I gave them
back to him and thanked him, requesting that he write to
you, telling you I have no use for such animals and did not
know what to do with them. For the kind of animals I am
looking for are quite different. I am in search of no other
animals, but only wish to study certain transformations,
how one emerges from the other. Therefore, I would ask
you not to send me any more animals, for I have no use for
them.
I continue my work and am still doing it, bringing everything to parchment in its full perfection. But everything I
did not bring, or did not find at the time when I cut short
my journey, cannot now, after so long a period, be similarly

rendered, or remembered, or imagined. And there are so many wondrous, rare things that have never come to light before, and which I will now not be able to bring to light. For the heat in your country is staggering, and many were surprised that I survived, and I have still not fully recovered from my malaria. Thus all my memory associated with that time—which even then had the quality of a dream—has become now all the more ephemeral in its proclivity to fade. And that is so much so that what I have preserved on parchment remains as the only tangible reality that I can summon of that time.

On the journey back, Mr. van der Lee, the sky raged for one entire week with storm, and I believed that God had set upon me, that he was pursuing me in the violent wake of the ship, and we all held fast upon the vessel as our only hope for life while day and night the storm raged, and the good captain, sallow, soaked and freezing, did not let go his place at the helm beside the helmsman. Though this I knew only afterwards, as you might guess, for during the storm I was confined to my own quarters, where never previously sick from motion, I was at that time quite ill. For my weakness from the malaria was still inside me, and that along with the tossing of the ship brought back my fever, and in my fever I believed, Mr. van der Lee, that I was beset upon by God, so filled as I was with remorse for all that had happened and perhaps as much so for what could not. It has been my pride for all my life to rely upon my good sense, and to engage the pragmatic view to carry me, and science to inform me, and God to guide and to protect me. But during those days and nights of storm at sea these went out of balance, Mr. van der Lee, and I came to believe that God was in pursuit of me for my weakness, and that the storm had been sent by His intention to fell me, and that the ship would be destroyed and everyone on board along with myself would perish, unfortunate as they had been to journey with me. I came to believe, too, that the sailors had been correct in their judgment of me as a witch. And I counted myself fortunate that the trials for witchcraft had been long since discontinued in the Netherlands, and that the last of these trials (it afterwards being deemed unlawful) had preceded me by a full 90 years. For were that not the case, I was convinced that I would surely be among those numbers of unfortunate women who were hung or burned or drowned. That is how distraught my mind was, Mr. van der Lee, from the fever and the storm. But then the storm cleared and the ship proceeded forward on a sea that was again calm, and we on board all settled back into its more gentle motion and continued that way for the remainder of the journey.

With that my mind, and my heart, too, became restored, and my days were spent again on deck, where I imagined I could catch the fading scent of the flamboyant trees, and all the other sweet smells of Paramaribo, and Marta, whom I brought back from your land to the Netherlands, and released from her condition of servitude, continued to nurture me throughout the journey with infusions of plants. These skills she had learned from her mother, who in turn had learned them from a Shaman in her former village of Kwamalasamoetoe, which in our language means the Bamboo Sand.

It is true I feel a longing for your land. In my ears there is still the sound of the rivers with their surface waters one minute placid, the next roiling. And my thoughts in some strange way are still carried forward by the sweep of those rivers.

There is great beauty in your land, I have never denied it, Mr. van der Lee; there is great beauty alongside the brutal harshness. I saw many things and many forms of life that I would elsewise not have seen, and I know you glimpsed and understood them, too. Your land has a multitude of small insects that are rare, and other creatures, fierce and strange and beautiful. I observed the habits formed by these creatures, and observed the way they have their own laws and their own proceedings, and these I regarded as metaphors for our own human lives.

I saw the swarm of ants devouring the spider, and the spider devouring the hummingbird. The Palisade Tree that is called the Tree of Paradise, the apple of Sodom that is red and poisonous, the thickness of the jungle with its tangle of vines, the rats, the storks, the armadillos and the lizards, the toucans and the parrots—all of these have I seen, Mr. van der Lee, and they have moved me. I felt, too, the heat that daily burned there, the heat that in the end I believe almost killed me. For the sun burns hotter there than a furnace, and hotter, too, than the strong clear fires used for boiling the sugar cane. But enough has been spoken of that heat.

It is that other heat I wish to speak of now, a heat capable of arousing in some unwilled and wild way. For it was that heat, too, that breathed itself into me, Mr. van der Lee, hot and needling and insistent. And perhaps you will now understand that you wish to recall to me what I have not forgotten.

"What is it you see? What do you see, Madame Sibylla?" How frequently you plied me with such questions, Mr. van der Lee. "What has taken you so far from your home?" you asked. "What keeps you as far? What do you yearn for to the point of dying?"

On that afternoon, Mr. van der Lee, when you followed me into the small forest, the one called Surimombo Forest, you plied me again with these same questions. And with other questions, too, while all the while the heat from the sun was burning me and the moisture in the jungle air was suffocating me. You wore a charm around your neck—untypical of the fastidiousness of your attire—it was a piece of bone, yellowish and slightly curved. You were telling me about the Cerro de la Compana, the mountain that sings like a bell, telling me that it was located south of the savannah on the rolling sandstone hills, and that we must journey there together to hear its bell sound. And I was in the Surimombo Forest and you had followed me and Marta was not with me and I told you again I had already made up my mind to cut short my journey and you went down on your knees before me, down to the leaves on their tiny stems shimmering blue-green on the jungle floor. And the perfume was overpowering from the delicate begonias, the caladiums, the fragile calla lilies, the red passion flowers. And you pushed in against the forest growth, Mr. van der Lee, no longer plying me with questions then, but saying to me instead, "I thought that you might—I thought that we might," and taking me down to the jungle floor with you.

But I must ask you now, as it seems to me I asked you then, there in that staggering heat—what is it that is expected? What can be hoped for now? when it could not be hoped for then?

I could not stay then, Mr. van der Lee, because the heat would have killed me, and apart from that your life on a sugar farm could not be my life. That has not changed. The entrancement that we shared cannot endure. There can be room in my life for only one thing, Mr. van der Lee, for only one thing that is passionate and irresistible. And the rapture that I seek is in the transformations that I study, and in bringing everything to parchment in its full perfection.

A light rain is falling now with the sun still shining. We call that *Leichter Machen*, or the *Lightening*. It is regarded as bewitching light, Mr. van der Lee, and sometimes it is called the love light or the lovers' light, or interchangeably the festival light. And if you stand at some strategic point you can see this light reflected on the waters of the canals still rippling with the falling rain, and to the eye it looks like countless lights reflected on the waters of the canals, and with the outlines of the bridges on each one. It is a fairy scene, Mr. van der Lee.

But when the rain stops, the strange light will disappear, and all will be as normal again, and no one will know what had been seen. There are visions like that, Mr. van der Lee. I did not answer your earlier letters because there seemed no more on my part to be said, and because I did not wish to give the impression that there was something to be hoped for or expected. I still do not wish to give that impression, Mr. van der Lee.

I write and ask you now to not send animals. For I have no use for them. That is, for the animals such as you sent previously. I wish only to study certain transformations, how one emerges from the other. And I therefore ask you not to send me animals, for I have no use for them.

But if you must send something, Mr. van der Lee, send butterflies, small caligo butterflies, diurnal butterflies and ricinis, sactails, jatrophas, moon moths, peacock moths, send primulas with nun moths, pale tussocks and pease blossom moths, tachinid flies and calicoid flies, owl moths and harlequin beetles, or send lantern flies, Mr. van der Lee, in a box that is filled up with the lantern flies, and make certain they are alive when you send them and can be kept living, so that when I open the lid, Mr. van der Lee, they will rise up like fire, and shoot out of the box like a flame, and that will delight me, Mr. van der Lee, and will remind me of that other fire that one day rose up inside me.

Ash City Stomp
Richard Butner

She had dated Secrest for six weeks before she asked for the Big Favor. The Big Favor sounded like, "I need to get to Asheville to check out the art therapy program in their psychology grad school," but in reality she had hard drugs that needed to be transported to an old boyfriend of hers in the mountains, and the engine in her 1982 Ford Escort had caught fire on the expressway earlier that spring.

Secrest was stable, a high school geometry teacher who still went to see bands at the Mad Monk and Axis most nights of the week. They had met at the birthday party of a mutual friend who lived in Southport. She had signified her attraction to him by hurling pieces of wet cardboard at him at two a.m. as he walked (in his wingtip Doc Martens) to his fully operative and freshly waxed blue 1990 Honda Civic wagon.

The Big Favor started in Wilmington, North Carolina, where they both lived. He had packed the night before—a single duffel bag. She had a pink Samsonite train case (busted lock, $1.98 from the American Way thrift store) and two large paper grocery bags full of various items, as well as some suggestions for motels in Asheville and sights to see along the way. These suggestions were scrawled on the back of a flyer for a show they'd attended the week before. The band had been a jazz quartet from New York, led by a guy playing saxophone. She hated saxophones. Secrest had loved the show, but she'd been forced to drink to excess to make it through to the end of all the screeching and tootling, even though she'd been trying to cut back on the drinking and smoking and related activities ever since they'd started dating.

That was one of the reasons she liked him—it had been a lot easier to quit her bad habits around him. He had a calming influence. She'd actually met him several months before, when he still had those unfashionably pointy sideburns. She pegged him as a sap the minute he mentioned that he was a high school teacher. But at the Southport birthday party they had ended up conversing, and he surprised her with his interests, with the bands and books and movies he liked and disliked. Since they'd started dating she had stopped taking half-pints of Wild Turkey in her purse when she worked lunch shifts at the Second Story Restaurant. His friends were used to hunching on the stoop outside his apartment to smoke, but she simply did without and stayed inside in the air-conditioning.

Hauling a load of drugs up to ex-boyfriend Rusty, though, was an old bad habit that paid too well to give up, at least not right away.

She compared her travel suggestions with his; he had scoured guidebooks at the local public library for information on budget motels, and he'd downloaded an online version of *North Carolina Scenic Byways.* His suggestions included several Civil War and Revolutionary War sites. Her suggestions included Rock City, which he vetoed because it turned out Rock City was in Tennessee, and the Devil's Stomping Ground, which he agreed to and did more research on at the library the next day.

"The Devil's Stomping Ground," he read from his notes, "is a perfect circle in the midst of the woods.

"According to natives, the Devil paces the circle every night, concocting his evil snares for mankind and trampling over anything growing in the circle or anything left in the circle."

"That's what the dude at the club said," she said without looking up from her sketchbook. She was sketching what looked like ornate wrought iron railings such as you'd find in New Orleans. She really did want to get into grad school in art therapy at Western Carolina.

"Of course, it's not really a historical site, but I guess it's doable," Secrest said. "It's only an hour out of our way, according to Triple A."

"So, there you go."

"This could be the beginning of something big, too—there are a lot of these Devil spots in the United States. We should probably try to hit them all at some point. After you get out of grad school, I mean."

"OK." It wasn't the first time he had alluded to their relationship as a long-term one, even though the question of love, let alone something as specific as marriage, had yet to come up directly in their conversations. She didn't know how to react when he did this, but he didn't seem deflated by her ambivalence.

That was how the trip came together. She had tried to get an interview with someone in the art therapy program at Western Carolina, but they never called back. Still, she finished putting together a portfolio.

The morning of the Big Favor, she awoke to a curiously spacious bed. He was up already. Not in the apartment. She peeked out through the blinds over the air conditioner and saw him inside the car, carefully cleaning the windshield with paper towels and glass cleaner. She put her clothes on and went down to the street. It was already a hazy, muggy day. He had cleaned the entire interior of the car, which she'd always thought of as spotless in the first place. The windshield glistened. All of the books and papers she had strewn around on the passenger floorboard, all of the empty coffee cups and wadded-up napkins that had accumulated there since she'd started dating him, all of the stains on the dashboard, all were gone.

"What are you doing?" she asked, truly bewildered.

"Can't go on a road trip in a dirty car," he said, smiling. He adjusted a new travel-sized box of tissues between the two front seats and stashed a few packets of antiseptic wipes in the glove compartment before crawling out of the car with the cleaning supplies. As they walked up the steps to his apartment she gazed back at the car in wonder, noting that he'd even scoured the tires. She remembered the story he'd told of trying to get a vanity plate for the car, a single zero. North Carolina DMV wouldn't allow it, for reasons as vague as any Supreme Court ruling. Neither would they allow two zeroes. He made it all the way up to five zeroes and they still wouldn't allow it. So he gave up and got the fairly random HDS-1800.

After several cups of coffee, she repacked her traincase and grocery bags four times while he sat on the stoop reading the newspaper. They left a little after nine a.m., and she could tell that he was rankled that they didn't leave before nine sharp. It always took her a long time to get ready, whether or not she was carefully taping baggies of drugs inside the underwear she had on.

Once they made it north out of Wilmington, the drive was uneventful. He kept the needle exactly on 65, even though the Honda didn't have cruise control. He stayed in the rightmost lane except when passing the occasional grandma who wasn't doing the speed limit. After he had recounted some current events he'd gleaned from the paper, they dug into the plastic case of mix tapes he had stashed under his seat. She nixed the jazz, and he vetoed the country tapes she'd brought along as too depressing, so they compromised and listened to some forties bluegrass he'd taped especially for the trip.

"You're going to be hearing a lot of this when you're in grad school in the mountains," he said.

She was bored before they even hit Burgaw, and her sketchpad was in the hatchback. She pawed the dash for the Sharpie that she'd left there, then switched to the glovebox where she found it living in parallel with a tire gauge and a McDonald's coffee stirrer. She carefully lettered WWSD on the knuckles of her left hand.

What Would Satan Do? Satan would not screw around, that's for sure. Satan would have no trouble hauling some drugs to the mountains. She flipped her hand over and stared at it, fingers down. Upside down, because the D was malformed, it looked like

OSMM. Oh Such Magnificent Miracles. Ontological Secrets Mystify Millions. Other Saviors Make Mistakes.

In Newton Grove, she demanded a pee break, and she recovered her sketchpad from the hatch. Just past Raleigh, they left the interstate and found the Devil's Stomping Ground with few problems, even though there was only a single sign. She had imagined there'd be more to it, a visitor's center or something, at least a parking lot. Instead there was a metal sign that had been blasted with a shotgun more than once, and a dirt trail. He slowed the Honda and pulled off onto the grassy shoulder. Traffic was light on the state road, just the occasional overloaded pickup swooshing by on the way to Bear Creek and Bennett and further west to Whynot. He pulled his camera from the duffel bag, checked that all the car doors were locked, and led the way down the trail into the woods. It was just after noon on a cloudy day, and the air smelled thickly of pine resin. Squirrels chased each other from tree to tree, chattering and shrieking.

It was only two hundred yards to the clearing. The trees opened up onto a circle about forty feet across. The circle was covered in short, wiry grass, but as the guidebook had said, none grew along the outer edge. The clearing was ringed by a dirt path. Nothing grew there, but the path was not empty. It was strewn with litter: smashed beer bottles, cigarette butts, shredded pages from hunting and porno magazines were all ground into the dust. These were not the strangest things on the path, though.

The strangest thing on the path was the Devil. He was marching around the path, counter-clockwise; just then he was directly across the clearing from them. They stood and waited for him to walk around to their side.

The Devil was rail thin, wearing a too-large red union suit that had long since faded to pink. It draped over his caved-in chest in front and bagged down almost to his knees in the seat. A tattered red bath towel was tied around his neck, serving as a cape. He wore muddy red suede shoes that looked like they'd been part of a Christmas elf costume. His black hair was tousled from the wind, swooping back on the sides but sticking straight up on the top of his head. His cheeks bore the pockmarks of acne scars; above them, he wore gold Elvis Presley-style sunglasses. His downcast eyes seemed to be focusing on the black hairs sprouting from his chin and upper lip, too sparse to merit being called a goatee.

"This must be the place," she said.

The Devil approached, neither quickening nor slowing his pace. She could tell that this was unnerving Secrest a bit. Whenever he was nervous, he sniffed, and that was what he was doing. Sniffing.

"You smell something?" asked the Devil, pushing his sunglasses to the top of his head. "Fire and/or brimstone, perhaps?" The Devil held up both hands and waggled them. His fingers were covered in black grime.

Secrest just stood still, but she leaned over and smelled the Devil's hand.

"Motor oil!" she pronounced. The Devil reeked of motor oil and rancid sweat masked by cheap aftershave. "Did your car break down?"

"I don't know nothing about any car," the Devil said. "All I know about is various plots involving souls, and about trying to keep anything fresh or green or good out of this path. But speaking of cars, if you're heading west on I-40, can I catch a ride with y'all?"

"Uh, no," Secrest said, then he turned to her. "Come on, let's go. There's nothing to see here." He sniffed again.

"Nothing to see?" cried the Devil. "Look at this circle! You see how clean it is? You know how long it took me to fix this place up?"

"Actually, it's filthy," Secrest said, poking his toe at the shattered remains of a whiskey bottle, grinding the clear glass into a candy bar wrapper beneath.

The Devil paused and glanced down to either side.

"Well, you should've seen it a while back."

Secrest turned to leave, tugging gently at her sleeve. She followed but said, "C'mon, I've picked up tons of hitchhikers in my time, and I've never been messed with. Besides, there's two of us, and he's a scrawny little dude."

"A scrawny little schizophrenic."

"He's funny. Live a little, give the guy a ride. You've read *On the Road*, right?"

"Yes. *The Subterraneans* was better." Secrest hesitated, as if reconsidering, which gave the Devil time to creep up right behind them.

"Stay on the path!" the Devil said, smiling. "Forward, march!"

Secrest sighed and turned back toward the path to the car. They marched along for a few more steps, and then he suddenly reached down, picked up a handful of dirt, then spun and hurled it at the Devil.

The Devil sputtered and threw his hands up far too late to keep from getting pelted with dirt and gravel.

"Go away!" Secrest said. He looked like he was trying to shoo a particularly ferocious dog.

"What did you do that for? You've ruined my outfit."

She walked over and helped brush the dirt off. "C'mon, now you've *got* to give him a ride." The Devil looked down at her hand and saw the letters there.

"Ah, yep, what would Satan do? Satan would catch a ride with you fine folks, that's what he'd do. Much obliged."

From there back to the interstate the Devil acted as a chatty tour guide, pointing out abandoned gold mines and Indian mounds along the way. Secrest had the windows down, so the Devil had to shout over the wind blowing through the cabin of the Honda. Secrest wouldn't turn on the AC until he hit the interstate. "It's not efficient to operate the air conditioning until you're cruising at highway speeds," he had told her.

That was fine with her; the wind helped to blow some of the stink off of the Devil.

A highway sign showed that they were twenty-five miles out of Winston-Salem. "Camel City coming up," the Devil said, keeping up his patter.

"Yeah, today we've rolled through Oak City, the Bull City, the Gate City, all the fabulous trucker cities of North Carolina," Secrest replied. "What's the nickname for Asheville?"

"Ash City," said the Devil.

"Fair enough," Secrest said.

They got back on the interstate near Greensboro, and Secrest rolled up all the power windows. When he punched the AC button on the dash, though, nothing happened. The little blue LED failed to light. Secrest punched the button over and over, but no cool air came out. He sniffed and rolled down all of the windows again.

He took the next exit and pulled into the parking lot of a large truck stop, stopping far from the swarms of eighteen wheelers. He got out and popped the hood.

"You guys should check out the truck stop," he said. "Buy a magazine or something." In the few weeks she'd known Secrest, she'd seen him like this several times. Silent, focused, just like solving a problem in math class. She hated it when he acted this way, and stalked off to find the restroom.

When she returned, he was sitting in the driver's seat, rubbing his hands with an antiseptic wipe.

"What's the verdict?"

"Unknown. I checked the fuses, the drive belt to the compressor, the wires to the compressor . . . nothing looks broken. I'll have to take it to the shop when we get back to Wilmington. You don't have a nail brush in your purse, do you?"

"A what?"

"A nail brush, for cleaning under your fingernails. Never mind."

"Don't forget me," the Devil said, throwing open the back door. He had a large plastic bag in his hand. Secrest pulled back onto the road and turned down the entrance ramp. The Devil pulled out a packaged apple pie, a can of lemonade, and a copy of *Barely Legal* magazine and set them on the seat next to him. Secrest glanced back at the Devil in the rearview as he sped up to enter the stream of traffic.

"What have you got back there?"

"Pie and a drink. Want some?"

"No, I want you to put them away. You're going to get the back seat all dirty."

The Devil folded down one of the rear seats to get into the hatch compartment.

"What are you *doing*?" asked Secrest, staring up into the rearview. The car drifted lazily into the path of a Cadillac in the center lane until Secrest looked down from the mirror and swerved back. She turned to look at what was going on and got a faceful of baggy pink Devil butt.

The Devil didn't respond; he just continued rummaging. Finally he turned and gave a satisfied sigh. He had a roll of duct tape from Secrest's emergency kit, and he zipped off a long piece. Starting at the front of the floorboards in the back seat, he fixed the tape to the carpet, rolled it up over the transmission hump and over to the other side, carefully bisecting the cabin. A gleaming silver snake guarding the back seat of the car.

"I get to be dirty on this side," he said. "You can do whatever you want up there." Then he picked up his copy of *Barely Legal* and started thumbing through it, holding the magazine up so it covered his face.

Secrest didn't argue. She looked over at him and noticed he was preoccupied with other matters. Secrest's hands, still dirty from poking around in the engine compartment, had stained the pristine blue plastic of the steering wheel, and he rubbed at these stains as he drove along.

She could see the speedometer from her seat, and he was over the speed limit, inching up past 70 steadily. He'd also started hanging out in the middle lane, not returning immediately to the safety of the right lane after he passed someone. Traffic thinned out as the land changed from flat plains to rolling hills, but he still stayed in the middle lane. Plenty of folks drove ten miles over the speed limit. That was standard. Secrest probably attracted more attention the way he normally drove—folks were always zooming up behind him in the right lane, cursing at him because he had the gall to do the speed limit. Now he was acting more like a normal driver—breaking the speed limit, changing lanes.

The Devil sat silently on the hump in the middle of the back seat, concentrating on the road ahead. The pie wrapper and empty can rolled around on the seat next to him. She watched the speedometer inch its way up. At 75 Secrest suddenly started to pull over through the empty right lane into the emergency lane.

"What are you doing?" she asked. Then she craned her head around just in time to catch the first blips of the siren from the trooper's car. Blue lights flashed from the dash of the unmarked black sedan.

The Devil leaned forward and whispered in her ear. "Be cool, I'll handle this," he said.

"Goddamn!" she said, and this curse invoked a daydream. In her daydream, she keeps saying "Goddamn!" over and over. Secrest is busy with slowing down, putting his hazard lights on, and stopping in the emergency lane. The Devil is not in her daydream. She pops the door handle and jumps out while he's still rolling to a stop, losing her footing and scraping her knees and elbows against the pavement as she rolls to the grassy shoulder. She stands up, starts running into the trees along the side of the road. As she goes, she reaches up under her skirt and peels the Ziploc from her panties, but it's already broken open. Little white packets fly through the air in all directions. They break open too, and it's snowing as she charges off into the woods. The trooper chases her, and just as the last packet flies from her fingertips, he tackles her. She starts to cry.

Outside of her daydream, the state trooper asked Secrest for his license and registration. He retrieved these from the glove compartment, where they were stacked on top of a pile of oil change receipts and maps. The trooper carefully watched Secrest's hand, inches away from her drug-laden crotch, as he did this. She was sitting on her own hands.

"Ma'am, could you please move your hands to where I can see them?"

She slid her hands out and placed them flat on top of her thighs.

The trooper took the registration certificate and Secrest's license, but he kept glancing back and forth from them to her hands.

"Nice tattoo, isn't it, officer?" the Devil said, pointing to the smeared letters on her knuckles. The trooper slid his mirrored sunglasses a fraction and peered into the back seat of the car, staring the Devil in the eye.

"Not really. You should see the tattoos my Amy got the minute she went off to the college. I won't even get into the piercings."

"Kids these days . . . ," said the Devil.

"Yep. What are you gonna do?" The trooper pushed his sunglasses back up on his nose and straightened up. "Well, anyway, here's your paperwork. Try to watch your speed out there, now." He smiled and handed the cards back to Secrest.

They stopped for gas near Morganton. There was a Phillips 66 there.

"The mother road," Secrest said.

"Last section decommissioned in 1984, and now all we have are these lousy gas stations," said the Devil.

"Ooh, 1984. Doubleplusungood," Secrest said.

"I'll pump," the Devil said. "Premium or regular?"

"Doubleplusregular."

Inside, Secrest got a large bottle of spring water, another packet of travel-size tissues, and breath mints. She stared at the array of snacks and the jeweled colors of the bottles of soda, trying to decide. Behind the counter, a teenage boy tuned a banjo, twanging away on the strings while fiddling with the tuning pegs.

It took her a long time to decide to forgo snacks altogether, and it took the teenager a long time to tune the banjo. She tried to think of a joke about *Deliverance*, but couldn't. Secrest went up to pay, and she headed for the door.

She went around to the side of the building to the ladies' room. The lock was busted. She sat to pee, carefully maintaining the position of the payload in her underwear. The door swung open and the Devil walked in.

"You know, I've been wanting to get into your panties ever since we met."

"Get the *hell* out of here, or I'll start screaming," she said.

"Oh, that's a funny one," the Devil said. "But I'm staying right here. You owe me."

"I don't owe you anything." She was trying to remember if she had anything sharp in her purse.

"Of course you do. Why do you think that cop didn't haul your ass out of the car? You have me to thank for that, for the fact that all that shit in your panties is intact, and for the fact that you're not rotting in one of their cages right about now."

"OK, for one thing, I don't know what you're talking about. For another, get out of here or the screaming really starts."

"What I'm talking about is all that smack you've got taped inside your underwear. The dope. *Las drogas.* I want you to give it to me, all of it, right now. That stuff is bad for you, in case you hadn't heard, and it can get you in a world of trouble."

"Screw you. You're not getting any of it. I was serious about the screaming part."

But then it didn't matter, because Secrest came in right behind the Devil. He spun the Devil around by the shoulder and kneed him in the crotch. It was the first time she'd ever seen him do anything remotely resembling violence. The Devil crumpled to the concrete floor.

"Screw you both," the Devil gasped. "I'll take the Greyhound bus anywhere I want to ride."

They checked in at the Economy Lodge in Asheville. Secrest checked the film in his camera and folded up an AAA map of downtown into his pocket and set out to see the sights.

"The historic district is a perfect square," he declared, as if he'd made a scientific discovery. "So I'd like to walk every street in the grid. I figure I'll get started today with the up and down and finish up tomorrow on the back and forth while you're at the university. Want to come with?"

She told him she was tired and crashed out on top of the musty comforter with all of her clothes on while the overworked air-conditioner chugged away.

She met Rusty at the Maple Leaf Bar. It had been less than two years since she'd seen him, but he had to have lost close to fifty pounds, and his hair, once a luxurious mass, was now thinning and stringy. He still got that same giddy smile when he caught sight of her, though, and he rocked back and forth with inaudible laughter. They walked back to his place on McDowell Street, where he gave her the $900 he owed her plus $600 for the drugs in her underwear. They celebrated the deal by getting high in his second floor bedroom, sitting on the end of the bed and staring out the gable window over the rooftops of old downtown as the fan whirred rhythmically overhead. After a few minutes, he collapsed onto his back, let out a long sigh, and then was silent.

She was daydreaming again. In her daydream, Secrest is out walking the maze, crisscrossing through the streets until he sees the Devil walking toward him from the opposite direction. The Devil's shoes look even filthier, and his goatee has vanished into the rest of the stubble on his face. His shirt is stained with sweat under the arms and around the collar, turning the pink to black.

"Not you again," Secrest says, kicking the nearest lamppost with the toe of his wingtip. "I was almost finished with walking every street in the historic district." He looks away, back toward the green hills of the Pisgah Forest to the south, then turns back, as if the Devil will have vanished in the interim.

"Yes, you're very good at staying on the path," the Devil says. "But now it's time for a little detour. Your girlfriend is sitting in an apartment on McDowell Street."

"Oh, really?" says Secrest.

"Yes, and the police are closing in, because an old friend of hers has ratted her out to the cops. They're probably climbing the stairs right now."

Or maybe he says, "An old friend of hers is dying on the bed next to her right now."

Anyway, the Devil reaches out and grabs Secrest's hand, shaking it energetically.

"Thanks for the ride, buddy," he says.

Then Secrest comes running up the street to save her.

King Rat

Karen Joy Fowler

One day when I was in the first grade, Scott Arnold told me he was going to wash my face with snow on my way home from school. By playground rules he couldn't hit a girl, but there was nothing to prevent him from chasing me for blocks, knocking me over and sitting on me while stuffing ice down my neck, and this was what he planned to do. I forget why.

I spent the afternoon with the taste of dread in my mouth. Scott Arnold was a lot bigger than I was. So was everybody else. I was the smallest girl in my first grade class and smaller than most of the kindergartners, too. So I decided not to go home at all. Instead I would surprise my father with a visit to his office.

My school was about halfway between my home and the university where my father worked. I left by a back door. There was snow in the gutters and the yards, but the sidewalks were clear, the walking easy. The university was only five blocks away, and a helpful adult took me across the one busy street. I found the psychology building with no trouble; I'd been there many times with my dad.

The ornate entrance door was too heavy for me. I had to sit on the cold steps until someone else opened it and let me slip inside. If I'd been with my father, we would have taken the elevator to his office on the fourth floor. He might have remembered to lift me up so that I could be the one to press the fourth floor button. If no one lifted me, I couldn't reach it.

I took the stairs instead. I didn't know that it took two flights to go one floor; I counted carefully but exited too early. There was nothing to tip me off to this. The halls of the first and the second and the third floors looked exactly like those of the fourth: green paint on the walls, flyers, a drinking fountain, rows of wooden doors on both sides.

I knocked on what I believed was my father's office, and a man I didn't know opened it. Apparently he thought I'd interrupted him as a prank. "You shouldn't be wandering around here," he said angrily. "I've half a mind to call the police." The man banged the door shut, and the sharp noise combined with my embarrassment made me cry. I was dressed for snow, and so I was also getting uncomfortably hot.

I retreated to the stairwell where I sat awhile, crying and thinking. In the lobby of the entryway a giant globe was set into the floor. I loved to spin it, close my eyes, put my finger down on Asia or Ecuador or the painted oceans. I thought that perhaps I could go back to the entrance, find the globe again, start all over. I couldn't imagine where I'd made my mistake, but I thought I could manage not to repeat it. I'd been to my father's office so many times.

But I couldn't stop crying, and this humiliated me more than anything. Only babies cried, Scott Arnold said, whenever he'd made me do so. I did my best not to let anyone see me, waited until the silence in the stairwell persuaded me it was empty before I went back down.

Then I couldn't find the globe again. Every door I tried opened on a green hallway and a row of identical wooden doors. It seemed I couldn't even manage to leave the building. I was more and more frightened. Even if I could find my father's office, I would never dare knock for fear the other man would be the one to answer.

I decided to go to the basement where the animal lab was. My father might be there or one of his students, someone I knew. I took the stairs as far down as they went and opened the door.

The light was different in the basement—no windows—and the smell was different, too. Fur and feces and disinfectant. I'd been there dozens of times. I knew to skirt the monkeys' cages. I knew they would rattle the bars, show me their teeth, howl, and if I came close enough, they would reach through to grab me. Monkeys were strong for all they were so small. They would bite.

Behind the monkeys were the rats. Their cages were stacked one on the next, so many of them they formed aisles like in the grocery store.

There was never more than a single rat in a single cage. They shredded the newspaper lining and made themselves damp, smelly-confetti nests. When I passed they came out of these nests to look at me, their paws wrapped over the bars, their noses ticking busily from side to side. These were hooded rats with black faces and tiny, nibbling teeth. I felt that their eyes were sympathetic. I felt that they were worried to see me there, lost without my father, and this concern was a comfort to me.

At the end of one of the aisles I found a man I didn't know. He was tall and blond, with pale blue eyes. He knelt and shook my hand so my empty mitten, tied to my sleeve, bounced about in the air. "I'm a stranger here," he said. He pronounced the words oddly. "Newly arrived. So I don't know everyone the way I should. My name is Vidkun Thrane." A large hooded rat climbed out of his shirt pocket. It looked at me with the same worried eyes the caged rats had shown. "I'm not entirely without friends," the blond man said. "Here is King Rat, come to make your acquaintance."

Because of his eyes, I told King Rat my father's name. We all took the elevator up to the fourth floor together.

My rescuer was a Norwegian psychologist who'd just come to work in the United States with men like my father, studying theories of learning by running rats through mazes. In Oslo, Vidkun had a wife and a son who was just the age of my older brother. My father was very glad to see him. Me, he was less glad to see.

I cared too much about my dignity to mention Scott Arnold. The door I had knocked on earlier was the office of the department chair, a man who, my father said, already had it in for him. I was told never to come as a surprise to see him again. Vidkun was told to come to supper.

Vidkun visited us several times during his residency, and even came to our Christmas dinner since his own family was so far away. He gave me a book, *Castles and Dragons, A Collection of Fairytales from Many Lands.* I don't know how he chose it. Perhaps the clerk recommended it. Perhaps his son had liked it.

However he found it, it turned out to be the perfect book for me. I read it over and over. It satisfied me in a way no other book ever has, grew up with me the way a good book does. These, then, are the two men I credit with making me a writer. First, my father, a stimulus/response psychologist who believed in reinforcement in the lab, but whose parenting ran instead to parables and medicinal doses of Aesop's fables.

Second, a man I hardly knew, a stranger from very far away, who showed me his home on the large, spinning globe and, one Christmas, brought me the book I wanted above all others to read. I have so few other memories of Vidkun. A soft voice and a gentle manner. The worried eyes of King Rat looking out from his pocket. The unfortunate same first name, my father told me later, as the famous Norwegian traitor. That can't have been easy growing up, I remember my father saying.

The stories in *Castles and Dragons* are full of magical incident. Terrible things may happen before the happy ending, but there are limits to how terrible. Good people get their reward, so do bad people. The stories are much softer than Grimm and Andersen. It was many, many years before I was tough enough for the pure thing.

Even now some of the classics remain hard for me. Of these, worst by a good margin is "The Pied Piper of Hamlin." I never liked the first part with the rats. I saw King

Rat and all the others dancing to their doom with their busy noses and worried eyes. Next, I hated the lying parents. And most of all, I hated the ending.

My father always tried to comfort me. The children were wonderfully happy at the end, he said. They were guests at an eternal birthday party where the food was spun sugar and the music just as sweet. They never stopped eating long enough to think of how their parents must miss them.

I wasn't persuaded. By my own experience, on Halloween there always came a moment when you'd eaten too much candy. One by one the children would remember their homes. One by one they would leave the table determined to find their way out of the mountain. They would climb the carved stairs up and then down into darkness. They would lose themselves in caves and stony corridors until their only choice, eventually and eternally, was to follow the music back to the piper. It was not a story with an ending at all. In my mind it stretched horribly onward.

Shortly after I met Vidkun, I wrote my own book. This was an illustrated collection of short pieces. The protagonists were all baby animals. In these stories a pig or a puppy or a lamb wandered inadvertently away from the family. After a frightening search, the stray was found again; a joyful reunion took place. The stories got progressively shorter as the book went on. My parents thought I was running out of energy for it. In fact, I was less and less able to bear the middle part of the story. In each successive version, I made the period of separation shorter.

I can guess now, as I couldn't then, what sorts of things may have happened to the monkeys in the psych lab. I suppose that the rats' lives were not entirely taken up with cheese, tucked into mazes like Easter eggs. As I grew up, there were more and more questions I thought of but didn't ask. Real life is only for the very toughest.

My brother went away to college, and I cried for three days. In his junior year, he went farther, to the south of England and an exchange program at Sussex University. During spring break, he went to Norway on a skiing vacation. He found himself alone at Easter, and he called the only person in all of Norway that he knew.

Vidkun insisted my brother come stay with him and his wife, immediately drove to the hostel to fetch him. He had wonderful memories of our family, he said. He'd spoken of us often. He asked after me. He was cordial and gracious, my brother told me, genuinely welcoming, and yet, clearly something was terribly wrong. My brother had never imagined a house so empty. Easter dinner was long and lavish and cheerless. Sometime during it, Vidkun stopped talking. His wife went early to bed and left the two men sitting at the table.

"My son," Vidkun said suddenly. "My son also took a trip abroad. Like you. He went to America, which I always told him was so wonderful. He went two years ago."

Vidkun's son had touched down in New York and spent a week there, then took a bus to cross the country. He wanted to get some idea of size and landscape. He was meeting up with friends in Yellowstone. Somewhere along the route, he vanished.

When word came, Vidkun flew to New York. The police showed him a statement, allowed him to speak to a witness who'd talked with his son, seen him board the bus. No witness could be found who saw him leave it. Vidkun searched for him or word of him for three months, took the same bus trip two times in each direction, questioning everyone he met on the route. No one who knew the family believed the boy would not have come home if he were able. They were all just so sad, my brother said.

So often over the years when I haven't wanted to, I've thought of Vidkun on that bus. The glass next to him is dirty and in some lights is a window and in others is a mirror. In his pocket is his son's face. I think how he forces himself to eat at least once every day, asks each person he meets to look at his picture. "No," they all say. "No." Such a long trip. Such a big country. Who could live there?

I hate this story.

Vidkun, for your long ago gifts, I return now two things.

The first is that I will not change this ending. This is your story. No magic, no clever rescue, no final twist. As long as you can't pretend otherwise, neither will I.

And then, because you once brought me a book with no such stories in it, the second thing I promise is not to write this one again. The older I get, the more I want a happy ending. Never again will I write about a child who disappears forever. All my pipers will have soft voices and gentle manners. No child so lost King Rat can't find him and bring him home.

Contributors

Christopher Barzak has published stories in magazines including *Nerve, Realms of Fantasy, Lady Churchill's Rosebud Wristlet, Strange Horizons, The Vestal Review,* and *The Year's Best Fantasy & Horror.* He recently completed his Master's Degree in English at Youngstown State University. He grew up in rural Ohio, has lived in California and Michigan, now lives in an attic back in post-industrial Ohio, has no pets to speak of, no longer smokes except socially, and likes to dance.

Richard Butner is a freelance journalist and short story writer. For some reason, he holds an M.S. in Computer Engineering (with an English minor) and a B.S. in Electrical Engineering, both from North Carolina State University. His stories have appeared in *Lady Churchill's Rosebud Wristlet, Scream,* and *RE Arts & Letters.* He co-edited *Intersections: The Sycamore Hill Anthology* with John Kessel and Mark L. Van Name. He lives in Raleigh, North Carolina.

Alan DeNiro's stories have appeared in *Santa Monica Review, Fence, Strange Horizons, 3rd Bed, Rabid Transit,* and elsewhere, and his work has been shortlisted for the O. Henry Award. He has recently completed a novel, *The Memory Palace of Ray Fell,* which concerns the perils of dating imaginary people.

Carol Emshwiller was a dreadful student. Just squeaked by with cs and a few ds. Failed freshman English and had to repeat it. Almost failed again. She went all the way through music school, playing the violin, but she had slow fingers so failed at that. She went to war. *All!* the men were gone, so, though she was a pacifist, she went with them. After war, she went to art school. First thing she didn't fail at. She always hated writing. It's too *hard.* But, like finally learning to love lobster, now lobster is her favorite. She's failed at even that, though. She's become allergic to it. Now she loves writing. She loves that it *is* so hard—that you never stop learning how to do it. Small Beer Press recently published her seventh and eighth books.

Jeffrey Ford is the author of the novels *The Physiognomy* (World Fantasy Award winner and a *New York Times* Notable Book), *Memoranda* (a *New York Times* Notable Book), *The Beyond* (*Washington Post Book World's* Best of 2001). His most recent novel is *The Portrait of Mrs. Charbuque,* which was published simultaneously with his first story collection, *The*

Fantasy Writer's Assistant & Other Stories. His short fiction has appeared in magazines (*Fantasy & Science Fiction, SciFiction, Event Horizon, Black Gate, Lady Churchill's Rosebud Wristlet, MSS, The Northwest Review, Puerto Del Sol*) and anthologies (*The Year's Best Fantasy & Horror, The Green Man, Leviathan 3,* and *The Journal of Pulse-Pounding Narratives*). Ford lives in South Jersey with his wife, Lynn, and two sons, Jack and Derek. He teaches Writing and Literature at Brookdale Community College in Monmouth County, New Jersey.

Karen Joy Fowler is the author of two story collections and three novels and is a frequent teacher of writing workshops. She lives with her husband in Davis, California. She wishes someday to have published more books than you can count on the fingers of both hands. She wishes this more often than she manages to actually make herself work on book number six. She's starting to think the opposable thumb is not all it's cracked up to be.

Greer Gilman's novel, *Moonwise,* is decidedly thorny. It won the Crawford Award and was short listed for the Tiptree and Mythopoeic Fantasy Awards. "A Crowd of Bone" is one of three linked stories, variations on a winter myth. The first, "Jack Daw's Pack," was a Nebula finalist for 2001 and the subject of a *Foundation* interview by Michael Swanwick. A sometime forensic librarian, Gilman lives in Cambridge, Massachusetts, and travels in stone circles.

John Gonzalez grew up in Battle Creek, Michigan, the Cereal Capital of the World. He spent much of his early life trying to escape, but the attack dogs seemed to anticipate his every move. After several years in graduate school and employment as a social worker, John landed a job as the house writer for Outrage Games, a videogame developer in Ann Arbor whose next game, the fantasy-SF action-adventure Alter Echo, is due out in August 2003. In 2001 he attended the Clarion Writers' Workshop. "Impala" is his first publication.

Glen Hirshberg's first novel, *The Snowman's Children* (Carroll & Graf), was published in December, 2002. His ghost stories have appeared in numerous anthologies, including *The Year's Best Fantasy & Horror, The Mammoth Book of Best New Horror,* and *Dark Terrors 6,* and have been nominated for the International Horror Guild Award and twice for the World Fantasy Award. *The Two Sams,* a collection of his supernatural fiction, will be published by Carroll & Graf later this year.

Samantha Hunt is a writer and artist from New York. Much to her delight, her stories and poems have appeared in *McSweeney's, Jubilat, Swerve, The Iowa Review, Literary, Colorado,* and *Western Humanities Reviews.* Her first play, "The Difference Engine," a story about the life of Charles Babbage, is currently in production. Hunt's artwork can be found at the New York Public Library. Of late, she is completing a novel.

Alex Irvine's first novel, *A Scattering of Jades* (Tor) appeared in 2002. His second, *One King, One Soldier* (Del Rey), is forthcoming, as is a short-story collection, *Unintended Consequences* (Subterranean Press). He has published short fiction in *Fantasy & Science Fiction, Asimov's, SciFiction, Lady Churchill's Rosebud Wristlet,* and in anthologies including *Starlight 3, Polyphony 2,* and *Live Without a Net.* He teaches English at Gardiner Area High School, in Gardiner, Maine—the home of Edwin Arlington Robinson—and lives in Portland with his wife, Beth, and their twins, Emma and Ian.

Shelley Jackson is the author of *The Melancholy of Anatomy,* the hypertext novel *Patchwork Girl,* and several children's books. She lives in Brooklyn.

Kelly Link co-edits the zine, *Lady Churchill's Rosebud Wristlet.* Her first collection, *Stranger Things Happen,* was nominated for the Firecracker Award and was selected as a best book of the year by Salon, *Locus,* and *The Village Voice.* She is working on more short stories.

Beth Adele Long's short fiction has appeared in *Lady Churchill's Rosebud Wristlet* and *Electric Velocipede.* She is a graduate of the Clarion Writers' Workshop and a former writer-in-residence at the Kerouac House in Orlando. By day she works as a graphic arts jack-of-all-trades for a fantabulous little company in Cape Canaveral. She lives in Florida and still complains about the cold winters, much to her northern friends' disgust.

Maureen McHugh (1959) has spent most of her life in Ohio but has lived in New York City and, for a year, in Shijiazhuang, China. Her first novel, *China Mountain Zhang,* won the Tiptree Award. Her latest novel, *Nekropolis,* was a Book Sense 76 pick and a *New York Times* Editor's Choice. Right now she lives with her husband, son, and two dogs next to a dairy farm. Sometimes, in the summer, black and white Holsteins look over the fence at them.

Susan Mosser has been writing for a while now and finds it to be just the very best part of sentience. By grace of unemployment, in the steamy wastelands of central Florida, she is writing two books (one novel and one mostly not) and ghost-editing a third, and lately has taken to scribbling bits of subtly rhythmic verse on gasoline receipts while driving. Susan is a graduate of the Clarion Writers' Workshop.

Ed Park is the author of a few published stories that have changed the way we see the world, two unpublished novels that haven't, an unpublished memoir in which every paragraph begins with "In," and two books illustrated by the fabulous Michael K. Carter. He is a senior editor at *The Village Voice*, where he reviews films, books, theater, and music. With Heidi Julavits, he co-edits *The Believer*. He contributes to the Canadian magazine *Cinema Scope* and belongs to the Harry Stephen Keeler Society, the New York Society Library, and the Duane Reade Dollar Rewards Club.

Christopher Rowe lives in Kentucky. His fiction, poetry, and essays have appeared in many magazines, webzines, and zine zines. He runs a small press, the Fortress of Words, and edits a zine, *Say . . .* He likes outside better than inside, brick better than vinyl, and made better than bought.

Dave Shaw's *Diving with the Devil* was awarded the Katherine Anne Porter Prize and will be published by University of North Texas Press in 2003. His stories have appeared in magazines and anthologies in England, Japan, New Zealand, and the United States, including *Best American Mystery Stories, The Southern Anthology, Literal Latte, Racing Home: New Stories by Award-Winning North Carolina Authors,* and *Stand Magazine.* He has received The Literal Latte Fiction Award, The Southern Prize for Fiction, a North Carolina Arts Council Writer's Fellowship, and other awards for his work, and he completed his MFA in Fiction Writing at UNC-Greensboro. "King of Spain" originally appeared in the *Greensboro Review.*

Vandana Singh was born and raised in India and now lives in the United States with her husband, daughter, dog, and innumerable books. She draws upon her background in physics and her experience as a woman and an Indian to spin wild tales of science fiction and fantasy. Her first published story appeared in the original anthology *Polyphony,* Volume 1.

Rosalind Palermo Stevenson's fiction and prose poems have appeared in *Conjunctions* (Web Conjunctions), *Washington Square, Skidrow Penthouse, Phantasmagoria, Literal Latte, Reflections* (published by the United Nations Society of Writers), *No Roses Review,* and *White Crow,* among other literary journals. Her prose poems "The Mara Axiom" and "Soul Murder" have been nominated for a Pushcart Prize. Her short story, "The Guest," won the Anne and Henry Paolucci fiction contest for Italian-American writing, and the *Negative Capability* annual fiction contest. Rosalind lives in New York City, where she is currently completing a second collection of short fiction.

Small Beer Press

Kalpa Imperial, a novel   1-931520-05-4 $16
Angélica Gorodischer, translated by Ursula K. Le Guin

A history of an empire that never was, by one of Argentina's premier novelists.

The Mount, a novel   1-931520-03-8 $16
Carol Emshwiller

"Best of the Year"—*Book Magazine, Locus, San Francisco Chronicle*

"Brilliantly conceived and painfully acute . . . deserves to be read and cherished as a fundamental fable for our material-minded times."—*Publishers Weekly* (starred review)

"[A] potent allegory about trading freedom for a soul-killing security . . ."
—*The Village Voice:* Our 25 Favorite Books of 2002

Report to the Men's Club and Other Stories   1-931520-02-X $16
Carol Emshwiller

"A daring, eccentric, and welcome observer of darkly human ways emerges from these nineteen motley tales."—*Kirkus Reviews*

"Elliptical, funny and stylish, they are for the most part profoundly unsettling."
—*Time Out New York*

Stranger Things Happen   1-931520-00-3 $16
Kelly Link

"At their best, her stories have the vibrancy, the buzzing resonance and the oddly insistent quality of dreams."—Andrew O'Hehir, *New York Times Book Review*

"An alchemical mix of Borges, Raymond Chandler, and 'Buffy the Vampire Slayer.'"
—Salon, Best Books of 2001

Meet Me in the Moon Room   1-931520-01-1 $16
Ray Vukcevich

". . .the thirty-three brief stories in *Meet Me in the Moon Room* defy categorization by genre. A few toy with the conventions of science fiction; others branch off from trails blazed by Donald Barthelme."—*Hartford Courant*

"Inventive and entertaining, these stories yield more emotional truth than much more comparatively realistic fiction."—*Publishers Weekly*

Small Beer Press Chapbooks

Bittersweet Creek   NOVEMBER 2003 $5
Christopher Rowe

Natural-born (or hard-earned) storytelling: crows, creeks, mountains, more.

Other Cities   NOVEMBER 2003 $5
Ben Rosenbaum

A dozen or more stories of cities not often found on maps.

Foreigners and Other Faces   JUNE 2003 $5
Mark Rich

Eleven stories from a widely-published author. Illustrated.

Lord Stink and Other Stories $5
Judith Berman

". . . intriguing works, displaying considerable range and a fine new voice."
—Locus Online

Rosetti Song: Four Stories $5
Alex Irvine

". . . an excellent introduction to the extended stylistic and subject palette of Irvine . . ."
—Charles DeLint, *Fantasy & Science Fiction*

Five Forbidden Things $4
Dora Knez

". . . a fine burgeoning talent."
—*Asimov's*

We also publish a twice-yearly zine. *The Washington Post* called it "tiny, but celebrated." We call it *Lady Churchill's Rosebud Wristlet*.

www.smallbeerpress.com